Xu Jian is the author of several fictional works, among them *Oriental Hada*, as well as essays and TV drama. He has also penned a number of works of reportage, including *McMahon Line* and *The Oriental Express*. *Swords of a Rising Power* won the first Lu Xun Literature Prize in 1998.

FROM INSIDE CHINA

—— • 中国报告系列 • ——

Cry For l ife

Seven Lost Letters

Real Marriage

Never give up on yourself

Son of the Nation

Wu Renbao: China's Most Eminent Farmer

China State Grid: The People Behind the Power

I Want to Go to School

Green Great Wall

Migrant Workers and the City: Generation Now

The People's Secretary: Fighting Corruption in the People's Party

The Battle of Beijing: On the Frontline Against SARS

Yingxiu: After the Earthquake

Fate of the Nation

The Great Disarmament

Zhongshan Road

The Summons of Centuries Past—Reflections on Hong Kong: A True Account

Swords of A Rising Power: A History of the Strategic Missile Troops of China

The Rejuvenation of Northeast China

Roads of Renewal: A Tibetan Journey

Tales from Tibet

The Oriental Express

From Inside China

SWORDS OF A RISING POWER:
A History of the Strategic Missile Troops of China

大国长剑

徐 剑 著

［澳大利亚］Declan Fry 译

中国出版集团

中译出版社

图书在版编目（CIP）数据

大国长剑＝Swords of A Rising Power：英文／徐剑著；（澳）迪克兰·弗莱（Declan Fry）译．—北京：中译出版社，2018.2
ISBN 978-7-5001-5518-8

I.①大… II.①徐… ②迪… III.①报告文学－中国－当代－英文 IV.① I25

中国版本图书馆 CIP 数据核字（2018）第 009431 号

出版发行／中译出版社
地　　址／北京市西城区车公庄大街甲 4 号物华大厦六层
电　　话／(010)68359376,68359827（发行部）；68358224（编辑部）
传　　真／(010)68357870
邮　　编／100044
电子邮箱／book@ctph.com.cn
网　　址／http://www.ctph.com.cn

总 策 划／张高里　刘永淳
策划编辑／范　伟
责任编辑／范　伟
封面设计／潘　峰

排　　版／北京竹页文化传媒有限公司
印　　刷／保定市中画美凯印刷有限公司
经　　销／新华书店

规　　格／880mm×1230mm　1/32
印　　张／12.375
字　　数／394 千字
版　　次／2018 年 2 月第一版
印　　次／2018 年 2 月第一次

ISBN 978-7-5001-5518-8　定价：80.00 元

中 译 出 版 社

CONTENTS

CHAPTER 1   The Spirit of a Great Country   7

CHAPTER 2   The Time in Changxindian   41

CHAPTER 3   The First Battalion of Asia   73

CHAPTER 4   The Rise of the Missile Troop   117

CHAPTER 5   Offering Blood Sacrifice to the Forests   157

CHAPTER 6   Walking out of the Mountains   185

CHAPTER 7   Mysterious Stories of the Mysterious Troops   213

CHAPTER 8   If My Sword Is Not Long Enough   257

CHAPTER 9   Our People, Our Land   300

CHAPTER 10   The Quivers of the East   332

CHAPTER 11   The Weight of Balance in the World   357

CHAPTER 12   Saying Goodbye to Nuclear Winter   386

With the passing tides of time, all glorious history will be washed away and fade; but so long as the spirit of a nation survives, the legends and songs of its heroes will live forever...

I dedicate this book to the thirtieth anniversary of the Second Artillery Corps of PLA!

Chapter 1

The Spirit of a Great Country

1. With the tension accumulating across the Taiwan Strait, China was on the edge of war. In a speech televised nationwide, President Eisenhower, from American army, threatened to turn Red China into another Nagasaki and Hiroshima.

Early winter, 1954. Shilin Official Residence, Yangming Mountain, Taiwan

Mr Chiang Kai-shek, in his mandarin jacket and unlined long gown, plodded out of the study towards the white-marble semicircle balcony of the presidential villa. Standing by the rail, he looked far into the distance. Across the distant sky, overcast and damp, the setting sun coloured the subtropical forests into an indistinct blood-red haze. A few returning ravens hovered over the coconut grove on the hillside, crowing hoarse and lonely. All these sounds and views gave Chiang, a man with little romanticism and a lifetime of war, a strong sense of melancholy and bleakness. He didn't like the winter on this isolated island at all. There was no discernible reason for it — though perhaps it was because his massive failure in the mainland was part of the last winter of his life. He extended his eyes as far as he could, over to the other side of the sea, toward his homeland, barely visible through the sea wind and fog. There was a kind of pain and regret in his heart which could never be relieved. He waved his hand gently, and the stolid guard standing beside him came forward and asked, "What instructions does your Excellency have?"

"Go and ask someone to drive off the ravens, their crows are driving me crazy…"

The secretary of the presidential office on duty had escorted Ye Gongchao, the Foreign Minister of the Kuomintang (KMT), inside. Chiang Kai-shek looked to Ye, and beckoned him to sit down.

"Brother Gongchao, are there any urgent matters?" he asked with some tenderness.

"Your Excellency, I have just received a phone call from the US ambassador Carl Lott Lank. The new Vice-President of the US, Richard Nixon, will visit us in December," Ye Gongchao said, submitting the report of the Foreign Ministry for Chiang's approval.

"Damn it! How much better can the new Eisenhower administration be than the previous Truman one? Upon coming to office, they retreated from Korea. The Americans are not real friends of the Republic of China."

This powerful Chinese man had been a dictator for almost his entire life, but when he interacted with the Americans, he always felt himself disdained, treated like a monkey. He could not forget, before the Dynasty of the Chiang Family collapsed, that Truman had colluded with Acheson to replace him with Li Zongren. And he could not forgive Eisenhower, the previous chief commander of the allied nations, for ending the Korean war and his dream of gaining the mainland back…

While Chiang Kai-shek read the report of the "Foreign Ministry", he asked in his gentle Zhejiang accent, "Nixon, this 39-year-old vice president… he used to be a senator… and has a young turk background… is he friendly to Republic of China?"

Ye Gongchao answered confidently, "You can put your heart at ease, your Excellency! This man was a lawyer before, and he was famous for assembling lots of votes for Eisenhower in the Southern states. As a strong right-wing person, he is totally unsympathetic to the Red's communism. Not to mention he is a rising new star in American politics, and he's got a promising future…"

"Good. Then we should bet on Mr Nixon. Inform all the relevant departments, and welcome him in accordance with the highest standards as our important guest. Now that the Communist Party of China (CPC) has been aggressive to us, we should settle the Mutual Defence Treaty of the US and Taiwan when the Vice-President visits us."

After Ye Gongchao left, Chiang Kai-shek's prior frustration and melancholy turned to excitement. The news about the upcoming visit of Nixon worked like a stimulant which injected into his enervated political veins.

Within a month, Richard Nixon arrived with his wife.

At the Taoyuan International Airport in Taipei, Mr Chiang personally welcomed the Nixon couple, despite his old age. The First Lady Song Meiling, who still kept her charm, personally acted as the interpreter. All of which indicated how much value Mr Chiang Kai-shek placed upon Nixon's first visit to Taiwan.

Richard Milhouse Nixon, a descendant of an 18th century Irishman who followed the gold-digging crowd to the American continent, was born in the little town of Yorba Linda near Los Angeles in 1913. Although his ancestors had been settled in the American continent for many years, they didn't realise their American dream of becoming farm land owners in the South. As a result, Nixon grew up a poor member of the underclass. He started to make his own way in life quite early, as a janitor and doorkeeper. He completed his study in Whittier College as a part-time student, before studying law at Duke University from 1934 to 1937. No doubt, his experience of struggling as a working-class man formed a solid basis for him to become a major Western politician. During the Second World War he joined the US navy and battled the Japanese fleets in the Southern Pacific tropical forests. After retiring from the army, he committed himself to politics, and was famous for his acute political acumen and great eloquence. He was elected as a Parliament Representative at the age of 34, and became a rising new star who later gained favour with Eisenhower, the five-star general. Nixon was subsequently nominated as the vice presidential candidate of the Republicans in 1952, and gathered a large number of votes for Eisenhower before he took office in the White House. Nixon became the youngest vice president in the US history. He represented the president in handling political issues many times and was trusted and relied upon by the president to a great extent. Even if Nixon has been in the White House for a limited period of time, he knew clearly that, in the eyes of the politicians in the White House and Capitol, Mr Chiang Kai-shek did not enjoy a good reputation; to receive such a grand welcoming ceremony made him confused and uneasy. Still, this did not affect the good feelings he registered at the first sight of this oriental emperor.

During the Nixons' stay in Taiwan, Mr Chiang made time to

accompany them for sightseeing tours around the beautiful island. One evening, in the official residence of the president, Mr Chiang entertained the Nixon couple with a family feast. When he spoke of how the KMT had intercepted Polish commercial boats to China twice, or the shelling of an oil tanker from the Soviet Union to China, Nixon applauded the defeated prior dictator who had dared to confront the Oriental red bloc. But Mr Chiang was not happy at all. He sighed and said, in a dull tone, "Your Excellency, what you don't know is that the Communist Party of China has assembled massive troops and artillery over the areas of Dachen, Yijiangshan Island, Jinmen and Penghu. They intend to destroy us overnight, and our survival depends on the protection of the US. There is an old saying in China, *there will be no intact eggs if the nest has been overturned.* The government of the Republic of China is ready to make counterattacks against the mainland, but without the settlement of the Mutual Defense Treaty with the US, we can't even get started! I am counting on you, Mr Vice-President, to labour this issue, if you would."

With some sympathy and consolation, Nixon said to Chiang Kai-shek, "Your Excellency, put yourself at ease. The Taiwan Strait is of strategic significance to the US in confronting the Reds at the front line — the US government cannot ignore this. I will make a report to the president once I return."

It can be said that, during his political career of more than half a century, Chiang Kai-shek had interacted with many American politicians, but there was always an irreconcilable cultural gap between the Americans and this oriental emperor. The arrogant Western politicians always harboured a sort of "oriental shortsightedness" when they looked to China. There was only one exception — Richard Nixon. As a result, he had formed a unique bond with Chiang Kai-shek, who was more than 20 years older than him.

During the subsequent few decades of his two terms of vice-presidency and presidency in the White House, he has always been the supporting pillar for the Chiang government, nestled away upon the isolated island of Taiwan. However, although the Chiang government succeeded with Nixon, they failed because of him as well. In the spring of 1972, Nixon flew to Beijing and shook hands with Mao Tse-tung, leaving Mr Chiang alone at the other side of the sea, a stranger to the historic event. Mr Chiang was so angry that he became sick. By the time of 1975, when Mr Chiang passed away, he was still complaining about the betrayal of Nixon. But that is a later story.

Several days later, in the Oval Office of the White House

Eisenhower, a tall but thin figure, was holding his pipe as he walked into the office. His most capable men in the cabinet, Vice-President Richard Nixon, State-Secretary Dulles and Secretary of Defence Wilson were already sitting there, waiting to meet him. Eisenhower strode to his seat like a soldier, glancing around at his subordinates as he sat down. The subtle smile on his face was filled with solemnity and wisdom.

Eisenhower declared the start of the meeting. He talked briefly about the content of the meeting, then titled his head to Nixon, sitting to the right side of him, his eyes full of trust and expectation. "Richard, could you please brief us on the current situation in Taiwan…"

While the Vice-President was making his report, Eisenhower would sometimes stand up from his seat and stroll around the room, sometimes gazing toward the picturesque views of the rose garden outside, sometimes at his cabinet members. This five-star general, elected as the president due to his reputation and character, a man who had successfully directed the Normandy Invasion and ended the Second World War with the allied nations, directed a foreign policy strongly coloured with the brush of anti-communism.

After Nixon's report, Eisenhower stood up immediately from his swivel chair, turned the globe of the world on his table and stared at the maple-shaped China. He said to Dulles, the secretary of state, "John, Taiwan is our unsinkable aircraft carrier at the strait of Malacca. We cannot accept the continuance of the current state of affairs. Talk with the Pentagon and come up with a strategy against China's penetration into Taiwan and Southeast Asia. We have already said that we could not exclude the possibility of using strategic nuclear weaponry during the Korea war, and now we must reiterate this…"

At the same time, on the eastern coast of the ocean, the people of China had just emerged from the bloodshed of the Korea war, content now to sit beneath the peace of the olive trees, enjoying the serenity and warmth of a peaceful life and nursing the bleeding wounds of the war. However, the US government, which harboured a strong prejudice against red China, and in spite of the shame of the war, had not corrected its view; on the contrary, the US government instigated the Chiang government in Taiwan to make provocations to increase the tension across the strait, fanning the fantasy that they would be able to land on the southern coast of China and recover the lost Chiang Dynasty.

On the June 25, 1950, the Korea War had just begun. Truman, the US president, sent the 7th Fleet to the Taiwan Strait. The

Fleet sailed into the Taiwan Strait, with 22 large warships and the "Midway" aircraft carrier as the flagship. They escorted the Chiang army many times and supported the Chiang air force in attacking and harassing the mid-south and southern part of mainland China. After Eisenhower took office, he went beyond Truman in his approach. When he was interviewed, he declared that the US supported Chiang in counterattacking the mainland; and if the mainland army attacked Taiwan, the 7th Fleet would join the battle to defend Taiwan with its modern defence systems. In addition, the Congress had passed acts to strengthen aid to Taiwan. For the time being, the tension accumulating across the strait was so strong that a war was on the verge of breaking out at any moment.

On the December 1, 1954, not long after Nixon had returned to the US after visiting Taiwan, the US government officially signed the Mutual Defence Treaty of the US and Taiwan with the KMT government in Washington. The Treaty was submitted to the Senate on the 6th of January and ratified on the 9th of February. At this moment, the US again picked up its truncheon, reassuming its role as the world's police and threatening China with nuclear weapons.

According to a disclosed document of the US government, file NSC-162/2, the then Defence Minister Charles Wilson had even organised for important officials in the Pentagon to attend a highly confidential meeting with the Joint Chiefs of Staff and Admiral Arthur on the USS Sequoia. At this meeting they decided that a policy of containment must be followed, but with more reliance on the new strategic deterrence of the air force. Soon, the commander of the Strategic Air Corps of the US, Curtis LeMay, bellowed at the world: "There is no suitable target for the SAC, but I can find a proper target in China, like Manchuria or southern Russia, to throw our nuclear bombs. In these poker games, we need to put out the bigger stake."

The Chairman of the Joint Chiefs of Staff, General Radford, was more straightforward when he submitted the Mutual Defence Treaty to the Senate for approval. He suggested to the president that, if there was a crisis on the Taiwan Strait, the US should use nuclear weapons against China.

As the representative of a new generation of leaders in China, Mao Tse-tung, who has been through the tough times when China suffered from the bullying and humiliations of the big powers, had a stronger sense of national justice and was more prepared for unexpected hardships. In the middle of January 1955, Chairman Mao ordered General Zhang Aiping, the Chief of Staff of the Southern China military area, to organise an underwater attack upon Yijiangshan Island, relying on intense aerial bombardment in coordination with the naval and military forces. Eventually they defeated the KMT army stationed on the island and liberalised it employing the forces of modern warfare. This success not only dealt a blow to the Chiang government in Taiwan but served as a kick in the arse for the cowboys in the US.

This action sent shockwaves through the US. President Eisenhower ordered the 7th Fleet to assist the KMT in retreating from the Dachen Island while he comforted Mr Chiang Kai-shek, proclaiming that neither Yijiangshan Island nor Dachen Island was important to the defence of Taiwan. He sent the secretary of state Dulles to Taiwan frequently and discussed counter strategies with Chiang.

March 6, 1955, White House, the Oval Office

Eisenhower was having a secret discussion with Dulles, who had just returned from Taiwan. Based on memorandums disclosed by the White House thirty years later, the two had secretly decided that, if the crisis on Jinmen and Mazu continued, they would apply nuclear surgery to Red China, rendering it a second Nagasaki or Hiroshima. Dulles delivered a speech at the Foreign Relations Committee of the State Senate, during which he declared emotionally: "Having spent three days in Taipei, I returned last night. We had a discussion with the Republic of China about our Mutual Defense Treaty. Today, the free world is confronted with a challenge which is more powerful than any before. Therefore, our government has decided to enforce a 'massive retaliation' strategy using 'new and effective weapons' to defeat any armed attack from China. We will spend what we can in order to gain the greatest deterrence possible."

Although Dulles' speech of "massive retaliation" and the "edge of war" received boos and hisses, the Eisenhower administration was stubbornly determined to enforce it. That same year, on the March 18, the US president, a former soldier, delivered a nationwide television speech. After some discussion of the situation across the Taiwan Strait and the penetration into Southeast Asia of the oriental bloc, this five-star general, who had commanded millions of soldiers and brought peace to humankind, suddenly cast a nuclear tornado upon humanity's roof. He subtly implied in his speech that nuclear weapons were not only strategic weapons, but that they could also be used to serve the cause of "peace". Between the lines, he was suggesting the waging of nuclear war against China — and that all ordinary Americans should be mentally prepared for that.

From that point on, the brinkmanship of the nuclear blackmail policy of the United States was officially developed, casting a dark cloud of war over the world: a nuclear winter had come to human-kind...

2. Mao Tse-tung, a great leader in oriental history, waves his strong arm: to avoid bullying in the current world, one cannot live without nuclear weapons.

Beijing, spring, 1955, in Fengze Garden, Zhongnanhai, the study of Mao Tse-tung

It was already early spring. The magnolia and winter jasmine outside of Zhongnanhai, the Chinese leadership compound, had just grown out their buds, waiting to bloom. A verdant green gently clothed the ancient capital.

While reading the traditional thread bound book of *Tolerant Study* essays at his large table, Mao Tse-tung waved the pen in his hand, commenting upon the historical notes *Miscellaneous Notes from the Tolerant Study* of the Song Dynasty's great intellectual, Hong Mai. Coming across something splendid, this romantic-poet of a politician could not help but read it aloud. Somehow, Mao Tse-tung, who held a life-long passion for reading, had developed a particular preference for this book of historical essays, which recorded the ancient classics and studies of ancient institutions, anecdotes and literary critics. No matter whether it was wartime or during one of his tours around the country after he took power in the Forbidden City, he would ask his secretary to take this book, and pick a few pages to read when he had some spare time. Sometimes, with great interest, he would select a few passages and give them to other high-rank officials to read, regardless whether they could understand them.

As Mao Tse-tung was enjoying his reading, his secretary on political matters, Tian Jiaying, brought a copy of reference materials from the Xinhua News Agency. From those confidential materials, which were only circulated around central power, there was a speech from Eisenhower about his intention to enforce a "massive retaliation" strategy against the Oriental Red Bloc. After reading this speech, Mao Tse-tung became livid—he slammed the paper on his table and stood up.

"A political hooligan! And with wild fantasies of becoming a global hegemony—it's a dream, complete bullshit." He turned to Jiaying Tian. "Please invite comrade Enlai here."

Premier Zhou Enlai quickly walked from Xihua Hall toward Fengze Garden. A great man who radiated humanity and held a life-long respect for Mao, he stepped into Mao's study and asked warmly, "Good morning Chairman, did you have a good sleep this morning?"

Mao replied in his strong Hunan accent, "Pretty good." Then he pointed to the paper which published Eisenhower's speech and said, with a serious look, "Enlai, have you had a chance to read it?"

"I have already sent it to a few senior generals and the Foreign Ministry, to develop a counter strategy…" Zhou Enlai had always gained the respect and appreciation of Mao, with his peerless astuteness and meticulousness, like the silent tolerance of a great housekeeper. Mao Tse-tung told him solemnly, "We must be faster. *The People's Daily* should issue an official editorial to reveal our position. Additionally, how are we developing and cultivating the talent necessary to develop nuclear bombs and missiles?"

"We do have the advantage in this regard," Zhou Enlai said confidently. "Qian Sanqiang has worked with the Nobel prize winner Madame Curie before. Yang Chengzong and Peng Huangwu returned from France and Britain, they are all famous radiation physicists. The other one, who has worked for the American father of the rocket, Dr Von Carmen, is missile expert — Professor Qian Xuesen. We have been trying to get him back to China via all available channels."

"Excellent!" Mao knocked on the arm of his chair in excitement. "Without the nuclear bomb, nobody will ever listen to what we have to say! So long as we have got the talents, and the resources, we can create miracles!"

Soon after that, while meeting a delegation from Finland, Mao was asked by a journalist about his comment on Eisenhower's "massive retaliation" strategy. Mao Tse-tung didn't lose his heroism and bravery as a great figure of oriental history in his reply, as he stood there and said, "During the 1940s, I told an American female journalist in Yan'an that nuclear weapons were just paper tigers. Today I am still credited with the phrase. No matter how powerful the Americans' nuclear weapons are, they can throw them at China and penetrate the earth. And certainly, this will be of some significance for our solar system; but in light of the size of the universe, it will hardly amount to anything…"

Mao Tse-tung's response was soon published in some major Western newspapers, receiving applause from Western society and some insightful men in Asia and Africa. By this point, China's project of developing nuclear missiles had already started, following a long and secretive journey of which hardly anyone was aware…

In the fall of 1955, Professor Qian Xuesen, the famous scientist who was remarked upon by the US Navy Secondary Chief Kimble as not being tradable even for five divisions, had returned to China as a result of the Chinese Foreign Ministry's efforts and those of a number of international academics.

Qian Xuesen was born in Shanghai in 1911. He followed his father to Peking at the age of three, and studied in the affiliated elementary school and middle school of the Normal University. At 1929, he was admitted to Peking Jiaotong University, and was sent to study abroad by Tsinghua University at the government's expense during the 1930s. In 1935, he was enrolled into the engineering department of MIT with the Boxer Indemnity. The following October, he transferred to the California Institute of Technology and became a student of Dr Von Carmen, a grand master of mechanics. They later became close partners. Qian subsequently got his PhD in aerodynamics and gained a professorship. During the Second World War, he took part in the Manhattan Project with his mentor Von Carmen, developing nuclear missiles. Von Carmen praised him as being the most talented and exceptional scientist in the field of rocket science. In 1945, when Von Carmen was employed by the US Air Force as Chief of the science consulting group, he insisted upon nominating Qian as a member, who later became one of the few foreign consultants. However, just like all the other students of the old China who wished to use science and technology to save the country, Qian had witnessed the sufferings of China under the big powers and experienced the pain of not being able to help the country. So when the five-starred red flag rose upon this unfortunate land, he felt as if he had seen the awakening of a major power that had lain dormant for over a hundred years. In spite of his mentor's persuasion and the happiness of the foreign land, he insisted upon returning and contributing to the construction of a new China. Kimble was furious upon seeing his resignation. He slammed the table, roaring, "No! No! He knows all the core secrets of the American missiles. One Qian could be as powerful as five marine divisions. I would rather shoot him to death than send him back to red China!" From then on, Professor Qian was under arrest and all his books and study materials were taken away; later he was imprisoned upon an isolated island, a victim of McCarthyism. Even so, this excellent scientist of the twentieth century didn't waver from his determination to contribute to the motherland. With Premier Zhou Enlai's solemn entreaties to the US and support from some American scientists with just minds, Qian was able to return to his motherland after five years of imprisonment. When Qian went back to China with his wife Jiang Ying and a pair of young children, he gave his mentor a monograph, *Engineering Cybernetics*. Professor Von Carmen told his Chinese student excitedly, "Now you have achieved more than me intellectually, go back and contribute to your homeland. Science knows no boundaries."

After Qian returned to China, the Defense Minister Marshal Peng Dehuai went to meet him, praising his patriotism and entrusting him with a number of important duties. Qian was appointed as the Director of the Fifth Research Institute of the Ministry of Defense, specifically responsible for the research and development of China's rockets.

Early spring, 1956.

The warm sunshine of spring drifted from the cold winter sky, melting the last remaining snow in the capital. The verdant greenery of spring brought the ancient royal city a new vigor.

In the dignified and solemn headquarters of the General of Staff of the PLA, Premier Zhou hosted a grand meeting for the Central

Military Committee. As these marshals and generals, men who had directed millions of soldiers, took their seats, Premier Zhou declared, in his usually gentle but exceptionally serious tone, that, "Today we have invited you here, not to be the teacher, but to be students. Now let's welcome Comrade Qian, who has just returned from the US to give us a lecture on advanced technology, and our plan to develop missile technology."

With a wave of applause, Professor Qian, who had just turned forty, stepped confidently onto the podium. Facing the Premier and the battle-hardened marshals and generals, Qian suddenly experienced an unprecedented feeling of excitement and heaviness, despite having been in similar situations with US five-star generals and other famous physicists many times. His lecture would reveal a fresh new field to these marshals and generals who came from Nanchang, Jinggangshan Mountains, Yan River and the Loess Plateau, and would lead to the promulgation of a vital new national defense strategy. Holding the heavy outline materials for his lecture in his hand he talked, with all his wisdom as a scientist, about the history of rocket technology from ancient times to the present. He also discussed new trends and developments in the technology, along with his vision of China's future missile development, visions which gained the full support of the sie marshals and generals. After the meeting, Premier Zhou personally submitted the briefs of the meeting to the Central Committee of the Party and Chairman Mao. Having pulled through the tough times of the wars, the leaders of the new China had developed historical acumen and foresight. They knew deeply and clearly the significance of China having its own nuclear weapons if it intended to regain its role in the world as a major power, as it had in history. Mao not only approved the report submitted by Zhou but, on the most sacred podium of the highest State Council of the Republic, voiced the aspirations of this oriental nation's determination to rise again.

"Today we must be stronger than yesterday. Not only do we need more planes and cannons, but nuclear bombs. In the world today, if we want to avoid bullies, these are necessities." A man of courage, he gave his predictions: "Within ten years it will be totally possible for us to have our own nuclear bombs and hydrogen bombs." Chen Yi, a Supreme Commander and diplomat, unable to resist his own poetically bold nature, waved his arms and said: "Do it! Even if we have to sell our pants, we must build our own nuclear weapons!"

General Zhang Aiping, the Deputy Chief of General Staff, a man appointed by Premier Zhou to be specifically responsible for the project, stated more clearly and vividly, "We cannot live without a stick to beat back the dogs ... "

The curtain was being lifted on a project which related to the future and status of the Chinese nation.

The Central Committee of the Party set up the Aviation Industry Committee, an organisation specifically responsible for high-end technology. Seeking an appropriate director for the Committee, the General Secretary of the Party, Deng Xiaoping, who had been working on the front line, vested his hope and trust in the Marshal Nie Rongzhen.

One morning in autumn, General Secretary Deng went to Marshal Nie's residence by car from Zhongnanhai, to visit his old friend while he was recovering from disease and consult him regarding the allocation of work. Three years ago, as the Chief of Staff of the PLA, Nie fainted and collapsed when he accompanied Marshal Peng Dehuai's tour around the suburbs of Beijing.

Later Nie was diagnosed with heart disease and high blood pressure which were causing an imbalance of the neural system in his brain. He submitted his resignation to the Central Committee of the Party in order to find time to recover from his disease. Now Nie had recovered, and the newly established republic was in urgent need of the talents of these marshals and generals in order to cure the heavy "disease" of a country which had lain ill it for hundred of years.

Comrade Deng asked about Nie's physical well-being in his heavy accent, holding big brother Nie's hands. "Good to hear you are recovering," he said in satisfaction. "Now the Central Committee is prepared to entrust you with a number of important tasks. Comrade Chen Yi has been assigned to the Foreign Ministry, and Comrade Peng Zhen is too busy to take on the responsibility of mayor of Beijing. So now that leaves us with two vacancies. Indeed, there is another vacancy also: to direct the use of military technology and equipment development. We would like you to choose one of these three options."

"I thank the Central Committee for trusting in me. I must admit to having had a strong interest in science ever since my teenage years. I would hope it may be possible to assume a role in charge of technology and missile development."

"Excellent," Comrade Deng said, in his usual decisive tone. "Then it's settled."

3. The Chinese government signals to the Soviet Union its intention to purchase nuclear weapons, but the Kremlin replies with silence.

By the end of the 1950s, the political honeymoon between China and the Soviet Union had come to an end.

The sun that had once sweetly shone and wandered between the two continents was now covered by the sudden cold wind rising from Siberia. For Nie Rongzhen, the newly appointed Vice-Premier in charge of the Aviation Industry Committee of the Defense Ministry, it was an inauspicious sign.

Not long before Nie recovered he had made contact with some famous scientists. Soon afterward he submitted the *Preliminary Opinion on Establishing a Chinese Missile Research Project* to the Central Committee of the Party. After Zhou Enlai's approval, the Central Military Committee resolved to begin developing missiles. But China's project still required the help of a big brother — the Soviet Union.

Early autumn of the same year, Zhongnanhai, Office of Premier Zhou

Although he was under intense pressure every day, Zhou put away the tasks at hand and told the Vice-Premier of the State Council Li Fuchun, with enormous trust: "Fuchun, you have a heck of a task in leading the delegation to Moscow. Not only do you need to settle 150 projects of technological and economic cooperation, but to be entrusted with the task of conveying the Party and Chairman Mao's request for assistance to develop our nuclear missiles to the Soviet Union…"

Li remained silent for a while and sighed. "I have already written a letter to the Chairman of the Soviet Union Council of Ministers, Comrade Bulganin, in August," he told the Premier in his heavy Hunan accent. "Usually Comrade Bulganin has been quite friendly to China, but this time his reply was rather ambiguous."

"He's not the one to blame. Bulganin cannot make the final decision — Khruschev's opinion is more important." With a serious look Premier Zhou continued, "Earlier this year, Marshal Peng and General Chen Geng mentioned this issue to the Chief of Staff of the Soviet Union, so the message must have been passed on. But the Kremlin replied with silence, without asking anything more. You have been in the Soviet Union for many years, and have a good relationship with them. I hope you can strive to settle it all."

"Premier, rest assured — I can guarantee you that I will see this task completed," Li said, standing up to leave.

"Good. When you return, I will personally give a dinner of welcome." Premier Zhou accompanied Li out of Xihua Hall, watching him go.

Several days later, the trade delegation arrived in Moscow.

It was a fine autumn day, all the maple tree ablaze; unexpectedly however, in this capital of the northern neighboring country, there came also a bout of snow that saw the Volga River clothed in silver.

The Chinese delegation did not seem to have any interest in admiring the stunning Moscow views. Assisted by the Chinese ambassador Liu Xiao and the commercial counselor Li Qiang, Comrade Li Fuchun signed 150 aid contracts with the Soviet Union. But the task Premier Zhou had entrusted him with remained a heavy burden.

One evening, in the magnificent banquet hall of the previous tsarist Russia's Romanov Dynasty in the Kremlin, the Premier of the Soviet Union, Bulganin, organised a feast to welcome Li Fuchun. Li used to study in France with Premier Zhou, and later continued his studies in the East University of the Soviet Union. Bulganin respected Li from the bottom of his heart and regarded him as an "expert on Soviet Union". He raised his glass of vodka frequently to Li, talking to him kindly in Russian.

"Comrade Li, the agreements are settled now. We have accomplished something great. In a few days, I will accompany you to the suburbs of Moscow for a hunting tour, and we can enjoy some rest."

Li however was not cheered by this kind offer. He extended his hands: "Comrade Bulganin, if the Soviet Union could offer China some assistance in building nuclear missiles, it would be of much assistance — far better than to go on a hunting tour!"

"I'm sorry," Bulganin answered after some hesitation. "When I wrote back to you I felt I had stated our position clearly. But as an old friend, I am still willing to have another conversation with Comrade Khruschev about the whole matter…"

"Fantastic! Then let's go hunting!" Li raised his glass to Bulganin. "To our friendship!"

Bulganin extended his glass to Li. "To my old friend!"

Several days later, Kremlin, Office of the General Secretary of the Communist Party of the Soviet Union

Nikita Khruschev was half bald and big-bellied. He wandered around his spacious and bright white office. This palace of power had seen its owner change no less than four times.

Although Khruschev had only been in office for three years, he was beginning to feel more confident in exercising his power. He sat atop the powerful seat of Stalin, a seat which could shake the entire earth; or perhaps his arrogance had simply blossomed as a result of occupying the red Palace which had once accommodated Peter the Great, Nicholas the First and the female Tsar Catherine.

Whether it was due to a naturally inherited chauvinism in Russia's blood, or because his family had come from the Ukraine's

Cossack family, Khruschev had a rudeness and assertiveness in his personality. During his first visit to the US he had argued with the American senators, taking off his shoes and banging the table, embarrassing the Soviet Union. Or in October of 1954, visiting China a month after his inauguration, he had found himself in a rather unpleasant exchange with Mao and Zhou on the issue of the Soviet army's retreat from Dalian and Lüshun. When Khruschev proposed building a long-wave radio station in China and extracting the resources in Xinjiang, he received strong resistance from Mao. No wonder then that from their very first meeting the two leaders held a subtle psychological grudge against each other — one which later developed into the "divorce" of the two parties.

"Comrade Bulganin, how can you become one of the Chinese?" Khruschev said as he talked to the chief of the Council of Ministers in his strong Ukraine accent, waving a stubby hand. "Do the Chinese comrades want to have nuclear weapons? You should convince them to come under the protection umbrella of our red family."

"Comrade Sergeyevich, could you please reconsider their request? This issue matters to the brotherhood of the two parties." Bulganin was kind but serious in his entreaties to the powerful secretary general. "Do we need to discuss this issue at the meeting of the political bureau?"

"All right, let's just follow what you have suggested, Comrade Bulganin," Khruschev said, waving his hand impatiently.

Watching Bulganin walk away, Khruschev was so angry he broke the pencil in his hand. He murmured to himself, "Let's see, Comrade Bulganin. I'll take you down … and then we'll see who the ultimate winner is."

At the next meeting of the Central Political Bureau of the Communist Party of the Soviet Union, it was the ideas and emotions of Khruschev that coloured the atmosphere and direction of the meeting. He stood up suddenly, spreading his hands in contempt, and said sarcastically, "The Chinese comrades are unwilling to take shelter under our nuclear protection umbrella and intend to build their own. In my opinion, they can't possibly succeed. In the end, they may not even be able to afford their pants…"

After that it seemed that there was no need for other people at the meeting to add anything else. In a society where power is highly centralised, everything will often be determined based on the personal idiosyncrasies of the leader, and this can lead the whole country to the abyss of tragedy.

For a couple of months, the Kremlin kept silent. Only when the delegation from China flew back did the Communist Party of the Soviet Union pass a perfunctory message to Liu Xiao, the Chinese ambassador in Moscow. "China can rely on the nuclear umbrella of the socialist family — there is not much meaning in having one or two more socialist countries equipped with nuclear weapons." They agreed to pick fifty Chinese students who were studying in the Soviet Union to transfer to majors in missile technology.

Maybe it was god who helped China. In the following year, the international political situation changed dramatically. The cold war had begun. The "peaceful evolution" strategy of Dulles took effect first in the red satellite states of the Soviet Union. It was Najib from Hungary who first showed defiance, before being followed by Tito from Yugoslavia. Khruschev encountered mockery and criticism for the first time when he visited the West. The hegemonic status of the Soviet Union in the international family of communism had been challenged. To secure its dominance at the upcoming International Meeting of Communist & Workers' Parties, Khruschev was in urgent need of the vote of China, a land with a population of more than 600 million. As a result, a year later, the highest power organ of the Soviet Union showed signs of concession to China's request to purchase nuclear missiles.

In the summer of 1957, the chairman of the Ministry of the Soviet Union, Nikolai Bulganin, telephoned the Russian general consultant in China and told him that the Kremlin was ready to welcome the representative group of the Chinese government to Moscow to discuss the sale of nuclear missiles. As a man who had always held a strong emotional attachment to the Chinese people, the general consultant in China could not withhold his excitement. "Call my driver as soon as possible," he told his interpreter, for fear he might forget. "I'm going to meet Comrade Zhou Enlai in Zhongnanhai!" History had finally given the Chinese people a chance!

4. By the side of the beautiful Volga River, a negotiation concerning the future of China's strategic missiles takes place.

Summer, 1957, by the seaside of the Beidaihe

This famous summer and tourism resort seemed to been bestowed with all nature's gifts. China's first emperor, Qinshihuang, left the famous site of the Qin Palace-on-tour at this holy place, neighbouring the Yan Mountains to the north and the Bohai Sea to the east. Emperor Wu of the Han Dynasty, who made conquests around the territory, had toured to Jieshi, causing Cao Cao to write a historical poem after his war towards the east: *I came* to view the boundless ocean/From a stony hill on the eastern shore/ *Its waters roll in rhythmic motion/And islands stand amid its roar.* And Mao Tse-tung had put a classic "ending" to this roll of poems dedicated to the sea: *The pouring rain falls on the silent swallows/As the white cream waves surge and roar to the sky.*

After the founding of PRC, the leaders of Party's central organs would come to work at this place every summer. It already seemed to be an open secret.

Marshal Nie Rongzhen popped out of the blue water, lying on the balcony of the villa while he looked over toward the sea. The sunny sky joined the blue sea in the distance, flocks of seagulls chasing after the white sailboats and merging into the far horizon. Amidst the view, a combined sense of bleakness and impending historical danger seemed to have arisen in the Supreme Commander's heart. Without wars and fights, all that he could see were the silence and serenity of heaven and earth. How did the Supreme Commander feel about this, having directed millions of soldiers? No one had ever asked him whether it was pleasure or a kind of loneliness.

Interrupting his meditation, his secretary Fan Jisheng suddenly rushed to him. "Commander, we have just received a notification from the General Office of the Central Committee. The Soviet Union government has agreed to have a discussion with our representative group. The Premier has asked you to return to Beijing right away."

Nie stood up instantly, just as if he had been commanding a squad of troops. "Telephone Chen Geng, Song Renqiong and Liu Jie immediately, and ask them to prepare the plans and materials for the negotiation. Let's pack up and head back to Beijing!"

Several days later, the delegation of China for the negotiations with the Soviet Union were officially set up in Beijing. Nie was appointed as the director of the delegation of more than thirty members. The Deputy Minister of Foreign Trade Li Qiang, Deputy Minister of Nuclear Industry Liu Jie and the Chief of the General Armaments Department of the General Staff Lieutenant General Wan Yi were all members of the group.

Just before the delegation departed Beijing, Nie went to Qinzheng Hall in Zhongnanhai to meet the Premier and receive his instructions. Nie reported to the Premier about their preparations for the negotiation, including the general principle of "Putting China's interests first and striving for foreign aid."

"But there will be no begging or anything which could disgrace China. And we will not reveal all the aspects of our current industrial ability."

After listening to his report, Premier Zhou nodded. "Good. I am in total agreement. The preliminary preparations made by the delegation are quite comprehensive. It was not a short while ago we made our request to the Soviet Union, and it can be said that there have been quite a few turns on this issue. Your task is not easy. Tell Comrade Chen Geng and Song Renqiong that our principles are, first, to buy; second, to request; and third, to learn. And we need to learn the technology as soon as possible and build our own nuclear missiles. I wish you success!"

Carrying the broad and glorious dream of the rocket, as well as the trust of the Central Committee and Chairman Mao, the delegation of China flew to Moscow and started their tough negotiations.

The views by the Volga River was at their most charming during autumn, but no one had time to be enchanted by the beautiful scenery. Rather, they quickly engaged in a long and difficult negotiation. The Soviet Union government had appointed the Deputy Chairman of the Ministry, Pervukhin, and a lieutenant general from the Defence Ministry to be responsible for receiving and corresponding with the delegation.

The Chinese never forgot that where they came from was a great country of courtesy. Before their departure, the delegation prepared Hunan embroidery handcraft as gifts for every member of the Soviet Union staff from the leaders of the state to ordinary working porsonnel with whom they would make contact. When the Marshal Nie gave Pervukhin the gifts for Khruschev, Vorochilov and Bulganin, Pervukhin answered in embarrassment, "Comrade Nikita Khruschev is taking a holiday at his seaside villa and cannot return for the meeting. He asked me to welcome you on his behalf." In fact, Pervukin had played an embarrassing role as the only remaining Vice Premier of the Malenkov bloc. He had no actual power to decide what to negotiate and what to relinquish. Pervukhin was only the receptionist, while Khruschev was behind the curtain. And everything had to obtain Khruschev's approval.

The delegation was separated to live in two different locations. Supreme Commander Nie, General Chen Geng and Minister Song Renqiong were placed in the villa on Belinski Street, which was of better condition, while the rest were arranged to live in a normal hotel.

The Soviet KGB was omnipresent. On the day of the group's arrival, the Soviet State Security Council immediately sent a colonel to the entrance of the hotel and monitored all the actions of the Chinese. The delegation found that, when they left the hotel, the colonel would sometimes make a telephone report to his superior. To avoid unnecessary troubles, the delegation decided not to discuss any critical issues of the negotiation in their rooms, instead discussing them during their walks outside. The most interesting thing was that the members of the delegation could not get enough food. For the first few days, the members living in the hotel all felt that there was not enough available. And there was no reply even after they complained. When the Chinese Ambassador Liu Xiao and the Deputy Minister of Foreign Trade Li Qiang happened to visit them they mentioned the problem. Li burst into laughter after hearing it, and the Deputy Minister, who was called "Expert on Soviet Union", told them a little secret, asking each member to put a few roubles under their plates after their meal. From then on, all the cooks and waitresses seemed to change their personality entirely, and took all of the nice dishes out to the Chinese.

The marathon negotiations were undertaken by the side of the Volga River. Nie directed the proceedings calmly. General Chen, along with Wan Yi, Song Renqiong and others who were responsible for negotiating the sale of the missiles led the experts in introducing the models of missile available. Although friendly laughs and handshakes were exchanged, the vigilance and gaps between the two age-old nations could not be bypassed. Sometimes some subtle thing would provoke disagreement.

During the negotiations, the highest military leader of the Soviet Union brought the delegation to the most modernised weapons factory in Moscow. But there were very strict restrictions imposed upon the members, which allowed only the Ministers and military officials with ranks higher than that of major general to visit. They were worried about the potential hidden experts in the group. Thus, throughout the 1950s and 1960s, there was a popular rumor that, in order to enable Qian Xuesen to visit the Soviet Union's weapons factory, Mao had joked with Premier Zhou that Qian could be promoted to a major general. During interviews for the preparation of this book, the author asked the secretary of Supreme Commander Nie, Fan Jisheng, Lieutanent General Wan Yi (who was already blind) and previous Minister for Foreign Trade Li Qiang more than once whether Qian Xuesen had ever been in the delegation. But none of them could recall whether he was with them. Maybe this rumor itself was only a story, but it does reflect the subtle and complicated relationship that existed between China and the Soviet Union from the perspective of ordinary Chinese people...

In early October, 1957, after 35 days of long and intense negotiation, the project plan for nuclear bombs and missiles was drafted by both parties. However, at this moment, Khrushchev, who had been hiding behind the curtain, suddenly stepped onstage. He conveyed the following message to Nie: *We are willing to give China missiles and nuclear bombs. But before that, can Comrade Mao attend the International Meeting of Communists & Workers' Parties at Moscow? We need his presence to support the entire meeting.* Between the lines, Khrushchev suggested that the final decision rested in the hands of China.

Just after National Day, Song Renqiong and Ambassador Liu Xiao flew back to Beijing and reported to Mao. When they walked into Fengze Garden after their long journey, Mao asked, in his Hunan accent, "Comrade Renqiong, how is your task going?"

"Chairman, everything is ready, the only thing needed now is your presence in Moscow," Song Renqiong answered with the same Hunan accent.

Following Song and Liu's report, Mao agreed to go. "We should give Khrushchev the honor."

On October 15, 1957, the agreement between China and the Soviet Union for the supply of missiles and nuclear bombs was finally settled.

5. The first batch of two P-2 missiles is sent to China through Manzhouli, but the nuclear bombs fail to arrive, despite repeated requests.

History has played a funny joke upon China.

China was the cradle of the rocket, which in turn signaled the dawn of the era for gunpowder-based weapons. And rockets and gunpowder, which were invented by the alchemists, constituted the sun of this new era. In the 12th century, when Genghis Khan swept through the Euro-Asia continent with the Mongolian Calvary, burning the castle of Moscow with rudimentary rockets and cannons, the entirety of Europe was still trapped in the long night of the medieval period.

During the 16th century, when the young Emperor Kangxi of the Qing Dynasty gave the Chinese-made rockets to Peter the Great of Russia, the Tsar treated the gifts like rare treasure. Russia was still struggling with helotism. A diligent ruler, Peter the Great learned from the West. Indeed, he was not resistant to the Eastern civilization either. Eventually, overcoming tremendous obstacles, Russia rose as a strong nation connecting Europe and Asia.

Although China had been on top of the world for thousands of years as a civilisation, after only one or two centuries of isolation by the Great Wall, the vision and breadth of mind of the Chinese had become blocked, hemmed in by the red walls of the palaces. And

Western civilisation, nurtured by the fruits of the Eastern civilisation, had left the Chinese nation far behind. The dramatic changes occurring in the world far surpassed China's own development.

The thousand year-long dream of the rocket dream, it seemed, would itself not be realised for another thousand years!

In the winter of 1957, the Chinese finally regained an opportunity to realise this dream again.

A secret military train from Russia carrying two P-2 missiles and other equipment travelled, bound for Manzhouli, China. After 300 years the rockets were returning to their homeland, two boxes of ancient missiles traded for two modern missiles.

Beijing, the General Logistics Department of the PLA

A witness to history, the retired former Head of the Equipment Department of the General Staff, Wan Yi, who had also been involved in negotiations with the Soviet Union, stood waiting to receive the carriage in Manzhouli.

The old veteran, blind and white haired, had worked for General Zhang Xueliang of the Northeastern Army during his youth, before working undercover for the Communist Party. After the Xi'an Incident, he fought with Marshal Peng on the grand Loess Plateau. By the end of the 1950s, at the Lushan Meeting, and following his involvement with Peng and Huang's Petofi Military Club, he had been through numerous political downfalls.

Though he is now 86, he is still quick-thinking and had a clear memory. Excitement arose from this senior general's heart when he recalled the extraordinary experience of the missile talks with the Soviet Union.

"At the end of 1957, the Soviet Union government sold two P-2 missiles to China. And the missiles entered China from Manzhouli. At that time, Chairman Mao and Premier Zhou, along with the entire Central Military Committee, had given this event tremendous significance, basically treating it as the treasure of the nation. Marshal Peng specifically asked me to receive the missiles in Manzhouli. After they entered China, we guarded them in ways we had learned from our old big brother the Soviet Union. To be fair, this brother did lend us a hand when we first started our missile project. Though there had been some very tough times during the bilateral relationship, some of which could be partly blamed on Khrushchev, we ourselves could not be totally absolved. Back then we put far too much emphasis on the convergence of ideology. What we overlooked was the national interest, which should be our biggest concern. It should be said that most of the people from the Soviet Union were friendly to China. And most of the missile contracts between China and the Soviet Union were carried out. Of course, our relationship with the Soviet Union deteriorated later, as agreements regarding the nuclear bombs were not performed. We had received a telegraph from Moscow saying that the model for the nuclear bombs would arrive soon, and I waited in Manzhouli for it with my colleagues several times. But despite repeated requests, they never came."

The reasons why the Soviet Union never sold nuclear bombs to China still remains an unsolved secret...

On August 19, 1990, the red flag having fluttered over the hometown of Lenin for 70 years, it suddenly fell from the Kremlin. The answer to the secret was finally uncovered from the confidential files of the KGB...

The last winter of the 1950s, the Kremlin

After kicking Bulganin, the Chairman of the Council of the Ministers, out of the politburo, Khrushchev secured his position in the Kremlin and was able to deliver orders as he wished.

One day, the Minister of Heavy Machinery Construction, Slaviski, responsible for nuclear weapons research, walked gingerly into the secretary-general's office, trembling. It was just before he was to make the determination to send the nuclear bomb model to China. Slaviski called Khruschev by his nickname, Serge-yevich. "Comrade Sergeyevich," he asked in a probing tone. "We have already assembled all the relevant parts for the nuclear bomb model to send to China. Comrade Secretary General, if you would please sign the final approval ... "

Khruschev took the approval document and put it on the side of the table. "What is your opinion, speaking from the side of the Heavy Machinery Construction Ministry?"

Slaviski was very good at guessing the ideas of his superior. He knew that, when Khruschev advanced his famous secretive report about Stalin's crimes to the 20th Congress of the Soviet Union Communist Party, it was Mao Tse-tung who stood up to criti-cize Khruschev, having previously attempted to criticise Stalin's mistakes. At the Bucharest Conference, Deng Xiaoping and Peng Zhen, as the delegates of the Chinese Communist Party, had argued vehemently with Khruschev, embarrassing him tremendously. According to rumors, during the last visit of Khruschev to China, celebrating the tenth anniversary of the new Communist China, he had again had an unpleasant experience with the Chinese leaders. So Slaviski said, taking a moment to prepare himself mentally,

"Considering our deteriorating relationship with the Chinese Communist Party, our belief is that we should not send the model to them, so as to avoid any later unnecessary troubles."

Khruschev drummed on the table with his two stubby hands, "This is a very good piece of advice. I must say, I agree with you completely." And he slapped Slaviski's shoulder as he moved forward, tearing up the document before throwing it into the bin.

At the very last minute, Nikita Khruschev had torn apart the honeymoon between the parties of China and the Soviet Union with his fat hands.

The people of both countries would pay a heavy toll for his rude conduct in the years to come.

Chapter 2

The Time in Changxindian

1. Upon the ruins of shame, a glorious history always rebuilds itself.

The Marco Polo Bridge and Changxindian area of the Yongding River were the first ancient city to be conquered by the Mongolian Calvary—indeed, they were also the place where the Japanese invaders fired their first shot...

On this unfortunate land marked by the shame of the Chinese soldiers, we again realised our rocket dream.

Changxindian, 30 km to the southwest of Beijing

For the young people of today, this place is only a faded memory which belongs to an unfamiliar history. Although the blood shed during the Great Strike of February 7, 1923 of the railway workers, organised by the Chinese Communist Party, had inspired a generation, all of these glories and tragedies had long since been buried in the yellow sand of the Yongding River's dried riverbed.

Digging beneath these layers of cold sand, there lies the most tragic history of the Chinese nation, and the darkest page of the Chinese army.

The clouds of time have faded away…

The ancient and clear water of the Yongding River flowed slowly from the Yanshan Mountains to the land around Beijing, just as the giant dragon flew over the ancient land of Yanjing (now Beijing) and left behind an ancient riverbed, nurturing the lives and soil of both sides, including the earliest major city constructed on the ancient Yanjing land—the Capital City of Jin, by the Yongding River.

In the year 1151—the third year of Tiande, during the Jin Dynasty—Wanyan Liang, the Prince of Hailing, expanded the old city of Yanjing toward three directions—the east, west and south. Based the design upon the ancient ruins of Youzhou from the Tang Dynasty and the southern capital of the Liao Dynasty, as well as the structure of the capital city Bianliang (today's Kaifeng) of the Song Dynasty, he built the biggest city of northern China. It occupied 22 square kilometres and had a population of hundreds of thousands, famous for its astonishing views and prosperity. The prince then moved the capital of Jin from Huining to Yanjing, marking the start of the city's glorious and tragic days as a royal city.

100 years passed as swiftly as a dream. In the year 1215, a tribe arose from the Hulun Buir Prairie of the eastern country. Led by Genghis Khan and his cavalry, they shattered the last sunset hanging over the palace of the ancient city of Yanjing. The fire of war burned out the dream-like prosperity of Yanjing, leaving ruins that would remain for a thousand years…

The Mongolians rebuilt the capital of Yuan Dynasty in Beijing, and used the gunpowder and rockets invented by the people of the

Central Plains in war for the first time. The era of gunpowder in human military history quickly replaced that of previous weapons. With the most advanced gunpowder weapons—the rockets of the time—an empire could rise to hegemony. The newly-born empire of Yuan rose from the Eastern horizon like a rising sun. Not only did they have the strength to shoot eagles, with what were then the most advanced weapons—rockets and cannons which covered a few hundred metres—they had also started upon their long journey to conquer the entire Euro-Asia continent.

In the year 1220, when the second son of Genghis Khan, Oködei, directed the Mongolian Calvary to attack the castles of the famous Middle Eastern city Baghdad, he used rudimentary rockets invented by the Chinese. In 1237, the Mongolian leader Batu swept northeastern Europe with his rolling Calvary. The thundering of cannons and rockets coloured the high red walls of Moscow, waking the Europeans who were still in deep in the sleep of helotism. A Mongolian Altan Ordo belonging to the capital city of Yanjing had conquered the Volga River…

However, a nation which indulges itself in the past glories of its ancestors will inevitably fall into decline. Within a hundred years, the imperial dream of the East had faded away. The Western nations, nurtured by Eastern civilisation, had surpassed the steps taken by the Chinese. Maybe it was the karma of history, after Genghis Khan's cavalry took off from Yanjing to wage wars against the Europeans, but in the first summer of the 20th century, the invading troops of Eight Powers set fire to the royal resort of the Qing Dynasty, burning down the last shreds of confidence and hope of the Chinese.

On July 7, 1937, over the Marco Polo Bridge from the Yongding

River, the Japanese troops in Wanping City fired the first shot of their invasion toward the Central Plains. The Chinese army, who had always been in a disadvantaged position, could not resist the humiliated urge to fight back, beginning the eight-year-long Anti-Japanese War.

The most glorious history is usually achieved by peoples from the most tragic lands.

In the autumn of 1957, with the approval of Premier Zhou, the Central Military Committee decided to build the first Training Centre for the Strategic Missiles of China in Changxindian, on the old site of the Central College of Marxism and Leninism.

Eventually, the Chinese stood up, and were finally capable of realizing their dream of the rocket in history.

2. China's best military officers gathered. In major news for the republic, captains become colonels, and lieutenants, battalion commanders.

1957, Autumn, Beijing. Headquarters of the Artillery Corps of the Central Military Committee

In a grave and dignified office building, the Commander of the Artillery Corps, General Chen Xilian, was in his uniform and concentrating on reading the list of leaders who would be establishing the Changxindian Artillery Training Brigade. With his pencil in hand, he looked upon all the familiar subordinates. But the forms were, in the experienced commander's eyes, somewhat disappointing. The highest level of education among all these "talents", selected from among all the levels of the Artillery Corps, was no higher than middle school. He put away his pencil and turned his head toward the Chief of Staff Major General Chen Ruiting, who was responsible for this special training task.

"Comrade Ruiting, are you telling me that these are the best assets of the Artillery Corps?" General Chen Xilian joked in the heavy accent of his hometown. "Did you leave the best for yourself?"

Chen Ruiting smiled bitterly and spread his hands.

"Commander, which aspect of our assets do you not already have knowledge of? A middle school graduate is indeed a major intellectual in the army." Having said this, the two generals burst into laughter. Yet they could not hide the silent bitterness in their laughs.

After a moment of consideration, General Chen Xilian told Chen Ruiting, as if he were giving an order, "Broaden the scope of the selection. We can pick up trainees from the freshmen of the Artillery School, or from among the first-class squad leaders. As for the cadres, I will make a report to Marshal Peng, tell him to select from among the entire army."

Thus the task of selecting the first group of trainees for China's first strategic missile troops Artillery Training Brigade began.

It was known to everyone that our army came from the Jinggangshan Mountain and the side of the Yan River. Although their heroic and disciplined steps had moved them far from the towering mountains and bleak yellow land, there still remained some of the farmers' blood running through the green corps, the military songs of the farmers floating just above them. Since the republic was only newly established, it was only natural that the army see their nature as farmers unchanged.

Perhaps because this was the first time China had had its own modern missiles, the selection standard for picking the soldiers who would be in charge of these weapons was cruel and harsh, a characteristic of that era. First, the eligible soldiers had to have an absolutely clean political background. There was no tolerance for any stains—they almost unearthed up to three previous generations worth of relatives. Some soldiers had the most outstandingly communist personal performance and family background, but could be precluded due to some minor problem in their social relationships. And there were some other soldiers with absolutely clean backgrounds and families who nonetheless faced a dilemma because of their girlfriend's social relationships. Their choice was between losing a glorious dream pursued by generations of soldiers and losing their beloved women. The young soldiers of the republic, with a strong sense of political mission, would usually choose the latter without hesitation, wading across any subsequent pain, unable even to look back to the love they had buried...

Lieutenant Huang, who was called by his colleagues "the handsome one in the office", did not escape this dilemma. A man with a carefree nature, he came from southern Jiangsu Province and started his military life battling with the Japanese. Later he went to Yan'an, the holy sanctuary of the revolutionaries, and studied in the fifth school of the Chinese People's Anti-Japanese Military and Political College. After graduation he joined the first division of the New Fourth Army in Southern China. Following the directions of General Su Yu, he took part in the famous 7 consecutive great victories in the middle of Jiangsu Province as a staff officer. During the Liberation War, he fought as the staff officer of the Eastern China Field Army and the section chief of the Shandong corps. He followed Generals Su Yu, Xu Shiyou and Tan Zhenlin for a long time, and was part of the famous Battles of Lunan, Laiwu and Menglianggu, during which he shot one of the elite generals of the KMT, Zhang Lingfu, and arrested Li Xianzhou. After the Huaihai Campaign he followed the army to Korea as deputy chief of the artillery corps. When he got the news that he would be working as a company commander in a technology unit with a battalion rank in the first Missile Training Centre as lieutenant, he could not withhold his excitement.

But one day, walking the long corridor of the office building, one of his close friends implied to him in a very subtle way that his assignment to Changxindian could be ruined. He was astonished, and asked his friend anxiously why. His friend did not want to talk too much about this, only referring to the complicated social relationship of Huang's girlfriend.

Huang felt inexplicably frustrated and disappointed. He had just turned thirty, and due to his intense military career, he was unable to deal with personal issues. He had fallen in love with a cadre who was originally a university student. Having had just this initial taste of the sweetness of love in the mortal world, he had felt the need to cut it off. Inevitably, he felt the strangeness of his fate. But the social values of the 1950s had influenced a generation's lifetimes, all their values and ways of thinking. He was no exception to that. Therefore he ended his love and made a choice he could never regret.

In the autumn among the blood red maples, he took his girlfriend for the last time to visit the Incense Hill.

In her Lenin style outfit, with a pair of white plastic framed glasses, the university girl was intoxicated by the burning view of autumn. She romantically gave him a twig with two maple leaves embracing together, red as the sunset. She prayed that their love could be as fabulous as the sun and burn like fire. But his hand froze between them, trembling. He wanted to take the twig but couldn't. He was tortured with regrets. Only then did his girlfriend realise the sorrow on his face. Everything became clear to her.

At the last moment, he moved his lips with great difficulty, and a few heavy words dropped from his mouth. "Please forget all about me. I am not worth your love."

There were no excessive explanations. There was not one word of promise.

He walked into the Changxindian Missiles Training Centre without ever looking back. He remained unmarried for life, and dedicated all his youth and his life to a career in building missiles for China…

But how could one forget his love? Now, as this man enters into the last phase of his life, he is living in an apartment with six bedrooms in the military compound by the Chang'an Avenue, with the last loneness of his life. On this old man's altar of fate there lies the model of the strategic missile which stands between the heaven and earth; while on the other side, there is a withered maple twig, covering a fading photo. After his regular morning and evening exercise, the old man often looks at the photo for a long time.

Under the sunset, there is the shadow of an old man crying. No one can tell whether it is out of sweetness or pain.

It is the tears of bitterness…

This story was told to me by an old man from that unforgettable age of missiles. The tragic love story touched my soul deeply, leaving me awestruck and confused at the same time. Our father's generation has contributed all of their youth and passion to what they valued, seeing it as the greatest ideal imaginable. To achieve that, they suppressed their personality and other pursuits, even sacrificing the love of their life. To the young people today, each of whom value their own unique personality, this must sound like a distant fairy tale.

Many times, the urge to interview this old veteran arose in my mind, but I never did so. On this ancient land, there isn't much space for secrets and privacy in the first place.

The idea of interrupting him has left my mind. But there remain lots of old men from the missile corps who could testify to the validity of the story.

In the same building of the Artillery Corps, the deputy section chief of Military Affairs, Major Li, was called to the commander's office by General Chen Xilian.

Major Li was a tall and slim man who was born in the land of northern China, a place which was famous for its many tragic heroes. The ancient and bleak Yanshan Mountains had gifted him with persistence and toughness, and the heroic nature of the man there had empowered him with straightforwardness and courage. His bright eyes reflected wisdom and the confidence and capabilities of a battle-worn soldier. Since the day he arrived in Yan'an, Li had established a long relationship with the artillery corps, who were called the God of War. Following General Zhu Rui, the father of the Red Army's artillery corps, who graduated from the Kraal Artillery Officers' School in Moscow, Li started as a trainee, then became a platoon leader and a company commander; subsequently he followed the Marshal Lin Biao into Shanhaiguan pass as a chief of the battalion in the first division of the Eastern Field Artillery Corps. They mastered the most advanced cannons captured from the Japanese troops and fought intensively for 100 days against General Chen Mingren of the KMT, who was from Hunan. With more than ten years of experience in the military, Li could tell that every time he was asked to meet the commander for a conversation, there would almost certainly be an important task waiting for him.

Li stepped into Commander Chen's office as a soldier. General Chen Xilian stared at this deputy section chief, a man no older than 30 years old, with a great deal of trust and expectation. He slapped Li's shoulder kindly and said, "We have decided to transfer you to the Changxindian Missiles Training Centre to work for the Artillery Brigade. That is where our most advanced weapons are, so you've got a bit of a task ahead of you. To match up with the Soviet Union army, you will be given a lower rank. Would you be unhappy with that?"

Li stood up immediately and answered steadily, "Commander, please do not worry. I promise you that I will complete my task."

This conversation forever and totally changed the young officer's life.

With the transfer order, Li later became the first battalion commander of an Asian missile corps. He packed up quietly, without informing his parents and wife, and took off to the Changxindian Training Centre in secret. At that time, the most outstanding soldiers of the entire Chinese army were gathered there. Those who later became senior officers of the strategic missile corps, like the General Li Xuge (the later commander of the Strategic Missile Troop of China), had all studied there.

During that period of time a division level officer became a colonel in the army, and a lieutenant becoming a battalion commander was big news. At one time, Major Li took part in an important military meeting. According to the rules, it was only available for officers ranked higher than colonel. But when the host introduced him as a battalion commander for the missile troop, he received a high degree of respect, not to mention envy.

3. A green military train carries 102 Soviet Union officers and men. Marshal Peng, who was about to meet his destiny, makes time to host a grand banquet for them.

In the winter of 1957, the first snow continued, steadily covering China. When the light of sunset eventually fell upon the snow, white met blood red, and the ancient capital Beijing revealed its elegance as a northern kingdom.

The sky over China and the Soviet Union shared the same winter sun, which was not as warm as the summer one, but still shone upon the helmet of the two nations' fate.

Lieutenant battalion commander Sherman came to China with 102 missile officers and men, with four P-2 missiles, following the order from the Defence Ministry of the Soviet Union to become a military trainer. The green military train that carried him ran through the massive Siberia plains. As the temperature dropped to minus 40 degrees, Sherman looked over into the distance as he travelled further and further from his beautiful hometown by the Don River. Views of snow-frozen forests flew past his eyes, taking him back to the distant memories of the earlier revolutionaries, who were expelled there and drew two long lines of life on the snow with their slides. At this point, he couldn't help but bemoan his own future. As a descendant of the Cossacks, his straightforward, candid and righteous nature rendered him unpopular in the army. Most of his old mates from the military academy had been promoted to captain or major general, while he was still a lieutenant in charge of a battalion. Indeed, his age would eventually put a tragic end to his military career. Going to China could be a good chance for promotion, but this red country in the east was too far away and unfamiliar, as if he would have been placing himself in an ancient dream or fairy tale.

When he awoke from his dream, a mass of blood red lay to the east of the sky, a yellow-red winter sun climbing slowly above the forests, colouring the window of the train. The orderly staff came in and told lieutenant Sherman that they would soon arrive in Manzhouli, the northeastern gate of China. A senior military officer of China would be waiting for all the Soviet Union officers there.

The train slowly entered the Manzhouli train station. Although snow and ice have already frozen the platform, Sherman could feel a warm sense of friendship and fun has been accumulating as he exited the train. Lieutenant General Wan Yi and Major Li were waiting on the platform. As a graduate of an university in Beijing and who had previously worked for the Party under Supreme Commander Zhang Xueliang, Lieutenant General Wan Yi spoke fluent Russian, which quickly dispersed any sense of unfamiliarity between the soldiers of the two countries in their hugs and handshaking. Lieutenant General Wan Yi, Major Li, and Lieutenant Sherman stepped onto the train towards Changxindian, Beijing. It was the first time Sherman had come to China. When their train arrived, the strict and comprehensive first-class guarding measures adopted along the railway made Sharman and his officers irresistibly excited and proud.

On the evening of December 22nd, the train arrived at the military base of Changxindian. However, when it came to unloading the carriage, there was a minor dispute between the two armies.

The Soviet Union army had brought four training missiles. Based on their previous experience, it was only possible to unload two missiles and the necessary ground facilities at most. But to maintain confidentiality, the Chinese army decided to unload all of the four missiles and ground facilities within one night. This sounded like a joke to Lieutenant Sherman, and he rejected the Chinese plan instantly. But Captain Sun Shixing and other leaders argued with him and presented a comprehensive plan, stating that they would unload all the missiles and ground facilities without scratching them at all before dawn. Lieutenant Sherman agreed reluctantly, hoping to embarrass the Chinese. He specifically asked a few Majors to take occupy central positions during the unloading task. Then he returned to his office and awaited the result.

This was in fact the first time the missile soldiers and officers of China and the Soviet Union had competed with each other in demonstrating their capabilities and determination. All the officers and men of the Artillery Training Brigade participated in the unloading task, taking hold of each position. The task was organised in an orderly manner. Even though the freezing wind of the winter night of Beijing cut through their bones and faces, the Chinese officers and men sweated during their task while the Soviet Union officers were so cold they had to rely on vodka. When Venus blinked in the night sky, bright light revealed itself across the horizon. All the missiles and ground facilities had been unloaded from the train, perfectly intact. After the staff officer of the Soviet

Union reported to Lieutenant Sherman, the first word that came out of his mouth was, "Impossible."

Lieutenant Sherman staggered outside, and saw the four missiles had indeed been placed inside of the towering missile operation room, along with the other ground facilities. This reality was enough to convince the passionate Cossack. He gave a thumbs-up, and said repeatedly, "My Chinese colleagues are marvelous! ... "

Arrogance and self-regard lowered its lofty head in front of iron facts; trust and respect were established in their place.

A few days later, Marshal Peng, who were stepping into the last stage of his glorious military career, made a point of hosting a grand banquet at the hall of the military committee, welcoming the 102 missile officers and men from the beautiful Volga River. Peng was originally the son of a Chinese farmer, and had only had three years of education in an old-style private school, though he had been through hundreds of battles. Just like many other high ranking officers who never enjoyed military academy experience, he could not escape the limits imposed by his experience. But as the only commander of the Party who had battled against the Americans in a modern war, he took his education in the theatre of the Korean War, during which he had witnessed soldiers who used their own bodies to block the American tanks. This only strengthened his determination to transform this farmers' army into a professional unit which could compete with any advanced country in the world. After coming back from the Korea War to the Central Military Committee, Peng initiated a historic journey of modernisation for the Chinese army, in spite of enormous difficulties and objections. Peng appeared to be particularly interested in the strategic missile corps, the most advanced part of the army.

That evening, the Soviet Union embassy's Office of the Military Attache' were greatly surprised by the people who attended the banquet from the Chinese party. More than ten people — Marshal Peng, Chief of General Staff General Huang Kecheng, Deputy Chief of General Staff General Zhang Aiping, Chief of Staff for the Artillery Corps Major General Chen Ruiting, and Chief of the Equipment Department from the General Staff, Lieutenant General Wan Yi, along with leaders from the Committee of Science and Technology for National Defence — attended the banquet. The event was hosted by General Zhang Aiping, who was famous for his air of intellectualism. Supreme Commander Peng, who used to be astute and quiet, delivered a speech. He talked humorously in his heavy Hunan accent.

"After touring around the world for a few hundred years, rockets, which were invented by our ancestors, have returned to their homeland. This is thanks to the Party and army of the Soviet Union, who provided us with the most advanced weapons available worldwide. An army which has mastered the nuclear missile is one which can truly say something meaningful in the world, and who truly can be called a powerful army. The Americans turned Nagasaki and Hiroshima into ruins with their nuclear bombs, and continue to threaten us. Once we have nuclear weapons, if they dare to attack, we will be able to bomb a giant hole on their territory as well. My comrades, we need to learn studiously from our big old brother, the Soviet Union, and master these weapons and technology as soon as possible ... "

Peng seemed to be exceptionally happy that night, though he was not usually good at drinking. Holding the strong Maotai liquor, he toasted the Soviet Union missile battalion officers table by table. Respect arose in the hearts of the Soviet Union missile battalion officers when they saw the Chinese Defence Minister's honesty, roughness and straightforwardness, and his remarkable achievement of successfully resisting the UN army in Korea.

It had been a long time since Peng had enjoyed such a good drink. That night, as he was helped out by two staff, he was already a bit drunk...

However, the Soviet Union officers were to stay in China for only three months. The Chinese Artillery Training Brigade was separated according to the number of officers from the Soviet Union, so that they could be taught in small groups. The Soviet Union officers taught the Chinese from up on the podium, with the aid of a Chinese interpreter. Among the Chinese officers, there were some who had studied missiles and nuclear weapons in the US, Britain and France, as well as technicians who had been newly selected from universities. These high-end talents sometimes raised difficult questions regarding the industrial technologies, which would render the Soviet Union officers speechless, astonished and embarrassed. Their knowledge went beyond the expectations of the Soviet Union officers.

Objectively speaking, the Soviet Union officers did provide enormous assistance to China in terms of missile technology. But, on the other hand, the sense of superiority of the Russians would affect the Chinese soldiers from time to time. The Russians always had hot blood, and they could never hide their affection for the slim Chinese women. Every weekend evening, they were most keen on the dancing parties. The Soviet Union officers would dance closely with the female doctors and nurses of the Chinese army. Soviet Union officers would harass the Chinese women after some vodka, and they would continue to do so even after repeated warnings from the Chinese…

But the Soviet Union officers would never be so warm and kind to the Chinese soldiers, who had little education.

4. The Chinese soldiers, who carried the blood of the yellow land, laid their hands, used to doing heavy chores, on the advanced weapons. And the training model missiles were made of carrot and soil.

Breathing heavily, Captain Sakharov rushed into the office of the deputy General Staff, Major Li's office and dorm room. He threw the training materials on Li's table, gesturing with his arms. "Comrade Zhang is no good. For a missile launching operator, his level of education is too low. He has to be replaced. Comrade Li, please find another to replace him."

With the assistance of the interpreter, Li eventually understood Captain Sakharov. Zhang Yuanqing was the copy clerk of the launching company, a young man from Sichuan who was sharp and responsive. He could be described as a decent intellectual in the army. And that was the reason that the party branch of the launching company had recommended him to take on the vital role of missile-launcher. Who else could replace him? Major Li struggled to think about this question, considering all the officers in the company; yet Zhang was still the most suitable one. Li kindly made Captain Sakharov a cup of black tea and handed him the apple peeled by the orderly. Then he told the Soviet Union officer, with a warm and friendly smile on his face, "Comrade Captain, please give me another half month. I will get Zhang to meet your requirements…"

Captain Sakharov was touched by Li's genuineness, and nodded to him quietly. Before he left the room, he saluted to Li and said to him decisively, "Comrade Major, as we agreed, you have half a month."

Major Li saw him off, and murmured to himself, "There is no joking in the army; we must ensure this will happen!"

Zhang Yuanqing was called to the party branch of the brigade by the orderly. Tears streamed down his face the moment Zhang heard that the Soviet Union trainer wanted to replace him.

In the social atmosphere at that time, once a soldier has been dismissed from such a glorious mission, it was not only a personal failure, but also a shame upon their family, even a whole group of people. Major Li handed a towel to Zhang, and seriously but brotherly patted his shoulders. "Wipe away your tears, you are a soldier, not a girl. How can you cry so easily? You are here to study on behalf of our motherland, our nation. No matter how difficult it is, you have to strive for success. Do not let our big old brother look down on we Chinese soldiers…"

Without harsh reprimand, without political preaching, the political education of the Chinese army was subtle, transforming the ordinary soldiers into heroes.

The Chinese soldiers did not believe in tears. Zhang Yuanqing wiped them away, and walked out calmly and confidently towards the northern horizon where the sun was rising. There he began a struggle in which he spared no effort…

Actually, the things holding the Chinese soldiers back was not just their low level of education. The training approach and exceedingly harsh confidentiality rules of the Soviet Army were also problematic. The missile weapons, the most advanced field after the Second World War, was also a brand new field for the Chinese soldiers. Usually an officer without a university degree could not master it without training for more than a year or so. However, the Soviet Union trainers only gave the Chinese soldiers three months. The trainers talked fast, and the interpreters translated fast as well. Before the trainees could take down all the notes, their trainers had already moved on to new topics. Moreover, there was also the "Catch-22" of the Soviet Union Missile Corps, which required that all the notes and training materials be registered and locked in safes after class. And there were no exceptions to this rule. Undoubtedly, this rule made it even harder for the Chinese soldiers with little education, and imposed enormous difficulties on their ability to review and assimilate the knowledge they learnt.

But every country and politician who has neglected the imagination, intelligence, passion and endurance of the Chinese nation will pay heavily for their mistake. The tough Chinese soldiers had been the heroes in the brutal wars, and in this peaceful competition of technology they were also smart and swift. After the class, with no notes to review, they tried hard to memorise during class; later a few people could combine their memories to create complete class notes for everyone's use. In addition, the Soviet Union trainers prohibited them from touching the facilities, and so they began using carrots and soil to build their own missiles, making iron sheet into ground facilities. Initially, the Soviet Union trainers showed contempt toward these game-like antics of the Chinese soldiers, believing that what they were doing resembled the building block games of childhood. However, after a month, they suddenly found out that these games only revealed their effects gradually. The Chinese soldiers had become better at commands, and their movements were precise. From this moment the trainers began to change their ideas about these soldiers from the yellow land ...

Zhan Yuanqing, the soldier on the blacklist of the Soviet Union trainers, knew that his last chance was only 15 days long. Apart from catching up, there was no other way out. He swallowed the bitter tears, and lost himself in study. Since he had never learned about advanced mathematics, he asked the university students for help in providing him with extra training. After the light went off at night, he started to review the things he had learned under his quilt with the flashlight on. Early the next morning, he got up and recited all the procedures for a missile launcher. He would memorise cards of testing rules wherever he went. Pictures of the control panels and lines were hung all over his dorm room, and he would draw more by himself every evening. After one hundred days of intense study and struggle, the light of rationalism swept through their hearts; the sun of hope rose. During the examinations organised by the Fifth Division of the Defence Minister and the Committee for Science a and Technology, Zhang drew the diagram with more than 3,000 lines and 10,000 conjunction points all by himself fifteen minutes faster than the Soviet Union experts; and he could recite the operative procedures of 500 commands without missing one word or mistaking one piece of data. He was called by the Soviet Union lieutenant engineer Puleo Brezhski a "living circuit".

Thirty years later, as the director of the Strategic Missile Corps Research Institute, Zhan Yuanqing went abroad to give lectures as a senior expert. If the Soviet Union trainer who had wanted to replace him knew about this, what would he think? Would he be embarrassed because he had belittled the young guy from the Dabashan Mountains, or would he be happy about the sweet fruits he had sown?

In the spring of 1958, ancient Beijing awoke from a long hibernation. After the tough struggle during the winter there was a prototype for China's strategic missile.

In March of the same year, right before the Soviet Union trainers returned, the trainees of Changxindian organised a launching mission. Apart from the fact that the missile could not actually be launched, everything proceeded as if it were real. In any case, the Soviet Union trainers were only monitoring. Marshals Chen Yi and Nie Rongzhen and General Huang Kecheng, along with all the relevant leaders from the Central Military Committee, showed up. Perhaps because they were too used to their old ways of battle with "millets and rifles", some senior generals from other divisions of the army also came to see the launching of the "treasure of the country". Marchal Nie also stood at the gates of the red courtyard with his guards, blocking the incoming sedans. Marchal Nie checked people's identity while warning senior officials.

"This is a top secret of the nation. If it is within your responsibility, please come and watch; but if it is not, I am sorry that I can only accept those with an authorised identity…"

An general from the Central Committee was stopped by Marshal Nie outside of the gate, forced to return to his sedan in disappointment.

Inside of the courtyard, several bamboo mats covered the dark green P-2 missiles. The Chinese officers involved in this mock launching were all stationed at their preordained positions.

Walking the narrow path beneath the plane trees, Marshal and diplomat Chen Yi joked with Senior General Huang Kecheng, who walked along behind him. "Senior General Huang, you'll have to open your eyes as wide as possible, because this giant is sharper than the big cannons of the Fourth Field Army when they went into Shanhaiguan."

Senior General Huang rebutted, in his heavy southern Hunan accent, "Marshal Chen, are you indulging in your poeticisms again?"

Chen Yi laughed. "No poeticisms this time, but I do have a few words to say. We fired a few shots at the Taiwan Strait, and the Americans said that it was a buzz from the mosquitoes. With these missiles, it will be the roar of lions and tigers. Hahaha!"

These battle-worn senior generals and marshal could not resist their excitement.

The Chinese officers who were doing their first mock launching achieved great success.

In April, Sherman had finished his short but productive stay in China and returned with his troops. During his one hundred days and nights in China, he had witnessed the peerless persistence and endurance of this army, an army through whose veins flowed the blood of the yellow land. He had felt the heavy history of this great country and nation.

Lieutenant Sherman waved goodbye to Senior General Huang Kecheng, holding back his tears, and departed with the green military trains. No matter how international politics changed, his experiences in China would always stay with this descendant of the Cossacks.

5. Coldness envelops the relationship between China and the Soviet Union. A Soviet Union major Squadron Leader arrogantly declares: "Without our help, the Chinese will be unable to launch their missiles."

In the last autumn of the 1950s, the currents of winter reached

Beijing earlier than usual.

The dense cloud coming from Siberia had enveloped the relationship between China and the Soviet Union, blocking out the sunny sky. The floating cloud morphed into a dark tornado as it tore apart the leaves of friendship in Beijing overnight…

The dense cloud overcast the political and diplomatic relationship of China and the Soviet Union, suggesting that the 10-year-long honeymoon between the two parties had officially come to an end, tragically ending the friendship between the two nations. The wind came from the north, but the origin of the tornado had been around for a much longer time.

When Khrushchev paid his second visit to Beijing, he spent a few days with the generation's oriental great man, Mao Tse-tung, in the swimming pool of Zhongnanhai. But the cooperation necessary to establishing a joint fleet and a long wave radio station were not settled by the waterside. On the contrary, a psychological gap between the two highest leaders had formed. Especially when it came to their attitudes towards Stalin, the two Parties had already adopted conflicting positions. It was only a matter of time before they would separate with each other politically.

Khrushchev made the first step. By sabotaging the sending of the promised nuclear bomb models and materials to China, he had already let down China. On top of this, international society had started to move in a direction which was disadvantageous to China.

In the summer of that year, the Soviet Union, US and Britain held an international nuclear arms control negotiation in Geneva. This was the first time humankind had raised the issue of prohibiting nuclear testing. In the following half century, there would be seventeen more arms control negotiations; nine of them would concern nuclear arms control. But the Geneva meeting did not achieve anything substantive — the positions of the three powers were too far removed from each other. The result of the negotiation was that nobody was responsible for anyone else's conduct or promises. And the Soviet Union would use this as a tool to pressure China...

In June 20, 1959, the Central Committee of the Soviet Union Communist Party officially wrote to the Central Committee of the Chinese Communist Party, informing them that the Soviet Union was undergoing a nuclear arms control talk with the US and Britain. Comrade Khrushchev would fly to meet President Eisenhower in Camp David. Therefore they had decided to postpone the delivery of the nuclear bomb model and materials to China. And whether the delivery would be made depended on how circumstances looked in two years time. Essentially, Khrushchev had already started to say "no" to the Chinese leaders.

In September, Khrushchev flew over the Atlantic, visiting the US as the secretary-general of the Soviet Union Communist Party and the Premier of the government for the first time. Because the ramp of the US could not reach the heavy and high plane he took, he had to climb down from the rope he had prepared himself in front of everyone, embarrassing the Soviet Union. But under the Statue of Liberty he still received the solemn welcome as a head of a state. After touring seven cities of the US, Khrushchev took the private helicopter of Eisenhower, who was originally a military officer, from the southern lawn of the White House down to Camp David, where the president's country villa was.

Camp David was located in the green forest of the Catoctin Mountains in Maryland, a ten-minute flight from the capital Washington. In 1930, President Roosevelt built a vacation resort for the president, a resort which occupied 6,000 acres in the picturesque mountain area. He also gave the resort a romantic and dreamy name, Shangri-La. President Eisenhower, who had spent his whole life fighting wars, was not a fan of this romantic name, so he renamed it "Camp David" — his beloved grandson's name.

Khrushchev walked into Camp David with Eisenhower, the two pairs of giant hostile hands temporarily joined. The US president told the owner of the Kremlin, "I am a soldier, and a soldier for life. I have fought more than once, but now I am not embarrassed to tell you that I am scared of war very much. And I am willing to spare no efforts to avoid it. Most importantly, I want to reach an agreement with you."

Khrushchev must have been touched by the genuineness of the US's five-star general. His eyes were full of tears, without the rudeness of a child of a Ukraine miner, and he said in a friendly tone, "Mr President, if we can reach an agreement, there will be no one happier than me…"

The US and the Soviet Union, the two major powers, shook hands at Camp David. From then on, Camp David became world famous as a symbol of peace.

20 years later, Egyptian president Sadat signed a treaty of peace with its long-time enemy Israel at Camp David; another 15 years later, Palestine president Arafat would sign a treaty of peace with Rabin, Premier of Israel, at Camp David.

And the American boy whose name was used by his president-grandfather later became the son-in-law of the great Western politician Nixon, and was allowed to meet Chairman Mao when Mao was in the final stages of his disease.

Of course, all of these are another story.

After touring around the US, Khrushchev came to China for the tenth anniversary of the PRC with the agreement reached in Camp David, which was of little substance. It was the last time Khrushchev would visit Beijing.

On October 1, China hosted a grand military parade in the world's largest city square.

The highest leader Chairman Mao, with his battle mates the seven giants — Liu Shaoqi, Zhou Enlai, Zhu De, Chen Yun, Lin Biao and Deng Xiaoping — entered Tiananmen to watch the parade. Hu Zhiming, who came from the forests of Vietnam, and Kim Il-Sung from North Korea, also showed up in the VIP box. Khrushchev talked to Mao cheerfully and humorously while pointing to Liu Shaoqi. "Comrade Chairman, is that big-nose guy your successor?" Mao, however, answered in a serious tone, "Did you see the little one over there?" Mao pointed to Deng among the crowd and continued, "He has toughness in his gentleness, and is indeed a promising one."

The two giants of the Eastern Bloc stood at the highest sanctum of power, waving to the soldiers and dancing crowds, though their visions had set out in different directions long ago. Before the celebration, China had been engaged in territory disputes with India over the eastern and western parts of their border. Without admonishing India over their offensive conduct against China, Khrushchev was on the side of Nehru. What annoyed Mao most was that, during the welcome banquet prepared by the friendly Chinese for him, Khrushchev, the rude Ukraine, called the Chinese, who had just been through a hard battle with the US, an "aggressive rooster". For Mao, what was worse was that Khrushchev even asked for a meeting with Peng, who just had disappeared from Chinese political arena, wanting to give him a present. What was this for? Did he actually mean that they had made a mistake in punishing Peng, or did he want Peng to defect? The Russian had no idea where he was — that he was in the Forbidden City, not the Kremlin. Clearly he was trying to intervene in the domestic politics of China. Therefore, when Khrushchev raised the issue at the welcoming banquet of building a long-wave radio station in Chinese territory, one which could keep contact with their Pacific fleets, Mao rejected him rather impatiently, his sense of nationalism badly hurt. "No, this is the last time I'll tell you, no." He continued angrily: "I do not want to discuss the issue anymore."

. . .

At the beginning of this troublesome autumn, more than 12,000 experts, technicians and military consultants from the Soviet Union left China, leaving their ongoing construction projects uncompleted together with various items of technology they had been working on, and the sweet but bitter memories of their time in China.

At the same time, in the Changxindian missile training base, the first Chinese missile battalion had already been built. When Lieutenant Sherman returned, there were only a few consultants remaining from the Soviet Union. After the order to leave China was delivered to them, an engineer, Major Batov, visited Major Li to say goodbye. The engineer had developed a deep emotional attachment to his Chinese colleagues. There was embarrassment and shame on his face as he packed away his materials. Walking out of the gate with his luggage, he held Major Li's hand tightly and said to him, in a sad and low tone, "I am terribly sorry, Major Li, but this is an order from my superior. As a armyman who has to obey his superior, I cannot help you anymore. I wish you all the best."

However, with his KGB background, Major Batov was unwilling to lower his arrogant head. He told Major Li in contempt, "Comrade Major, I can tell you honestly, without our help, your missile project can never be completed."

Hearing this, Major Li felt his blood rise. Having grown up in Northern China, a land of heroism, he would never yield to any difficulties. His face turned red as he pointed to the door.

"Comrade Major, please leave now. I appreciate your help. We have an old saying in China — the earth will keep spinning without anyone in it. The Chinese armymen are totally capable of sending our missiles to the sky, just wait and see."

After the military consultants of the Soviet Union had left, all that remained for the Chinese missile battalion was a *Guide to Military Affairs of the Soviet Union Army*. Looking at the empty building for the Soviet Union consultants, Major Li and his officers and men from the first missile battalion no longer had any assistance left. An individual, a nation could not rely on another's sympathy; but once all his means have been cut off, there comes the chance for him to strive for survival; and through the hell-like experience of pain and struggle, one can gain a new life in the fire, like a phoenix...

The Chinese armymen never believed in God or salvation. Major Li swallowed the bitterness along with his soldiers, and led the Chinese missile battalion on into the tribulations of the next stage.

6. Before leaving China, a Soviet Union expert gives an important lesson to the Chinese nuclear physicist Zhu Guangya.

The Friendship Hotel, Beijing. Apartment compound for the Soviet Union experts

As one of the last Soviet Union experts to leave China, nuclear physicist Nikola (for reasons of security I can only give his father's surname) was walking around his room in great anxiety. He divided the red curtains from time to time, expecting to see the Chinese nuclear physicist, Zhu Guangya. Last night, Zhu telephoned him and told him that he would see Nikola off at the hotel. During his two-year-stay in China, Nikola had enjoyed the happiest time of his life. He relished the cooperation with his Chinese colleagues, especially with Dr Zhu Guangya, who had graduated from the US University of Michigan. They had developed a strong friendship. As Nikola was prepared to work hard in China and contribute to its missile project, the two parties' relationship deteriorated. But he knew that the Chinese nuclear industry was still in a stage of infancy, and the leading young Chinese physicists were talented and had a strong academic background. With some help, they could quickly achieve great things. So he valued this last meeting with Dr Zhu very much. As the Chinese saying goes, once you leave the village, you will never encounter the same shop again.

Time passed while Nikola kept looking over to the crowd downstairs, sometimes with hope, sometimes with frustration.

As he looked at his watch and divided the heavy curtains, the slim figure of Dr Zhu suddenly entered his horizon. "Thank god, you finally came."

Zhu Guangya was from Yichang, Hubei province. He was born in an intellectual family by the side of the Yangtze River. Just like many other young people of the old times, he harbored an ambition to save his nation through science. So he left the country and the Yangtze River area to study abroad. He was first admitted by Nanjing Central University and Southwest Associated University, where he was instructed by the famous Chinese physicists Zhou Peiyuan, Wu Youxun and Wu Dayou. In 1946, as recommended by Wu Dayou, he went across the ocean to study at the University of Michigan for a PhD in nuclear physics, along with Tang Aoqing and Li Zhengdao. In 1949, he was granted a doctorate in nuclear physics and stayed at the university to teach. However, an ambitious patriot, as the bright sunlight of the new China arose over the eastern coast, he felt the urge to return. In 1950, in spite of the objections of his American mentors and colleagues, he insisted upon returning to serve his country. After participating in land reform in the old revolutionary base areas for a year, he was assigned to the physics department of Northeastern University. During the negotiation in Panmunjom, he acted as a senior interpreter for the Chinese army under the order of Marshal Peng, his Michigan accented English shocking the US General Clark.

In 1955, Zhu taught in the physics department of Peking University as he turned 30. Two years later, he was transferred to the Atom Science Research Institute by the Minister for Nuclear Industry. Along with the founding father of the Chinese atomic and hydrogen bombs, Deng Jiaxian, he became a critical figure in the development of China's nuclear weapons. Like many of the scientists who quietly contributed to this area, Zhu worked in a highly confidential area for a long time, not showing up in any international academia forums. Later, Li Zhengdao and Yang Zhening, schoolmates of Zhu Guangya and Deng Jiaxian, won the Nobel prize. But their names were hardly known to the Chinese people. Only once Zhu was nominated as the deputy Chairman of the National Chinese People's Political Consultative Conference in 1993, at the Second Plenary Meeting of the 8th National Political

Consultative Conference, did his unusual experience reach other members of the conference who had read about him. Subsequently, with a vote of 96%, he was elected as the deputy Chairman. Showered with applause from all around the hall, he stepped out of the mysterious curtain and onto the splendid podium of the Great Hall of the People. After half of century, he had met the world again.

However, in the early 1960s, Zhu did not enjoy this glory. You could not distinguish him from the crowds on the street as he walked along, a slim figure in his ordinary old-style Zhongshan suits. Only his bright eyes reflected the particular sophistication of his education and exceptional manner. On this day, he was riding his old bike in a rush from Nanyuan to the apartment compound of the Soviet Union experts. When he arrived he ran to Nikola's room, breathing heavily. As he pushed the door open, without any greetings, he started to apologise.

"I am terribly sorry, Professor Nikola, for making you wait for me."

"Not a problem, Dr Zhu. Nanyuan is far away. Thank you for coming."

"It's nothing — since you have helped us so much."

"Good comrade Dr Zhu, we don't have much time, so let's save the small talk. Regarding the technology for the atomic bombs, we have offered you very little material. These questions have been discussed during our work. And there are some other key points that I need to talk with you about, just to raise your attention to them for your later research."

As he talked, professor Nikola brought out a piece of paper and drew a simple diagram. "You must take good care of the crash field problems for these two kinds of materials ... " Nikola said, pointing to a section of his diagram.

Professor Zhu listened to him quietly, nodding his head from time to time. He would occasionally make a few comments when he was confused. Two scholars of different colours, countries and languages, sharing an important lesson together in their intellectual discussion.

After the conversation, professor Nikola walked over and picked up the few pieces of paper containing drafts for the atomic bombs and shredded them to pieces, flushing them down the toilet.

Without any fake or pretentious words, nor even a shred of paper, this upright Soviet Union scientist left China. But he had left behind a genuine mark in the home of the oriental dragon, lighting the fire of knowledge for the Chinese scientists, helping them to hold on to the sun of China.

At the last moment, Professor Nikola hugged Dr Zhu tightly. Zhu's eyes were filled with tears.

"Professor Nikola, I wish you a safe trip. Please take care."

"Thank you! I wish the Chinese comrades good luck. I will be waiting for a big explosion by the side of the Volga River."

Chapter 3

The First Battalion of Asia

1. China had come to a crossroads of fate again. In the old site of the military camp of Ma Bufang, the former so-called King of the Northwest, the first missile battalion of Asia makes its first step.

In the last year of the 1960s, those Chinese who had experienced the tough times of the young republic had eyes filled with the shadow of hunger.

It was a good year for agriculture originally. But, in that beautiful tale of utopia, the Chinese nation, who used to be good at rational thinking, spread their wings of imagination, and waved a ridiculous tale of the 20th century. As a result, the steady steps of the young republic gradually fell into a dark swamp. At a time of great urgency for the Chinese, the big country to the north had shredded the agreements and taken away all the experts, demanding the repayment of loans from the Korean War. Undoubtedly, this had cut off a life-saving straw for China.

Again, the Chinese had come to a crossroads of fate ...

One gloomy day, a mysterious military train departed from Beijing and ran through the Hexi Corridor towards ancient Liangzhou with the only strategic missile battalion on board.

The train ran fast through the dark night along the ancient silk road.

It was deep at night, and the western plains was deathly silent.

The stars were blinking their mysterious green eyes while the wind blew heavily. Occasionally, one could see groups of gazelles following the train. The wheels of the train roared as it lanced through the silence of the night. The commander of the battalion, Major Li, did not want to sleep at all. Watching the sleeping soldiers in the train, he felt the heavy burden laid upon his shoulders. As the train sped through the darkness his mind returned to a few months ago in Beijing…

After the establishment, with the approval of Premier Zhou, of the Changxindian strategic missile training base, the Central Military Committee decided to transfer the first strategic missile battalion to the remote northwestern military base of Liangzhou to undertake training for the purpose of launching the first short-range strategic missile.

Before their departure, Major Li was called to the headquarters of the Artillery Corps. Major General Chen Ruiting grasped his hand and said to him with enormous expectation, "Comrade Li, you are leading the first strategic missile battalion of Asia. Chairman Mao and Premier Zhou have great expectations of this troop. Please tell the soldiers to train themselves hard and not fail their reputation as the No. 1 Battalion under heaven."

Major Li nodded with firm determination. In his burning blood, an unprecedented confidence surged and roared. This was a chance which all ambitious officers longed for. But not everyone had Major Li's luck…

History had granted him a piece of land upon which to build the glory of his life.

As the dawn broke the darkness, this piece of land was becoming more and more clear. Li looked into the distance as far as he could, to the towering ridges of the Qilian Mountains in the south, like the strong and hard back of a knight who had spent too long in the sun. The broad Tengger desert to the north had extended its golden curves, coloured by the blood-red rising sun—like groups of battle-worn soldiers throwing eternal questions to heaven.

This piece of land had carried many of the nation's glories and shames. It is a bleak piece of land which has buried many soldiers who dreamt of peace.

The train arrived at a military camp in Liangzhou by sunset. Upon arrival the soldiers saw an old military dorm, with thick mud walls more than ten metres high. The wall enclosed the camp in a square court a few miles wide, the poplars so tall they almost pierced the sky.

Since the Qin and Han Dynasties, this had been an important military base. General Li Guang from the Han Dynasty defeated the Huns here, but eventually he killed himself when the Hun's armies circled him. During the Qing Dynasty, it was called Mancheng city. Zuo Zongtang used to base his army here and crushed the rebelling Muslims of Hui in the Xihaigu area. Before the founding of PRC, it again became the military camp of Ma Bufang, the King of the Northwest then. Many soldiers of the Red Army who were sent to conquer the west were buried here.

Perhaps it was a coincidence of fate that history had made the first Chinese strategic missile battalion start here, a piece of land with too many glories and blood and tears. The first problem facing the soldiers of the battalion was a set of P-2 missile facilities with missing pieces and a lonely *Guide to Military Affairs*.

During the meeting for the officers of the battalion, Major Li walked around the humble room for a long time, knocking on the table hard with his fist. "Do it!" he told his subordinates. "Even at the cost of our lives, we cannot afford to be looked down upon by the Russians."

A group of literate officers were organised to edit training materials. They pooled their notes from Changxindian together, and considered each paragraph carefully. Their work formed the first guide book for missile-launch training. In the winter of the Hexi Corridor, there were no romantic views of cows and sheep revealed from the grass by the wind. In the strong and heavy wind, a sand storm was cast over the western sky, all nature's power freely whipping the old camp. The freezing coldness threatened the soldiers of the battalion, who had no heating facilities. But these farmers' soldiers from the yellow land, who were famous for their toughness in the harsh environment, used their bodies to fight the nature. Bian Mingyuan, who was from Sichuan, a famous "heaven on earth", was the most educated member of the battalion. He took on most of the responsibilities in editing the guide book. Since he had grown up in the south, he had never experienced the harsh coldness of the plateau. His hands and feet were covered with chilblains and swelled like a steaming bun. When the chilblains started to bleed he used a piece of cloth to tie his pen up tightly. With every line of words he wrote, a trail of blood was left on the paper. Through the hard fight of an entire winter, the first 300,000-characters guide book for missile-launching was completed. When the soldiers held the book, they could not help bursting into tears.

With the guide book completed, the missile model and launching platform, made from galvanized iron sheet and cables which were actually ropes, was completed, looking just like the real thing. The soldiers of the first missile battalion used their tough hands to propel the modernisation of the Chinese army, having begun from the most primitive stage.

Looking at the honest soldiers, Major Li saluted them solemnly, his throat choked with emotion.

2. Premier Zhou tells the leaders of all the military areas, tears in his eyes, "I am here as a beggar. Our strategic missile troop is hungry."

Although it could be said that difficulties in the military training could be overcome, the famine, caused by natural and man-made disasters, pushed the battalion into desperation.

The food stores were exhausted. The standard 100 grams of food for every meal and two meals a day could no longer sustain the soldiers' bodies. The amount of people suffering from liver diseases was increasing. And there were an increasing number of people collapsing in the training grounds. The deputy chief of the technology section was a first lieutenant who was transferred from the Artillery Academy. To leave more food for the soldiers, he only ate a little food with some wild herbs, and eventually ended up with a severe liver condition. Even so, he struggled to remain in training, until he collapsed and died. No longer would he open his eyes again to see his white-headed mother who was waiting for him in his hometown.

The number of the soldiers was decreasing everyday. Major Li had to send a platoon to the Qilian Mountains for hunting gazelles, rabbits, wild chickens and sparrows. They had to dig for wild herbs to mix with barley for food. One Sunday, the deputy chief of the transportation section, Meng Ling, led a few soldiers to the snowy mountains of Qilian, hoping to hunt for something to improve the soldiers' diet. For the past few months, in order to let the soldiers have more food, he forewent food for months. He searched around for targets when suddenly he saw, through the brown-blue smoke, a group of gazelles running. He chased them over multiple ridges until the gazelles turned into an illusion. But he did not realise this until it was too late and he had lost himself in the boundless Tengger desert. Exhausted, he lay in the desert forever.

A highly confidential telegraph reporting that the strategic missile troop containing the most advanced technological talent was starving was laid on the desk of Premier Zhou.

Premier Zhou had never relaxed his frowning eyebrows, given the shocking number of starving people all over the provinces. The report of casualties from the strategic missile troops due to starvation became another heavy burden, making Premier Zhou frown even more. He read the report several times, his hand trembling, as if he were carrying a load thousands of kilo heavy. He walked around his room, then pushed his window open. As he looked up to the sky of Zhongnanhai, a breeze blew away the clouds in the sky. The Premier turned around and told the military secretary, Zhou Jiading, who stood by, "Jiading, prepare my car, let's go to the expanded meeting of the Central Military Committee."

Premier Zhou walked into the meeting hall looking grave. The hall fell silent. The leaders of the third division of the Central Committee and all the military commands were surprised, since usually the Premier would walk in and greet them with a kind smile on his face, and even an occasional joke. Today he walked straight to the rostrum solemnly and took a seat. Everyone was staring at the Premier's serious face, wondering what had happened. Gradually, the applause stopped as the Premier motioned with his hand. Lin Biao, who replaced Marshal Peng at the Lushan Meeting and handled the daily tasks of the Central Military Committee, said in a gentle Hubei accent: "Now — please welcome the Premier's instructions!"

"Today, I am here, not to give you instructions, but to beg from all of the commanders." Premier Zhou waved his left arm, injured during the war, a grave look upon his face.

The commanders and commissars from all of the military commands were astonished. Had the Premier became a beggar? The atmosphere of the meeting immediately turned solemn.

The Premier took a few pieces of paper from his pocket, and waved them at the senior military officers. "We received this telegraph this morning," he said in a rather painful tone. "A few days ago, a strategic missile troop broke the rules at their station. The soldiers picked the leaves of the local trees, which damaged them and was reported by the locals to the provincial government. After investigations of the provincial task force, it was found that the troop had run out of food a long time ago. People had starved already. But the soldiers knew that the entire country has been under great difficulties, so they didn't want to report to their superior about their situation. When they heard that the leaves could be used as food, they..."

Premier Zhou's eyes were full of tears, and his throat was choked with sadness. "What a troop! What a group of soldiers!"

The meeting hall went silent. The leaders of the military were guilty of not knowing the situation of their own subordinates before the Premier did. They looked at the Premier quietly.

As Premier Zhou calmed himself down, he said in a gentle voice, "I have talked to the Minister for Food Security by phone. With what little storage we have now, we cannot afford to lose any of it, in case of emergency. So today, I am here to ask for help from you. Please lend me a hand, please!"

All the people were listening to the Premier in silence, with an unspeakable bitterness surging up in their hearts. The Premier of such a great country had to beg personally for help!

In the early 1960s, any food in China was life-saving. With every extra half kilo, one more life could be saved. For the military officers who have been through the Long March, they already knew how vital food could be. At this critical moment, what should they do? The topics of the meeting had to be changed to the food shortage problem. The heads of all the military commands expressed the view that, since the country has been undergoing extreme difficulties, the military should handle their own affairs without adding troubles to the country that could make it harder for the Premier. The food shortage of the strategic missile troop could be resolved by donations from all the military commands. Many phone calls and telegraphs had been made from Beijing to the headquarters of each of the military commands. Soon, the food donated by all the military commands had been sent to the northwest by train.

The train carried the food begged for by Premier Zhou rushed through the northwestern plain day and night. It passed Xi'an,

Tianshui and Lanzhou on its way towards ancient Liangzhou. It was intended to arrive overnight, bringing much needed food to the soldiers there. However, something unexpected happened.

That day, at sunset, the train stopped by a quiet station for water supplies. The soldiers who guarded the train were eating solid food on the platform. Suddenly, a group of people crowded around them with bags, baskets and basins. They circled the train and the stronger young men took one bag of food and ran away. The weaker women, elders and children just tore bags and put the raw rice and flour into their mouths while screaming...

The guards were not able to stop them. They could only call the leaders of the military for instructions.

A colonel who used to be in the past Eighth Route Army took the call. Shocked by the news, he lifted his fist. "Damn them, how dare they rob the military supply? Hurry up and..." But his heavy fist didn't hit the table. It was too difficult for him to make a choice. In this dilemma, on one side it was the soldiers who had run out of food, and on the other side it was the gods of the foodless army.

The anxious voice from the other side of the phone continued: "Commander, what should we do? Please hurry up, they've almost taken all the food."

The colonel put down his fist helplessly. "Let them take it. The people are starving as well. Please tell the chief of the battalion to distribute the rest of the food to the people. As for the army..."

The phone call ended.

The event was discovered by the local government. They arrived at the site overnight and explained the situation to the local people. By sunrise, the people who took the food had brought it back to the station. Some of them took the hands of the guards. "Comrades, we are terribly sorry. We didn't know that you had been starving for days. We have committed a crime ... "

Actually, among the people who returned the food, many of them had lost some of their families to starvation. Even as they returned the food, their elders and children were still starving.

The food was transported to the missile battalion. When the soldiers unpacked the bags, they found loads of food coupons and notes scattered around. There were food coupons for 5 kilos, 2.5 kilos, and also half a kilo and lower. There was a note left by a little girl in third grade. The words she wrote left the tough soldiers in tears: *Dear uncle soldiers of the People's Liberation Army, I was among those who robbed food that night. I was hungry, so I grabbed a few bags of rice with my clothes. When I heard that you hadn't had anything to eat for days, I burst into tears in regret. Now I return your rice to you, along with the food coupons which I have saved. Please do not dismiss it over such little food. Could you forgive me?*"

These were our people, who were the gods of the army.

3. The core power organ of Zhongnanhai begins a debate as to whether or not to build nuclear weapons. The Marshal and diplomat, Chen Yi, says, "Do it! Even if we have to sell our pants, we must build our own atomic bombs."

Marshal Lin Biao was even stronger. "Even if we were burned in fire we would need those weapons."

In the hot summer of 1961, Mao, Jiang Qing and Li Na went to Lushan Mountain again, living in the newly built convalescent villa of Lushan No. 1.

The setting sun was reflected in the Lulin Lake while the birds flew by. In the evening mist and fog surrounding the peak on which the Imperial Tablet Pavilion stood, it seemed that the peak was growing higher, revealing its steepness and long history. Along with the breeze came the sound of drums and waves, as if they were whispering something to the people.

Mao didn't like this luxuriant and modern building. The Lushan No. 1 villa occupied more than 10,000 acres. For whatever reason, he still believed that the villa named Meilu, which used to be the residence of many past heroes, could better inspire his aspirations and romanticism…

In the hard summer three years ago, on this very mountain, he had sacrificed the armour of Marshal Peng in order to turn the extreme left-wing around. However, there was a radical change following that event, which later became a movement against the right-wing. It caused China to slip into a leftist extreme, generating the terrible famine that lasted for three years. In front of this harsh reality, Mao criticised himself at the Central Work Conference and the public meeting of 10,000 in Beijing. Then he voluntarily stepped back to the second tier and let Liu Shaoqi, Deng Xiaoping and Premier Zhou stand at the front tier and handle the daily work of the State and State Council.

At this moment, the great man of a generation, Mao Tse-tung, was standing on the Huling peak of Lushan Mountain, looking over to the Long River. He wandered casually along the Bull Peak. He composed a poem for Jiang Qing's photo at the Immortal Cave. All these showed some romanticism, similar to the poem that went, *I picked a chrysanthemum at the eastern fence and saw the southern mountain.* He didn't know that, among the decision-makers of the central power organ, there was an ongoing debate about whether the nuclear weapons project should be continued.

Huairen Hall, Zhongnanhai

The sunlight of the first winter of the 1960s entered the traditional royal courtyard. Soviet Union style Jim stopped at the front gate, and the heads of the centre of the party, Liu Shaoqi, Zhou Enlai, Deng Xiaoping, Chen Yun, Lin Biao and Chen Yi walked into that splendid hall which had determined the fate of China many times. The causal life on the Bull Peak of Lushan Mountain and what lay inside of the high red walls presented a stark contrast. The Chairman of State, Liu Shaoqi, commanded the heads of the Central Military Committee and some leaders of the State Council for a meeting, to discuss the construction and development of the Chinese nuclear industry. In his heavy Ningxiang accent, Liu Shaoqi asked, "Enlai, everyone is here now, shall we begin?"

Premier Zhou nodded his head, smiling and respectful, and started the introduction of the meeting. "The Chairman is out for a vacation. Today we gathered a few vice Premiers charged with economic development and heads of the Central Military Committee for a meeting, to discuss about how we are going to develop our nuclear industry under the current circumstances. Please tell me your opinions."

After the initial silence, there was disagreement between the ones responsible for economic development and the military officers. The former were working on the front line of the Chinese economy, supporting the food and clothing of a country of 600 million. The irreversible damage and trouble left by the Great Leap Forward and natural disasters had already left the national economy in distress, putting these great "managers" in a tough situation. They argued that, during the current distress, when the country was in desperate need of assistance, to extract a large amount of money to develop missiles and atomic bombs would inevitably burden the country heavily and affect the recovery of the economy. They suggested the project be discontinued temporarily. But those who had experienced the war were thinking of the country's strategy and status in the world. They argued that only with missiles and atomic bombs could China secure its status as a great power internationally, solving the problem of the sanctions and nuclear threats of the US-led Western bloc. Their suggestion was that, even at the cost of less food, the missile project should be continued.

Chen Yi was sitting on the sofa, listening carefully to the comments made by the few senior comrades from the economy development department. He became more and more unsettled. After his interactions with other foreign politicians and senior military officers, this Marshal and diplomat who had taken over the Chinese Foreign Ministry realised that, if China could not join the nuclear club, no matter how big its population was and how much territory it possessed, nobody would care about China. The nuclear balance could be achieved only if China possessed nuclear weapons. As a Supreme Commander who combined the nature of a soldier and a romantic poet, his hometown Sichuan had gifted him with an honest and loyal nature. What was revealed more in him was the blood of a soldier — very little of the smoothness of a politician. Regardless of the era, a politician of his kind would gain a good reputation among the people. But in this unpredictable and complicated time of political struggle, the more a politician was inclined to his personality, the easier it was for him to make a tragedy of his personality — or of the time.

He put on a serious look and stood up instantly, his face turning red. "Do it! Even if we have to sell our pants, we must build our own nuclear weapons."

Compared to Chen Yi's straightforward and honest character, Marshal Lin Biao, who was famous for being quiet but a quick-thinker and who had replaced Marshal Peng as the Defence Minister, had lost his interest in war and invested more of his attention in political struggles—perhaps it was because of the example set up by his predecessor Peng, or because history had already granted him such an opportunity. He was striving to transform the Chinese army into a political army, to gain the favour of Mao. As a result, Lin changed when he took power in the military. At the meeting that day, his opinion about the missile project came from his blood-worn battle experience over the decades. Though he seldom made jokes, in this matter, one of great importance to the status of the Chinese nation worldwide, this noted general, who later became a traitor, was as calm and smart as he used to be when he directed the Liaoshen and Pingjin Campaigns. He threw out an important but obscure comment: "We need the atomic bomb, even if we can only start a fire with firewood; even if we were burned in the fire we must acquire them ... " Afterwards, many military officers were confused about his words. How could this marchal, who was called by foreign military critics a commander of no defeat, feared by the KMT, say something as if he were a layman—the atomic bomb could not be lit by firewood. Supreme Commander Lin, this time you were, technically speaking, only ignorant.

What was reflected in Lin Biao's comments were the general unfamiliarity of the Chinese senior military officers with modern weapons. The opinions of the military and political leaders were in sharp disagreement. Both parties had concentrated their eyes on chairman Liu Shaoqi, the Premier and Comrade Xiaoping, in the hope of gaining their understanding and support. But these three could not rush to conclusions. Instead, they felt they should send someone to investigate the current state of the Chinese nuclear industry, then let the Centre of the Party make a decision. Liu Shaoqi telephoned Chairman Mao to report the disagreement to him, as well as the opinions of the Premier, comrade Xiaoping and himself. Chairman Mao agreed with him. Regarding the problem of who should be sent to the investigation, Liu Shaoqi asked Marshal Nie, "Commander, who do you think is the most appropriate?"

"The deputy Chief of Staff, Comrade Zhang Aiping is the most suitable one. He has been responsible for this task."

"Good. Then it is settled. After his investigation, please send the report to the Centre, and we will discuss it later."

. . .

That thirty-year long time has passed swiftly, an unusual period of time already buried by the dust of history. But when it came to this topic, General Zhang Aiping, who was in his old age, was still excited.

In the summer of 1999, by the side of Shichahai Lake, in an old courtyard of the previous royal family

The sunlight of the summer pierced the red curtain stubbornly, as if it wanted to talk to the host of the home. The general who had followed Premier Zhou for four decades and personally directed the Chinese Aerospace cause, Zhang Aiping was still in his uniform. His slim figure radiated heroism and energy. When he was interviewed by the researchers of the Party's history, he started talking about the debate over the missile project that had occurred in the high-level policy-making organ at that time. He said calmly, "This problem cannot be blamed on anyone. Stuff like atomic bombs and missiles are very complicated. At that time, when the Soviet Union sent back their experts, the Party Centre had already considered whether we should continue the project. Because nobody had a clue. Since the Second World War, both the Soviet Union and Germany had undertaken nuclear bomb projects. But neither of them were successful. Only the Americans succeeded, and they dropped one each at Nagasaki and Hiroshima. It was not easy to develop advanced technology. When the Centre was debating this issue, actually they couldn't make it clear. Eventually they decided to send someone to investigate, and that was the background for me accepting the task. Actually, I didn't understand what the atomic bomb was. So I asked Comrade Liu Xiyao, the Vice-minister of the National Committee for Science. He was an engineer student at university. We went to the west together..."

General Zhang's memory was enlivened as he mentioned the old time, as if returning to an unforgettable period...

In the fall of 1961, General Zhang followed the order of the Centre, with Liu Xiyao and Liu Jie, Minister of the Second Engineering Ministry, along with other relevant comrades from the General Staff and Commission of Science, Technology and Industry for National Defence. They visited factories, mines, and research institutes in western China.

At that time, China had already formed foundations for the nuclear industry, and the research into nuclear weapons had made some progress. Some engineers, experts and technicians from abroad and trained by China transformed their usual quietness and timidity, promising to General Zhang that, so long as they had the support and directions of the Party Centre, they would complete constructions at the front tier while maintaining a good relationship with all the relevant parties. They promised that, by 1964, they would be able to produce an atomic bomb.

This was a very ambitious plan. The US, the Soviet Union, France, and Britain each spent four to eight years completing the project. But our nuclear experts promised three years, revealing the courage and ambition of the Chinese. The determination of the Centre came from the solid support of the people. After a month of investigation, Zhang Aiping and Liu Xiyao submitted the report, *About the General State of the Construction of Atomic Energy Industry and Related Problems*, to the Centre of the Party. The report stated that China had already formed a solid basis for nuclear industry. So long as the Party Centre provided directions, with its own leaders giving instructions personally, and all the supporting services were maintained, by 1964 it would be possible to produce nuclear weapons and conduct nuclear experiments.

In late autumn of that year, osmanthus bloomed and spread its fragrance all around Zhongnanhai, the maple trees red as fire. The General Secretary Deng Xiaoping convened the meeting of the Secretariat of the Central Committee to discuss the report submitted by Comrade Zhang Aiping. Liu Shaoqi and Premier Zhou attended the meeting as well. Comrade Xiaoping was full of passion about this grand project. He agreed with the report completely. As he pointed out at the meeting, "We can't afford to lose the atomic bomb. Without it, nobody cares about what we have to say."

After the discussion and approval of the Secretariat, Deng left a comment on the report before it was submitted to Mao and Liu:

If you have no time, it's enough if you can please read the first page and the first half of the second page. When Deng later met the representatives of the nuclear industry, he told them passionately, "The Party Centre has made its decision, just do your job wholeheartedly. If you succeed, the contributions are yours; if you fail, the Secretariat will take responsibility."

As the General Secretary working at the front line, Deng harboured the breadth of mind, wisdom and vision of a great politician. During that tough era, the support in developing Chinese nuclear weapons was of great significance.

History remembered this unusual period of time.

Chairman Mao quickly approved this important report, emphasising that we should be determined to work on the advanced weapons immediately. If Khrushchev refused to give us the technology, great. If he did give it to us, the debt would be hard to make good. He joked he would grant Khrushchev a ton of medals.

4. An ordinary soldier collapses on the launching field of the great northwest. His remains are kept with the ashes of the founders of the republic.

In the quietude of Zhongnanhai, the Party Centre executive organ revealed its grand ambition and bravery, which undoubtedly gave hope to the first battalion of Asia. But in the distant deserts of the west, the first generation of Chinese strategic missile troops still faced some difficulties. The harsh natural environment, a placed of limited oxygen and extreme coldness, encroached upon the bodies of the young soldiers gradually. It was a battle of determination and coldness, youth and time, mortal body and iron ...

Zhao Cangku padded towards the launching field, following the green team. He was raised by the side of Hutuo River, and carried in him the heroic legacy of history's old Northern China heroes. He was honest and straightforward in nature and 180 cm tall. With his tall figure and dark complexion, his cheek was as red as the red sorghum on the Central Hebei Plains. His eyes were especially big and bright. Since he joined the first strategic missile battalion and became the number one command-deliverer, he had developed a sense of holiness. Because he was tall, strong, and ate a lot of food, he was called the "Three Bigs" by his comrades. This day was the first training session. It involved some mock launching procedures after the battalion was transferred to the west. A leader from the Artillery Corps was coming to the session. For some reason, Zhao felt his feet were as heavy as a thousand kilo sand bag, too much for him to lift. Cold sweat was rolling down his face and mirages were before his eyes.

The mysterious wing of the Sun flew over the desert of the north-west China swiftly. The giant green missile was standing under the snowy peak of Qilian Mountains, just like a sword lancing through the sky, representing the elegant head of a nation which had suffered too many disasters and misfortunes.

The head of the battalion, Major Li, stood at the position of the commander, with every command-deliverer of each technology section in position and following his directions. The leader from the headquarters in Beijing was impressed by the skillful operation of these soldiers, who had had less than a year's independent training in the northwest. The generals, who were not used to revealing their emotions, showed comforting smiles. A leader from the Artillery Corps stepped into the launching field to check the operations of each command-deliverer one by one. Suddenly, a tall soldier ran up to him.

"Report chief, please give your directions, sir!" The general saluted him in return, while observing this imposing soldier, who was taller than him, with unyielding eyes. He could not help but say, "What a guy!" before turning to Major Li.

"Major Li, you are good at finding people. You have someone here who could be an honour guard. It is indeed as the old saying goes: a strong general will not have weak soldiers."

The general held Zhao's hand and asked him kindly, "Young man, how old are you?"

"Twenty, but I haven't celebrated my birthday yet." Zhao's timid look reflected the pride at the bottom of his heart.

"How is it going now — do you have enough food?" The general was thinking about the food shortage and how Premier Zhou had gone begging for them.

"Please put your mind at ease, chief. Now we can eat as much as we need. I have five buns and a bowl of porridge at each meal … " Before Zhao had finished, Major Li interrupted.

"What a bold young man, how dare you lie in front of the chief?"

He went on and told the general, "This guy has lost more than five kilos during the recent training. Originally he was as strong as a tank. His food was reduced from five buns each meal to two, and now he can only eat one. I often see him covering his stomach with his hands, so I ask him what's wrong. He said he had eaten too much. We had no clue about this."

"Was he sick? Is it better for him to have a physical check in Beijing?" The general asked with concern.

"Once the launching session is over, I will have the doctor

accompany him to Beijing," Major Li replied.

Zhao had come to realise the severity of his condition to some degree. In 1961 when he first came to the missile battalion, it was during the time of the three-year natural disaster. Even though Zhao himself had to consume lots of food to support his body, he saved some of his rationed food for his comrades-in-arms. As his malnutrition worsened, he started to experience pain in his stomach. Everyday after dinner, he walked to a valley in the mountains, and leaned on a tree, pushing the branch of the tree against his liver to alleviate the pain. After some time, drops of sweat would roll down his face. Soon enough, other soldiers of his section had discovered this secret and followed him. They asked him why he did it all the time after dinner. But he replied that he was only practicing his operations and posture by the old tree. But everyday before sunrise, when the moon was still in the sky and Venus revealing its blinking smile by the eastern horizon, Zhao had to pull his sick body to the well and fill everyone's basin with water. This was said to be one of the four daily tasks of Zhao. Perhaps, realizing that there was not much time left for him, Zhao, the son of a farmer, had decided to use his short life to construct its last glory.

One golden autumn on the launching field, while the tragic setting sun caressed the eternal desert, the soldiers of the first Chinese missile battalion found themselves stepping over a thousand-year-long loneliness. With innumerable generations of soldiers and after endless days and nights, eventually the solemn and holy moment for the mock launching had arrived. The commander was giving orders determinedly and calmly in the underground shelter: "Two hours from now!" "One hour from now!"

The No.1 command-deliverer was standing in his position with a serious look, following the orders of the commander, pulling up the missile precisely.

As the missile reached a 45 degree angle, it suddenly stopped. The commander asked loudly, "No.1 command-deliverer, what's wrong?" At this moment, Zhao was already extremely weak. His tall and skinny body leant on the base of the missile, with the light of the sunset piercing his eyes. All he could see was a mass of blood red, sweat dampening his uniform inside and out. But his hands, which were thin as a skeleton, still held tightly to the operating bar. When he heard the voice of the commander, Zhao regained his consciousness and tightened his belt, replying with all his strength, "The No.1 command-deliverer is here…"

"Please follow the orders!" From the receiver there came the voice of the commander again.

"Understood."

The green missile was slowly pulled up and finally stood up on the foundation. It was like a bow of the orient, waiting to shot the Greater Dog star in the sky. "Three minutes from now!" "Ready for launching! Ignition!"

A trail of yellow fire burst out form the tail of the missile, carrying the toughness and heaviness of the nation and its pain and happiness up into the sky. Apart from not activating the missile, the entire ignition process was a complete success. As the soldiers cheered the success and hugged each other in tears, Zhao Cangku fell to the ground…

His comrades-in-arms circled him and lifted him into the ambulance. They happened to find a hard board tied to his stomach, covered by his hands. When his clothes were removed, everyone was shocked. Under Zhao's chest, there was a wide leather belt, under which iron sheet was pressed against his liver. Due to long-term friction, the iron sheet was smooth and bright while Zhao's clothes was covered with trails of blood.

Looking at this soldier in his last moments and thinking about him pressing braches against himself alone after dinner, about how he had brought washing face water for everyone despite being sick, many soldiers cried, "Cangku, why did you have to hide this from us?...Why?"

Exhausting his last shreds of energy, Zhao told his comrades in the army, smiling, "Don't cry, the ignition was successful... everyone... should be happy."

Suffering from the late stages of liver cancer, this young soldier had reached the final moments of his life...

When the news reached Zhongnanhai, the life of this ordinary rocket soldier brought great attention from the Premier. He ordered the staff to tell the PLA General Hospital to do their best in saving the soldier. But the warm hands of the Premier were unable to support this shooting star which had shone for just a little while. Even so, he had obtained an honour which ordinary soldiers could never get. His remains were kept in the Babaoshan Revolution Cemetery along with the founders of the republic and other important figures.

Thirty years later, during a cold rainy Pure Brightness Festival, in order to make a TV show telling the story of this young missile troop, I paid a visit to the Babaoshan Revolution Cemetery, the last stop of life, to find the final home of this young soldier. In the thriving green pines and cypresses stood a room made of white jade. Inside the room, a carved box contained all the happiness, sufferings, sweetness and bitterness of the young man. Although the soul of the young man were faded by the rain of time, his pure and bright eyes were still filled with happy and bitter memories. Perhaps he was thinking about his childhood, or the last movement on the launching field, or he was just looking into the distance for his white-headed mother on the yellow land.

5. On this ancient oriental land, we built the "gloried bomb", developing our nation's dignity. It was the foundation of blood that propelled the secret development of Chinese strategic nuclear weapons.

In September 1964, the first atomic bomb of China was ready to explode and was already counting down its final seconds.

That year, reunited under the flag of self-reliance, the Chinese nuclear engineers and technicians produced the first installment of qualified enriched uranium and the first qualified set of nuclear parts. The oriental land's first atomic bomb had revealed its mysterious face. Chairman Mao was enormously grateful for this achievement. On the sixth of June, led by General Li Jue, they undertook the last trial for denotation in the desert area of Qinghai province. It was a success. All the heads of the government and military, including General Zhang Aiping, Vice Minister Liu Xiyao, along with the first generation of the Chinese nuclear physicists — Zhu Guangya, Wang Ganchang, Peng Huanwu, Guo Yonghuai, and Deng Jiaxian, smiled in comfort as they attended the trial. It signaled the end of the production of the first atomic bomb of China, which was completed in shame and bitterness and hard battle over four years.

To remember the national day of shame on June 1959 when the

Soviet Union rejected China's request for the atomic bomb model, the Chinese nuclear missile experts named the first atomic bomb and missile "596", to let their descendants remember this dark day.

As part of the ground facility for the atomic bombs, the first nuclear trial field of China was constructed in the giant Lop Nor by the side of the Peacock River. The huge steel tower which was used to support the atomic bomb "stood brighter than a thousand suns in combination", 102.4 metres high and 180 tons. As the tower stood in the middle of the desert, more than a thousand animals, all for the purposes of military and civil use trial projects, were delivered to the trail field. With everything ready, all that was needed was a final order from the Party Centre and a good sunny day.

September 16 and 17, Xihua Hall, Zhongnanhai

The thriving cherry-apple trees covered all over this ancient royal courtyard. Branches of blooming begonia extended their friendly arms to the windows as the refreshing breeze of autumn carried the fragrance inside, a golden season of harvest just around the corner. Premier Zhou had convened the special committee for a ninth meeting to discuss the first nuclear trial. He Long, Li Fuchun, Li Xiannian, Lu Dingyi, Bo Yibo, Luo Ruiqing and Zhang Aiping came one by one to his little meeting room under the begonia tree. After the greetings, they got straight down to business. After hearing a report on *The State of Work and Arrangements for the First Nuclear Trial* made by Zhang Aiping and Liu Xiyao, Premier Zhou put aside the materials in his hands and looked around at his familiar old subordinates. He said gently, "Let's focus on the issues for the first nuclear trial. Comrade Aiping and Xiyao have talked about them, so please give your opinions … "

The Chief of Staff and General Luo Ruiqing, who was called the shadow of Chairman Mao by the Western media, stood up instantly. Since he had taken on roles as the secretary of the Secretariat, Minister for Public Security, Chief of Staff, and others, this General was at the peak of his time, responsible for military and political matters and close to Mao. Although Marshal Lin Biao, the first Vice Chairman of the Central Military Committee and Minister for National Defence, was handling the daily work of the Central Military Committee, he was not interested in the military training after having damaged his nerves during the war — he could not face sunlight. So he entrusted all these affairs to Chief Luo, while concentrating fully on guessing the mind of Chairman Mao. He kept observing the most sophisticated, sharp, doubtful and passionate eyes of the highest one in Chinese politics, and he set up the political flag of personal worship like a magician.

The Western military critics were all confused about Lin's transformation from a military commander to a political one. Under these circumstances, General Luo had to take on all the responsibilities of military training, which turned him into the most solid supporter of Chinese nuclear weapon development. He asked Premier Zhou with respect whether or not they should conduct the trial in October.

The Premier stared at Chief Luo. "The weather is not suitable. Maybe we will not conduct it this year. Prepare a plan for the next year, and submit it to the Chairman Mao."

After the establishment of the republic, Marshal He Long has been in charge of the sports industry. After Marshal Peng was replaced during the Lushan Mountain Meeting, his role started to change as he was gradually promoted to deputy chairman for the

Central Military Committee after Lin Biao. Since Lin was not in a good physical condition, he was responsible at the front line. He advised upon the national security perspective, stating "We need to consider the factor of attacks from the US and the Soviet Union after the explosion."

"Regarding this question, I have discussed with Marshal Chen Yi and we have asked Foreign Affairs Minister Qiao Guanhua to carefully evaluate the potential overseas reaction." The Premier answered confidently, "As for the trial, the first thing is that we must do it now, even at a cost. Khrushchev said we were not capable, but we succeeded anyway, which may draw the Imperialists' attention and see them attack us. But we must also tell the world that we have ended the hegemony of the two major powers. On the other hand, it's also a way to demonstrate the international status of China to the world. There will not be much difference in doing it this year or the next, it's only a matter of opportunity. If we do it this year we'd have to make up our minds by the end of September."

Luo Ruiqing took out some materials from his bag, and said worriedly, "Recently, the Minister for Public Security has found out from the US media's *Business Weekly* that the country to the north is planning to sabotage the Chinese nuclear industry."

"Then we need to make good arrangements for air defence. Talk to Air Force Commander Liu Yalou and put the air force into the base." The Premier turned to He Long.

Luo Ruiqing continued, "After the explosion, there will be some turmoil. The first one affected will be the Japanese. If the US and Soviet Union are going to attack us, they will have to face the consequences. That's something we can learn from Dulles. We can also have some 'edge' policy."

Finally, He Long advised the Premier, "We need to prepare a few plans for the explosion." The Premier nodded. "If we conduct the trial at the end of October, we need to make the decision on September 25. I will gather more materials and do some research, then await the decision of the Party Centre."

A few days later, the Premier came to the study of the Chairman. The afternoon sunlight poured down the pebble path of Fengze Garden, and the cassia trees were blooming and fragrant. He saw Mao's secretary Tian Jiaying sorting out books.

"Comrade Jiaying, did the Chairman wake up from his nap?"

Following the voice of Premier Zhou, the tall figure of Mao emerged. "Is Enlai here?" He was carrying a traditional thread-bound book of *Han Fu* as he walked out of his bedroom. "Recently I have read through Mei Cheng's *Qi Fa*. His critical spirit was like a dagger or spear, cutting straight through to the essence."

Premier Zhou elaborated on Mao's words, talking about essays of the Han Dynasty. "The essays in the style of *An Elegy on Encountering Sorrows* were constrained too much by formalities, which left them with very few superb ones. People like Jia Yi, Yang Xiong and Mei Cheng could be said to be the great literati of that time. Speaking of Mei Cheng, he came from my hometown Huaiyin."

"The great essays always come from people in the south of the Yangtze River."

"No, no! Only the people of Hubei and Hunan are the real talents..."

"Hahahaha..."

Mao's brilliant mind came back from distant history to reality. "Enlai, what is the international situation like now?"

"After President Kennedy's assassination, President Johnson

intended to intervene in the southeastern Asian countries. He has been increasing the American troops in Saigon. The three countries of Indochina could soon become the hot spots of international politics. To the north, according to the comrades focusing on eastern Europe, the status of Khrushchev is now unstable. It's possible the Kremlin may change its owner."

"Good. That situation works to our benefit."

"Chairman, now we have a difficult situation at hand. Regarding the detonation of our first atomic bomb, and whether we should set it up this year or next year, we are waiting on your decision."

"Of course this year would be better. For one thing, it may facilitate the process of Khrushchev's losing power — didn't he say that we were incapable of making one? But now we Chinese have made one by ourselves anyway. For another thing, since the US has sent their army into Indochina, targeting us, the explosion of our atomic bombs could be a deterrent to them."

"Good, then we will do as you have instructed ... "

The Premier stood up and left. Mao watched him leave, his eyes filled with trust and high expectations. Their friendship had withstood the test of time.

After returning to Xihua Hall, the Premier immediately convened He Long, Chen Yi, Zhang Aiping and Liu Xiyao for a meeting. He declared confidently, "I have reported to Chairman Mao and Shaoqi, and they agreed with the first plan. The Chairman specifically told me that the atomic bomb was for the purpose of threatening others, not necessarily for actual use. Since it's for the purpose of threatening others, the earlier it's exploded, the more threatening it will be. So now your task is actually more difficult." He turned to Zhang Aiping and Liu Xiyao. "You need to ensure this information is kept secret. The ones who are not supposed to know about it shall remain ignorant. The decision-makers are limited to the two Vice Chairmen of the Standing Committee, the Central Military Committee and Comrade Peng Zhen. During this period, you two must not write any letters, expect for the purpose of your responsibilities. And do not make any phone calls related to person affairs.

"Chief Chen, from now on, do not allocate them to foreign affairs. Do not let any information leak out."

Chen Yi nodded in agreement. "We will strictly follow the Premier's instructions."

After that, the Premier made further arrangements for the transportation of the atomic bomb, air defence and diplomatic conflict. He specifically told Marshal He Long that the Anti-Chemical Weapons Army of the Lanzhou military area should be sent to Dunhuang, assisting the local government to help keep people in their houses after the explosion.

After the meeting, the Premier asked for the director of the Nuclear Explosion Commanding Office, Colonel Li Xuge. He said to him, "After you return, report to me once you have settled the correspondence code and ciphers."

In the eve of the National Day, the general commander of the nuclear trial field, General Zhang Aiping, flew to the Malan Base with his associates. On October 3, the atomic bomb for the first trial was transported to the trial field in several installments.

On October 10, general commander Zhang Aiping sent the director of the Nuclear Explosion Commanding Office, Colonel Li Xuge, to Beijing by special plane with highly confidential documents planning the pre-explosion preparations, arrangements for air defence, and secure evacuation in case of an unsuccessful trial. Li submitted the documents directly to Premier Zhou's office in Zhongnanhai. After the approval of Premier Zhou, the documents were sent to the Chairman Mao for urgent approval.

The Chairman and the Premier agreed that the explosion time for the first atomic bomb of China should be 12 pm, October 16, avoiding the scheduled visit to China of the King of Afghanistan on October 19.

However, the Heaven seemed to intentionally give the Chinese another obstacle just as they were closing in on historical glory. The unpredictable climate of the desert area embarrassed many famous meteorologists. At 4 pm of October 14, the general commander discussed the weather with the meteorologists. Most of them believed that the fifteenth would be a good sunny day. Only Zhu Pinde, an ordinary weatherman at the base, believed that there would be strong winds coming in on the fourteenth, which could reach speeds of up to 14 to 16 miles a second. But with his low rank as a weatherman, his advice was not given sufficient attention. In the evening, the atomic bomb was placed on the tower at 7:20 pm. Just as Zhu predicted, strong winds arose at night along with rolling sand. And the speed of the wind exceeded 18 miles a second. The sand carried by the wind blackened the entire sky. Luckily, they had had a prior experience of strong winds, which allowed them to avoid the shock. At 2 pm, the weather forecast predicted that the wind speed would slow down and the sixteenth would be a sunny day. The detonation time was scheduled for 3 am of October 16 by General Zhang Aiping. When it was confirmed that the sixteenth would be a good sunny day, this General, who had dedicated all his life's energy to the Chinese nuclear missile cause, felt relived.

At 8 am in the morning, two engineers climbed up to the tower for the last procedure before the full installation of the atomic bomb—application of the detonator. Then General Zhang told Colonel Li, "Contact Beijing now, and report to the Premier with the secret codes—Miss Qiu is sitting by her dressing table, and she will braid her hair at 8 o'clock." Shortly after he went to the master control station to check the state of the electricity. Then he drove to Fangzhuang, to see the Anti-Chemical Weapons Army off. Not until 2:30 pm, did he return to the observation shelter, which was 60 km away from the explosion site.

At the same time, in the bleakness of Lop Nor, everything went into silence while the tower containing China's first atomic bomb stood against the sky. All the people involved in this trial were moved to the shelter as they waited for the most glorious and holy moment nervously. Only the breeze was gently caressing the airplanes, tanks and cannons.

The important confidential call had been put through to the red telephone in Zhongnanhai, Beijing. General Zhang Aiping held the receiver. "Is it the Premier speaking? This is Zhang Aiping. All the preparations for the trial has been completed, and the power has been activated as well. Whether or not we should go on, please give us further instructions."

From the other end came the confident and solid voice of the Premier in Beijing. "The Party Centre has decided the explosion time should be at 3 pm today. We wish you success!"

General Zhang made the last half hour of commands determinedly.

"Ten minutes from now!"

"Three minutes from now!"

At 2:59 pm, one operator from the master control station acti-vated the major transmission switch, which sent the explosion into its last countdown.

"10 … 9 … 8 … 7 … 6 … 5 … 4 … 3 … 2 … 1 … Ignition!"

On the ancient bleak plains, there burst out a streak of strong dazzling light followed by an earth-shaking explosion. The massive and imposing mushroom-shaped cloud shot up into the sky, the white fog spreading as the epic tide's red wave expanded, like a burning sun shattering the sky, or the explosion of a volcano, shooting up into heaven and forming a formidable mountain.

An oriental goddess descended upon the China Land; the trembling of the East started at the peak of the earth.

General Zhang was standing on the slope, looking over at the rising mushroom cloud. The battle-worn general could not resist his excitement, and tears came to his eyes. At this moment, the capable Colonel Li had connected the special line to the Premier's office and handed the phone to General Zhang. Zhang reported to the Premier tearfully, "Premier, we succeeded! Our atomic bomb was detonated successfully!"

Marshal Nie and Minister Liu Jie were waiting with Premier Zhou in Xihua Hall, excited beyond words. But Premier Zhou's first words to Zhang from the other end of the phone were, "Is it really a nuclear explosion?"

Zhang Aiping covered the receiver and turned back to the famous nuclear physicist Wang Ganchang. This doctor, who had graduated from the US, nodded his head with confidently and calmly, saying that it was indeed a nuclear explosion. When he heard this affirmation from General Zhang, the Premier said with great happiness, "Excellent! I congratulate all those involved in the atomic bomb project and the nuclear trial on behalf of the Centre of the Party, the State Council and the Central Military Committee. I will report this exciting news to the Chairman Mao immediately … "

The subsequent samples taken by planes and other data confirmed that the first atomic bomb had been detonated successfully.

6. The trembling from the East shocked the whole world. The US President Johnson cancelled his weekend vacation. Khrushchev said goodbye to the Kremlin in celebration of China's success.

When Dr Yang Zhenning knew that it was the Chinese themselves who had detonated the bomb, he cried as he ran to the bathroom of his lab, "Chinese … Chinese … "

A U-2 surveillance aircraft took off from the Clark Base in the Philippines, flying along the Pacific Ocean through the tropical forests of southeastern Asia towards the remote frozen northwest of China, the roof of the world.

From the late 1950s, there were continuously U-2 surveillance aircrafts from the US infringing the southeastern coast of China. They even reached the top of the Haihe River in Tianjin, but were shot down by the Chinese air defence, shocking the American cowboys. This advanced product of high technology had been shot down by the young Chinese air force. The foreign journalists in China asked Marshal Chen Yi in surprise, "What secret weapon did the Chinese use to shoot the U-2 down?" Chen Yi replied humorously, "We used a bamboo stick to poke it down."

However, this time the U-2 was sent by the Pentagon to follow the "Hump route", which was both the most familiar and the most feared. They took use of the blind area of the Chinese radar and entered the western desert area to take sample from the dust. Although this flight was full of difficulties and unpredictability, the Americans wanted to take their chances. Because Washington was still waiting for the final result of the first atomic bomb explosion of China.

Catoctin Mountains, Maryland, US

The autumn sunlight poured down into the forest, the maples leaves falling in the breeze. With the dark green mountains reflected in the giant lake, the whole picturesque view looked like some kind of fantasy world.

The 36th president of the US, Lyndon Johnson flew to Camp David with his family, away from the harassment of the real world, hoping to spend a happy weekend with them. While Johnson was enjoying the serenity of nature, a helicopter landed on the grassland of Camp David. The State Secretary Dean Rusk, Secretary of Defence McNamara and the Director of CSI McCormick came out of the helicopter. The three most important officials of the White House had come to David Camp together. Johnson had the feeling that there must have been something significant happening, otherwise the three of them would not bother his routine weekend holiday at Camp David. Just as he predicted, the State Secretary Dean informed him: "Mr President, I am terribly sorry to report to you that the Red China have exploded an atomic bomb." Johnson turned to Defence Minister McNamara and McComick. "Is this report true?"

McNamara spread his hands helplessly. "The Pentagon and CIA have both received the news. It's definitely true."

"My God." Johnson felt his relaxed state of mind evaporate. He said, trembling, "It's an unfortunate day for the free world."

"Newspapers across the US have posted the news from the Red China. There's panic across the nation. I think you had better issue a declaration and tell the public that the US is strong and capable of defending itself," Rusk said.

"Good idea. We should return to Washington right now."

Johnson returned to his housekeeper to get back, muttering to himself, "These goddamned easterners!"

That night the US president showed up on TV. Though he tried to present some calmness and confidence as the leader of a great country, his Texan face could not hide the gloom and heaviness in his heart. In a deep voice he spoke to the American people.

"I am telling all the citizens of the US, this is not something that need startle you. Based on our investigations, it has been proved that at around 3 pm, there was a low explosivity trial... We must not overestimate the military significance of this event."

Returning to the Oval Office, Johnson found himself unable to cheer up. The President's secretary for news had delivered the latest copies of the *Washington Post* and *New York Times*. As the President turned over the newspapers, the articles from Reuters and the Associated Press stood out:

Reuters, Beijing, 16th: *Today China exploded an atomic bomb at 7 o'clock Greenwich time, joining the international nuclear club. China is the fifth country to explode its own atomic bomb. The* announcement was made 24 hours after Moscow declared that Khrushchev had resigned.

Tonight, we saw the happy Chinese people running cheerfully on the streets.

Associated Press, Washington, 16th: *The news that the Chinese Communist Party has joined the nuclear countries comes as an even greater surprise to the American people, given the news of Khrushchev losing power at the same time. According to an official US source: Khrushchev has left, China has exploded an atomic bomb, and Mao Tse-tung is sailing smoothly.*

Johnson threw the newspapers away in anger, walking back to his bedroom. That night, even with the aid of a few sleeping pills, he could not sleep.

A few days later, the American airplanes gathered a sample of radioactive dust and returned it to the US. The Pentagon submitted the sample immediately to the Atomic Energy Committee to be tested by experts. They discovered that the Chinese used uranium 235 for the fission, instead of plutonium 239. These scientists, with their sense of national superiority, had to admit in surprise that the technology used by the Chinese was very advanced.

This unexpected result caused a great reaction all across the US. The Defense Minister McNamara delivered the test results of the Atomic Energy Committee to the President. After Johnson had read through it, he fell into silence. Then he told the secretary of Defense, "The US cannot remain silent anymore. We should send the 7th Fleet into the South China Sea to demonstrate our position."

"Mr President, do you want to prove the strength of the US, or the fear?"

"Naturally, our strength."

"But this is already clear to Mao. He used to say that the US is a paper tiger, although it was strong."

"No matter what Mao has said, we should not show weakness in front of the Red Chinese."

Science is boundless. Although US politics had tried to narrow the effect of this event as much as possible, the nuclear physicists who had been involved in the Manhattan project all wrote essays and made statements, giving recognition to the Chinese atomic explosion.

Reuters, Washington, 22nd: *Officials have announced today that China's nuclear technology is more advanced than expected. The US Atomic Energy Committee issued a declaration yesterday, stating that there were signs to suggest that China has adopted the uranium 235 fission device. This is contrary to previous suppositions that the explosion used plutonium, which could be produced by one nuclear reactor.*

Associated Press, Washington, 22nd: *This journalist has invited the nuclear physicist, Philip Eberson, from the Dale Carnegie Institute, to talk about the significance of this declaration. Eberson said it was already a great achievement that they had used uranium 235, which is difficult to control during fission, instead of plutonium. "We have to be more serious when we deal with the Chinese Communist Party," he said. "No matter what method they have used, it was not completed by a backward nation in a shower basin... Their technology is much more advanced than we had expected."*

Associated Press, Washington, 23rd: *Nuclear physicists believe that, by using the uranium 235 fission device, the initial stage of the Chinese nuclear industry has exceeded the Russians, British and French. These three nations adopted plutonium initially, only later using uranium 235. As far as design is concerned, it is superior even to the atomic bomb which the US dropped on Hiroshima.*

MIT, the US

The Chinese physicist, Nobel Prize winning Professor Yang Zhenning, had been fully concentrated in the lab, with no idea of what had happened outside. That day, his American mentor and colleagues rushed into his lab with flowers.

"Yang, congratulations to you and your country."

Dr Yang was a bit confused. "Why?"

His American colleagues were shocked. "Mr Yang, why don't you know about the news?"

One American handed the *Washington Post* to him, the top headline stating clearly: *Red China Successfully Explodes Their First Atomic Bomb*. Hot blood suddenly rushed to Yang's head. He grabbed his colleagues' hands in excitement, and said, trembling, "Is it true?"

His American colleagues nodded with a smile.

A wave of tears both happy and bitter emerged from Dr Yang's eyes, streaming down his face. This Chinese scientist, who had experienced great honour in his life, could no longer control the excitement. His throat was choked with emotion as he hugged each of his colleagues, saying in a hoarse voice, "Thank you! Thank you!" Then he left his colleagues alone and cried, "The Chinese... the Chinese..." He ran to the bathroom to let the tears of happiness and bitterness flow.

This was the sound of a shame which had been suppressed for ages!

These were the tears of a nation which had accumulated over many years!

Standing in the political and historical isolation between the US and China, Dr Yang had never imagined that his best friend from his youth and classmate at middle school and university, Professor Deng Jiaxian, would be among the crowds of scientists on the trial field.

History always likes to play jokes upon mankind. When the experts and soldiers were conducting the nuclear trial in isolation, they didn't know that the huge explosion would later become the salute celebrating Khrushchev's farewell to the Kremlin. Ten hours before the nuclear trial, the previous Secretary General of the Soviet Union Communist Party, Nikita Khrushchev, had lost the battle against the Brezhnev bloc and was excluded from the Kremlin. He was forced to retire to the walled national villa in Dalneye Village, Peterov, which was 20 miles to the west of Moscow. On October 16, when Khrushchev was sorting out his documents and personal belongings, his secretary revealed that news had just been received of China's nuclear explosion. His lips pursed, Khrushchev could not speak a word. He felt that he was being teased by God. At the most unfortunate moment of his life, even worse news had come to cast salt on his political injuries.

Four years ago, Khrushchev told the world, smiling, "Without the assistance of the Soviet Union, the Chinese cannot explode their atomic bomb." Mao mocked him by saying that, if the atomic bomb were successfully detonated, he would grant Khrushchev a ton of medals.

Whoever laughs last is the winner. But the winner was not Khrushchev, the descendant of Cossacks; the winner was Mao, a descendant of the dragon. That night, in the lonely walled villa, Nikita Khrushchev drank bottles of Vodka, drunk as if he were dead...

He has never been so drunk.

7. China becomes the hometown of the rocket. The first missile battalion of Asia sends a made-in-China rocket out into the universe, realising a thousand-year-long dream.

On Premier Zhou's way back from his visit to Africa, he went to visit the No.1 battalion in the deep desert.

The No.1 battalion had finally escaped the low ebb of its destiny and the time. The first successful explosion of the first Chinese atomic bomb had undoubtedly equipped the strategic missile battalion with a two-blade sword. As the carrier of the Chinese atomic bomb, the strategic missile and the quality of the soldiers who mastered it had naturally become the centre of the world.

As China awoke from the poverty and sufferings of the three-year natural disaster, the soldiers of the No.1 battalion showed up again in front of the people, emerging together from the hellish sufferings.

They came from this unfortunate land of heroes, but their steps had gone beyond this ancient hot land...

It was the harvest season of the golden autumn. The soldiers of the No.1 battalion had launched the first made-in-China strategic missile, using equipment made by their own hands.

During the early autumn, in the huge desert under the infinite blue sky, the rocket soldiers in yellow could be seen traversing the yellow sand through the yellow wind. The first generation of Chinese strategic missiles had been set up at the launching foundation. At sunset, an oriental sword stood glistening under the bleak sunset. Major Li and his first missile battalion all had their own roles. Major Li walked into the launching command car with his gun and belt. Holding the phone, he felt, from some unknown power, the gloomy eyes of past generations of Chinese soldiers buried in the sand staring at him. He was giving directions on behalf of generations of soldiers and a strong nation. Major Li sent out all the directions to his subordinates in a determined voice.

"Ready in an hour!"

"Ready in 30 minutes!"

"Ready in a minute!"

"Ignition!"

The green missile was like a giant dragon who had lain low for a long period, carrying the heavy wings of an unfortunate nation and its only hope. It stirred the clouds and waters, gushing burning fire and flying into the sky towards a target thousands of miles away in the distant desert.

After many minutes, a huge thundering sound came across the distant desert. According to the reported data, the first made-in-China missile had hit its target precisely.

The sunset that day was particularly red. On this land of great military significance, an ancient nation rose from the unfortunate yellow land, finally realising its rocket dream, stepping across the nuclear gap and gaining the nuclear shield which was brighter than a thousand suns.

The Central Committee of the Party and Chairman Mao sent

their congratulations to the No.1 battalion.

Not long after that, when Premier Zhou returned from Africa, on his way back he passed by the northwest. He heard the missile troop was conducting a missile launching, and he specifically asked the pilot to stop by at the base. Despite his exhaustion after the long trip, he wanted to visit and congratulate the soldiers of the missile troop personally.

It was a cloudless sunny day in the desert. Another launching trial had begun.

The troop entered the trial field full of confidence. The missiles stood against the sky and the bleak desert seemed to be solemn and serene. The frozen atmosphere suddenly became active and cheerful, as a few sedans came from the distance and stopped by the gate. "Premier Zhou has come to see us!" The good news spread around every corner of the launching field like the wind of spring. Accompanied by General Yang Chengwu and the deputy commander of the Artillery Corps, Premier Zhou came to visit the soldiers at 5 pm. Standing in front of the green missiles, the Premier waved his inflexible arm and told them to "Be serious and meticulous, be comprehensive and reliable, and avoid all risks." These three admonitions have been the mottos and standard for all the soldiers of the strategic missile troop.

Afterwards, the Premier drove to the command post on Aobaoshan Mountain, to observe the entire view of the missile launching field from higher land. Following the earth-shattering blast, a green missile arose from a sea of fire, carrying the dignity of a nation and its dream of a strong country toward its distant target.

"We succeeded!" Premier Zhou stood up and applauded. He shook hands with everyone and congratulated them. The entire launching field was submerged in happiness and pride. The Premier walked into the apron of the launching field, taking photos with the first generation of pioneers. This was the only photo of the Chinese missile troop and the Premier, a moment captured and immortalised in history!

Chapter 4

The Rise of the Missile Troop

1. In the summer of 1966, the headquarters of the Chinese strategic missile troop are constructed in Beijing. General Xiang Shouzhi changes one of the characters in his name and commits to work for the Chinese missile cause.

In the early spring of 1964, the last snow on the northern plains had just melted, and the steps of spring came rushing to China.

In the office of the Central Military Committee, in the guarded old red Royal Residence in Beijing, a highly confidential military meeting was held. The battle-worn Supreme Commanders and generals of China had made the most important decision of their life: to construct the first Chinese strategic missile base.

A year later, after repeated investigations, the report for constructing the first missile base in the northern mountain areas was placed on the table of the leaders from the Central Military Committee. Afterwards, the then deputy Chief of Staff, General Zhang Aiping, investigated the northern forests with people from the General Staff and Artillery Corps. After treading deep into the virgin forests of China, they set up the central point of the first battling field of China, a place that would become the stage upon which the opening curtain of the missile soldiers in the mountains would stand...

On September 28 of the same year, when the red document from the Central Military Committee to organise China's first missile base was sent around, tens of thousands of soldiers from the entire 88 units of the PLA started to gather secretively in the depths of the giant forests.

In the desolate forests, the first strategic missile troop of China began to gather. As one troop arrived at the mountains, others followed. After decades of effort, a few generations had sacrificed their passion and youth to build many different camps for the strategic missile troops where they could fight, defend, store supplies, and live.

The tribes of the Chinese strategic missiles had risen in the forests of eastern China.

However, this mysterious troop was not born at the right time, but in a time of chaos.

In the summer of 1966, a red tornado of the times overcast the sky of China.

At around this time, an unusual event happened in Chinese politics, an event of great significance for the Chinese historians.

In the autumn of 1965, Chairman Mao returned to Jinggang-shan Mountain with various feelings in his heart, accompanied by Wang Dongxing and secretary general of Jiangxi Province Fang Zhichun. He wrote down a sentence in his wild free style scribble: *My ambition is higher than the cloud as I return to Jinggangshan Mountain.* He stood on Huangyangjie, enjoying the view of the millions of mountains of China. He heard the faded thundering sounds of cannons from Huangyangjie, a heavy and tragic sense of history and time rolling towards this senior man...

38 years ago, in the deep forests, Mao raised a flag of retaliation against the old world with his comrades, beginning the great achievement of his life: to overturn the Jiang Kai-shek's rule, and establish socialism in the new China. As he carried the strong vigour of the Forbidden City to conquer the entirety of China and return to the old place, a sense of loneliness borne of great achievements followed him. The sky was as blue as the ocean, the mountains still and dark green, the clouds unpredictable and the water still running peacefully. The only difference was that this was no longer the damaged and troubled old China, but a new and vibrating world.

At the originating place of the revolution, Mao had found a new power and motivation for China. Facing the complicated politics of China and the world, his life impulse from when he used to joke with the American journalist Edgar Snow that he was "a monk roaming around with a broken umbrella" had arisen again. Choosing a role as a nation's leader perhaps put him through more sufferings than ordinary people encountered. After he came down from Jinggangshan Mountain, Chairman Mao commenced his second cause — to initiate a ten-year-long "cultural revolution".

......

In the summer of 1966, people's passion towards politics had already pushed the hot temperature in Beijing to an even higher degree. As Chairman Mao stood on Tian'anmen and waved his hand, an oriental great man, he met the young Red Guards eight times, which led to a series of "revolutionary tie storms" around the whole country. According to an incomplete survey, this unusual chance for free travel around the country lasted more than a year and involved over 100 million Chinese people. Many people walked, rode on a train, or took a sedan or carriage to Beijing and Shanghai for a trip to Shaoshan Mountain and Jinggangshan Mountain, worshiping the holy revolutionary site of Yan'an and looking piously for the resting place of their soul and idealistic spirit. If not for the physical boundaries between different countries, the fearless Red Guards probably would step out of China and bring the fires nurtured in Jinggangshan Mountains to every corner of the world.

If the ten-year-long disaster had been a historical calamity for China, taking the nation to the brink of collapse, it may also be said that this event had led the Chinese to deeply reflect upon themselves, and to the glory of the open door policy 20 years later.

But during the dark days, the craze for revolution and idol-worshipping far outweighed China's concern for international status.

Ziguangge, Zhongnanhai

The ancient tall cypresses covered the royal courtyard's red walls and yellow roof. All the cicadas on the trees were silent. There was no wind at all. The sultry weather was as hot as the political atmosphere, causing the Premier to frown. A great number of old cadres from the central through to local level were taken down under the chaos of rebellion from the Red Guards. Those naïve and enthusiastic young people debated in the Great Hall of the People day and night, and in persuading them to leave, Premier Zhou had exhausted his heart and body.

. . .

A red-labelled document from the General Staff was placed on the spacious and bright table of the Premier. After the discussion of the Central Military Committee, they decided to organise China's first strategic missile troop using the few missile armies originally controlled by the Artillery Corps. As for the name of the head-quarters, the opinions of the Central Military Committee and the General Staff were that the missile troop should have a name equal to that of the US strategic air force and the Soviet Union strategic rocket army. Finally they decided to name it the Strategic Rocket Army of China, submitting the name to the Premier for approval.

As Premier Zhou read through this confidential document which would set the foundation for China's major role in international society, his frowning eyebrows relaxed and a smile appeared on his face. He picked up the phone.

"Please contact comrade Zhang Aiping." The red special line on his desk was soon connected.

"Is this comrade Aiping? It's Zhou Enlai. I agree with your report. As for the name of our strategic missile troop, I'm inclined to call it the Second Artillery Corps. Please let the Special Committee of the Centre discuss the idea."

"No problem, Premier," Zhang Aiping replied from the other end.

Actually, at this moment, the members of the Central Nuclear Weapon Special Committee had been scattered. General Luo Ruiqing, who supported the development of nuclear weapons, was removed from his position in the General Staff. He could not live with the personal worship and the little red book advanced by Lin Biao, as well as Mao's attempt to take Marxism to extremes. Mao turned his back on Luo indifferently when he was replaced by Yang Chengwu. As one of the two deputy Chairmen of the Central

Military Committee, Marshal He Long was moved aside as well, accused of being a "big warlord" and "big bandit".

Even so, the Centreal Special Committee approved the advice of the Premier after meeting.

On July 1, 1966, the Chinese Communist Party celebrated its 35th birthday. A red-labelled document approved by both Premier Zhou and Chairman Mao was officially announced in this ancient oriental land, as the headquarters of the strategic missile troop was being built in Beijing.

After Chairman Mao's approval, the deputy commander of the Artillery Corps, General Xiang Shouzhi, was appointed as the commander of the Second Artillery Corps. Just like other senior generals of the PLA, General Xiang's great achievements were not learned from any military academy, but in the "university of war". This man, who had grown up by the Jialing River, was granted the perseverance of the mountains and the talents of war from its rich culture. In 1934, Marshal Xu Xiangqian led the fourth division of the Red Army to build the revolutionary base in Sichuan and Shaanxi Provinces. At the age of 16, Xiang said goodbye to the relatives of his hometown, and joined the No. 33 division of the Red Army, which was organised by people from Xuanhan of Da County. And he had experienced the great but tragic Long March. Among the list of PLA senior officers, Xiang Shouzhi had been in school only twice, the 2nd School of the Chinese People's Anti-Japanese Military and Political College, and the Senior Military Academy, which was set up by Marshal Liu Bocheng following the Korea War. Considering the craze for diplomas back then, this was nothing compared to others. But in the university of war, from a soldier to a commander, he didn't miss a step. From the Anti-Japanese War to the Liberation War, as regimental commander, brigade commander and the division commander of the army of Liu Bocheng and Deng Xiaoping, he followed the Marshal Liu Bocheng and the political commissar Deng Xiaoping across the Taihang Mountain and the Yellow River. He had leapt into the Dabie Mountain, which would lead them to fight for the middle land; looked down on the militarily significant city of Wuhan by the Yangtze River, moving towards the great southwest. Perhaps it was because of his journey from soldier to general that he had been able to wipe out a battalion of the US during the Five Battles of the Korea War, when he directed the 40th division in Seoul. Later, in the front troop of the fifteenth division, he annihilated the 38th regiment of the US south of the 38th Parallel after a ten-day long battle. During the famous battle of Shangganling Mountain, he directed the entire division to defend the critical site of the western wing and effectively worked with the main force of the Chinese army and the friendly forces, costing the US more than 25 thousand lives as they retreated. This was one of the greatest achievements in military history, such that the successor of the famous General Barton of the 8th Division and the last commander of the allied force, General Clarke, requested a meeting with the Chinese commander of the Battle of Shangganling Mountain when the treaty was signed in Panmunjom. Of course, his wish was not satisfied, but the Pentagon added this Chinese general to their database.

Following the end of the Battle of Shangganling Mountain, General Xiang was promoted to Chief of Staff of that division, and then later deputy chief and chief of the division. After he returned, he was sent to the military academy set up by Marshal Liu Bocheng to study. The ever-victorious army he had led disappeared mysteriously, caused all kinds of guessing from foreign military critics, even strange stories and fantasies. During the 1980s, when this army showed up again with brand new equipment out of the blue sky, they represented themselves as the new trump division of the PLA in front of foreign military delegate groups. The American generals who had battled with them during the Korea War said repeatedly, "Good, good!"

Surely, this was the story for the successors of General Xiang.

However, at that time, when he had just stepped out of the PLA Military Academy, he was appointed by Premier Zhou personally to be the director of the first strategic missile research institute. The Premier valued him, perhaps because this general who was just over 40 years old had just battled the American cowboys in a modern war. The wisdom and bravery of the senior Chinese military officers had made their mark on the arrogant American generals. Thus the Premier had entrusted him with the task of training the first generation of talents for the Chinese strategic missile troop. Upon the day of appointment, General Xiang no longer tasted any flavour in his meals or had any sleep at night. He changed one of the characters in his name and committed himself fully to the cause of China's strategic missile.

Not long after the order to appoint General Xiang first commander of the Second Artillery Corps was given out, he was involved in the blast of the times, before the people for the newly set up headquarters of the strategic missile troop had arrived. As with many other senior officers in China, General Xiang could not escape the fate of living in the prison known as the "cowshed", deprived of his position as commander. The wheels of history would move on for another ten years before he recovered his commander position at the Second Artillery Corps in 1975.

For an individual, how many ten-year periods does a man have? As a general who was in his prime, it was a much heavier pain to be deprived of his power and soldiers — far worse than being defeated by his enemies, as the time and chances left for him were limited.

Spring of 1992, Nanjing

The verdant Chinese parasols were like layers of luxuriant umbrellas. They covered the high class villas besides the old presidential residence that had house senior officials of the KMT. The bitter winds and miserable rains of time had worn these residences out. But the high surrounding walls and the iron gates still proclaimed the exalted position and identity of its owner. After the rain of the spring, our camera crew relied solely on the vague memories of the driver to find the residence of the prior highest military officer of the Eastern China area, General Xiang. We inquired at every house on the way, though there was seldom any people or cars in the quiet villa era outside the noisy city. Obviously this is a place which is barely visited by ordinary people. General Xiang, who had just retired from the commander position of Nanjing Military Area, accepted our interview. Although he was wearing a grey suit, he was still in a pair of a military trousers, not hiding his affection for a decades-long military life. His tall figure made it hard for people to connect him with the people from the Three Gorges area of Sichuan Province. With his smiling face, it was hard to imagine that he could be the General who was famous among the US army during the Battle of Shangganling. Instead, people would only treat him as a kind and friendly man of their father's generation. Actually, in the army of the republic, the more senior ranking a man is, the more they can be friendly and kind to people, without pretentiousness. It is the people who do not have a high ranking but pretend to be sophisticated that are actually shallow, making it hard for you to approach them or respect them. Perhaps because he had just retired from his longtime service, or because of the integration of his life with the strategic missile troop, General Xiang was particularly talkative that day. We talked from morning to evening. He felt that the most memorable time of his life was not the battles or his time as the highest commander of Eastern China, but the sixteen years of tough times in the Chinese strategic missile army. He said in excitement, "I joined the Red Army at the age of 16. From the revolutionary base of Sichuan and western Hubei Province, I took part in the Long March. After joining the force in Huining, I went to the Chinese People's Anti-Japanese Military and Political College in Yan'an to study. Then I followed Commander Liu Bocheng and political commissar Deng Xiaoping to the front line of the Anti-Japanese War. During the Liberation War, I directed my troops across the Longhai Line with Liu and Deng, leaping into Dabie Mountain. After I returned from the Korea war, once I had just stepped out of the military academy, the Premier personally appointed me to be transferred from the chief of the 15th Division to the director of China's first missile institute. I changed one of the characters in my name to show that I would commit myself fully to China's missile cause. It can be said that my time with all the soldiers and officers of the Second Artillery Troop was the most memorable of my life, the time of which I'm most proud. All the soldiers used their bodies to propel the modernisation process of the Chinese army…"

After the interview, the senior general gladly took the pen and wrote a calligraphic scroll, *the Shield of Peace, the Guardians of the Country*, for all the soldiers of the Second Artillery Troop. That evening, the senior general was quite happy, and took out some Maotai liquor to treat me at his family banquet. During dinner, there happened to be another general visiting, transferred from another major military command. But General Xiang asked his wife to talk to the other general, which left me confused and fearful. So I urged him to accompany the other guest, but he is not a man interested in socialising. He said to me, "Try the dishes, try the dishes. Let's have a drink together for all the soldiers in the Second Artillery Corps." He insisted on having dinner with me, an ordinary scholar. Only afterward did he go to see the General. Instead of saying that this affection was granted to me out of sympathy, it would be better to say that it was granted as a result of the unusual time he had shared with all of the rocket soldiers ...

There were a lot of regrets that needed to be sated in his life journey.

2. A mysterious army disappears suddenly overnight, and the military satellite of the US comes to find their trace six times a week. The former KGB headquarters telegraph to their military officers stationed in China.

Politicians around the world had opened their eyes to see the Cultural Revolution happening in this Eastern country. Obviously, what happened during the 1960s was confusing to the blond and blue-eyed Westerners—a country of 5,000 years of history, a great nation who had created a splendid oriental civilisation, could somehow shut down their factories and drop their axes, letting the land waste and fighting for an imaginary political ring, even at the cost of causing a turmoil with guns and cannons.

Compared to those politicians who were overly concentrated on the political arena of China, the practical Western military circle was focusing all the time on all the movements of the army, which had experienced the Long March unknown to any other armies. But they discovered that even these people, who were the pillars of the country, were as solid as rocks. Not only did they maintain the stability of the country, but they also became the solid red support of the three Indochinese red governments in the forests in South-eastern Asia, defending against US intrusion. What concerned them most was that there were signs to show that a new army of service had arisen on the oriental land. And their leaders' names would show up in the newspapers in Beijing from time to time.

The famous world military magazine, *Jane's Defence Weekly*, pointed out that, according to military observers, though red China was undergoing the sufferings of the Cultural Revolution, the legendary Red Army was still a great world army. As confirmed by reliable sources from Reuters and AFP from Beijing, a new army was recently added to the PLA. But this new army disappeared as soon as they showed up, without leaving any clues as to their whereabouts. *Jane's Defence Weekly* was famous for its reliability. As a result, its report about Chinese military issues raised the attention of the two major world powers.

Washington, the US, the Pentagon

The Defence Minister McNamara was sitting before the bright and spacious desk, turning the terrestrial globe that lay atop it. As the globe turned, it stopped right at the tropical area of southeastern Asia, just next to the Red China that lay on its horizon. Every time when he looked at this piece of giant forest so many young American soldiers had lost their lives, he felt a sense of unspeakable gloom and helplessness as Defence Minister.

Although in front of the president and his subordinates he tried hard to present his loyalty and toughness, when he was alone, there was always the image of all those white-headed mothers screaming "Return my son!" in the anti-war parades haunting him.

What had shocked him particularly was, after the aggravation of the Vietnam War, in a small gathering among the important officials of the Johnson government and their wives, he had met the previous first lady, the wife of the most respected President, Jacqueline Kennedy. The beautiful and elegant lady seemed to have recovered from the hugely unfortunate event of two years ago. She was holding an expensive cocktail, and walked to him like a goddess. She said to him, "Hi, Robert! How are your wife and children?" He nodded and greeted her on behalf of his wife and children. They clinked their glasses, and she told him with a serious look, "Robert, you know I am not interested in politics. But as an old friend, I have to tell you, the US government has to stop this goddamn Vietnam War. It was not the original intention of President Johnson."

McNamara rolled his eyes and said, "Honorable First Lady, now it is the time of Johnson, not of Kennedy. I am only following the instructions of the president ... "

Jacqueline's eyes were full of tears. She felt tremendously humiliated. She put her glass on the table, her right fist tightened, and hit the US Defence Minister while crying, "You have to stop the killing. I hate this country, I hate the US ... "

The Defence Minister being hit by the former First Lady was

explosive news in the US. Some anti-war activists made great use of the event. What really broke his heart was that Jacqueline was against the war — the First Lady he respected most, who had refused to take off her blood stained red coat when the president was assassinated, in order to boost up the American spirit. Her dignity had astonished the entire world. If she was against the war, and hit him regardless of their friendship, it was indeed a great shock.

His instincts told McNamara more and more that the Vietnam War was no longer in the US interest. But as he was in a high position, responsible to the American people and the President, he naturally killed the sound of conscience in his soul.

In April of 1995, during the 20th anniversary of the end of the Vietnam War, McNamara was in his 80s. He suddenly published his memoirs and gave his regret for making the wrong decision about the war. It caused a huge reaction in the US. Many veterans and their surviving relatives could not forgive him, and some people also thought he had insulted the US. Of course, this was a later story.

In the autumn of 1964, with the vehement lobbying of the US ambassador in Vietnam, President Johnson sent the US army to Saigon to support the Yanting Wu government and contain the waves of communism expanding from the forests of Indochina. In this way, he mistakenly pushed the US into the black swamp of war in Vietnam, and left an irremovable scar on the national spirit of several generations.

On February 7, 1965, the Vietnam armed forces were led by the former Secretary General Ruan Wenling and the current Chairman Li Deying. They began the Pleiku Battle in the forests, attacking the US airport unexpectedly. They killed 235 American soldiers and destroyed 31 airplanes, causing a shock in the US. On that day, Johnson immediately convened a cabinet meeting. A decision was made to increase the US force in Saigon. In the evening, the president delivered a TV speech nationwide, stating that the US would never ignore the youth who lost their lives in the forests of Vietnam. The Vietnam Communist Party would pay a heavy price for their brutal and violent actions.

Two days later, the Americans went across the traditional separation line of the war, starting a blanket style bombing and shooting in Guangping Province and Donghai City in northern Vietnam. A large number of unarmed civilians were killed, and casualties were counted by the thousands. Subsequently, the Pentagon recruited a large number of soldiers and officers, rapidly increasing their force in Saigon to 200 thousand and peaking at 530 thousand.

The massacre caused huge anger and shock among the Chinese Communist Party and Chinese people. Mao and his battle mates, Liu Shaoqi, Zhou En'lai, Zhu De, Chen Yun and Deng Xiaoping stepped onto Tiananmen Gate Tower, shaking hands with Ruan Mingfang, the chief of the delegation group of southern vietnamese representatire and Huang Bei, the northern Vietnamese Charge d'affaires and interim in China. They gave China's support to the justified struggle of the Vietnamese.

A few months later, Mao returned to Dishui Cave in the Shaoshan Mountain for a rest. He received information that Ho Chi Minh would pay him a visit secretly. Chairman Mao decided to meet him in his own hometown. This friend of China who came from the forests of Vietnam accompanied him, touring the beautiful autumn views of Mao's hometown.

After the farewell at Lushan Mountain in the summer of 1958, they hadn't seen each other for several years. Ho Chi Minh's beard had gone white, which made him look even older. This echoed Mao's poem — *if heaven had feelings it would age as well.* Once they met, Mao went straight to business: "When a friend comes, it is such a pleasure! Chairman Hu, we are family, so we can talk as family. I understand your situation, just tell me what you need."

Chairman Hu took out a piece of paper from the pocket of his worn Zhongshan style suit. After reading it, Chairman Mao asked the Chinese air defence, engineering and telecommunications to provide assistance in secret.

Mao put the paper on the table, and said determinedly, "Good, let's do what Chairman Hu has required. I won't be a believer all my life — let's fight the Americans again … "

China sent its army to the forests of northern Vietnam secretly. 320 thousand sons and daughters of the Chinese people and 50 billion dollars' worth of goods, materials and military supplies were sent across the border to the green forests.

The American satellite flying over the Pacific Ocean had discovered the movements of the Chinese army heading towards the Indochinese forests. McNamara has already realised that this was a war which they would never win. From the outside, it was a war between the US and the Vietnamese Communist Party. Actually it was a war between the West, led by the US, and the two giants, China and the Soviet Union, who stood behind the Vietnamese Communist Party.

However, what concerned the Defence Minister of the Johnson government was that the new army of China had just shown up before disappearing in the eastern forests. What kind of army was it? What was its nature and quality? Had it already invaded the Indochinese forests? Or was it hiding in the dense forests of the mountains in China? It was the nuclear missile technology controlled by the Chinese that worried McNamara the most. If this army was newly equipped, it was definitely not good news for the US. However, due to the long-term hostile relationship between China and the US, the two countries had not yet established a formal relationship. To rely on the intelligence obtained by the military officers in the US embassy was no longer possible. They could only rely on the satellite in the sky. McNamara picked up the phone: "Contact the joint conference of the Chief of Staff."

"Hello General Taylor, this is McNamara."

"Hello Minister," General Maxwell Taylor, the Chairman of the joint conference of the Chief of Staff, replied.

"The red Chinese have recently set up a new army but it just disappeared ... "

"We noticed it," Taylor answered straight away. Because he wrote *The Uncertain Trumpet*, which publicly objected to the Eisenhower government's massive retaliation policy, he had resigned from his position. Later he was promoted to a significant position by President Kennedy.

"Tell the air force to adjust the tracks of the Explorer and Giant Bird satellite and strengthen the monitor over red China."

"Very well."

So exploring and investigative satellites were sent into the sky as the existing US satellite changed their tracks at Vandenberg Air Force Base in the US. In some areas of China, sometimes people could see a shooting star-like bright spot rushing through the sky over their head. Some who were romantic would take it to be a fallen star. Some would take it to be an airplane. Nobody ever imagined that it was the satellite which passed over China every Saturday…

By the side of the Volga River, Moscow

The former National Security Council was located beside the Dzerzhinskiy Square in a gigantic building whose cold colour represented the solemnness of the biggest spy organisation in the world. But this day, the former leader of the KGB, Andropov, was not in a light mood at all. He came out of the sedan which the KGB had carry him to and from work, taking the lift to the luxuriant office with thick red carpet and oriental handcrafts on the third floor. This senior official of the Soviet Union Communist Party, who had rich diplomatic experience and a literate quality, spoke up: "Please invite all the directors to my office."

In a short time, the KGB's high-level military officers with medals of the Soviet Union Red Army, major generals and lieutenant generals, walked into the office of the head of KGB. Andropov politely asked everyone to take a seat. Facing this gentle but solemn superior officer, these well-trained KGB officers had to show some fear and respect. Andropov said in a melancholy tone, "Comrades, I have just returned from the secretary general, Brezhnev. The far-east border-control army has been in confrontation with the Chinese army by the distant Heilong River. A border war cannot be avoided. But I have to tell everyone, with regret, that the Chinese Communist Party have just set up a new army. If they have formed a rocket army with substantive force, then the consequences would be unimaginable. This was exactly what Comrade Brezhnev worried about the most. The first division must investigate this new army of the CPC until there is clear information about its nature…"

Two years later, there was a war between China and the Soviet

Union over the Zhenbao Islet and Diaoyu Islet. When the Central News and Film Studios of China were shooting the documentary *The Crimes of the New Tsar*, it specifically stated that the KGB telegraphed the military officers of the Soviet Union Embassy to make clear the nature of the Second Artillery Corps. The spies planted by the Soviet Union Embassy in China were specifically asked to make clear the movements and locations of the headquarters of the Second Artillery Corps. Among the files of the cases about selling military intelligence which were uncovered by China, it was proved that at that time the KGB had been searching for traces of the strategic missile troop in China.

So, where has this troop been hiding?

3. China was trapped for ten years in chaos. While the masses were crazed by cults of personality and leader worship, the silent rocket soldiers were setting the foundation of blood for the modernisation of the Chinese army in the remote mountains and deserts.

Major Li, who had been promoted to the Chief of the Logistics Department of the missile troop, said farewell to the soldiers of the No.1 Battalion with whom he had spent six years. He then was transferred to the first missile troop of China.

From the west full of sand storms to the huge plains covered by snow, he faced the second stage of his missile career. Compared to the bleak northwestern region, this place represented a long winter. As he looked into the distance, he saw mountains and valleys high and low, all part of a silver dreamy world. But this romantic dream of snow plains was frozen here, as the high white birches were shredded by the strong wind, revealing their dark and dry trunks. They looked like layers of giant pines covered in beautiful glazed ice, like silver tents in a kingdom of fairy tales. As the waist-deep snow blocked his way, he heard the wonderful sounds of nature which could never be deciphered, singing between heaven and earth.

But as a man who has been in the battlefield for a long time, Major Li had lost his poetic romanticism, and had to look directly into the eyes of the brutal reality. If it could be said that there was still an ancient camp for them in the huge desert area, something which gave the soldiers a sense of home, then here they had to start all over again, with the soldiers having to build the camp with their own hands. At that time, there was no camp for the troop. So the soldiers had to find shelter under the snow, and the only shelter they had were the green tents. The heads of the troop could enjoy some privileges, but the biggest luxury for these former officers of the Red Army or Eighth Army was sleeping in a wretched temple. Despite the harsh conditions, the officers and soldiers of the strategic missile troop used their bodies and blood to set the foundation for the modernisation of the Chinese army.

The prior commander of the Second Artillery Corps, General He Jinheng, was transferred to these frozen plains from the headquarters of the Artillery Corps in Beijing. He was originally from the green Jiaodong peninsula, and had committed himself to the Eighth Army in the Anti-Japanese War. With his tall and slim figure, he was a handsome man. As a cadre ranked in the deputy corps, when the trains carrying military supplies had arrived, he unloaded the bags and equipment along with the other soldiers, causing him to sprain his back. After two shots of injections from the doctors, he went back and continued to unload the supplies along with the others. The soldiers were impressed by the silent acts of the leaders, and so no matter how many difficulties they encountered, they endured them quietly…

It was the engineer soldiers who faced the toughest situation, since they had to build silos for the missiles.

The older people who had been living in the area all their life said that they had never seen such heavy snow as they saw that winter. The soil was white; the river was white; the sky was white, even the sun was frozen—just like a snowball rolled by children in a fairy tale world, hanging by the slim branches of the birches. When the snow on the ground was frozen solid, cracks appeared in the ground. As the rain and snow attacked the soldiers, the construction team took shelter in a valley, without a camp. Under the heavy snow, all that they had was a tent to protect against the coldness. Even when the temperature dropped under minus 20 degrees and the strong wind was blowing from the swamp, the soldiers still had to carve out a path through the mountains, drilling through the ground with explosives and build the battle field for the missiles.

At that time, Wu Guoshun was the leader of one of the engineer platoons. The platoon he directed were doing construction works in the frozen world. The soldiers rolled around in the muddy water, saying that it actually felt better for them to work in the snow instead of sleeping in the tent, because the tent was not as warm as the tunnels of the construction site. After work, with all the mud on their bodies, they could only boil a kettle of hot water in the shack, and wipe their bodies with the water. At night, soldiers of the same section would squeeze together with their coats on and covered by a quilt for warmth. The next morning when they woke up, the towel they used during the night would be frozen into an ice ball and a thick layer of snow accumulated on their quilt and coats. Some soldiers from the southern area were tortured badly by the brutal and willful acts of nature. The hands of some soldiers were swollen due to the coldness, and their feet were frozen and leaking pus— they could not even take off their shoes at night, because if they did, blood would seep from their feet. Even so, nobody complained. Their biggest wish was sacrifice their youth and bodies to light up the burning fire of the modernisation of the Chinese army. Colonel Wu Guoshun, who later became the political commissar of a missile brigade, said in memory of that unforgettable period of time, with tears in his eyes, "The only request of the soldiers at that time was, 'Platoon leader, let's not return to the tent during the night. We can sleep with our clothes on in the tunnel, it's warmer here.'"

As the deputy chief of the logistics department of this troop, looking at these sons of the Chinese people use their young lives to propel the modernisation of the Chinese army, Major Li felt a strong sense of guilt. After some discussions with the heads of the troop, they decided to set up their camp first. The entire troop, from top to bottom, used the trunks of the birches to build wooden houses and red bricks to set up rooms. Finally, before the heaviest snow of the winter arrived, the soldiers said goodbye to the tents, and lived in rudimentary houses, which became their settled home.

Compared to the frozen black soil in northeastern China, the situation of another missile troop of China in the mountains of northern China was not much better.

Fu Xunyi, who graduated from Shanghai Jiao Tong University by the Huangpu River, joined the missile troop with 60 other top graduates from Tsinghua University, Peking University, Harbin Military Engineering College and Northwest University.

At that time, for these intellectuals who were ranked "Nine" in the whole society then, their first task was not how to exercise their expertise in missile design and weapon operation, but to reform their world views to align with those of the workers and farmers. The model of integration was simple. They had to be as one of the soldiers and use their bodies to carry the air drill, struggling for modernisation.

Wei Xunyi was raised in a small town in southern China, and had a simple life. He moved smoothly from elementary school and middle school to a famous university. He could not remember ever having done any heavy labour work. But this time, as a way of "purifying his soul", he had to reform his life, using the hardened skin on his hands and the stinking sweat all over his body. The engineering team to which he was transferred was assigned to build the battle field for the strategic missiles. In order to keep it confidential, the location of the troop was five or six kilometres away from the cave depot of the missiles. Everyday, when the morning light had just broken the sky, they'd have to complete a task in the dawn light. It was almost like a religious ritual: greeting and taking instructions from the great leader Mao, then doing the morning exercise, which was followed by washing at the river side. After breakfast, they started the toughest work of the day. As they walked in queues with the spades, they sung the most popular songs of Chairman Mao's words on their way to work on the battlefield for the missiles. The more risky one's task was, the better "their minds were said to have been transformed", which would make it more likely for them to be transferred to the teams of their own expertise. By sunset, exhausted, they had to walk for five or six kilometres on the path of the mountains. As they saw the sun emitting the last streaks of its light, it seemed to be hard for them to find the final destiny of their lives.

When they returned to their camp, which could not really be called a "camp", reality crushed all their beautiful fantasies. Without a showering place, they could only take a basin of cold water from the river to wipe off the mud on their bodies. During the summertime, it might have had some kind of idyllic romanticism; however, when the frost and snow had covered the plains, this romanticism could only be felt as the cruelty of life. Especially in the remote areas, the soldiers could only build a soil shelter no higher than their waists upon the bleak plains. They had the ground as their bed, the night sky as their quilt. When they slept, they had to put on their cotton coats and hats, then cover the quilts with another layer of plastic. When they woke up the next morning, they were covered in a layer of white frost.

In this harsh living and working environment, Wei Xunyi, along with another more than sixty university graduates from all around the country, had all made a choice in life. Some had given up in front of the difficulties, some had made another choice, but most had chosen to stay, using their youth and bodies to build up the first strategic missile troop of China. This generation of pioneers of the strategic missile troop, they eventually stepped into senior leading roles of the troop. Wei Xunyi, who used to be a student back then, has become a senior engineer with a Senior Colonel military rank in the strategic missile troop.

In the deep forests of southern China, an engineering team, which had just left the flames of war in the tropical forests in southeastern China, dug into the remote mountain areas. Led by the Regiment chief Shi Fubao and political commissar Shan Chenglin, they commenced building silos for the missiles. This heroic team raised the red flag on the land of Northern China, and became one of the seven major engineering teams which assisted in the Vietnam War, constructing roads, bridges and tunnels in the deep forests of northern Vietnam despite the bombing of the US B-52s. With their efforts, many underground tunnels were built for airplanes, hospitals and the centre of the Vietnam Communist Party. Chairman Ho Chi Ming called them the "iron army", and they left a glorious page in the history of the anti-US Vietnam War.

After they returned, the Cultural Revolution was at its height. But they quietly set their pioneering steps in the primitive forests. When the army entered the distant little town occupied by ethnic minority groups, they could sense a traditional serenity and enjoy the idyllic views. Many residents of the villages were still living the ancient life, wearing self-made clothes and walking around without shoes. Even the County head, who was wearing the most luxuriant shoes, only had a pair of sandals which were made out of abandoned tires. When the military officers and their wives came here, they also brought outside information and civilisation into this little county, awakening the local girls and women's desire for beauty. Meanwhile the soldiers were living in the valley, which was 60 or 70 miles away from the county with no connecting roads. They spent all the years with the drillers and battled tens of thousands of landslides, debris flow and collapses. Many of the soldiers never entered the county in four years, quietly coming and leaving—some of them even left their bodies forever there.

25 years flew by.

When the bell of the New Year sounded in 1994, all the soldiers of this heroic team lifted the "August 1" army flag, shot through with American bullets, for the last time, to receive the inspection of the chiefs. They were filled with complicated feelings of happiness and sadness. According to the order of the Central Military Committee, this heroic team would be integrated into the strategic missile troop and have their original designation removed. When the last regiment chief Zhang Baochun and political commissar Zhang Gushun solemnly handed over the military flag immerseing with the blood of the soldiers and the smoke of gunpowder from the tunnels to the troop's commander Major General Ge, the soldiers were all in tears, even though they had been through 25 years of tough battles in the tunnels.

From the time of entering the forests during the Cultural Revolution period, 25 years of efforts, blood and lives were mixed with the cement of the construction of the strategic nuclear missile project.

However, at this moment, they were saluting to this land of hot blood for the last time.

In one of the cemeteries for martyrs, covered by azaleas

This heroic team, which was famous for overcoming the toughest difficulties, were all well-equipped and ready to say a final goodbye to the seven soldiers who had eternally slept there beside the battlefield of the missiles.

The tough battalion commander spread a big bowl of white liquor to the sky, and the political instructor offered an elegiac address on behalf of all the soldiers. They carried seven white wreaths and fresh azaleas to the martyr's tombs. The battalion commander tried seven times to light the match but failed. The battalion commander seemed to feel something and he kneeled down suddenly, crying in a sad tone, "My good brothers, if you do have your souls in heaven, please receive our offerings … "

All of a sudden, the clouds cracked and the sun came out, and the wind and trees stopped. Sunlight the colour of blood overcast the martyr's cemetery, and the burning wreaths became many black butterflies flying towards heaven …

Zhang Gushun, the last political commissar, who came from Shandong Province, was still excited as he talked about this part of the tragic history, when the army was building silos for China's strategic missile troop during the toughest period of the Cultural Revolution. "I came to the forests in 1968 during an unusual period of history, going from being a soldier to the political commissar. I never left this heroic army for even one day. On that day, when I handed back our flag with the battalion commander, my feelings were very complicated. I was happy, but I wanted to cry. I felt relieved, but I also found it difficult to say goodbye. When I say relief, that was because we had to meet the God of Death all the time. When I say it was difficult to say goodbye, that was because we had offered the 100 youths to these forests, and the battlefield of the missiles. 25 years — how many 25 years can one have in his life?"

This was the soldier of the republic — the spine of the republic.

4. The cloud of war haunted the border between China and the Soviet Union, causing enormous tension. The owner of the Kremlin places his hand on the highly confidential black box containing the switch for the nuclear missiles.

The construction of the battlefields for China's strategic missiles was undertaken in tough times.

However, by the distant Wusuli River and Heilongjiang River, the two Parties of China and the Soviet Union finally came to war in Zhenbao Islet on March 2 of 1969 after long-term ideological battles.

Actually the small piece of land, Zhenbao Islet, was not recorded in the early maps of China and the Soviet Union, because its history had only begun after it was formed by rivers in 1915. Because the original part of the islet was on the Chinese side, near the major channel of Wusuli River, it was connected with the Chinese territory during the dry season. Therefore it was naturally supposed to belong to China. But ever since 1966, due to ideological battles between the two countries, the tension at the border finally developed into war. The Soviet Army belonging to the KGB had beaten the Chinese fishermen and soldiers with wood sticks many times. According to a survey, from the 15th of October 1964 to the 15th of March 1969, there were 4,189 instances of provocation by the Soviet Union, which caused injuries to many Chinese border residents and soldiers.

At the dawn of March 2, 1969, there were a group of Soviet Union soldiers who invaded Zhenbao Islet, with the seven soldiers led by captain Iwan entering more than 200 metres into Chinese territory. Consequently, there was a serious confrontation between the two armies. During the scuffle, the Soviet Union started to shoot and several Chinese soldiers died. Thus the Chinese army fought back, and killed the seven people led by Iwan, which led to the commencement of armed confrontation between the two countries.

The battle of Zhenbao Islet was escalated by periodic armed conflicts. The Soviet Union gathered their army immediately. Until the summer of 1969, they convened 55 divisions of one million solders on their side of the border. While focusing on the Northern

China and Beijing military commands, China also increased their total military force at the 4,000 km border line to 5 million, including the official army and production and construction groups.

Some western military observers said humorously, Mao has extended the ocean of the people's war against the fully equipped Soviet Union red army of Brezhnev. It was said that, during the height of the war, the abandoned phone line between the heads of the two countries was employed again. The lady from the Kremlin asked directly for Mao to pick up the phone in perfect Chinese; but the Chinese receptionist from Zhongnanhai asked, "Who are you?" The chief secretary of the Kremlin said, "Please ask Comrade Mao to answer the phone, our Secretary General Comrade Brezhnev wants to talk to him." But the Chinese receptionist lady flew into a rage. "You goddamned revisionists, who are you to talk to our great leader?" Then she hung up the phone. The last chance for a talk between the heads of the two countries was lost.

After this, the heads of the confidential Office criticised this receptionist, "This is an important matter between the heads of the two countries, how dare you scold them without asking for directions from your superior?"

The receptionist cried, her absolute separation of love and hatred unable to be understood.

Xihua Hall, Zhongnanhai

Premier Zhou got up with only two hours sleep after having worked day and night for the 9th National Congress of the CPC. Outside the window, the morning light shone and the birds were singing. But, his heart loaded with worries for the country, the Premier was not cheerful at all. There was enough mess and troubles caused by the Cultural Revolution already for this great manager. Yet the Polar Bear to the north had presented millions of soldiers at the border, threatening the security of China. The Premier would ask about the status of the event every day.

At this moment, the Premier was sitting by the spacious desk, on which *the Reference Materials* of Xinhua News Agency had been placed by his military secretary Zhou Jiading and Wang Yanan. A paragraph circled in red by the secretary had drawn the attention of the Premier: *Extracted from The Times, journalist of the US, Taylor reports from London: Based on information from the CPC's important source here, the tension between China and the Soviet Union could lead to a major border conflict. It is said the intense situation between Beijing and Moscow is approaching an extremely dangerous degree. According to the diplomatic society of London, it is understood that some important figures of the military and political circle of Moscow are proposing secretly that they should attack first with nuclear weapons. Based on this information, the responsible ones in Kremlin have refused to take this action. Because using nuclear weapons would permanently damage its reputation around the world, and would drag the Soviet Union into a never-ending war of the people…"*

A few months ago, Shevchenko, a former senior KGB official who had defected to the US revealed in the *New York Times* that there was such a proposal in the Kremlin. The nuclear missiles from the Soviet Union's 35 bases had already targeted the Chinese missile base and major cities. The Strategic Rocket Army of the Soviet Union was on full alert.

At 3 pm, Premier Zhou went to Zhongnanhai by car. Chairman Mao was sitting on the sofa in his study, concentrating on the *History of Ming*. He wrote a wise comment on the upper edge of the classic.

What the Premier worried about most was how the Chairman was sleeping.

"How was your sleep last night, Chairman?" he asked.

"I have to rely on pills."

"Chairman, based on the reports of foreign media, the Brezhnev bloc has the intention of applying nuclear surgery to our missile bases…"

Mao seemed to want to avoid this topic intentionally. He picked up the few copies of the *History of Ming* on the table, and knocked on them with a red pencil.

"There was a piece of advice from the Emperor Zhu Yuanzhang who had a counsellor named Zhu Sheng. Although he was only a scholar originally, he was full of strategies. When Zhu Yuanzhang asked all the ministers how to become an emperor, Zhu Sheng offered nine characters: *Build the wall high, store the food more, take the crown later*. It was very wise and profound. I will change his words in a minor way: *Dig the hole deep, store the food more, do not be a hegemon*. What do you think?"

As they talked about history, Mao has already stated his strategy against the military pressure of the Soviet Union in these characters. This was a rare insight into the charisma and courage of the great man of a generation. Premier Zhou was impressed by Mao's talent and knowledge. He said in excitement, "Chairman, you have turned rocks into gold, the rotten into the wonderful. I will carry out these instructions soon."

Mao smiled and said, "I got my inspirations from the old piles as well. As to Brezhnev wielding the nuclear bomb, as I have already said, the atomic bomb is a paper tiger. I was not scared, and I don't think he would do what is forbidden. They have it, but we have it, too."

As the Premier stood up and said goodbye, Mao moved forward on the sofa and said, "Enlai, we are in need of more talents. How are Marshals Chen Yi, Ye Jianying, Nie Rongzhen and Xu Xiangqian? You can ask them for advice on the border conflict with the Soviet Union."

A few days later, Qinzheng Palace, Zhongnanhai

Marshals Chen Yi, Ye Jianying, Nie Rongzhen and Xu Xiangqian were invited out even though they were affected by the political struggle during the Cultural Revolution. The four supreme commanders looked at each other after surviving the sufferings, and Ye said humorously, "Chief Chen, I see you look good today. It seems that the bullets from the Foreign Minister did not put you down."

Chen Yi laughed. "I was not scared of the bullets right in front me, but I am worried about the back stabbings." The other three commanders all understood the implications of Chen's words. Xu, who was the more prudent one, said, "All right, let's not talk about this. More discussion about it could see us end up saddled with 'capitalist roader' hats."

The marshal-diplomat was still candid and honest though. "What's to fear? I am not afraid. Can they control everything without going out of their door? Now, let's see who is in charge today."

Ye interrupted and changed the topic. "Today the Premier asked we old men out of our retirement, what's the matter?"

As they talked, the Premier walked up to them. He shook hands with them and asked, smiling, "Are the chiefs still good?"

Chen was still mad. "What's good? It's already lucky enough for us to be meeting here alive!"

Chen's words seemed to make the Premier sad, as he looked gloomy, as though he were guilty to Marshals Peng Dehuai and He Long, who could not make it. He said in a low voice, "I firmly believe that it won't be long before all this has come to an end, and everything will be back to normal. You four were selected by the Chairman personally."

Knowing that they were chosen by the Chairman himself, the four commanders became excited again.

The Premier said slowly, "Maybe you chiefs have already heard of it, after the Battle of Zhenbao Islet, but the Soviet Union pressured our eastern and western borders with millions of soldiers. And most of their nuclear missiles have targeted our missile bases and important industrial cities. Please have a meeting this week about the international situation. And come up with an agreement and a memorandum, for the reference of the Chairman and the Centre."

Before their departure, the Premier told them solemnly, "This meeting should be led by chief Ye." Then he turned to Chen Yi, "Chief Chen, you have to see the doctor as soon as possible."

After repeated reminders, the Premier eventually left, but the four commanders still stood in the cold wind to see him go. From this, one could see the deep friendship between them.

The efficiency of the four commanders was surprisingly high. Shortly after, the first judgment they made was that, with the tension at the border, though it was possible there would be conflict, the Soviet Union would not invade China on a massive scale. The reason was that during the Spring of Prague last year, in order to quash the reformists of Dubcek, the Soviet Union mobilized 25 divisions of half a million soldiers, ultimately presenting

55 divisions of a million solders at the border. If they truly wanted to invade China, they would have needed at least 100 divisions — 3 million soldiers. To achieve this, they had to mobilise all the troops stationed in their territory plus all the troops stationed in Eastern Europe, which would still be less that what was required.

The analysis from the four commanders made the Chairman and the Premier relieved. And the time has proved them right.

On September 2nd, 1969, Chairman Ho Chi Minh of Vietnam passed away. This much respected politician of red communist international society left a heavy political task to the heads of China and the Soviet Union. He hoped the two old brothers would stop fighting each other. This last political statement was almost like the last word of his life, deeply touching the hearts of the two parties.

The Chairman of the Council of the Minister Kosygin decided to attend the funeral of Chairman Ho in Hanoi to meet Premier Zhou, despite the insistence of the Defence Minister, who declared that they should apply a "surgical" nuclear attack to China. However, what he didn't expect was that, to avoid meeting him, Premier Zhou said farewell to Ho's remains in advance secretively. So when Kosygin visited Hanoi, the Premier had already left. Then Kosygin had a brave idea — he should meet Premier Zhou in Beijing. The Kremlin had extended the olive branch to China. However, when Beijing received this message, it kept silent. Before Kosygin left Hanoi, he hadn't received any confirmation. He had to inform the Chinese embassy of his flight route, in the hope of a miracle. Only when his plane has arrived at Dushanbe, the capital of Tajikistan, did he receive the confirmation from China agreeing to a meeting. So Kosygin turned back, and flew directly to Beijing.

As Premier Zhou met Kosygin in Beijing, the tension at the

border started to decrease.

At the same time, the 37th president of the US, President Nixon, was eager to step out of the swamp of the Vietnam War. He declared in Guam that the US's military expansion in Asia had ended. He expected to unfreeze the gate to China, shut for nearly one third of the century. Kissinger stated clearly in his conversations with Dobrynin, the Soviet Union ambassador in the USA, that he was against the idea of using nuclear weapons on China, because he was worried that it might hurt the innocent. The *Washington Post* even exposed the Soviet Union's secret intention to use nuclear weapons on China. The whole world was watching the missile launcher at the border between the two countries with baited breath. The black wings of the God of Death were flying over the heads of the two nations. Borzhnev felt that he had been betrayed by the Americans. In front of the eyes of billions of people all around the world, his right hand left the Pandora box with the nuclear code, trembling…

5. Zhou, who has been struggling to maintain the country's stability during a bout of serious illness, told Marshal Ye, "Our swords are not long enough. The development of the missile troop should be faster, otherwise I cannot rest in peace."

Premier Zhou was too old to hold on.

In the summer of 1973, the Premier entered the final stages of his life. The cancer tortured the century's greatest politician like a demon. The sufferings from the cancer and the struggle to maintain the country had exhausted his energy. His Zhongshan suits seemed too big for his skinny body. The handsome face which was called "the most handsome in Asia" by the female journalists in

New Dehli was covered with pigment from age. It gave people a shocked sense of pity. As to the two bright eyes under his eyebrows, they seemed to be deeper and more grave with worry and anxiety.

It was the night before the 10th National Congress of the CPC. The Premier was still worried about the future of China, even in hospital. The Gang of Four, led by Jiang Qing, rose again after the death of Lin Biao, and had accelerated their plan to control power. Although, with the consent of Chairman Mao, comrade Deng Xiaoping was promoted to the State Council, the Gang of Four were determined to arrange for more of their followers to enter the State Council through the National Congress. Therefore, the Premier insisted on handling the personal assignments of the National Congress by himself, and got lots of old comrades who were taken down back to the Central Committee, forming a solid foundation for the turning of Chinese history later.

In August 1973, the 10th National Congress of the CPC was held in Beijing as scheduled. Mao and Zhou both attended the congress, despite their heavy illnesses. Perhaps because of his earlier concern about the Chinese missile troop, which was still in its "youth", or because of the status of China in international society, Premier Zhou specifically spent one day participating in the discussions of the military during the 5-day term of the congress.

When Liao Chengmei, the Deputy Commander of the Second Artillery Corps, delivered his speech, the Premier interrupted many times, asking him how many soldiers the Second Artillery Corps had, how training was going, how many times had they performed trial launches, were they able to fight a real war? After receiving affirmative answers, the Premier nodded happily. He said continuously, "That's good, the history of our missile troop is still short, but with their achievements, I feel comforted."

Seeing the Premier has been so concerned about the developing missile troop, many old battle-worn generals were so touched that they had tears on their faces. Many prayed in their hearts, "Premier, please take care of yourself."

There was a time when the Premier held a conference of the Science and National Defense Circle. After he looked around without seeing delegates from the Second Artillery Corps, he asked the hosts of the conference loudly, "Why didn't the comrades from the Second Artillery Corps take part in the conference?"

The hosts looked at each other without an answer.

"Inform them immediately of the conference," the Premier said seriously. "This is our new army, and also the symbol of the PLA's modernization. It represents the image of our country as a major power. How can we have this meeting without them?"

During this conference, when the Premier realised that the Second Artillery Corps did not have a chance to do actual trials launches, he instructed the General Staff and the Committee of National Defense, "We must arrange the Second Artillery Corps to be part of the launching trials at the satellite base. From squad leader level up. If the Second Artillery Corps do not operate, they are just empty artillery. During the trial period, you have to teach them until they become capable."

503 Hospital in Beijing

The last snow of the winter had not melted away completely, and the ancient capital city was still hibernating in between the frozen sky and earth after a long winter. Only some branches of wintersweets produced buds, suggesting the approach of spring.

Marshal Ye Jianying walked into the long corridor of 503 Hospital heavily. His staff had brought the Premier's favourite white lily. As a commander who had followed the Premier all his life, Ye realised that there was not much time left for the Premier, having watched him weaken day by day. The Chairman was not much better than the Premier. After Lin Biao's event, the old man seemed to have aged overnight. All kinds of diseases followed one after another due to old age. The callous times had deprived him of his former heroic charisma. Witnessing the deeds of the Gang of Four, Marshal Ye was worried deeply about the future of China.

When he met the Premier, these two battle mates, dating back to the Eight One Nanchang Uprising, shook hands silently. Staring at the white and sparse hair of the Premier and his gaunt face, a sense of bitterness brought tears to Ye's eyes. He said to the Premier, sobbing, "Premier, are you recovering?"

The Premier shook his head quietly, but his bright eyes still retained optimism and confidence.

"You have to relax and take care of yourself."

The Premier sat up and said to Ye, who was acting as the Chairman of the Central Military Committee, "We are all supporters of historical materialism, so we have to face the end and transformation of life. Marx has issued me a notice. The development of the strategic missile troop should be faster. Otherwise I cannot rest in peace, even after having met Marx."

Staring at his old superior from Nanchang Uprising, full of emotion, Marshal Ye nodded silently.

However, at the same time, in the headquarters of the strategic missile troop, due to the power struggles between different factions, there were severe confrontations between the leaders. An expanded meeting of the Party Committee of the Second Artillery Corps had been going on for nine months without any progress. The Deputy Chairman of the Central Military Committee, Supreme Commander Ye Jianying, went to Jingxi Hotel angrily by car.

Emerging from the car, Ye was unsmiling. He walked up to the rostrum with a serious look, and pounded on the desk: "I am not here to deliver a speech. I am here to dismiss the meeting. It's time to end it. A meeting lasting for nine months must be some kind of world record. I don't care what your backgrounds are. What are you arguing for? We are all revolutionary comrades. But we have been struggling with each other for more than 200 days — do you know what the soldiers have been doing…"

Ye came angry and left angry. Many were shocked by his having pounded on the table. Some high-ranking officers who had followed Ye for many years said they had never seen Ye so angry in years.

The Supreme Commander was angry for the swords of China!

6. Ten years of chaos leaves the Chinese nation permanently scarred, but the Chinese strategic missile troop rises through the suffering.

1976 was the Year of Dragon.

In astrology, the time when the dragon raises its head brings endless disasters to earth. This seemed to be a part of nature's cycle and was recognised by the people, though even now nobody has solved its mystery…

That year, the Chinese had lost three great men in succession — Zhou Enlai, Zhu De, and Mao Tse-tung. Yet under the heavy clouds of China, there suddenly came a fine golden autumn.

History eventually ended the tragic ten years of suffering the Chinese had undergone. China had hesitated for two years before it restarted its process of industrialisation under Deng Xiaoping during the Third Plenary Session of the 11th CPC Central Committee. And so, in 1976, China recovered its motivation to develop.

18 years had passed by.

In reviewing the history, the tides of our emotions can be calmed. As we stand by the turning gate of the new era and look back on an age of suffering, we can go beyond all our personal or familial feelings of gratitude and resentment, and reconsider this part of history.

Needless to say, the Cultural Revolution was a huge tragedy for the old generation of the Party's leaders and the ancient Chinese nation. It dominated the lives of billions of Chinese and crushed their souls and characters. And this problem may still be passed down for a few more generations. However, from another perspective, if it were not for the extremes of the Cultural Revolution and Deng's period of reflection in Jiangxi Province, we could not achieve our current understanding and the 15 years of glory of the open door policy.

In particular, we should see that, although the Chinese nation was pushed to the edge and the people were left with permanent traumas, they still kept the country moving and their consciences intact. Especially for the soldiers of the missile troop, who had been living in the remote mountains and deserts, they used their youth and ideals to direct the difficult path of the Chinese army towards the world.

On October 1st, 1984, when the mysterious Chinese strategic missile troop first walked out of the curtain, the whole world looked at them in surprise and envy.

History was frozen at this moment.

Chapter 5

Offering Blood Sacrifice to the Forests

1. As the political commissar, staring at the soldiers who had been fighting in the forests for 20 years, his eyes were full of tears: "We must set up a monument for you!"

In the summer of 1993, the forests in southern China's mountain areas

On the rolling mountain road leading towards the deep forests, a team of high class military SUVs travelled, a line of police cars at the front. The views of the steep mountains, silent forest, running streams and distant fog were like a bleak picture flashing by the windows of the cars. If it were treated as a destination for camping, people might be impressed by these wonderful works of the nature. But if it were treated as the last destination of one's youth and life, how would one feel?

But brutal reality often leaves people with no choice. In the remote forests, there lived a tribe of missile troop which was accompanied by loneliness.

The newly appointed Political Commissar of the Second Artillery Corps, Lieutenant General Sui Yongju, came to visit this uncompleted battlefield for strategic missiles after rushing through thousands of miles. In the giant cave, which was full of the pungent smell of gunpowder and dust, a group of barebacked soldiers were doing construction work. As the sweat rolled down their dark backs and the black mud grew deeper than their knees, they battled the rocks with determination and persistence. The blare of the drills in their hands joined together, forming the last sound of the remote mountains.

Major General Ge Dongsheng, the commander who accompanied him, watched the soldiers work. He said with deep emotion, "This team of soldiers have been fighting in this forests for 25 years. And they have contributed greatly to the construction. More than 100 sacrificed their lives, with hundreds injured. Many have spent all their lives after their recruitment here. They came quietly and left quietly. Some have never even been to the nearby town!"

Lieutenant General Sui, who had been in the engineering team of the troop, was in tears. The touching view in front of him seemed to have taken him back to the distant years. This high-ranking officer, who had the blood of the heroes from the land of Shandong in his veins, had spent a long time during his military life with the engineering team of this troop. In the heroic team he had led, they had experienced the bloody battles in Korea and the heavy snow on the black soil; withstood the battles in Vietnam and broken through the border by Kunlun Mountains; before sacrificing their youth and blood in the remote mountains and deserts for the Chinese strategic missile cause. With his great achievements and noble personality, which were formed after his long-term of service in the army, Sui was promoted to a leading role in the strategic missile troop.

As he looked at these soldiers, who still kept their childish smiles, this old general seemed to have recovered his beautiful life as an ordinary engineering soldier. He stepped forward, and grasped one soldier's hand tightly despite of all the mud on his body. "My good comrades, you are the heroes," he said. "In the future, we will set up a monument for you on every strategic missile battlefield. We will let the mountains and history remember you forever ... "

A few days later, in the Headquarters of the Second Artillery Corps in Beijing

Sui Yongju, the political commissar who had returned, and Lieutenant General Yang Guoliang, the commander, decided that once the constructions in the mountains was completed, they would invite all the honourable soldiers, veterans and the relatives of those who had died, to come for a summary commendation congress, and engrave the silent heroes' names on the monuments in golden characters ...

In the summer of 1995, the summary commendation congress was held as scheduled. When those veterans, disabled soldiers on wheelchairs and relatives of the martyrs came back to the field they had known during their youth, they fell into tears, seeing the missile caves, which were as heavy as the mountains ...

After thousands of cracking sounds of fireworks, and the solemn military orchestra, many monuments were erected in the forests against the sky ...

They had tied their souls to the forests, and offered a blood sacrifice.

2. The American strategic air force sent their soldiers to bases by airplane, but our rocket army soldiers were famous for their rare spirit of persistence and toughness, propelling China outward towards the world.

In the 1980s, in the headquarters of the US strategic air force in Omaha and the Peterson Launching Centre in Colorado

Since the 33rd president, President Kennedy, there had been the construction of underground silos across the forests and deserts of the US. Thousands of missiles were standing in the mountains and the giant plains, each of them targeting an important target in a hostile country. They stood like sharp swords monitoring the whole world, ready to react in minutes at the command of the president. With their nuclear missile storage, they could annihilate this blue planet three times over.

Perhaps because most of the nuclear missile bases were hidden in remote areas away from the civilised cities, they were all equipped with first class service facilities. But the harsh and dull conditions made the American soldiers helpless. They were too used to a comfortable life. Those things which were against the rules, like homosexuality and self-harming, were uncommon in the military. To ensure a fast reaction and the nuclear threat of the army, the US strategic air force adopted a duty system of shifts. Every weekend, the operators and commanders of the nuclear missiles were carried by Black Hawks to the silos from the headquarters. After they had finished their tasks, by the scheduled time the following weekend, the Black Hawks would bring another group of people on duty to the silos while bringing back the earlier ones to the headquarters. When the earlier ones returned for the weekend, they drunk it through. It was hundreds of miles between the silos and the head-quarters, but the American soldiers transformed the loneliness of guarding the missiles into the pleasure of youth and life.

Compared to the pleasant life of the US and the former Soviet Union soldiers, the situation of China and the nature of its army as the people's army destined the soldiers of the Chinese strategic missile troop to face different starting points to those of the US and Soviet Union competition. They started in a completely primitive situation, and used their hands to move the wheels of modernisation forward toward glory.

This historic transcendence was achieved with great effort.

When the open door policy made the Chinese people step out of the gate of poverty, the pursuit of money or pleasure in life was no longer treated as a sin, yet the soldiers of the strategic missile troop in the remote mountains still went on silently. They lived in the houses built by yellow soil and trunks. Even the most luxuriant head offices of the company or the battalion were no more than a soil house or a linoleum tent. When they returned from the construction sites during the winter, the soldiers covered with muddy water had to bring buckets of icy cold water from the frozen stream and wipe their bodies. There was a five or six mile distance between the construction sites and the canteen. During the snowy days, by the time the cooks brought the warm food to the construction sites, it had already turned cold. When landslides blocked the roads and bridges, the food and vegetables could not be transported into the mountains. So they had to rely on a ration of food, and it was common for them to eat rice with soy sauce and chili.

If the harsh living conditions had developed the persistence of the soldiers, then the construction works were a strong test and practice for their determination. Because the tunnels underground leaked heavily, it was damp and cold downside. The soldiers had to work in their cotton-padded coats for the whole year. At the end of each shift, the coats would be totally drenched with sweat and muddy water, weighing more than ten kilos. During the summer time, the sweat and muddy water caused skin diseases for more than 70% of the soldiers, making them unbearably itchy and eroding their skin; during the winters, the cotton-padded coats were frozen into silver armour from outside but the inside part were still warm, so every time it took several people to take down one's coat. The three shift working schedule each day, which lasted for years, was a heavy burden of tasks for them, and it left them with few weekends and rest days. Each day, their working hours exceeded 12 hours on average; when it came to building the concrete slabs, they could not sleep for several consecutive days; many of the soldiers would be sleeping when they held the drills, and when they woke up, they had to work again. Some also sat by the side of the tunnel for a rest, but they quickly fell asleep. An old general from Beijing asked a 16-year-old soldier, "What is your biggest wish?" This soldier, who was younger than his grandson, replied without hesitation, "Just give me a week-long vacation and let me have enough sleep." Hearing such a simple and natural request, the general burst into tears…

Late autumn, 1993

At a construction site which was just completed, a group of soldiers were about to depart and take off their muddy wet cotton-padded coats. They picked up a few pieces of brown rocks from the inside of the tunnel silently, as a final souvenir of their military service. After four years of heavy labour, they have developed silicosis to different degrees. As compensation, they could only get one or two hundred *yuan* each month, although the illness in their bodies would accompany them for a long time. Some grassroots cadres would "smite the table and jump to one's feet to express their indignation" for the health compensation money of the disabled, or dead soldiers. During the 1980s, even if the military trucks hit the peasants' cows, they would grant the owner seven or eight hundred *yuan*. Many soldiers sighed, *Are our lives worth less than a cow?* Even so, they had no regrets, and still tied their lives to the forests...

Zhang Jianguo, who was raised by the water of the Xiang River, was originally the chairman of the student union in Xiangtan University. The tough culture from his hometown gifted him with a tough personality. When he graduated from the university, the provincial government extended several offers to him; there were quite a few positions available for a graduate of philosophy to choose from. But he was only interested in the missile cause. When he realised that the strategic missile troop recruited at his university, this graduate, who always wished to serve the country, firmly let go of the comfortable working conditions in the capital city of the province and walked into the huge forests without turning back. As he walked into the green square array of the soldiers, he became an engineering platoon leader, directing his soldiers to work in a dangerous tunnel, and quickly completing his transformation from an idealistic young intellectual to a qualified soldier. A young military writer who was touched by this stark contrast of life choices during his youth, asked the platoon leader, "As a university graduate of the 1990s, how do you feel about your life since you have been labouring heavily each day?"

Zhang Jianguo answered proudly, "Your question reminds me of Rousseau's words — if it were not he who would go to hell, who else would? History had chosen us."

3. The biggest wish of the soldiers who built the silos for the missiles was to look at them once.

A green military train rushed down the Yunnan Plateau, breaking through the dark fog.

That year, I had just turned 16. Above the sky of the republic, there was already a blood red crack in the iron curtain of the ten-year chaos. A hopeful dawn was about to fall on China. But we, a group of students who couldn't find a way to serve the country, had to forgo the shattered university dream and join the army, revealing a romantic and great chapter of our life.

It was totally accidental that I joined the strategic missile troop, and it was also a mysterious temptation. It was early winter, and a team of soldiers had come to recruit in my hometown. The label they revealed there definitely shocked the people: the special force of China. And they had strict political requirements — not only did the candidates have to be red from the root, they would go back three generations, not tolerating any stain on their family history. With this requirement alone they struck down many arrogant and ambitious young people. That year, so many signed up that it set a record for our town. The future it promised seemed quite attractive. On the coasts of southern China, there were tall elegant coconut trees, and the wind caressed the tides of the sea. Young people who were born in remote mountains were naturally attracted to the ocean they had never seen. Given one in twenty were chosen, the competition was fierce. Some even tried to reveal other's family histories in order to get themselves in. I was first precluded from the physical check due to my age, and later was precluded because of my father's expulsion during the Cultural Revolution, even if he joined the revolution at the age of 13. It seemed to be hopeless for me. If it were not for the platoon leader, Wang Aidong, who valued my writing skills, I might have lost my chance with the army.

The train was running fast on the red soil plateau under the blood sunset.

My hometown has long since disappeared, and the smiles and voices of my families have become vague. It was the first time I had travelled far away. I was looking for the horizon of my life as I looked up to the picturesque views on both sides of the railway through a half-closed door of the carriage. Actually nobody knew whether this military experience would bring us glory or suffering. Once we stepped out of the red soil land, we felt the expansive sky and earth. In this large world, there were very few people who could hold on to the rein of their own life.

However, our actual destiny was not the southern coast of China, but the green forests rolling like the ocean.

The train stopped at a tourist attraction site in the south suddenly, and the platoon leader told us we had arrived at the end of the railway and had to change to cars. As we came out of the rain, hundreds of military trucks were waiting on the platform. We drove for a whole day into the mountains in the rain. At midnight we reached a place where we could only see a streak of sky, with both sides overshadowed by mountains. It was a long valley, with a bright stream in front of the dormitory, which was built with grass and bamboo fences. It was an idyllic view of Eden. But the next morning, when the sounds of the birds woke me up, I got up and found, to my astonishment, that I was inside of a primitive forest. I was far away from the world, with only the rain, ancient trees and sounds of wolves and monkeys near me. The remoteness and gruesomeness of this area was much worse than the Yunnan Plateau. Thus, a group of men who grew up in the remote mountains were shocked to find themselves crying together in a bigger and more remote mountain area. The romanticism and poeticism from last night was long gone.

These were the last tears of a group of young boys before they walked into the real men's square array. It also formed the last remnants of a desire for vanity before they started their life in the mountains...

Many freshmen asked the platoon leader who took them from their hometown, "Aren't we the special force of China? Why do the special forces live in mountains and grass houses?" When the regimental commander of the freshmen heard this, he became furious: "We special forces specifically work to build the silos for the missiles. If we do not live in the mountains, what do we do? Damn it, bring these young freshmen to the tunnels and get them to experience it..."

So we were taken to one of the tunnels under construction. Inside, it was filled with the smoke of gunpowder and dim yellow light. It was always possible for a landslide to happen here. A group of soldiers were drilling barebacked, despite it being winter. The cadres from the company said some of the soldiers had been here for four years, but they hadn't even been to the small town, all they had been doing here was drilling in the mountains.

Needless to say, their today would become our tomorrow.

I spent four years in this engineering team. From an ordinary soldier to an officer, I took part in the great project of building a great wall under the forests. And I witnessed the adventures in the tunnels of my young battle mates who came with me by train, and their moving and tragic life tied with the mountains. But until I was transferred to a superior organ of the military away from this troop, me and my battle mates had never seen the missile which we had imagined for days and nights. So when I became the news correspondent for this famous strategic missile troop, I made a request to my superior that I wanted to interview the missile troop and take a look at the swords of the orient in the middle of the mountains.

That night, I lived in a military camp beside a battle field. Toward those real missile soldiers who could personally operate on the missiles, we had developed a sense of envy and jealousy since joining the army. It was not because they had better living conditions than us—they lived in standard barracks while we lived in grass houses. Although we undertook construction works while they did training, we expended more energy; their daily food was worth 3 *yuan* while ours was worth no more than 1 *yuan*. What was more important, in front of those female nurses in the hospital, it seemed that only they were the handsome princes with white horses, while we engineering soldiers were like some dirty and scruffy peasants. No matter whether it was about seeing the doctors or seeking love, seldom did we have any warmth of love or the chance to feel like the winner. A leader who accompanied me to the interview seemed to understand my feelings. The same night he promised to take me to see the missiles underground the next morning. That night, I could not sleep. The longing eyes of my dead battle mates who had lost their lives in building the battle fields for missiles always flashed before me …

The next morning, sunlight came down from the top of the mountains through the pines, colouring the stream red. I walked into the underground sanctum palace of the missiles in a rush. As I looked up to the green missiles which were like ready swords, I could not help touching them, wishing I could hold them in my arms. At that moment, I burst into tears — for me, for history, and for my battle mates who would rest in the mountains forever …

However, the majority did not have this luck.

In the steep mountains of China, there were many soldiers of the strategic missile troop who had planted their life deeply into the giant ocean of forests, the frozen plateaus, the deep valleys, the deserts, the remote forbidden places, away from their families. Having experienced the cracks of the sky and earth, and made blood sacrifices, many battlefields for the missiles were completed, breaking different records of national defense construction. After they were honoured with gold medals by the army, they left for a new construction site. From a soldier to a regimental commander, all they wanted was to look at that giant missile. But the biggest regret of their life was that none of them had ever seen it. They were the real missile soldiers who have never seen the missiles.

In this mysterious brigade, a pair of Wang brothers' tragic story of looking for a chance to see the missile could shatter people's hearts and gain people's respect. The elder brother, Wang Changgui, was from Dengzhou, Henan Province. He was born in this place, which was famous for natural disasters and corruption. During his youth, he had witnessed a good deal of poverty and hunger. But these sufferings formed his tough personality. After he joined the army in 1976, with his tough life experience, he became famous for being able to overcome difficulties. He was lucky enough to have the last chance at being directly promoted from soldier to cadres, and became a platoon leader in the engineering team. When he returned to his hometown, everyone there would praise his achievements, glorifying his hometown. His younger brother was a fan of the military since he was a child. When he heard that his elder brother was an officer in the strategic missile troop, which operated with the most advanced weapons, he would follow his brother around and ask him to tell him about the missile whenever he was home. However, every time Wang Changgui faced the innocent eyes of his younger brother, he felt embarrassed and guilty. He didn't know whether he should tell him that he was only the platoon leader of an engineering team which was building silos for the missiles. He was not a glorious rocket soldier yet. It was not known whether it was due to his dignity or his discipline as a soldier, or because he didn't want to let his younger brother down, but Wang Changgui would either avoid the questions or just answer in a vague way. Actually, he has never seen the missiles. This regret upset him all his life, until his soul was taken to the grave.

It was rainy and windy day in late autumn, and Wang Changgui had just sent away his wife, who had come to the army for a honeymoon. He stood on the platform in loneliness, tears rolling in his eyes. When he waved goodbye to her, neither of them could have realized that this would be their last goodbye.

It rained heavily that night. For no particular reason, Wang Changgui suddenly started to talk about his life and struggles from poverty to the army with the deputy platoon leader Jia. After all the sufferings and his difficulties in finding love, he finally was able to marry a beautiful, kind and considerate female worker. This late happiness was just about to start. After having finished talking about his short life story, his young life was about to end in tragedy. Once he finished drilling the last row of holes, he went to put in the last installment of explosives. Before the blasting fuse was burned out, it exploded. Other soldiers shouted, "Platoon leader, where are you?" When they rushed into the cave, it was dark. The platoon leader was lying in blood, his chest blown out, and covered by shredded stones…

Outside the cave, streaks of lightening cracked the heavy layers of clouds and coloured the heaven and earth red. Tornados arose while the rain poured down. The sky cried mercifully for a shooting star from the earth.

Wang Changhua, who was just a second year high school student, came to the army with his father and pregnant sister-in-law after a long journey, to handle the funeral of his brother. Facing the missile storage cave which cost his brother's life, he eventually understood that his brother was not a missile platoon leader, but an engineering platoon leader who had built the battle-fields for missiles. Unable to resist the complicated feelings in his heart, he burst into tears…

That night, the family did not raise additional requests to the regimental commander who came to visit. Their only wish was to place Wang Changhua in his brother's position.

Wang Changhua became an engineering soldier, as he had wished to. In the beginning, he worked in the platoon of his brother. Later the leaders thought he was the only son left for the Wang family and the cave was under constant danger of landslides, so they allowed him to learn to drive and became a voluntary soldier. But when the lifelong regrets of his elder brother at not being able to see the missile became his own, he decided to take a turn in his life.

On that day, he had just heard about the completion of the underground cave that cost his brother's life. It was a chance for him to deliver something into this secretive, forbidden place. So after he entered the forbidden area and started to unload the truck, he avoided the two lines of guards. But right before he stepped across the gate of the cave storage, he was found out by the monitors. The guards were ready to send him to the security section. Only at this moment did he start to regret his recklessness. However, when he cried and talked about his story, the group of soldiers were so touched they cried. After the approval of their superior, they made an exception for him and shined the green light to this missile soldier who has never seen the missiles. They led him into the missile storage cave, which was decorated like an underground heavenly palace. He touched the missile, covered with his brother's blood. Looking at the giant green missile, the soldier knelt down suddenly, tears all over his face. His voice was choked with sadness.

"Brother, you can rest in peace. I finally come to see this missile on your behalf… "

The guards beside him burst into tears as they stood listening.

4. Loftiness is the tombstone of the lofty. The death of a hero is only a glory for a moment — what follows his death is an ancient lament.

Hu Dingfa was gone forever.

He took the biggest shame and grievance of a man into the cold cemetery, and also left the last glory, honor and satisfaction of a hero to the earth which he could never take with him…

It was a cold spring with unpredictable weather. In front of these caves where he had been battling with the soldiers of the second battalion, Hu Dingfa, the one who replaced the company commander of the fifth company, suddenly decided to bring his white headed mother, wife and daughter to the army for the spring festival. He hasn't had a vacation in four years. In order to finish the digging task earlier, and to ensure the security of the soldiers, Hu spent all his time on the construction site and would not stay elsewhere. Originally, the early spring and winter were the harshest times of the year in this area. There was rain without any glimpse of the sun for days. Once you stepped out, you would be standing on snow and muddy water. There were very few relatives of the soldiers who were willing to visit the army during this period. But Hu took his family here at this time and arranged for them to live in a cabin beside the construction site. They accompanied him all the time during his stay on the construction site. It seemed that he intentionally wanted his family to witness how he and his battle mates were able to conquer the magic caves. Since his mother and wife's arrival more than 20 days earlier, he could not get one day off to stay with them for a trip to the town 30 miles away.

At noon, his wife had already set up the dishes on the table outside of the cave and was waiting for him to come out of the cave. The platoon leader on duty also urged him to go out soon and not let his wife wait for too long. But he started to inspect every construction position and arrange for the plan for the next shift.

Suddenly, a disaster dropped from the sky, as a giant rock

weighing 800 kilos fell down and struck him ...

The soldiers circled him and removed the giant rock. Company Commander Hu initially could still stand up and tell them, "I'm fine, just go back to your work. I need to go to the toilet." The soldiers patted him to get rid of the dust, and there were no injuries at all. But a surge of blood shocked everyone — this was the last bit of blood Hu shed in the tunnel, and it didn't come from any part but his heart, which became the last monument of Hu on the missile battlefield.

The Battalion Commander Zhao Xinze rushed down once he heard of the news, and he grabbed Hu in his arms. He said in tears, "Company Commander Hu, please hang on there ... "

The ambulance rushed through the mountains to the hospital. Hu, who lay in the arms of the battalion leader, said only one sentence on his way to the hospital — "I felt a bit stuffy." He left in a hurry, without any second words, nor even the chance of saying goodbye to all the soldiers in his company. But he left with relief and calmness, without fear, regrets, worries or heart-broken reluctance.

"Company Commander Hu, please wake up, look at me," Zhao Xinze cried out, shaking Hu's body. The doctor sitting beside him kept calling out, "Hu Dingfa, you can't leave now!"

"Company Commander Hu ... Company Commander Hu ... " Zhao drummed on the bed in the ambulance, struck by the grief of losing Hu, and lost his sanity. Zhao's hand was hurt and began to bleed. As the ambulance passed the valley, there was a hoarse voiced cry.

Can anyone ever understand how much grief and guilt Zhao had to withstand?

The first time Zhao met Hu was when Hu was transferred to the second battalion led by Zhao, and Hu was appointed as the company commander of the fifth company. Honestly, Hu didn't impress Zhao at the first meeting. As a big and dark guy who grew up in northeastern China, Zhao didn't think Hu, a short-built and thin guy from Sichuan province, always with a smile on his face, had any of the character belonging to a military officer.

On that day, there was an engineering meeting in the battalion. All the company commanders had arrived, leaving Hu alone absent. Everybody had waited for him for a long time but just couldn't find him. The few orderlies of the battalion could not find him in the tunnels either. Zhao didn't want to keep waiting, and he was ready to declare the meeting started. Hu walked inside at this moment with his body covered with muddy water and his shabby cotton coat.

"Why do we need to have a meeting when the construction works are so pressing?" he said, smashing his security hat on the table and cursing. "Why do you still have the time to talk empty words? If there is anything important, why can't we talk on the construction site?"

Zhao was quite angry. Since everyone had waited for so long, he started to curse before he made an apology. Zhao pounded on the table and said, "Hu Dingfa, shut your damn dirty mouth."

"Why are you so mad? Your mouth is not clean either," Hu said, having his chance after the battalion leader swore.

The other few company commanders were all from Northeastern China and quick tempered, and none of them had valued Hu much. In a rush, they dragged Hu closer and beat him. Hu suffered some pain. The meeting that day ended unpleasantly.

When they had calmed down, Zhao began to feel worried. This could bring him big trouble. In the army, the most forbidden thing was to fight, and the consequences were severe. If Hu reported this to their superior, Zhao and the others would definitely be punished, and he would lose his position as the battalion leader. He ran to Hu and apologised to him. But Hu said, "It's fine. I have already forgotten about it. I did some wrong as well that day."

Though he did not pay much attention to his personal affairs, he was concerned about his subordinates all the time. One day, a voluntary soldier from the fifth company had his wife and baby come to visit, and they were just about to leave. Hu came by and saw them off. After the greetings, he asked, "Did you arrange for the cars?" That soldier said, "I did. The drivers said the cars are in tight supply and asked us to figure out something else instead."

"Damn them. It's 30 miles on the mountain path, how can a woman overcome this?" He turned away and said, "Stay here, I will go and find the battalion leader."

Hu rushed to the battalion office angrily with his neck turning red. As soon as he saw Zhao, the battalion leader, he began to roar.

"You officers don't have any sympathy. Our soldiers have sacrificed all their youth here, even their lives. Now their families are suffering. How can a woman with a baby walk 30 miles on the mountain path? Are you going to send a car for them? If not, I will report this thing to the brigade office, the Second Artillery Corps and the Central Military Committee…"

Zhao's eyes became wet, and he seemed to feel this short company commander become taller suddenly. He could tolerate the beatings on him, but he could not withstand the grief of his subordinates. He was a real man with a soft appearance but a hard determination.

The Jeep Zhao had taken from the hospital parked outside of the fifth company alone. As a man with a naturally dark complexion, he walked out of the car with a dark and iron face. Facing the longing eyes, he didn't want to say anything and walked straight to the place where Hu died. Sequences of yellow lights extended deep into the cave. "The fifth company, I have helped your commander out of this cave but I was not able to bring him back. What can I tell you now?"

The soldiers stood behind the battalion leader. Nobody wanted to step forward. Nobody wanted to be the first one to be hurt badly.

God was unfair. He forced the soldiers to accept the most unacceptable reality. After hardening their hearts, the battalion leader and the political commissar gathered all the soldiers of the fifth company, and struck down the last defence of everyone's heart...

"Company Commander...Company Commander Hu..." The giant forest rolled like the ocean as the calls reached the distant mountains, the valley echoing with hoarse cries.

The fifth company was overwhelmed by tears.

A soldier knelt down on the ground, pounding on the rocks with his bare hands as if he were crazy; even the blood didn't make him aware of his injuries. There was no other way for him to let out the grief and pain of losing his company commander.

The soldiers could not forget the black rock which took the company commander's life all of a sudden. They took the mallets and ran into the tunnel, hitting it while tears streamed; as the mallet hit the black rock, so did the tears and blood from their hands. "Give our company commander back, give him back..." That sinful black rock turned into a pile of dust in the mad cries of the soldiers.

Hu's wife was accompanied by a female army surgeon as she walked into the hall set up for Hu's memorial service. Her husband was in a brand new uniform and lying peacefully among the flowers, some make-up on his face. She threw herself on her husband and embraced his cold body, crying with all her strength, "Dingfa, how could you leave me and our child alone in such cruel way…" Before she finished speaking, she felt a strong dizziness, as if she had walked into darkness and passed over.

Hu's face was always filled with the honesty of a son of the mountains in Sichuan, how could they give him so much make-up? He was such a kind and passionate man after all, how could he be so cold? He loved her so much, how could he not answer her after she called him so many times? This must not be her Dingfa. She felt that she was dreaming. A dream of her childhood, her youth; a bitter dream, a sweet dream, a happy dream, and a shattered dream. It was like a movie flashing before her. Before she knew Hu, perhaps the Goddess of destiny had already tied her happiness and sadness as a woman to this family. Hu's elder brother was a tailor in his hometown, who made a living by making clothes for people. After he married and had a son, his life was happy. But still, he spent much of his life traveling around. The later father-in-law of Hu's brother valued Hu's tailoring skills, so he forced his daughter to be his apprentice, in order to give her a skill to rely on in future. With many people's persuasion, Hu's brother eventually agreed to take this girl as his apprentice. He thought this girl was pretty, gentle and diligent, with a good character, so he liked her very much and felt lucky that he had found such a good assistant. However, they had all ignored the most realistic problem—a single man and woman who had to spend so much time together travelling outside would have a great deal of space, but also hidden temptations.

The night was dark and windy, and it was raining as the cold wind blew. The temperature dropped dramatically. Hu's brother and his female apprentice had a late dinner after working late. They had hot pot and some white liquor to defend against the coldness. Perhaps it was because the strong liquor had provoked their hot blood, or it was because he had been separated from his wife for too long and needed the warmth of a woman, but at midnight, he approached his apprentice's bed. That day she had had some drinks and was drunk. When a man loses his rationality, he could become a bad wolf — and how could a weak woman defend herself against a bad wolf? In a wild fire, a girl can lose her innocence and confidence.

The next morning, when she reflected upon what had happened the night before, it was too late. She was a tough woman who valued her virginity more than her life. The incident last night meant she has been sacrificed. The bright blue sky and sunshine disappeared in her life. She had thought about death to prove her innocence. She bought a bottle of pesticide and drunk it up. If not for Hu's brother, who found her in time, he would have been dragged into court. With her attempted suicide, Hu's brother became worried. He had to chew on the bitter fruit he planted himself. He fixed his eyes on Hu Dingfa, who became an officer in the army.

He sent a telegraph and asked him home.

It was the first time Hu had met his brother's female apprentice, and he was attracted by her beauty and gentle, considerate character. After a whole year of exchanging letters, they decided to get married.

The first night for them was mysterious. When they revealed the veil of the forbidden fruit, Hu found out his wife was not as pure as he had imagined. He asked her what had happened. She told him honestly with tears. Hu rushed out, and spent all night under the cold moon, throwing cigarettes ends all around.

The next morning, Hu walked back to his house as if he had aged overnight, and told his wife seriously, "It was not your fault — so long as it will not happen again, I will love you with all my heart." His wife burst into tears and threw herself into his arms.

Then he asked his brother into his room and pointed at his nose, "You monster, I am telling you now, the bitter wine you brewed I will drink up for you. But if you try to touch her in the future, I will shred you into pieces. Remember that, I will definitely do what I said … " She felt lucky that the God of Love gifted her with a real man who was tolerant. But the mercy of God, for all its generousness, was also short-lived. Before she could actually enjoy this happiness, it was taken away cruelly …

The memorial service was held under a sad and heavy atmosphere.

The soldiers of the fifth company cried themselves half to death. On that day, even if warm food was served, nobody touched his chopsticks. It was actually better not to console them, because once you started to comfort them, they all started to cry again. The soldiers missed their commander so much. Usually when they had their meals, Company Commander Hu would sit with them and talk about the tunnel or tell them stories. In the same canteen, at the same time — but the commander was gone, and who could share their meal with them? Once they opened their mouth, tears dropped down. Those who comforted the soldiers could resist the sadness, but the more they tried to comfort the soldiers, the more they found themselves crying with the soldiers…

Not long after the memorial service, Hu's wife returned to their hometown with the kid. On that day, all the soldiers of the fifth company accompanied her to visit the place where Hu died, to say a final goodbye. She placed the first class medal and a bunch of fresh azaleas on the ground. Kneeling down, she cried in hoarse voice, "Dingfa, I am going home with the child, leaving you here to guard this mountain and the battlefield alone. Every year at this time, I will burn paper money for you with mother…" She stood up slowly, and turned to the soldiers. "I cannot come to visit you in the future. Nor can I wash your clothes and bring you water. I can't see you sweet young brothers anymore. I will say goodbye to you here, you must take care…" In saying this, she kneeled down to the soldiers again.

The soldiers circled her and helped her up, crying, "Sister, you shouldn't do this, you shouldn't do this…" At this moment, they all cried in the tunnel together.

It lasted for ten minutes.

The next morning, the newly appointed Company Commander Hou Quanwen led the soldiers to the tunnel, standing at the place where Hu died, and offered a bunch of flowers and bowls of wine to him. With the most ancient but serious sacrifice ritual to honour the hero, Hou declared in his heavy Gaomi accent, "We are going to work again. We hope you can bless all the brothers of our company, who will conquer this mountain on your behalf…"

5. Everyday before entering the tunnel to work, he would leave a note to his parents. When he retired from the army, the notes had accumulated to a whole box. With a match, he burned all

the memories of his youth in the mountains of southern China.

The trees of the mountains in southern China turned green then withered, repeated in cycles. As time flew, four years of military service passed away. Another autumn with blood red maple trees came again, another year for some soldiers to retire.

Wang, who was from the plains of western Sichuan Province, was just a high school student when he joined the troop at the age of 17. He was the only son of his family. Since he was a child, he liked literature very much. But he failed the college entrance exam by one mark. So he joined the strategic missile troop and gave up his dream of becoming a military officer. However, year after year, the heavy construction works for national defense shattered his dream of entering the military academy. Facing the cruel and hard reality that many of his battle mates had died in the tunnels, he had to hand his life to God. This young man, with the sensitive character of a poet, had to leave a note to his parents everyday before he entered the tunnel. All the notes were pressed under his bed. If he could return safely, he would store the note carefully, as part of his bitter or sweet memories. The next time he entered the tunnel, he would leave a note again. It lasted for four years, and he never gave up doing this. Until the last night of the four-year period, he finished writing the last note and got ready to enter the tunnel, suddenly, he heard the news that the company commander had declared he was going to retire. He couldn't help crying while holding that note.

One blood sunset evening, a rare sunny day in the forest. The last bit of the sun was brushed red across the western sky. Taking off his uniform, Wang came to the missile storage cave which was called "the Valley of Terror" with the box of notes he had written. Kneeling down piously, he lit a match with trembling fingers. While he burned the notes, he read them and cried, "All my dead battle mates, all the Gods of the Mountains, thank you for blessing me and keeping me safe for the past four years. I am going home tomorrow. I can no longer accompany you. Please take care. So long as this battlefield is here, you will never be lonely … Goodbye … " He worshiped these magic mountains, with these notes of his adventurous memories all turned into black butterflies flying into the sky …

As the sky darkened, so did the forest, till there was only one last brush of blood reddening the western horizon.

This was the sacrifice ritual of the youth, the beauty of cruelty.

Pure Brightness Festival, 1994

Just before the large strategic missile battlefields were officially completed, I returned to the strategic missile troop in the remote forests of southern China where I had had my adventures.

The rain of the first month of spring fell down with the wind of the mountains. After the hibernation of a whole winter and a year's cycle, the mountains regained their vigour and greenness. The bunches of azalea on the dark green mountains were blooming like fire and sunset, indicating the once glorious lives of the soldiers resting there. But the mountains were silent. The noise and glory of yesterday were long buried in the red soil, leaving only a few partridges singing a lament that accompanied the soldiers forever.

In the spacious and solemn martyrs' cemetery, there were more than 100 soldiers who had sacrificed themselves for the missiles over two decades. The pine trees and grass were thriving, while the graves had collapsed; bunches of wild flowers and wormwood grew out of the cracks of the graves, which had suffered in the wind and rain. The falling leaves and dust were gradually turning each of the graves into flat ground. The cement tombstones with golden characters were eroded by time and fading away, just like pairs of bright eyes darkening.

Who could remember they used to have their youth and glorious achievements? Who could remember they used to suffer in this remote and giant forest?

I placed bunches of blood red camellia in front of their graves, the names on the faded tombstones staring at me like pairs of vague eyes. In this cemetery, there lay many battle mates of mine who had taken the same train with me from our hometown, my familiar leaders, and those freshmen who I couldn't name. Tears obscured my eyes, and I could no longer see those faces clearly. I could only chew on the heaviness and bitterness of time alone…

A life should not have too much vanity and noise. It was not intended to carry a heavy and uptight mask. They were all sons of the peasants originally, with dark skin coloured by the sun and soil. They came to this place quietly and left in a hurry, without expecting anything in reward, without hoping to take anything away. Even if they died here, and lay beside the battlefield forever, they would support the wings of the republic as loyal soldiers.

They were not born as heroes. Because in every era, there is always a group of soldiers like them from this nation, which has been through many disasters.

They were not symbols of loftiness. Because the rolling world, this ancient country, always uses its own way to extend its spirit. History may remember a great man, but it cannot remember the hundreds of thousands of ordinary soldiers who assisted the great man. Especially for this nation, which was forgetful, a dead man cannot count on the living to remember him. Only the silent times will direct their spirit into the mountains and the blood of the nation…

The rain stopped, and a brush of blood red pierced through the clouds and revealed the veil of fog over the mountains, exposing a bright and beautiful world.

The setting sun lay between heaven and earth. On the fields, the sounds of the peasants who were plowing the land echoed. In the forest, young people from minority groups were singing love songs which enchanted the birds. All these seemed to be a picture of an idyllic Eden from the kingdom of fairy tales.

The heaven and earth were in serenity, and the noisy world was so attractive. I said goodbye to the martyrs' cemetery and walked down the mountains, my feelings complicated.

Chapter 6

Walking out of the Mountains

1. During the age of insanity, the No.1 order from Deputy Commander Lin Biao saw much of the republic's money sent into the remote mountain areas.

Let's turn the clock back to the last cold spring of the 1960s.

Beijing, inside of the red classically-styled quadrangle courtyard near Maojiawan

The high walls were like iron bars on the earth, leaving the pain and happiness of the world outside, and concealing tightly the nobleness, sophistication, mysteriousness and darkness of the prior royal residence inside. Lin Biao, who has been afraid of light and preferred quietness all his life, pushed the idol worship of the Chinese to an extreme after a long time of planning and waiting since he replaced Marshal Peng in the summer of 1959 on Lushan Mountain. He placed the oriental great man Mao Zedong on a holly sanctum, and struck down all his strong competitors. Eventually he was able to stand on the peak of Chinese politics from behind a

Xu Jian

mysterious and dark curtain. At the 9ᵗʰ National Congress of the CPC that year, Lin was added to the Party's Charter as the second leader and the successor of Mao in an abnormal way.

Back then on the battlefields, the prior victorious general, who had directed millions of soldiers, saw a massive victory in the political struggle. In the earth-shattering loud prayers from all around the nation—"Enjoy good health, and be healthy forever"—he felt as if he was the legal successor, and the countdown before he stepped onto the highest point in the Forbidden City had started...

After the 9ᵗʰ National Congress, Marshal Lin was refreshed, energetic and ambitious. He took a leave from Mao and left Beijing, excusing himself to tour around the old revolutionary areas. He first visited Shaoshan, the hometown of Mao; then he drove to Jinggangshan Mountain and returned to Huangyangjie. After this, he visited Five Wells, to refresh his memory of Mao's battle at Luoxiao Mountain. Finally he stopped at the high-class villa by West Lake. Washing off the dust of political struggle, he enjoyed the paradise-like views of clear streams, bright moonlight and pine trees.

Accidentally, at the same time, Mao came to take a vacation in Hangzhou as well. They met each other unexpectedly. After they had excluded Liu Shaoqi, Deng Xiaoping, and other important leaders from the central power circle, Lin became Mao's most (and only) trusted successor. Otherwise, Mao would never have left the country to him.

Actually, considering the history between Mao and Lin as a whole, during the few decades from Jinggangshan Mountain to the Lushan Mountain Meeting in 1970, objectively speaking, the appreciation and value given to Lin by Mao was much more than resentment. Not to mention at Luoxiao Mountain during the 1920s, when Mao appointed Lin, a 24-year-old, as the Chief Commander of the First Corps of the Red Army, and was personally developed and trusted by Mao; and especially the Battle of Pingxingguan Pass in 1937, in which Lin directed his soldiers to annihilate the division led by Itagaki, encouraging the Chinese army, led by the CPC, in the Anti-Japanese War. What surprised Mao even more was that, even this guy from Hubei province, who had only taken 100 thousand soldiers out of Shanhaiguan Pass, already had an army of millions in three years when he returned from Northeastern China. The size of the army, the quality of their supplies, and their bravery could all be called strong. Moreover, they had fought from the northeastern to the southern border, and occupied half of China. Even though Mao asked him first to fight in Korea in 1950, he excused himself with illness, and received a cold reception for a period of time. But when Marshal Peng was struck down in July 1959 on Lushan Mountain, he started to handle the daily works of the Central Military Committee. He used all his intelligence from the war in the political construction of the army. He was the first one to propose "learn and apply flexibly and it will take effect immediately", invented the "peak theory", and he initiated the personal worship of China. Again, he gained Mao's favour.

In February 1964, during a reception event for Mao, he praised Lin's "four number ones", as it was a new discovery and invention of Lin, and also appreciated Lin's approach to "Study the words of Chairman Mao and put emphasis on four parts". In searching for more chances to step higher, he eventually got to the top of the power step by step.

That day, in a high-class classically-styled villa not far from West Lake, Deputy Supreme Commander Lin, who had hurt his nerves during the war, was in a fine outfit. The dark green military uniform covered his slim figure; under the red hat, a pair of eyebrows were cast above the sharp eyes. Lin was looking at this building, which was more elegant and classic than the one in Maojiawan, with the green pond covered by lotus and pavilions. The images of the buildings were reflected in the water, generating some poetic feeling.

The secretary approached them quietly. "Chief, the Chairman will arrive here soon."

Lin stood under the eaves of the main building, circled by his staff, and waited for Mao.

Soon, the Red-flag brand car of Mao stopped. From inside there came a tall and strong man whose shadow had cast itself over two thirds of the century. He held Lin's hand and turned to his staff. "How is your Chief Lin going recently?" He didn't call Lin the deputy chairman, but followed the old way of addressing him from the wartime, narrowing the distance between them.

Shaking his head, Lin said, "As usual, not good or bad."

The Chairman said with concern, "You need more rest. The working schedule can be flexible."

Lin answered, "Thank you, Chairman."

Mao and Lin walked into the living room. Mao sat on the sofa and lit a cigarette. He said to Lin, "You were not in Beijing during this period. After Zhou's meeting with Kosygin in the airport, the tension at the border has been relaxed. But you have to tell Huang Yongsheng the defense in the northern area cannot be relaxed. It is an open area, and I am very much worried."

When it came to war, Lin's eyes brightened. "Put yourself at ease, Chairman. If the Soviet Union dares to attack, they will definitely be trapped in the ocean of a people's war, as you have planned…"

After Mao went, Lin was left in contemplation.

Reflecting on his conversation with Mao, he thought of the pair of eyes which could see through everything, yet didn't show any sign of negative feelings. In the past, even though he was placed in the deputy commander position, and was called by the foreign media the second leader of China, he understood that all that he has been doing was just following Mao, the real emperor, to rule others. Whether he was powerful or not, whether his orders could be effective, all depended on Mao. Lin decided that he would use his own political career as a bet. Even if the Chairman blamed him, he could be excused by the imminent threat without incurring too much negative effect on himself. Therefore, after two days of consideration, the usually prudent Lin set up an outline, and asked his staff to contact his old subordinate Huang Yongsheng, who was the Chief of General Staff, by the red telephone line.

On October 18th, 1969, in following Lin's directions, Huang summarised Lin's oral orders into a highly confidential red-headed document, and filed it to the entire army under the name of *No.1 Order of Deputy Chairman Lin*. According to this order, the whole army was to be combat ready, in order to defend against attacks from the enemies. And the army must produce the anti-tank weapons faster, and organise capable leading teams which could occupy commanding positions. With the leaders of all levels in ready positions, all the circumstances were to be known and reported in time. At the same time, the *No.1 Order* also required the governments, schools, factories and residents of major cities to be relocated in more remote rural areas.

The next day, receiving the *No.1 Order*, all the soldiers and residents of China started to move, just as had happened in the rural

revolutionary bases. It was no less than another solemn and stirring Long March. Of course, after Lin sent out his *No.1 Order*, he
didn't forget to report to Mao by phone as a meeting's minutes.

When Mao received the report, his mood turned heavy and
serious. Lin was still like how he had been during the years of war.
Such an important thing should be reported first. He lacked the
prudence for the Party, the people and the army. Was it done out
of emergency and innocent mistake? Or it was usurpation? Mao
kept smoking, and walking around his study. He could not make a
final decision in a short time. Eventually this senior man sorted out
his complicated thoughts, and used his unique thinking to solve
the issue. He waved his pen and commented on the report in wild
script, "Burn it."

It was an order which carried much weight. With this spirit, even
the greatest general would be fearful. Huang, who had just taken
the position as the Chief of General Staff, didn't have the courage.
He transferred Mao's comment immediately to Lin in Hangzhou.
Lin thought for a moment and replied to Huang and the entire
army, "Good, burn it." With a minor change, the tone was totally
different. There was no sign of blame from the Chairman.

Lin's order was burned, but the effect of it on China at that time
didn't disappear, and the Chinese paid heavily for it.

The old generation of revolutionaries were struck down and
expelled from Beijing. Liu Shaoqi, who was already dying, was
escorted to Kaifeng, Henan Province, Deng Xiaoping and Chen
Yun were sent to Jiangxi Province, Chen Yi was relocated to Shiji-
azhuang, Ye Jiangying went to Changsha, and Tao Zhu was sent to
Hefei…

A large group of third tier modernised factories were relocated to remote forests in mountains based on Lin's principle of "Scattering throughout the mountains and caves"…

Tens of millions of city residents were forced to move to rural areas, leaving a permanent scar on the history of the republic…

An ancient country had suffered an unprecedented disaster in an insane age, a great nation forced to swallow the bitter fruit of an era.

2. The hard fruit of an era had been chewed on by the strategic missile troop for 15 years.

The *No.1 Order* of Lin generated a green apple at the time, leaving the soldiers of the strategic missile troop in the remote mountains for a long time.

That year, the developing strategic missile troop was affected by Lin's principles of "Scattering throughout the mountains and caves", all of them sent to camp in the most remote mountains and deserts. The purpose was to fight the big nuclear war earlier. But the tension at the border quickly disappeared, and the pigeon of peace flew over the blue sky of the republic. However, the soldiers of the strategic missile troop were undergoing a quiet war against the harsh natural environment in one of the most remote areas on earth.

Deep in the mountains of northern China

A path devolving around the mountains extended into the distance. Along the way, there were sometimes some native people scattered on the tops of the mountains. There was no end for the road extending into the forests. No people were living in this region tens of kilometres wide. But one of the strategic missile troops, the most advanced army of China, set up their first camp here. The soldiers came first, followed by their families. They had no cities or shops to rely on, and certainly no factories or schools. To move an army here was no less than to move a small society here. The head of a missile troop was responsible for all kinds of matters, no matter how trivial they were, including the jobs of the families, the schools for the kids, even the fights between a couple. Because the local residents didn't have the concept of trade, and they kept an eternal and rudimentary lifestyle of farming. As a result, the vegetable and meat supplies of the soldiers and their families became a big problem. Often, they had to purchase vegetables from the nearby town more than 100 kilometres away. During the summer time, when the food arrived, the meat and the vegetables had all gone bad. This forced the soldiers to build their own farm, producing the supplies for themselves. But the most annoying thing was the jobs for the families of the soldiers. Those women who didn't have anything to do for a long time would experience a great deal of trouble. First of all, there were the financial problems of their families. These officers were far from supporting their families solely on their own salaries. Especially for the first few years, their income was not high and they had to carry their debts to the war or till their death. The army did their best to set up grocery shops, photo shops, barbershops, and kindergartens in the community. But all these places could only hire a limited amount of people. While the number of families increased, the problems became more serious. The heads of the army had to contact the shoes factories in a small city which was hundreds of kilometres away, to set up a joint venture together. They had settled lots of the families overnight, but the shoes factories only operated half the year and stopped for two or three months due to a lack of materials or low sales. The families still had nothing to do and wandered around. The heads of the army were worried and the officers were angry. But nobody could solve the problem in a fundamental way.

A little town in southern China

It was probably the smallest town in China, only five or six hundred metres long and a hundred metres wide. There was only one main street in the town, with the natives' unique stilted buildings on both sides showing the remaining characteristics of an ancient history. A clear and green stream was running around the city. Obviously, this was a distant border city with no industrial foundation at all. When the strategic missile troop first arrived here, even the staff of the local government were not used to wearing shoes. The army brought the little town modern civilisation and concepts of modern life. The girls of the town all followed the wives of the soldiers in dressing themselves up. But they had to face the cruel reality that, due to the size of the town, the jobs it could provide were very limited. Once they had stepped into this town hidden behind the mountains, they became unemployed. Some of the employed families were just doing the things that nobody in the town wanted to do—the wife of a deputy regimental commander followed her husband here from southern China. While her husband was a decent man in the army, even with the special approval from the county government for her to get a job in the little town, the head of the town, a man from the minority group, was very embarrassed. He told her, "I am terribly sorry, the only vacancy in town was janitor at the hospital." The deputy regimental commander grasped his hand tightly, and thanked him repeatedly, "I understand your difficult situation. Thank you!" The wife of the deputy regimental commander officially started to work in the hospital. But her job was not supposed to be done by a human. Everyday she had to clean the surgery room and wash the blood-stained sheets from obstetrics. Initially she vomited upon seeing it. And she cried in front of her husband. But after all this, she still had to work. Because she was already luckier than others' wives. As the wife of a deputy regimental commander, she had an official job. Day after day, year after year, she became used to it.

The wife of a chief of logistics came from Sichuan, the land of paradise. Since she followed her husband here, her husband had tried hard to find her a job, which was a butcher in a food station in the county. Luckily, she was strong and was used to hard labour in the countryside. As she was able to eat fine food, it was still better to be a butcher here than labouring in the countryside as a peasant. Everyday at 4 am, she had to start to work in the darkness. Along with other male butchers, she had to boil the water, and then slaughter the pigs. In the beginning, when the pigs snarled, she was frightened. Later, with more experience, she was no longer frightened. The only problem was, when she walked on the street with her blood-stained and oil-soaked butcher uniform, her husband's reputation was hurt and he showed some anger. As a woman from Sichuan Province with a fiery character, she was upset as well. "How can you dislike me for this reason? Find me another good job if you can."

This group of wives of the officers could not even get the most low class jobs. But they were very considerate and didn't want to trouble the heads of the army. They volunteered to work as sand-carriers. They would stand in the waist-deep water and do the works of a man. Many of them developed illnesses after such heavy labour. Some men from the army would shed tears in front of them …

In a lonely village primary school in the deep forest

More than just children from the minority group gathered here. Only since the establishment of this primary school did they have the chance to learn to read. But its teaching time and quality did not appeal to many of the families of the army. The kids from the mountains would come to school at 8 am with their cows or goats. When the herds were roaming on the grass, they returned to school. The class started at 10 am, and ended at 12 pm. In the afternoon, there would be two more teaching hours. But during the busy farming season, the teachers had to harvest, so the pupils ran free. Usually pupils from three or four grades were taught together. When they graduated, it meant that their childhood had ended. In this school of the mountains, the children of the officers studied with the local children. Their fathers' generation came from a high class educational background and operated the most advanced weapons of China, but their children had to walk for more than ten miles each day to study in a village school. Basically, they would only study for half of the day and play for the rest. There was not even one college student among these children of the officers. The fathers who had a high education felt they owed a heavy debt to their children which could never be returned.

Young Zhou Fang, who was 7 years old, waited for his father to come out of the forbidden area with her bright eyes wide open. When she was four, she came to the mountains with her mother and her younger brother from a village on the Yunnan Guizhou Plateau. Her mother couldn't find a job, so she had to open a small shop outside of the forbidden area. Zhou Wengui, her father, was an engineer in the army. As for her, she had to walk for six or seven miles on the mountain—climbing over a hill and crossing a valley with steep slopes and a devolving path. An uncle would walk with her if he was going to buy vegetables. But usually she always walked the long way by herself. The mountains were high and the forest was dense. There were many animals around. Initially she was scared. During the summer, when there was suddenly a snake blocking her way, she cried and ran back home. Of course she didn't make it to school that day. On a rainy and windy day, she would get all wet and fall on the ground. But gradually she became used to it. The years in the mountains made a young girl mature at an early age. It had been three years since she arrived here, and her only wish was to ask her father to take her to the town which was 100 miles away, just to take a coloured photo. It was a Sunday, early in the morning, and her father promised her that he would take her to the town by car once he had finished checking the construction sites. But after a long wait, the only thing that came out was an ambulance, which carried her father to the hospital outside of the mountains. On that day in the morning, Zhou Wengui, engineer of the army, was suddenly hit by an egg-sized stone falling from above while he was checking the construction site. The stone shot through his security hat. He didn't stand up again. When little Zhou Fang arrived at the hospital with her mother, it was her first time in town. But it didn't leave any sweet memory for her; on the contrary, it became a dark day in her childhood. She stood by her father's dead body with her mother. Her mother had already passed out after crying so hard.

She cried, her heart broken, "Dad, wake up, wake up. Didn't you say you would take a photo with me? I'm here, I'm here...."

Her dad could no longer open his gentle and smiling eyes. The pain of losing her father in childhood left a deep trauma in her heart. From then on, a flower withered, an innocent and joyful child became silent. Nobody ever heard her sweet laugh. She spent all her day listening to the teachers with her head low, and walked with her head low. She didn't speak one word, as if she were mute. The pain of the dead was quietly imposed on the little girl.

When the first "summer camp of the light of the rocket" was held along the beautiful seaside of Qingdao, Zhou Fang was invited as a special guest following a personal request from the heads of the Second Artillery Corps. This little girl who grew up in the mountains never faced the giant ocean. It was the first time for her to chase after the cheerful waves of the sea. Her bright eyes were full of tears, as she shouted at the ocean, "Dad... "

Only at this moment did the people see a smile return to her innocent face.

3. During the last days of Premier Zhou's life, he told the head of a province who came to visit him, "There is a missile troop stationed in your province. It was their life that I worried about the most. You guys from the provincial committee must care more about them ... "

General Li Xuge made a historical full stop for the period of the missile troop's stay in the mountains.

In the spring of 1983, by an order signed by Deng Xiaoping, the Chairman of the Central Military Committee, Lieutenant General

Li Xuge, the prior Deputy Head of Department of Battles from the General Staff was promoted to the deputy commander of the strategic missile troop.

That morning, Li went to work in the headquarters of the strategic missile troop in Beijing for the first time. As he came out of the car and stared at the place which was the last stage of his military career, he inevitably felt astonished. The headquarters was separated into three parts. The Command was stationed in a small guest house, which was built 30 years ago. The building was already too old, with outdated office equipment. There were seven or eight people squeezed in one office with no space to work. Many documents were piled up in the cabinets in the corridor. It was not only unsafe, but also unsuitable for training. To imagine the status of the army from the status of its headquarters, it was easy to infer that the army must be in no better a position.

The most advanced army of China had been wandering at a "manageable" level. Since the first day of his assignment, an ambition to change this situation completely had arisen in the general's heart.

In the evening, when he returned to the military compound, his wife Ms Geng Sumo, who used to be a military reporter, asked him in her usual humorous way, "How do you feel on the first day of your new job?"

"It was unbearable!"

Actually he was not unfamiliar with this strategic missile troop. During his 40 years of military service, most of his time had had something to do with it.

Lieutenant General Li was from Luannan, Hebei Province. In 1943, the Japanese invaders adopted the policy of "Kill all, burn all, rob all" in northern China, and turned the eastern Hebei Province into an ocean of blood and fire. At that time, Li, who was only a 16-year-old middle school student, decided to join the army and serve the country. He started his military life under General Li Yunchang's direction. The battles turned a young student who was supposed to go to school into a strong soldier. During the Anti-Japanese War, his young talent stood out. Since he was young, Li was keen to study. He always maintained an exceptional sensitivity to new things. When his army occupied Yutian county in Hebei province at 1945, he got a bike from the Japanese army. It was the first time for him to see this foreign thing. One evening, he learned to ride it and kept falling. He rode it to Luannan, his hometown, to visit his parents, and returned the next morning. It was more than 200 miles as a double trip, and his battle mates could not imagine how he achieved it. This kind of interest remained in his blood until his old age.

During the Liberation War, he was promoted to the Chief of General Staff for his regiment at the age of 23. After he took part in the Pingjin and Liaoshen Battles, he fought with Ma Bufang and Ma Hongkui with a battalion on the giant land of Northeastern China. He defeated the primary force of Ma near Liupan Mountain and Lanzhou, which washed away the shame of the West Division of the Red Army who had lost to Ma.

After the liberation of the mainland, the Americans started a war by the side of Yalu River after the Chinese had just had a taste of peace. Li followed the army to Korea again. He was transferred to the Command's military training section as the chief from the Chief of Staff for the regiment. By the end of the Five Battles, the commander of the allied force, General Clarke, was forced to negotiate at

Panmunjom. After the end of the war, he returned with the army.

In 1954, following the order of the Central Military Committee, he was transferred to the Department of Battles of the Central Military Committee as a staff officer of the General Staff, responsible for the special force. Since December 1957, after he was trained in Changxindian, he was in charge of the tasks for the missile troop.

In 1964, he worked under General Zhang Aiping as the director of the Nuclear Trial Office. This secret operation shocked the whole world. And he listened to Premier Zhou's instructions many times, and was deeply influenced by the old generation of revolutionaries. These all formed a solid foundation for him to work with the strategic missile troop. During his 20 years of working experience with the General Staff, Li was not only equipped with a meticulous working style, but also exceptional wisdom and courage. When he was entrusted with responsibilities, his courage and abilities could not help but reveal themselves.

In 1969, during a critical moment between the conflicting armies of China and the Soviet Union, something happened in Xinjiang. As someone who had reserved his opinion about the Cultural Revolution, Li was expelled from Beijing to lead a newly established division to defend the border in Yili, where people of past dynasties were exiled.

It was just his luck to be leaving Beijing when the wicked were in power. Once the order was made, he moved his whole family, including his three young daughters and mother-in-law, who were already 65 years old, to Yili, the penal colony. His family were ready to bury themselves there without ever returning to Beijing. With peerless strategy and foresight, before the army started to build new camps, he asked them to carry construction materials and sanitation facilities from Beijing and Tianjin after discussion with his deputy, in order to change the local living customs. Many people were confused about his decision, since it was against the tradition of the PLA to not try and survive in harsh conditions. But after witnessing the improvements of the local living conditions, and enjoying the benefits, they had to admire the old leader's foresight. What was more impressive was that, with his management talent, he regulated his army, which was formed by people from many different units, into a disciplined and strong troop. Some of the people who had chosen the wrong line in the Cultural Revolution were entrusted with important tasks, so long as they were capable. Many people were impressed by his abilities to lead the army.

At the end of 1970s, one of the famous "Three Yangs" in the Chinese army, General Yang Yong, was appointed as the Commander of the Urumchi Command. When Yang inspected the army, he appreciated Li's works and was ready to transfer him to the military committee of the command. Accidentally at this time, the order to transfer Li back to Beijing from the Central Military Committee had arrived as well. General Yang, who valued Li's abilities, even kept the order down. When another commander called General Yang, he joked, "Commander Yang, aren't you too bold to withhold an order approved by Deputy Chairman Deng?"

Yang laughed on the telephone. "We are in urgent need of talent. Everywhere is the same. Moreover, I have reported to the Central Military Committee to put Li on the candidate list for the Deputy Chief of Staff of our Military Area Command. It is the border area that needs him more." The candid and stubborn commander Yang withheld the order for two months, until the Central Military Committee pushed him harder, and he let Li return to Beijing.

History eventually granted Li a space to make use of his abilities. Not long after he came to the strategic missile troop, Li drove more than 10 thousand miles to the northern mountain areas and southern forests to investigate the living conditions of the missile troops there, including their material life, cultural life, facilities and the accumulated problems of the families' employment and schooling. These problems were far more severe than he had expected. Pictures of struggles emerged before him.

In a launching battalion in the tropical forest of Southern China

Ever since the arrival of the army, they have been living in grass cottages, which were built on the former site of a farm of Reform through Labour. For the past few decades, the cottages were never repaired. The walls were made out of soil, which was cracked. During the winter, cold wind would enter the cottages; during the rainy season, water leaked inside heavily. When it came to consecutive rains, even with all the basins and bowls, they were not able to contain the water leaking into the cottages. Some soldiers even put a raincoat on the quilt while they were sleeping, or just sat through the whole night. The officers described their cottages as if they had "bent down its waist, leaned on its stick, untied its hair and dropped tears", which was really a vivid analogy.

In the deep valleys, in order to receive the TV signals from CCTV, the soldiers of the entire company would hold the TV and carry the antenna while running around on the mountains—from the bottom of the mountains to the slope, then to the top. But they could only hear the sounds or see the pictures. Finally they were all disappointed and shouted at the mountains to let go of their disappointment.

After the first snow in the northern mountains, a group of soldiers carried water from the frozen stream barebacked to wipe their bodies.

Watching this scene, Li felt tears of bitterness obscure his vision. He seemed to have seen the last few months of the Premier, when he was concerned about the living conditions of the strategic missile troop.

The cold spring of 1975, Beijing

Premier Zhou, who was very sick, was approaching the end of his life. However, he was still worried about the economy, which was on the edge of collapse.

One day, two major leaders of a province came to visit Premier Zhou after reporting their work. After asking about the living conditions of the people in the old revolutionary areas, border areas and poor areas, the Premier encouraged the two leaders, with much concern, "You must have confidence, and believe that the difficulties will eventually pass away." When the time allowed by the doctor for visits had come to an end, the two leaders were full of tears and reluctant to say goodbye to the Premier. They prayed for his health. And the Premier waved to him in his bed.

Suddenly, the Premier's hand stopped in the middle of the air, as he said, "Please don't go yet, I have other things to tell you." The two leaders turned back and looked at the Premier with deep feeling. "There is a missile troop stationed at your place, it is the treasure of the country. Their life is my biggest concern. You folk from the provincial government should take more care of them," Premier Zhou said, his skinny hands gently holding theirs.

The two leaders could no longer resist the tears in their eyes.

They nodded to the Premier with their throat choked by complicated feelings.

Every time when Li thought about this unforgettable scene, he always felt the holy commission and responsibilities entrusted to him.

However, how to get the strategic missile troop out of the mountains was a question that had been recognised by several generations of leaders but remained unsolved. It involved not just the Second Artillery Corps alone, but also the strategy of the entire country and the army.

But finally, the spring breeze of the reform and open-door policy had come to the remote mountain areas of China. With the approval of Deng, the Chairman of the Central Military Committee, the investigation team for strengthening the grass-root level construction sent by the Headquarters, had come to the mountains and deserts where the strategic missile troop was stationed. After seeing the soldiers of the 1980s still living in shabby grass cottages or tents, and many of them drinking water from the rice field and taking showers by the river during the winter, they were deeply shocked, some even bursting into tears out of guilt. A few white-headed section chiefs said with much emotion, "The modernisation of our army was built on the flesh of the soldiers from the Second Artillery Corps. We had never imagined how harsh their living environment was!"

A female Section Chief from the Budget of the Ministry of Finance couldn't help but cry and hug a soldier after she had seen her son working in the muddy water with soldiers of his age in shabby cotton-padded coats, their meals poor and insurance inadequate to support any normal construction work.

4. In the mid-1980s, Deng reached out to the world.

Following the change of strategy of the Chinese army and a disarmament policy which reduced the amount of soldiers by 1 million, the strategic missile troop started to move out of the remote mountains.

In 1986, history was no longer stubborn.

Since Deng, the general designer of the reform and open-up policy, had pushed open the gate of the Forbidden City, which had been closed and dusty for a hundred years, the Chinese had stepped into a new era of joining the world.

In the middle of the 1980s, the world was fairly peaceful, though there were still wars going on in some corners, and even some areas around China had not recovered their charming blue sky. However, the Chairman of the Central Military Committee and a great politician, Deng Xiaoping, made a judgment full of wisdom and foresight: the next world war would not come in the following twenty years. He required the entire Party, army and country to focus on economic construction, making use of this rare window of world peace. In the Eastern Hall of the Great Hall of People, after analysing the international situation in front of all the important leaders of the Party, army and the country, this oriental great man of 82 pointed out that the army had to change the prior guiding principles from fighting a big nuclear war to focusing on economic construction during peace time. He reached out to the world, and the Chinese army was reduced by one million soldiers. Before that, in the third national population census of 1982, the Chinese government had measured the total number of the army at 4.23 million. This oriental great man, with the courage of an era, advanced the disarmament policy earlier than the world-wide wave of disarmament in the second autumn of the 1990s by seven years. Were it not for all kinds of changes in the international balance of power, Deng could have made this decision even earlier.

Actually, ever since he had started to take charge of the army, he had been focusing on a much more efficient and sharp form of military construction, waiting for the change of power balances in the world. In 1974, when he returned for the first time, he was praised by Mao as someone who "Hides his needle in the cotton, and has strength disguised as weakness." When he was appointed chief of the General Staff, he had been focusing on the modernisation of the Chinese army, and confronted heavy pressure to reduce the number of soldiers. Within one year, the army was cut by 13.6%. Two years later, when Deng returned again, he pushed the reduction with even stronger determination, facilitating the transformation of the army's guiding principles in order to build a stronger army.

History undoubtedly had given the Chinese soldiers a second chance.

Actually, in real life, every one of us is granted an equal chance at certain opportunities. But usually when the God of destiny visits us, we might be in the neighbour's home, while some of us have stayed home and grasped the opportunity tightly, walking into the glory of their life and history.

However, the chances granted to a nation or an individual may not be many.

In 1985, Li Xuge, who had already been promoted to the commander of the Chinese strategic missile troop, grasped the historical opportunity granted by the time. No leader had allowed the missile troop to get out of the mountains, nor was there any mention of it in any red-headed document, but Li gleaned this understanding from the change of the army's guiding principles. He believed the army must consider their plans in the long term, and create a comprehensive war system which relied upon middle- and small-sized cities. A document from the State Council and the Central Military Committee which talked about the separation of battlefields and dormitories had inspired him to let the missile troop get out of the mountains. He realised that the time and opportunity to solve all the old problems fundamentally had arrived.

Deep at night, the meeting room of the Party branch in the headquarters of the strategic missile troop were still bathed in bright light. These generals who had been through difficulties and challenges from different eras could not resist the excitement in their hearts. The problems which the old leaders had struggled with were showing signs of resolution. A consensus was quickly reached: the missile troop should walk out of the mountains and open the horizon of military construction in a wider space.

After getting rid of the historical fetters of "Scattering throughout the mountains and caves", the strategic missile troop said goodbye to the narrow world where they had been trapped for so long and stepped into the middle and large cities. In this way, the guiding principles of the strategic missile troop were transformed from a closed type to an open type. The determination for changes from the Party committee of the Second Artillery Corps was supported and affirmed by the Central Military Committee. General Zhang Aiping, who was the prior Deputy Chief Secretary of the Central Military Committee and Defense Minister, had lent them enormous support. And General Hong Xuezhi, who was the prior Deputy Secretary-General of the Central Military Committee and Chief for Logistics, had also helped them in solving detailed financial problems.

From the spring of 1986, led by the Commander Li Xuege and Political Commissar Liu Lifeng, the heads of the strategic missile troop and leaders from the four divisions had covered every tribe, unit and valley through the southern and northern borders, and solved 230 important problems which worked to the benefit of the soldiers.

In the summer on the deserts of the plateau, the imposing snow peaks had transformed into spacious and infinite deserts. During the rainy season of the forests, the pouring rain whipped the dark green mountains. In order to relocate the army to small and middle cities on time, Commander Li and Political Commissar Liu had to visit the local governments before the army entered any county, an idea that gained strong support from local government.

As time flew, the vigorous green covered the mountains beside the battlefields. The "Hope Project", which lasted for six years in the strategic missile troop, eventually brought the missile troops an eternal spring.

Many modern military barracks were erected in small and middle cities, and the majority of the army's headquarters had been moved to cities in standard barracks. The multi-functioned cultural facilities formed an important part of the soldiers' life. When the music was started in the deep mountains, the soldiers' rough singing inspired their feelings; when a wave of new culture and ideas from Deng's open-up policy reached the deserts, the breeze of the metropolis entered into the remote regions. In the bowls of the grassroot soldiers, the prior "pickles in rice porridge" was gone, replaced by delicious new dishes. When the soldiers needed to shower, the old scenes of "relying on a bucket in the summer and a pot in the winter" had become history. With the solar energy water heaters and standard bathrooms, the young guys were able to be cleaner and tidier. When some veterans who had lived and fought with the missile troop for many years returned, they gladly found out that the bleak deserts had already changed into a fruitful and beautiful garden for the soldiers.

A series of policies which favoured the harsh regions were promulgated. After the approvals of the State Council and the Central Military Committee, the officers of the strategic missile troop would receive allowances higher than to their ranks. This meant that a battalion commander of the missile troop could enjoy benefits equivalent to those of a deputy regimental commander in a normal army. The soldiers and officers stationed in harsh environments like remote mountains or plateaus would obtain compensation—a lieutenant's income was equal to a captain's income stationed in Beijing. And the military academies would apply special admission policies to the children of officers stationed in remote and harsh regions. Once the fruits of material construction were transformed into mental motivation, exceptional energy could be released. The loss of soldiers' faith back in the old days when the strategic missile troop were trapped in the remote mountains was long vanished in the depths of historical record. The contrast between the grassroots level and the executive organs was narrowing down. Many university graduates considered being a platoon leader in the launching battalion the first choice of their career, the reason being that, so long as you had abilities, you could use them there and be valued.

By the end of 1994, according to the comprehensive quality survey and analysis of the strategic missile troop soldiers made by the political department of the Second Artillery Corps, although affected by the strong tides of commercialism, 95% of the grass-roots officers were content, a rare situation for any army in the world.

5. The Western military satellites didn't seem to notice the great migration of the green square array.

The Chinese soldiers would not enter the 21st century carrying hardship. The barracks, which matched the high technologies of the army, had tied the hearts of the soldiers.

Pairs of surreptitious eyes flew over the sky of China.

Ever since the Chinese strategic missile troop had come out from the curtains of history, the spy satellites never stopped searching for the most advanced part of the Chinese army. Especially when this troop had just got out of the forests and travelled through China and revealed their launching trials publicly, the Western media would base their reports on satellite photos.

It could be said that, in this world, the actions of every country and every nation could not escape the eyes of others. But the spy satellites which regularly crossed the sky of China had ignored the steady steps of the strategic missile troop who were walking out of the forests and getting closer to the middle and smaller cities. Perhaps because they had been in a harsh environment for a long time, enduring hardship seemed to be synonymous with the Chinese. Therefore, when all the barracks with modern facilities were erected suddenly in the cities, the western military analysts ignored this newly emerged group. However, for the missile troop, which has been used to living in mountains for decades, this historical migration became a turning point in their life. The employment and schooling problems which had troubled generations of soldiers had passed, along with the problems of inadequate showering and drinking water, and no TV or newspapers. For them, the luxury of taking helicopters and cars to report for duty enjoyed by the American strategic air force and Russian strategic rocket army was no longer a distant and impossible dream. At least they could take cars to report for duty on the battlefields, and no longer needed to be troubled by landslides and snowstorms blocking the roads, or insufficient food supplies.

Many facilities which matched the most advanced weapons operated by this army had been built, and this, along with the mysterious and powerful land of the strategic missile tribes, attracted more and more hot blooded men.

On the land of Shaanxi, there were the clouds and willows of the Ba River. The dust and wind of the time had buried this piece of land, which was immersed in the bloodshed of history. The faded smoke of gunpowder had formed terracotta warriors for the entertainment of people. However, the military spirit of defending the country was always boiling hot in the blood of this ancient nation, which had been through so many disasters.

Not far away from Li Mountain, the graduation ceremony of the highest academy of the strategic missile troop was going on. More than one hundred undergraduates and graduates were granted the rank of lieutenant in advance before voluntarily settling themselves in Qinghai-Tibet Plateau. They were making a vow under the solemn "Eight One" military flag.

For the past decade, the rate of military academy graduates obeying their transfer orders was 100%. There were more than 1,000 graduates who were sent to the forbidden areas of history, bringing vigorous green to a place that was hardly visited by the breeze of spring. They would follow the steps of the prior soldiers who sacrificed their bodies to build the battlefields, and create new achievements as a new generation of rocket officers.

History would be rewritten in their hands.

Chapter 7

Mysterious Stories of the Mysterious Troops

1. The unrevealed secret of when General Zhang Aiping attended foreign affairs. Premier Zhou searched his pockets personally and asked him with much concern, "Have you taken the documents?"

Deng Yingchao complained to her husband, Premier Zhou, that he had concealed nuclear trial secrets from her.

Early autumn, 1964, Zhongnanhai, Beijing

The blood red fire ball which had been hanging in the sky for thousands of years struck Yan Mountains, which was cast in a dark blue fog. The burning fire at the western horizon had coloured the land of Beijing in red, and also the green waves of Zhongnanhai.

The sunset burnished the ancient maples trees in red, indicating the arrival of another golden harvest season; the glorious end of the day suggested there would be a bright dawn for the four-year long project of the atomic bomb of China.

Evening had come and the lights were just going on in Beijing.

The light from Qinzheng Hall emerged through the windows. Inside of the meeting room, Premier Zhou had gathered the members of the Special Central Committee, He Long, Chen Yi, Luo Ruiqing, Zhang Aiping and Liu Jie for a last special meeting on the confidentiality of the nuclear trial. Sitting in the middle of the meeting room, the Premier looked around at these old familiar subordinates. He waved his right arm and told them seriously, "The Chairman has agreed to conduct the trial in October, and the time is approaching. The confidentiality is a vital issue. We are not in the small liberated zone anymore, now we are on the stage, and they are in the darkness. Don't spell it out before we can do it. If we leak it and they come to attack us, then it would ruin all our plans. This minor illness I have is widely known. Who knows — if one more knows about it, he may take it as a news. I hope you will not talk about it at home, and do not tell anyone. My wife Comrade Deng Yingchao is an old Party member and a member of the central committee, but I will not tell her what I am not supposed to. Anyone who is not supposed to know shall remain in the dark. Not everyone who attended the meeting a few days ago needs to be informed of this. The matter which has been decided is limited to the standing committee members, the two Deputy Chairmen of the Central Military Committee, and Comrade Peng Zhen."

Under Premier Zhou's directions, the meeting studied the evacuation and air defense matters in the trial region in detail. At the end, General Zhang Aiping, who was specifically appointed the general commander of the trial, came to take leave from the Premier. "Premier, I have to attend a foreign affair tonight, so I have to leave early."

Premier Zhou looked at his Shanghai brand watch. It was past dinner time, and he nodded gently, "Comrade Aiping can leave earlier. Let's determine the final two problems … "

General Zhang Aiping picked up his file case and was just about to salute the Premier and leave when Zhou stood up suddenly. "Please wait a moment, Comrade Aiping. Check your pocket to see whether there is any paper that you may have scribbled on. They have to be taken out."

Under the Premier's request, General Zhang Aiping searched through all of his pockets in front of everyone. The Premier nodded when he saw they were clear. Then he pointed to Zhang's file case, and asked with much concern, "Are there any documents inside? If there is, they must not be taken to foreign affairs. From tomorrow on, Comrades Aiping and Liu Xiyao shall not attend any foreign affairs … "

A Premier of the People's Republic, a manager who was responsible for 800 million, his meticulousness was historically peerless. It was the luck of the Chinese people, but also their misfortune, since it formed part of the reasons for his early death due to disease.

Time flew in a hurry.

…

Late autumn, Xihua Hall, Zhongnanhai

The old cherry-apple trees had produced many fruits.

General Zhang Aiping, who had successfully directed the first nuclear trial of China in the deep deserts of Lop Nur, returned to Beijing and visited Premier Zhou and his wife Deng Yingchao.

Zhang Aiping's face had been darkened by the sun of the desert in a few months. However, in between his eyebrows, the excitement of great achievements could not be hidden. In order to thank this general whose achievements had helped China to settle its status among all the nations of the world, the Premier invited him to have dinner with them at home. During dinner, the Premier raised a glass of fragrant Maotai liquor and toasted with Zhang Aiping. "Aiping, you have accomplished a great event, and this one is for you!"

"It was all because of your directions, Premier."

"The primary determination was settled by the Chairman. I only did some detailed works." Zhou had never forgotten to place Mao at the highest position. The piousness and respect came from the bottom of his heart.

"For the successful explosion of China's first atomic bomb!"

"For our strong motherland!"

The Premier raised his glass and drank up.

Sitting beside him, Comrade Deng Yingchao kept putting more food in Zhang's bowl while she said, smiling, "Aiping, I have to criticise you. After you have done such great things, Enlai came home with his mouth shut tightly, not leaking a clue to me." She shot a glance at her husband with some hidden bitterness. "This has been his old problem for a long time, I will just leave him alone for now. But how about you, even you didn't say anything…"

"Sister, you have blamed the wrong person. It was the Premier's order not to tell anyone," Zhang explained to her.

"It was me who asked them not to tell their wives and children, this is the rule of confidentiality…" The Premier saved General Zhang.

"You two always help each other, and treat me as an outsider." Deng Yingchao smiled, showing her understanding.

This was a true story which has never been published by any

magazines. From this trivial thing, which seemed like the sort of thing that would not happen to the Premier of a large country, it could be inferred that the older generation of leaders had put much value in the confidentiality of this mysterious army and had been strict in this regard. Therefore, when the fog of history had faded away, what remained were many stories about this mysterious troop…

2. This was a piece of forbidden land. This was the world of men. The only female in it was a piece of stone.

A great valley went across the mountain areas of northern China, as if it was a deep and ancient wrinkle left by nature. When the cars entered the valley, they seemed to enter a semi-open tunnel, with steep and high walls on both sides. The dark black cliffs had been engraved with the chronology of thousands of years. When it was sunny, there was no light in the valley, leaving the valley in darkness. When the sunlight over the top of the mountains had broken through the clouds, a streak of gold was cast down through the gap, reminding the people in the valley that there was still a sun in the sky.

Although this valley was essentially no different from any other valleys in the big mountains of China, there was no entry without a special permit. Even the emperor or heavenly king would have been stopped by the guards of the valley, which was a military forbidden area. Since no one could get close to this area, it had a gloss of mysteriousness. Some local residents or hunters who mistakenly entered the adjacent forest, were caught by the sentinels. After their backgrounds were checked out, their eyes would be covered by a black mask and escorted out of the area after turning a few circles, thus made him unable to know the directions. It was supposed to happen in the movies or legends, but it actually happened in this mysterious forbidden area, which made it even more attractive. Therefore, there were always curious people looking inside by the gate or attempting to get inside, even at the cost of their life. They were all stopped by the iron bars eventually, without seeing the truth behind the white clouds and smoke. Thus, there were many legendary stories happening in this mysterious valley…

In the spring of 1992, with a special permit, I was able to live here for half a month. Why did this valley become an important military base? Because it involved top state secrets and core military intelligence, I cannot say anything here. I can only say that there was treasure more valuable than the pandas stored there.

Actually, after living in the valley for a period and unveiling its mysteriousness, it turned out not to be so secret and magical as people had imagined.

In the giant forest, under the mountains, there was hidden a men's world, an iron barracks of national defense. In a few decades, the valley seemed to have become a kingdom of males, without any women. On this wonderful land, they were accompanied only by the moon in the night sky, and the female beasts with bright eyes in the dark forest, which spread some sense of the female side.

Maybe because this valley would never be visited by women, the soldiers could have more freedom. They were so unrestrained that, in some circumstances, they could expose their strong bodies as they wished, without worrying about women's eyes. During the summertime, when they jogged under the morning sunlight, they could just wear their dark green military shorts, leaving their bare backs against the blood red sun while drops of sweat rolled down. This group of men seemed to have just emerged from the huge heavenly palace of their mother, without any embarrassment in front of women. In the evening, by the sunset, a brush of cold sunlight coloured the bright stream outside of their camp in red. The soldiers who rushed to take a shower there could strip themselves without hesitation, and reveal their bodies of Adam in the arms of nature. There were only the bears, wild boars and antelopes drinking water in the distance to look at them in astonishment, confused as to why their neighbours in the mountains had returned to their childhood ...

In this world of men, their life and mindset were so causal and simple that all the things relating to women, including female dormitories and bathrooms simply didn't exist. Many officers joked, "Our world is supposed to involve getting the women to leave." However, there eventually came a day they were caught unguarded and had to swallow the bitter fruits of their own simplicity as women entered the valley.

During that summer, an art troupe of the army from Beijing had come to the valley to give them a performance. There was a famous singer and a group of beautiful as angels dancers. Although the performing time didn't last long, these women already had the soldiers, who hadn't seen any women for a long time, in panic and confusion; what was more, there was only one washroom for men in the valley—what could these women do when they needed to use the toilet?

The highest chief of the troop, the head of the logistics department, prayed quietly for no more troubles, given that these actresses would not stay in the valley for more than half a day. But things on earth are always strange — the more you hope, the more likely the opposite will happen. Right before the beginning of the performance, that famous singer needed to use the toilet, which worried the highest chief a lot. The slope was too far and too dangerous with all the beasts and snakes around; after some consideration, suddenly it came to him that he should mobilise half of a company to set up a circle of 500 metres wide with each of the soldiers facing the mountains, and inside of this circle another circle of 200 metres wide should be set up in the same way. And they could give several sheets to the female soldiers and let them hold it while other female soldiers did their business. It was an absolutely safe plan, with the soldiers guarding in the two outside circles.

When I first heard of this, I thought it might just be a joke. But the regimental commander who told me this story didn't laugh at all, and he raised his right hand and swore to Chairman Mao that it was not made up. Actually he was the company commander whose soldiers were asked to form the circles. He said, during the performance that day, seeing those pretty and fragrant girls, the soldiers were astonished and turned dumb—they were so timid that they couldn't even hand over the tea to their female comrades. When they were watching the show, all of them sat uptight, without laughter or judgment, let alone any reckless or unrestrained behaviour. They were sitting there watching, almost coldly staring at them, as if they were not appreciating the girls' dancing and singing, but worshipping an idol like the holy Mother of God.

Only at the end of the performance could these men wake up from their dreams and applaud with all their energy; only when the actresses said goodbye to them and the soldiers were in tears could you feel their innocent, genuine and honest characters.

The actresses quickly disappeared from the forest, but the discussions and sentimental attachments they had left to the soldiers lasted a long time...

It's hard to know whether it was because of an accidental grant of fate or an oversupply of female soldiers in the Headquarters, but for a period of time, the Headquarters sent a squad of female soldiers to the valley. Initially, the heads of the regiment didn't reject that, and they thought that perhaps with some warmth of women, the life of the soldiers in this valley could be more interesting. However, the reality was not that simple and beautiful. No matter how innocent and honest the soldiers were, they had to face the truth that the soldiers had been suppressed for too long, with the wings of their youth burdened so heavily that their burning hot blood and unsettling soul had to find way to let go of the anxiety. As this squad of cheerful young girls like a group of larks arrived, the serene and monolithic life formed over many years for the men here was changed.

In the beginning, these groups of young men, who had been in the army for three years and never been to town, were always avoiding the girls out of timidity. When they encountered them, before any words could come out of their mouths, their necks would turn red. If they sat in the same row with the girls to watch a movie, it would be even more uncomfortable for them, with their hands sweating and feet trembling. However, these groups of young female soldiers who grew up in the cities never took these matters seriously. They acted like some proud princesses boldly showing off the beauty of their youth. Usually, their sanitation pads should be considered private and kept in their dormitories, but they ignored the existence of the male comrades and hung them under bright daylight, revealing their private lives and also their shallowness.

These things certainly provoked the curiosity and imaginations of those soldiers who had stayed in the valley for too long. Initially, they just approached them and had a look. Later, it became worse. There were always female soldiers reporting to the leaders that the things they hung on the trees often got lost within seconds. The regimental commander was an experienced man, and he knew what had happened, and was always able to catch the perpetrators. But he still kept the incidents low, without digging deeper. And he told these girls politely, as an older brother, that such intimate things should not be hung in the camp.

There was another incident that compelled him to try and rebuild the serenity of the men's world. That night, the regimental commander went out to check the guards. He saw a young man approaching a pretty young girl in the duty room. In their eyes was reflected a timid affection. They were close enough to kiss each other. If it were during the usual time, the commander would have asked the soldier out and criticised him vehemently. But it was late at night, the lights had gone off a long time ago — what were this single man and woman here talking about? However, on that day, this regimental commander, who regulated his army strictly, kept down his anger and politely told them, "It's late, you should leave your unsaid words to tomorrow…"

It was a threat which did not seem like a threat, and he was harsh as though he were not harsh. In seeing the commander's cold eyes, the male soldier turned red instantly. For a couple of days, he would leave once he saw the commander, and he didn't have the courage to look at his eyes again. The criticism had its effect. However, the most primitive but fundamental way was to separate the men and the women's worlds.

One day, a leader from the Headquarters came to inspect the military's forbidden area. The heads of this regiment all requested the removal of this squad of female soldiers. The leader smiled helplessly. He had meant to give some warmth of women to this lonely men's world, but in the end had done the opposite.

The beautiful female soldiers disappeared forever after their short presence. From then on, in this green valley, there was never any talk of the longing for women.

A young breeder even told me humorously, "In our valley, probably even the mice are all male. The only female animal — an old pig has also eloped with a wild boar from the mountains." He said that that old pig had given birth to three baby pigs that autumn. In a month, the three little pigs grew up with thicker hair than other pigs and could easily jump over the bar. Even if the breeders had thought of many ways to stop them, they could still do it.

One morning, when he got up to feed the pigs, he found that none of the old and young pigs were there. He asked the soldiers to search around the camp, but they still couldn't find them. A soldier who had gotten back from duty told him that he had seen a tall and strong pig covered by mud screaming in front of the swinery early in the morning. He thought it was just an escaped pig, so he didn't pay much attention. At that moment, the breeder finally understood that the three little pigs were fathered by the wild boar in the mountains. They had returned to the forest with the wild boar ...

In the forbidden area, there will never be women.

But it was women, the mother of mankind, who gave birth to men and raised them up. Instead of allowing many horny soldiers to keep those porny pictures of actresses, it would be better to build an elegant, pure and holly statue of the Mother of Mankind, to accompany the soldiers and make them understand that, even if they were undertaking tasks lacking in interest, it was all for the safety of their mothers. In this way, there would be holy fire lit in their anxious blood. Therefore, they invited a sculptor from the city and carved a beautiful young mother from the stones of the forbidden area.

From sunrise to sunset, once the soldiers stepped out of their room, the first thing they saw would be the female statue of a holy mother standing in the shadow of the willows. And they could find peace in their unsettled life, with a sense of responsibility rising in their heart. When there was more sense of serenity, there was less anxiety.

This was the only woman in the kingdom of men, a woman made of stone.

3. The iron law of the military forbidden area was that it only allowed entrance by proof of authorisation, not identity. The commander was stopped because he had left his authorisation behind, and a deputy regimental commander had to ask the security section to lead him inside.

A green military jeep was heading to the military forbidden area from the headquarters.

Commander Jia was sitting beside the driver. He saw a giant forest on the mountains covered by snow. The lazy sunlight of the winter was cast on the mountains of northern China, revealing their dark ridges stripped of their green coats by the strong wind. The dry branches were full of glazed ice. On the way to the forbidden area, ice had frozen the path after a snow storm. In the mountains, which were rarely visited by cars, it appeared to be even more quiet and lonely. The only thing he could feel was the mysterious sounds of silence in the northern kingdom after the snow. Even with the tire chains, the jeep kept slipping, which made the trip very difficult. The 50 kilometres of mountain path between the headquarters and the forbidden area usually cost them one or two hours, but it already had taken them four hours, and they were a long distance from the valley.

Commander Jia kept looking at his watch from time to time. If it were the usual time, he would have started to curse. This sturdy man started his military career fighting the Japanese. He had a rough and candid character, and was a naturally tough soldier. He was especially strict in regulating the army. And the tenet he valued most was that a soldier should die standing rather than live kneeling down. And a disobedient soldier was not a good soldier. When the Premier entrusted him with the most valuable assets of the republic, he suddenly felt the heavy responsibilities on his shoulder. Ever since his appointment, he had never ignored them. At the start, he gave his instructions to the guards: "The country has entrusted us with something more valuable than gold. I am here to set up an iron rule with you — anyone who wants to enter the forbidden area must have authorisation. Without if, even the emperor of heavenly king cannot be let in. And I am no exception. I hope all of you can tie your life to this valuable asset. So long as we are alive, it must be here; whoever tries to enter forcefully must be arrested; whoever wants to cause troubles intentionally is to be killed without exception…"

For the past few years, under Commander Jia's strict regulations, the troop had developed an impartial and incorruptible manner. Every Monday, when the shuttle bus stopped at the first sentinel at the gate of the forbidden area, the guards would insist on checking everyone's authorisation, no matter whether he knew or didn't know the officers or soldiers. If any one of them did not have the authorisation, he would have to step out of the bus and would not be allowed inside. If there was no bus or car to return to the headquarters, he had to figure his own way out or just walk back. Similarly, when the shuttle bus left the forbidden area on weekends, authorisation had to be checked out, and without it one could not return. Commander Jia was very proud of his system, and frequently praised the guards at meetings.

However, he didn't expect that, on this day, he himself would be caught by the rule he had set up. In the morning, when he was going out, his wife said to him, out of consideration for his safety, "It is a long distance? Given that the road has frozen, why don't you go after it turns sunny?"

"Stop nagging at me you old woman, no matter how slippery the road is I still have a car to take. It's already so much better than staying in an ice hole when we attack Changchun. There's such a large group of soldiers in the valley, what if they get cold or don't have enough food? I have to go there and have a look, otherwise I cannot sleep well at night. Hurry up and bring my clothes to me ... " Commander Jia seemed to be criticising his subordinates instead of talking to his wife. As his wife had to put his clothes together in a hurry, she didn't put the authorisation into his pocket.

The Jeep ran down the devolving road, until the first sentinel was in front of them. With their dark green helmets and black machine guns, the guards was crafted into solemn sculptures by the snow.

Waving the small flags in their hands with their white gloves on, they were a picture full of beauty and power, composing the alert line for the forbidden military area.

The sentinels knew that, under this beautiful and picturesque forest, there was hidden a great underground palace which contained the "thunder and lightning". Generations of sentinels would only repeat one sentence, after they had inherited the red flags from their predecessors: "We only recognise the authorisation, not the person."

The Jeep came forward slowly.

The sentinel who was in position stood at attention in the most standard way, the flag in his hands in a horizontal position. The Jeep stopped, and the sentinel said in an impartial voice, "Chief, please show your special authorisation."

Commander Jia reached into his pocket, but it was not there. His secretary stepped out of the car in a hurry, and said, smiling, "This is the commander of our troop, and he came specifically to visit you guards here. He left home in a hurry and forgot to take his authorisation. Given it's such a long and difficult trip, could you please let us in now? I will get it for you after … "

The sentinel saluted to the secretary with a cold face, and replied without hesitation, "I am sorry, Chief, I cannot let you in without the special authorisation—this is the rule. No matter if it is the real or a fake commander, I will only recognise the authorisation, not the person. I hope you understand."

"You damn soldier, this is my authorisation and I am the commander's secretary." The secretary started to show his own power. "It is such a freezing day, and the road is slippery. It's lucky that the chief could even make it here. Please call your regimental commander, I will talk to him ... "

Commander Jia was looking at what was happening in the Jeep quietly. As the highest commander of this troop, he felt very pleasant. An ordinary sentinel daring to stop a chief who didn't have his authorization — it meant that the concept of guarding the national treasure was deeply entrenched in their blood. If I, as the commander, could not possibly get in without authorisation, then other people could not get in, even if they had wings. After Commander Jia was rejected, he stepped out of the Jeep and saluted to the sentinel who was performing his duty. He grasped the sentinel's hand tightly, "Young comrade, what is your name?"

"My name is Zhang Chunliang, Chief," he answered instantly.

"Good. What you did is right! If you dared to stop my car, then you would dare to stop the emperor of heavenly king. With guards like you protecting the iron gate, I know I can sleep well." He turned back to his secretary and driver, "Do not put this young comrade in any difficulty; let's go back according to the rule. Once we've got our authorisation, let's come back."

"But you haven't inspected the work, Chief. Have we come in vain?"

"We will do the inspection. Given these sentinels, I can award them a full mark."

After Commander Jia arrived at the headquarters, he called the leaders in the forbidden area right away to award all of the sentinels at the first guarding position. Especially, he said, the sentinel who stopped his car, Zhang Chunliang.

Perhaps someone would say, because Commander Jia was such a high level leader and he rarely visited the forbidden area, the ordinary soldiers didn't know him, and so he was stopped at the gate.

Hence it could be argued the event was not representative. But then what of the soldiers' attitudes towards their direct commander? Did this impartial manner work in China, a country that values connections?

Ten years later

The rain was pouring endlessly.

The storm whipped the forest and the trees were struck by lightning, leaving the people trembling. The devolving road was quickly covered by the pouring rain and fog, making it hard to see even if the car lights were on. The scariest thing was the unexpected rushing landslides, which would suddenly throw people passing by down to the bottom of the valley.

The deputy regimental commander and his driver drove back in the darkness after the meeting at the headquarters. When the meeting was dismissed in the evening, the weather was still fine. The comrades at headquarters all tried to talk him into staying longer, given that it was a rare chance for him to come out. They suggested he should watch a movie or something else to relax, or just have dinner before going. But he said it was only a two hour drive in the mountains, and that if he was fast he could reach there in no time. Who could have expected a storm? As the sky turned dark, a giant piece of ice was cast down like a collapsing mountain. It was as scary and dangerous as an adventure in life.

Given they could only drive off and on, the trip of two hours took them four hours instead. At 9 pm, they finally reached the first gate of the forbidden area. The sentinels were standing like stones in the storm. The regimental commander's car stopped. With the pouring rain and howling wind, the voice of the sentinel became lower, but it reached through the window: "Please show me your special authorisation."

As the deputy regimental commander searched his pocket, he realised he had left it in the drawer when he washed his clothes that morning. The driver and the sentinel were from the same town, and they were quite good friends. The driver said to the sentinel, "It's not someone you don't know, this is the deputy regimental commander. You see him everyday. Could you please make an exception and let us in ... "

The sentinel shook his head and said, "Although we came from the same town and I know the deputy regimental commander, I will only recognise the special authorisation, nothing else." The driver was anxious and angry. "You fool, nobody is as stubborn as you. We haven't had dinner, and it's cold as well ... "

The sentinel stepped closer to the window, telling the deputy regimental commander seriously and impartially, "I am sorry, commander. I can only follow the rules in handling this situation." After he finished, he made a phone call. "Hello, is this the security department? I am calling from the No.1 sentry. The deputy regimental commander has left his special authorisation behind, and was stopped here. Please come and take him inside."

In hearing this, the deputy regimental commander wet his eyes. He walked outside of the car immediately, and told the sentinel, "I see your clothes are all wet. Come inside the car and avoid the rain. You'll get warmer. Let me take on your duty."

The sentinel refused the offer. "Thank you, chief. I haven't checked out your identity yet. How can I let you take on my duty?"

From the No.1 sentry to the camp, there was another dozens of miles of distance. When the security department came to take the deputy regimental commander inside, it was already midnight.

The next day, the deputy regimental commander declared to a meeting of the entire regiment that he would reward the sentinel who kept him outside of the gate for half of the night cold and hungry a third-class military medal.

Not long after, a comrade from a Beijing higher task force requested a look at the national treasure stored in the forbidden area. It was the last day before they had to leave the headquarters, so they could not possibly obtain a "green card" from the security department. Led by the relevant staff, they drove together in a team to the valley. Just as they arrived at the No.1 sentry, the sentinel stopped them in the same way—they had to show the special authorisation, otherwise they had to return. The staff did their best to convince the sentinel, but the sentinel didn't consider their words at all. Even after they had talked to the highest leader in the valley, they received the same answer. The staff from high office, who were used to being flattered by their subordinates, were extremely embarrassed and called the regiment's higher authorities in Beijing in anger. However, the reply they got was neither permission nor rejection: "You are not responsible for the things in the valley, perhaps you are not supposed to visit there…"

They returned in anger and frustration. As they left, they said, "People here must have become dumb after spending too long in the mountains; they have lost their flexibility…"

Was this the only military base which dared say no to a superior? Were the soldiers who had never been to the town the only people who dared say no? After an old general heard of this story, he said with complicated feelings, "They are no less outstanding than sentinels from any other army in the world."

4. A rare snow storm had blocked the road. The wives and children of the soldiers and officers who had come for a spring festival holiday could only say "take care" to their husbands on the phone.

The trains running from Beijing to western China would only stop at Zhengzhou for 15 minutes.

Ms Cui Yanqing, the section chief of design from Ouli Digital Group in Zhengzhou, was squeezing the hard seat section of the train while she held her 3-year-old daughter's hand and carried a large luggage bag. It was the spring festival season, when millions of migrating workers were all in a rush to return home for spring festival. The gate of the train was already crowded, without any order or courtesy—all that mattered was strength and luck, and whoever got inside was the lucky one. These were the travelers of China. Seeing the crowds in front of them, several sisters who came to see her off said to her, "Sister Cui, maybe you shouldn't go, how can you get on the train?"

Cui turned back to her friends while she kept pushing forward. "No, I have to go. My daughter is already 3 years old and still doesn't know what her father looks like. I know he is a man eager to excel, so he hasn't had a vacation in three years. And I am only free for these ten or twenty days." Holding her daughter in her arms and carrying the luggage bag in the other hand, before she could make it to the gate of the train, a group of strong and rude men pushed them aside. The time left for them was limited. Seeing a soldier sitting by the window in his uniform, she suddenly said to him, "Please, could you take this, my husband is a soldier as well…"

Before the soldier could answer her, the child and the luggage bag were forced into his hands. Her daughter was frightened in the stranger's hands, and she screamed, "I want mummy, mummy..."

Cui hardened her heart and turned to the crowds who were pushing to the gate. She said to her friends, "Don't just stand there, come here and push me inside..." After some effort, a fragile woman was eventually moved to the gate with her friends' help. But at this moment, the siren went on, and the male attendant was going to shut the door. Cui was scared and her face turned white. Her friends cried, "Don't shut the door, her child and luggage are all on the train!" The male attendant, either because of his mercy or because he had realised the seriousness of the situation, extended his arm and dragged Cui onto the train. Before she could stand still on the train, it started to move slowly.

After this shock, Cui's limbs were left powerless and her body was sweating. Looking around, she saw her daughter was still in the soldier's hands. After she asked all the way through, she moved bit by bit and finally pushed herself to her daughter after ten minutes. Once the little girl saw her mother, she burst into tears. "Mum, I want mum." Cui embraced her daughter as she struggled out of the soldier's hands. Tears fell before she could say thank you to the soldier.

To hand over the red string of love to a soldier meant suffering from the eternal drifting of life; to hand over the happiness and hope of a woman to the distant military camp meant that the waiting would become indefinite.

The train was too crowded and the air inside was unbearable, a mix of the smell of people's bodies and smoke. The corridors were full of people standing, and even the space under the seats was full of people lying down. It was hard to find a place for one person to stand. Cui stood in the carriage for a whole night with her daughter in her arms, until she felt her energy was exhausted. She couldn't tell what kind of power was supporting her thin body.

In the summer of 1982, Cui graduated from the Radio Department of Peking University. At that time, given her youth and beauty, she faced lots of rosy temptations. Some digital companies in Beijing valued her and offered her great conditions to work in Beijing. However, the surging new waves from the coast of Southern China deeply attracted this young student who had grown up in Northern China. She was determined to go to the south and came to a large joint venture digital company. Two years later, she was promoted as the manager of the design section. With her elegance and beauty, plus her exceptional capabilities, she became the target of many high class young men. The arrows of Cupid kept shooting toward her.

But nobody had expected she would finally throw her red ball to Gao Guoqian, an engineer who was undertaking mysterious tasks for the strategic missile troop in the deserts of Northwestern China. He was a young military officer who grew up by the Yellow River and was also her classmate. Perhaps it was that the bonds formed in tough times were much more genuine than those established under the neon lights. But when some of her university friends or colleagues threw her warm smiles, she rejected them politely.

Marrying a professional soldier meant that she was tied to the heavy chariot of family responsibility. No matter whether this chariot ended up trapped in a swamp or running on a smooth path, as a wife, she had to help her husband to pull it forever, despite the difficulties.

Cui had no choice. Her husband was the only son in his family, and his old mother was in Zhengzhou. As an ambitious man, he was deeply attached to the "Oriental magic fire" which was 1,000 times brighter than sunlight. So the task of taking care of his mother would have to be given to Cui, who was in Shenzhen. However, given the long distance and her worries about her mother-in-law, the only solution was for her to be transferred back to Zhengzhou. When she talked about this idea with her colleagues, they said in surprise, "Shenzhou is not a place where you can just come and find a good job as you wish. What you are doing here is great and is valued by the boss. With the local support here, you will regret it if you return to the north." When her boss heard of it, he tried to persuade her to remain. "No, I can't let you go," he said genuinely. "It's too big a loss for the company. As a condition for you to stay, I can arrange a position for your husband and you can ask him to withdraw from the army."

Cui shook her head with a bitter smile. She knew very well that her husband loved his military career more than his life. Her determination to quit could not be changed. At her farewell party banquet, her boss told her in front of all the managers, "This position will always be kept for you. No matter when you come back, you will always be welcomed ... "

Cui was transferred back to Zhengzhou and worked as an ordinary member of design staff in Ouli Digital Group. She took up the double loads of her career and her family. On the one hand, she had to take care of her mother-in-law. On the other, she had to work hard in her own field, since she was just transferred and had to start everything again to gain recognition. Performing heavy daily chores and care responsibilities, Cui accomplished great achievements in her career. The Ouli sound system she developed was rewarded with the best product award by the Industry Ministry and quickly took over the market, which saved the company from death. And she was also promoted to section chief.

As an intellectual woman, what Cui expected was not to accompany her husband, but the matching of their careers. As his wife was accomplished in her career, it formed an intangible pressure on him. In order to achieve something in the mysterious northwestern land, and support the soul of the rising power, Gao Guoqian didn't return home for three years, even when his daughter was born or his mother passed away. All these were left for Cui to bear, so that when her mother-in-law breathed her last breath, she said, "It's better to find a good daughter-in-law than have a good son."

Cui, however, understood her husband very well. When someone asked why she didn't have any complaints, she even defended him. "Although I didn't know what he was doing, based on my instinct, I could tell that it was more important than anyone..." Because of her lack of regret, she handled her mother-in-law's funeral while taking care of their one-year-old daughter.

All the past would fade away.

After two days of hard journeying, the train eventually reached the final stop. When she and her daughter walked out of the station, tired, she imagined that her husband would be waiting for them at the gate—before they departed, she has already sent him a telegraph. As the strong wind of the west attacked her, she felt pain on her face. The wind cut like a knife. Cui searched around the square while carrying her daughter and heavy luggage, hoping to see her husband in the crowd. But she was disappointed—the people in the station were long gone, and her husband was nowhere to be seen. They were still more than 50 kilometres from the station to the army's headquarters, how could a woman with a child manage to get there? Out of desperation, she had to look for soldiers near the station. Perhaps it was God's work, but after some time she happened to see a military car which was from her husband's army. And the driver was sympathetic and agreed to give them a ride. The mother and daughter had to sit in the car, frozen by the cold wind. Several miles away from the headquarters, the driver had to let them off due to some emergency. They had to walk through the snow. When they eventually arrived, it was already sunset.

After they went through all of this, what awaited them was a cold room. Her husband was not in the headquarters but in the forbidden area conducting a special trial. He could not possibly get out within ten days. Therefore, not only could he not pick them up, but he couldn't come out and meet them. Looking at the lonely room for the visiting families, tears of bitterness surged up. Cui, who would not normally shed one, could not help bursting into tears …

The 10-day period was only a short moment of her life, but for a woman who was waiting for her husband it was almost like 10 years. As the family of the officer, they were not allowed to go inside of the forbidden area; otherwise Cui would have flown inside long ago. They waited and waited until, the night before her husband could get out, there came a rare snow storm. The ice and snow blocked the road — even with tire chains the car could not move. Cruel nature seemed to be testing the loyalty of the couple by coldly setting up a mass of frozen river between them. The waiting wife took her daughter everyday out to look into the distance in the hope of seeing her husband. But they were disappointed every time. Their feelings were getting heavier each day. She hated this cruel snow storm, and she complained about nature's cruelty. She had been waiting for a reunion with her husband for three years, but this dream was eventually shattered and swallowed by the snow plains.

On New Year's Eve, Gao Guoqian was celebrating the new year with other soldiers in the forbidden area, while her wife and daughter were in a small and cold room waiting for a man who could not return. When all their hopes became luxury, the wife had to call her husband in duty room with her daughter. "Hello, Guoqian, did you have your dinner?" Her gentle and sweet voice came through the phone.

"I just have had my dinner with all the brothers. How about you and our daughter?"

"We had your favourite dumplings. Come, let's have a toast!"

They used the glasses in the office as wine glasses and hit them over the phone. Afterwards, they fell into silence. From the phone came the crying of the three year old. She grabbed the phone from her mother and said to her father, who she had never met, "Dad, please come back. My mother and I miss you so much."

"Good girl, I miss you as well. Sing a song you've learned in kindergarten for dad."

"OK. Listen, dad. 'I have a good father, a good father…I have a bad father, a bad father…'" A child's voice started to sing.

The husband and wife who were listening on both sides of the phone burst into tears.

After January 5 of the lunar calendar, Cui's 20-day long holiday was over. Before she left, she could only convey her true love on the phone, sobbing, "You take care, we have to go…"

The little one said goodbye to her father, who she had never met, and left her doll in the temporary visiting room of the families. She told her father on the phone, "Mum and I have been waiting for you, but you didn't come. So I left my doll here for you. When it gets warmer and the snow melts, you can take the doll with you when you come back from the mountains…"

The husband on the other side of the phone who was telling his wife not to cry burst into tears when he heard the voice of his daughter. The tears of the soldiers and their wives were the heaviest. But it was the weight of having traded the delight of being with their families. Can you understand the softness in the soldiers' hardness? Could you blame their coldness when they appeared to be indifferent?

The wife left and took away the disappointment, and left an empty space behind.

The daughter left and took away the fantasy, and left a child's innocence behind.

5. The nuclear ruins of Nagasaki and Hiroshima were indeed terrible, but the chiefs who had been stepping inside of the nuclear gate were not afraid, though their names could never be published.

November, 1994, Washington, the US

In order to celebrate the upcoming 50th anniversary of the end of the Second World War, the US Post Bureau issued a set of stamps which reflected the Second World War. One of them was a rising mushroom cloud, and in the footage there was one line saying, "On August 7, the explosions of atomic bombs facilitated the end of

the Second World War." However, they didn't expect the nationalism of the Japanese would be hurt by this tiny stamp. The Foreign
Minister of Japan protested to the US government, and the Deputy
Premier and Foreign Minister Kono Yohei delivered a speech to
all the foreign journalists in Tokyo, requesting the US government
to take notice of the trauma suffered by the people of Nagasaki
and Hiroshima after the atomic bombing. And the victims of the
atomic bombing in Nagasaki and Hiroshima held a large demonstration to protest against the Americans who had provoked painful
memories of the disastrous day. Premier Murayama, who had just
taken office, frequently had phone conversations with US president
Clinton, asking them to consider the psychological tolerance of the
Japanese people.

A tiny stamp was able to cast more clouds and rain on the diplomatic relationship between Japan and the US after their relationship had suffered from the trade war ...

The White House urged the Post Bureau to cancel the issue of
this stamp, fearing it might otherwise end the political honeymoon between the two countries, which had lasted for a third of
a century. President Clinton personally intervened, asking them to
reissue it with some other content.

Due to the interventions of the President and White House, the
independent American cowboys had to compromise, agreeing to
cancel the one of the atomic bombing.

A diplomatic storm caused by a tiny stamp was solved. However,
the fear caused by nuclear weapons remained — as if once they
stepped through the nuclear gate, it would always mean war and
death ...

But on the oriental part of the planet, there were four senior colonel engineers who had to step into the nuclear gate almost everyday, interacting with the nuclear ghost that was described as "1,000 times brighter than the sun". But due to the secretiveness of their career, their identities were hidden — even their names were confidential and would never be allowed to be made public. However, their academic achievements and substantive accomplishments were top secret even among the top secrets, which destined them to be anonymous heroes who stood behind the curtains all their life. So when we met them, apart from the meeting of souls, we had to adopt vague language to maintain that confidentiality, even at the cost of losing part of the power of their touching stories.

Early 1960s, Harbin Military Engineering College

In this biggest military academy in Asia, two students from Southern China were about to graduate. There were two options in front of them: to stay in the academy to teach, and no doubt they would be successful if they followed this well designed path; or to go to Western China, where the Chinese mushroom clouds were about to rise, and which meant that reputation and wealth would be irrelevant to them. These two young graduates, who were full of surging passion for building a strong country, chose to go to west without hesitation.

At the same time, in Tsinghua University in Beijing, one of the highest set of learning of China, hundreds of senior students had gone through strict political background checks which only a lucky few passed. They were sent to a highly isolated and confidential location to build the Chinese atomic bomb.

Four young students who came from different areas had walked into a remote mountain area for a common cause, starting a great and splendid career that would exhaust their life.

The Goddess of Destiny didn't leave them alone on this bleak soil, and they had many opportunities to return to the senior research departments in the cities. But an old general's words had deeply influenced the choices of their life.

The old Red Army soldiers from Luoxiao Mountain said excitedly, "Don't underestimate the cause here, even Premier Zhou knows all about your works. Do not mention the issue of leaving — let's promise each other, we are ready to have our own memorial service here. A great man can bury himself anywhere."

The old general had buried himself in the yellow sand of this giant desert, while the four students had planted the roots of their life in this desert, where only rose willows and splendid needlegrass survived. The winds of time had frozen their hot blood, turning their black hair to white frost. Their old classmates were all famous intellectuals or professors, but they remained anonymous forever.

Even if their scientific achievements had gained national awards, they could not be published. As they approached the autumn of their life, they could have returned to the cities and found a place in their beautiful hometown to enjoy the retired life. But because they had learnt too many state secrets, they couldn't move to the places they wanted, instead remaining at the abandoned place year after year. Their life would end with a tragic but splendid comma at this place. They had no regrets, because they had improved the status of China in the world with their youth, passion and intelligence. However, their biggest regret was that their children could not follow their path and be educated as they were. Some of them dropped out of middle school because they just couldn't keep up.

Since there were no factories or government organs there, the employment of their children became a worry. A girl may be able to marry someone and leave this place; but it would be hard for a boy to find a suitable wife. Some had to marry a countryside girl and became the locals there...

In this giant desert, there was one among them who was an exceptional graduate of Harbin Military Engineering College. He was handsome and 1.80m tall, but left the place in a carved box...

Everyone said he worked to death. When he died, he was only 48 years old. On the track of his life, 48 years old was just at the prime, but he died. Just as he came to this world, he left quietly, without taking a piece of cloud nor a mass of glory. He came from a poor farmer's family, and he lost his mother at three. It was all because of his personal struggle and the student loans of the Party that he got through middle school and was admitted into Harbin Military Engineering College, a school which was not easy to enter. When he graduated, he abandoned the option of staying in Beijing and undertaking atomic research in a comfortable environment, instead walked into these bleak plains, just to light up the "Magic fire of China", which symbolised the dignity of our nation. After decades of hard work, perhaps because he had to work for a long time in the dark underground, or perhaps because he had to step over that nuclear gate frequently, a man who used to be active on the basketball ground and never needed medicine didn't have any healthy organs when he collapsed, and had developed liver cirrhosis, a swollen spleen, diabetes, and arteriosclerosis. How much he had to pay...

Now let's tell the tragic stories which his wife and eldest daughter told us in tears. His wife said, "We had a similar background. He lost his mother at three and his father when he was in university. My father died when I was seven, and my mother passed away when I was eighteen. Both of us had a tragic life. We have been married for twenty years, but we spent no more than five years together. He didn't come back when the three children were born. He spent all his time working, experimenting, no matter whether it was Sunday or holidays. He never talked about what he was doing, even if he had been awarded. Only when the report and rewards were sent home did we know about it. He coughed up blood a long time ago, but he wouldn't tell anyone, because it might delay his work. I am used to the tough life, so I never counted on or relied on him. In the end, he coughed up lots of blood, and passed out in the cave. When he was alive, he didn't even have the time to take a photo. After he died, we couldn't find a photo of him. Eventually we found one in his files, which was taken in a meeting when he made a speech."

His eldest daughter said, "When my dad was about to pass away, I wanted to be transferred back to take care of him. But he said that he didn't want to trouble the Party. My dad didn't leave us with any property—his only wish was that we should study hard. Even if we couldn't get into university it didn't matter, we could still teach ourselves and learn something real, which would make us useful to society."

His wife continued, "What made him sad all his life was that he was a university graduate, but none of his three children made it to university. The children grew up in the mountains with him. If he entered the forbidden area, it would be another week before he could come back. So he never had time to teach the children. When he heard that our eldest daughter didn't get into university, he cried in the hospital. He was a tough guy, and at that time he was so sick but he didn't even make a sound of pain. But he cried for that. He was sitting on the sofa, head lifted, trying to avoid me seeing his tears. Before he died, he sighed, 'All in vain!' That was because his experiment has produced lots of data, but only the last step was missing…"

He didn't regret dying in his prime. His only regret was his experiment, which was only one step away from success. He had done much for the Chinese nuclear missile cause, but had caused irreversible trauma to his family.

The autumn of 1992, by the Huangpu River

Shanghai Jiaotong University, which was as old as the century, had reached the 80th anniversary of its establishment. The scientists who had come from this oldest set of learning of China returned and gathered at the university, offering their fruitful research to the school. Among the alumni scattered all around China, there were a few technicians who were invited from the Chinese strategic missile troop. Compared with other alumni, they didn't have any fancy professorship, or any monographs that could match their value or achievements, or any honour that made them prestigious worldwide. Everyday when they walked into the nuclear gate, they repeated a detailed and meticulous testing. Their hair fell out because of their long term exposure to nuclear radiation. But they promoted the honour and dignity of a nation with earth-shattering blasts in the mysterious forbidden area. When the school introduced them to others, some established alumni grasped their hands tightly. "You have done so much for the rising of our nation, you are the pride of our school…"

Their university would never forget them, nor the republic.

They received an escort over 500 kilometres. The task of guarding the special facilities, which were much more valuable than pandas, was no doubt honourable and splendid for the soldiers. But there were many hidden tragic stories behind this mysterious army.

A green military train rushed out of the giant valley secretly, as if a dragon with wings which held the setting sun and rising moon in its mouth had flown over plains, mountains, rivers and villages, towards its nesting place.

Wherever the special train arrived, it enjoyed a guard befitting a head of a state. Along its line, the police cars would clear its path; way train had to stop while the express train had to change to another rails. Through every forked road and every important city or village it passed, the public security department and armed police would guard along the way. There was a mysterious army who had been living on this special train and was specifically responsible for escorting the strategic missile troop. In the eyes of ordinary people, they were the luckiest of the time, given that they could not only travel around the country with the best guards, they could also obtain the rarest honour and glory. However, once you stepped deeper into the hinterland of this mysterious army, what was behind the imagined honour and glory was actually some unexpected tragedy and commonness.

This special train seemed to be nothing special compared to the ordinary passenger trains running on the railways. Apart from its special facilities storage, the space left for the soldiers was only 14 square metres. However, this small cabin on the railway became the ark for the transportation soldiers when they travelled around. All the passengers, attendants, cooks and mechanics of the train were the soldiers of this army. During the long trip, every soldier was only a passing guest, each of them with their own work. The cooks on the dining car had to cook for more than ten times every day to provide food for the soldiers on board; and the mechanics also had to check and maintain the train at every station; the operators had to start the engines, power generators and air conditioners, and they had to check the temperature of the special facilities every hour. During their escorting tasks, the rules were clearly set out: all entertainment was forbidden, including playing cards, chess or listening to music, even reading novels. Therefore, along the long railway, what was left with the soldiers was loneliness only. The sounds of the wheels hitting the railway had shattered more than just romantic dreams, but also their longing for their families...

The transportation soldiers on this special train required special characters and an iron determination.

During the summer time in northern China, with waves of heat rolling, the ground temperature broke 40°C. A special military train stopped at the special line near a seaside city. In the distance, the sea surged up with layers of snow-white waves, which rushed along the golden coast. Lots of tourists went to the sea and enjoyed the serenity and nature. Although the noises on the earth were endless, the soldiers of the train were not allowed to step down. The burning sun and the firing ground has baked the train like a giant steamer. The soldiers' clothes were dampened by their sweat until layers of white salt emerged on their clothes, but none of them complained. Many soldiers who had just walked out of the mountains were eager to see the beauty of a seaside city, shower under the salty refreshing sea wind, and pick up some shells on the beach, realising fantasies from their childhood. However, the military rules were like an intangible fence, and nobody dared to ask for a tour outside of the train. They waited on the special line for three days and four nights. Sitting down in peace and imagining became the soldiers' way of travelling. When the train left this seaside city slowly, the beautiful imaginations of the soldiers about the ocean were still stored in their memories…

The most lonely task was when two or three soldiers had to undertake an escort task alone for thousands of miles. As the freight train ran through the mountains, among all the cargo carts, there was one for passengers. Four soldiers were using their own kerosene stove to cook. In the light of the fire, the chicken soup noodles radiated an inviting smell. The four soldiers were just about to eat with their bowls and chopsticks. Suddenly, with a sharp stop, the stove was knocked over and the delicious noodles spread all around. The four soldiers could not help but burst into tears. They hadn't had anything to eat in two days. It was a special task of escorting one single carriage, and it was master sergeant Qing Zhixi and three of his new recruits who formed the squad. In this situation, they were alone in performing the duty, without assistance alongside the railway. Since their carriage was mixed into the train, there was nobody who would tell them when to depart, when to arrive or how long they should stay in one stop. Sometimes they had to wait for days. In the toughest situation, they couldn't have water or food. Given that a cargo train could not be stopped at a passenger's platform, even if they could get half a bucket of water from the neighbouring residents of the station, they had to use it carefully, sometimes having to save the water for cooling down the machine instead of drinking it. When there was no water left for them to cook, they could only munch on the instant noodles or have some bread to get over the long and lonely journey…

If the suffering of the transportation soldiers on the railway was the loneliness of life, then for those soldiers who had been driving to escort the freight trucks across the country, there was more physical and mental pain.

Night fell quietly. The land was in silence. The world which had been noisy for a whole day eventually returned to hide in the dusk. A long line of special task trucks rushed into the dark night, commencing their long journey. Because of the confidentiality, this mysterious escorting team for special facilities was destined to have their journey during the nights. The long dark nights and long journey was a special test for the soldiers' bodies and determination. Given that they were entrusted with the heavy responsibilities of the country and the nation, every soldier in the mysterious army could not have one moment of rest or relaxation. When they got too sleepy at night, even if they had to eat some dry chili or stab needles on their laps or bury their head in the snow, they would still open their eyes in alertness.

This night was the fifth night since their departure. After they had passed Ghast to Worry, Hawk's Beak Cliff and Ten-hundred kilo Abyss, what was in front of them was a frozen slope of 35 degrees and one kilometre long, which blocked their way like an icy peak. During the daytime, they had to be careful when they passed the frozen slope. It was even more difficult to pass it during the night—the slightest carelessness and they would fall into the cliff. The Deputy Battalion Commander Song Shuli walked out of the truck and had a look around the land. He gathered all the soldiers together and said, "What we are carrying here is a national treasure. Even if we have to pull it through with ropes or carry it with our shoulders, we have to move it across this frozen slope." In the dark night, the soldiers dug sand, stones and tree branches from the bottom of the ice and placed them under the wheels. But the trucks still slipped. Many soldiers then removed their coats and placed them on the icy road, trembling with coldness. With one person leading the way at the front and another two holding the triangular wooden structures to push the wheels forward, it took them four hours to pass through one kilometre safely...

One day, a big freight truck entered a little town in northern China, surprising many local people who had never seen a truck like this. They wondered how the soldiers could drive a train carriage around on the road. Lots of people came to inspect the truck. Master Sergeant He Wenxi, the acting deputy company commander, looked out from inside of the truck. Views of the yellow land which was his hometown were before his eyes. How familiar he was with the hometown accent, people and views. His foot left the accelerator as the truck slowed down. The soldiers beside him said, "Since it's a rare chance for you to pass by home, why don't you get out and visit your wife?"

"No," he said, shaking his head. "We are on duty now, I can't break the rules by leaving the truck..." His wife *Yuan* was hospitalised for two months because of typhoid fever one year ago. Although her life was saved by the doctors' efforts, she lost her health. As a young woman, she had to quit her job and stay at home. She had sent lots of telegraphs to He Wenxi, asking him to come back and take care of her. But he couldn't, since he was busy with his works. Now he had passed his home, if he could walk inside and see his wife, talk to her, she would be more than delighted. However, as a member of the special transportation motorcade, all their routes were confidential, and they were not allowed to stay anywhere. He Wenxi could only have a glimpse of his home before driving ahead. But accidents always happen in real life. When his truck was just about to leave the town, he saw his wife *Yuan*, and *Yuan* also saw her husband in the truck. As one sat in the truck and the other stood outside, the couple had a sad conversation, the window between them.

"Wenxi, why didn't you tell me that you were home."

"No, no, I am just passing by on duty."

"Can you stay home for a few days?"

"Not at the moment, I have to go now ... "

"Then, where are you going?"

"I can't tell you, it is a far-away place. Please do not tell others that I have been here, since we have strict confidentiality rules. Take care, I will come home for spring festival ... "

His wife stood there, sobbing. He Wenxi could not look at her as he stepped on the accelerator. The truck rushed ahead like an arrow. From the rearview mirror, he saw his wife standing exactly where she had met him like a statute, waving her hands to him. His eyes were wet with tears.

Since these soldiers had been spending all their time travelling thousands of miles across the country to perform escort tasks, their life was like that of a drifter. They didn't know when they had arrived in the army, when they would go home, how long they could stay there, or whether their wives could see them after they finished their tasks. There was a lack of time and chances for communication between the couples, and thus the conflicts and misunderstandings in their families often troubled the soldiers.

Liu Qigui, a voluntary soldier, received a subpoena from the town court upon his return from an escort task. This veteran has spent 14 years on the railway escorting line. While he was travelling all the time, he could only contact his wife on and off. But his wife didn't want to live such a life, so she filed for divorce three years ago. But he had to travel around all the time, he couldn't find enough time to handle his personal life. Eventually his wife took a lawsuit to court, and only in the situation that the judge was going to give a judgment in his absence did he hurriedly return home. However, before the final judgment was made, he had to return to the army for another task. When the judge asked his wife whether she wanted to continue, she saw her husband, who had gotten thinner. Heartbroken, she said helplessly, "Alright, it seems that I'll have to stay with him for life ... "

In the evening, after she had wiped away her tears, she had to see her husband off at the train station.

6. In order to complete the task entrusted by Premier Zhou, the first generation of the strategic missile troop became lost on the huge plains as wranglers, their blood and families had already been localised completely.

The old clouds of war had gone far away.

The rolling gunpowder of war went off.

A mysterious military forbidden area was revealed in the huge wildness. In the astonishing underground palace, there were special missile facilities which could transform into thunder and lightning. Thus, it became an important target and received much attention.

During that tough pioneering time, Premier Zhou, who had

exhausted all his life's energy on the modernisation of the Chinese army, asked the few chiefs responsible for the strategic missile troop to come before him.

"The confidentiality and security of the underground caves are no small deal," he told them solemnly. "You should select some exceptional officers who have returned from the Korean War and ask them to be wranglers—they can be special guards without uniforms."

Therefore, overnight, a group of veterans who had just returned from the battlefields of the Korean War took off their yellow uniforms and said goodbye to their mothers in central plains and girlfriends in eastern China, arriving at the huge wild plains far from their hometowns to commence their nomadic life as wranglers alongside the local minority groups. As special guards, they and the local herdsmen protected the national treasure in another way. No matter whether it was some strangers who appeared, or some guests taking photos, or malicious eyes intending to provoke troubles between ethnic groups, none could escape their alert gaze...

Dear reader, please remember this army who were not in uniform.

With a shotgun, a whip and a tent, they drifted around with the herds, the sadness and happiness of life boiling in the aluminum pot. During the winters, they drank on the snow in the wilderness; during the summers, they drank the melted water flowing in the dried river bed from the snow peak. Often, there was one person with a herd and a tent, following the clouds. He fought on his own, and was accompanied by eternal time, walking towards the place where the sun rose. From outside, there seemed to be some romanticism and fun in this life. However, for these soldiers who preferred their military life and had left their army, who could no longer see the disciplined marching steps or the familiar horn, and could no longer return to the red poppy fields in their hometown, it was anything but. Undoubtedly, this was a great loss and pain in their life. But this group of battle-experienced veterans didn't regret planting roots in this huge wilderness. The sun on the plateau bronzed their skin, and the women of the plateau gave alien blood and wild beauty to their descendants.

They had forgotten about the work songs of the boatmen on the Yellow River, and their hometown accent by the Qinhuai River in region south of the Yangtze River. A moving tent replaced their prior dreams of having their wives and children on the heated sleeping platform. The dry and burning seasonal wind turned the first generation of missile soldiers into lost wranglers in the wilderness. Their accent, way of life and appearances were all localised. When facing them, it was hard to imagine that they came from the central plains…

They had many choices as to how to spend their life under heaven, why did they have to choose to plant their life in this wild plateau with air of insufficient oxygen? These quiet men who had been through the wars could only say one thing: "It's in order to complete the task entrusted to us by Premier Zhou, and for the safety of that forbidden area." The seasonal winds on the plateau passed by again and again, and the cycles of time turned around and around. Most of those first generation wranglers had entered into the last stage of their life. Some of them had already buried themselves in this border land, leaving only their eyes fixed on their hometown.

In the summer of 1994, Jiang Dongxian, the deputy chief of the pasture, who was among the first group of people settled on the wilderness, led the writer from Beijing for an interview to an anonymous slope facing the sun. On the slope, there stood rows of soil cottages belonging to the old soldiers. They walked down the ridge, feeling that they could still hear the orders of battle. Deputy Chief Jiang pointed to a grave to the east and said, "That was the grave of my prior Platoon Leader Zhang Chunyuan. We had been in the Five Battles in Korea and struggled out from under the bodies of our battle mates. After we returned, he was engaged with a rural family in his hometown in Shandong Province. She was a pretty girl. And they were just about to get married, but he had to take off his uniform and come to this remote and sparsely populated plateau. In order to stop the girl having to suffer, he rejected this engagement despite the blame and has never been married since. Later, when we were drilling a hole in the mountains, he died in a landslide. On the day of his funeral, the ground was frozen, so we couldn't bury him. We had to use explosives to bomb a hole, and placed him inside. The next year, during the Pure Brightness Festival, I visited to burn paper-moneys for him. The snow and ice on his grave had melted, revealing his shoes. I cried at that time, and dug out some soil and sand to cover his shoes with my hands. After a few years, I visited him again. His small grave was rubbed clean by the wind on the deserts, revealing his shoes again. His flesh had not decayed, because it was dry and cold. That day was Children's Day. I told a group of pupils with me: 'Children, on this slope, there lies a martyr. I will lead you to visit his grave. Everyone should carry a bag of soil from the bottom of the mountain.' When the children climbed the slope, they burst into tears when they saw his shoes. They put down their bags of soil and formed a small grave for him to avoid the rain and wind. Here we call it soil-covered grave. It gets smaller whenever it rains. So every year during this festival and Children's Day, the children would come here to bring soil for him. It has been a few decades, and the children have grown up. Some have left the plateau, some stayed here. They named the martyr in different ways, from uncle Zhang to grandfather Zhang. But their visits to the grave have never stopped. Now our pasture has money, some people suggested we should build a cement grave for him. I thought about it many times, but decided to keep the soil-covered grave. Because people would come to visit the martyr every year and remember these anonymous heroes, and history will also remember them forever…"

Readers, please remember this army without uniform; please remember these mysterious guards who were lost as wranglers…

Chapter 8
If My Sword Is Not Long Enough

1. A piece of historical information: According to an authoritative military magazine from Britain, "The Chinese strategic missile troop has had a period of hibernation." General Zhang Zhen pounded on the table, "I have been in the army for decades — an army which has not fought a war in half a year! It's a joke."

The last spring of the 1980s, Beijing

The sun of winter has just come out from the grey clouds, and started to heat up. There came waves of wind from early spring to the northern land of cold currents and snow storms, awaking the ancient capital city after a long winter. The willows revealed some yellow colour while the locust trees burgeoned with fresh shoots. After ten years of Cultural Revolution, the Chinese people started to adjust their coordinates to the way ahead. Under the directions of Deng Xiaoping, the general designer of Chinese reform and the open-door policy, they moved their steps with difficulty into lines with other world civilisations. And the army which came from

Luoxiao Mountains and the Yan River had to face novel opportunities and challenges in the new era.

Warm sunlight gently cast itself over the tall and imposing office building of the General Staff. Three armed soldiers who stood there still symbolised the solemn and inviolable power of the Chinese Army. With a thick red wall like a historical border monument, it separated the peace here and the noise outside, revealing a mysterious elegance and dignity.

In the bright and spacious office, General Zhang Zhen, who was the Deputy Chairman of General Staff of the PLA, was reading the documents from the commands across China. This old general had walked out of his hometown in Pingxiang, Hunan Province and had taken part in the Long March. Although he was already in his sixties, with his hair whitened by time, his slim but strong body still kept the standard manner of a soldier. During his military service, after the republic was established, he was promoted from the Chairman of Staff of the 3rd Field Army under Supreme Commander Chen Yi to the first Battle Head. From the Head of Logistics to the Deputy Chairman of General Staff, most of his military life was dedicated to the training of the Chinese Army, which made him familiar with the modern development of foreign armies and the Chinese one. Armed with such familiarity, he had developed a strong and clear sense of crisis.

On that day, in the high pile of documents on the general's table, an excerpt from a British authoritative military magazine submitted by the military intelligence department had attracted his attention, unsettling him. According to this report, based on an anonymous source and the western military analysts, the strategic missile troop of red China had made great progress despite the ten years of the Cultural Revolution. However, compared to the reaction time of 3 to 15 minutes for the US strategic air force and the Soviet Union strategic rocket army, the Chinese strategic missile troop, the most modernised army of China, had had a long period of hibernation, which concerned the CPC. During the half year gap before the new soldiers were recruited and the veterans retired, the Chinese strategic nuclear power had almost lost its strength. If red China did not change the situation in a short time, their position in international society and their status as a major power would be greatly weakened …

This foreign military magazine was famous for the reliability of its sources, and its accurate analysis. It was greatly valued by many senior military officers worldwide. From an outsider's perspective, they observed the Chinese strategic missile troop with a Western sense of superiority. However, this report indeed had pointed out the weakness of the Chinese army. The ten years of the Cultural Revolution had expanded the gap between the Chinese Army and the foreign armies, which was originally narrower. A fresh new sense of crisis had made the old general feel that we could no longer lose any chances.

Soon after, he led a group of people personally to inspect the Chinese strategic missile troop. When their observations confirmed the analysis of the foreign magazine, the old general sighed. He picked up the special red phone line on his table and said in his heavy Hunan accent, "Please connect to General Li Xuge, the Battle Head … Hello, is this Comrade Xuge? It's Zhang Zhen. Please come to my office."

"Certainly, Deputy Chief Zhang, I will be there soon."

General Li Xuge, who had led a field army in Xinjiang for seven years, had been transferred to Beijing to be the Deputy Head of Battle in General Staff. He continued his old cause of developing the Chinese special force. From the day when the strategic missile troop was established in Changxindian, he had taken part in this great project. As a result, he had developed deep affections for this most advanced part of the Chinese Army, and his life could never be separated from the troop.

General Li Xuge drove from the Battle Department to the Headquarters building. He was not surprised at the problem raised by Deputy Chief Zhang. As the head of a department which was primarily responsible for the development of Chinese nuclear power, he had been in the missile troop many times, and was very familiar with all the glories and weaknesses of this army at all its stages. After he had read through the report of this foreign military magazine, he told Deputy Chief Zhang confidently, "The analysis of the foreign military observers is correct. The problem of hibernation has been troubling us for many years. It is a difficult old problem that has gone unsolved for a long time."

General Zhang Zhen pounded on the table and stood up. "How can it be, an army not fighting for half a year? I have been in the army for decades, it is a joke. Don't underestimate this problem. You should come up with some suggestions for solutions with the army as soon as possible, and solve this problem."

Deputy Chief Zhang had set out the final date for a resolution, which indicated that this problem had reached a stage where it had to be solved.

The god of fate seemed to entrust General Li and his generation with the heavy responsibility of pushing the strategic missile troop into a new era. Soon after, General Li was appointed as Deputy

Commander of the Second Artillery Corps. Later he was the commander for another seven years, and personally led the army to a new historical glory.

2. The wise eyes of the Chinese soldiers had gone over the gate of the 1980s. We had realised that our swords were not long enough in the world's strategic battlefield. A new sense of crisis motivated the strategic missile troop to embark on new developments and excel.

Beijing, an old small residence

The old quadrangle courtyard immersed in the sunset seemed to be exceptionally beautiful and powerful. The autumn sun falling on west Yanshan Mountains cast its last brush of tragic red upon the 100-year-old tree in the courtyard, colouring its dry trunk and setting up a stark contrast with the vigorous green leaves.

In the early spring of 1993, the retired Commander of the Second Artillery Corps, General Li Xuge, was going to spend his later years in this small classically-styled courtyard. Although he had left his beloved military career, the retirement of the old general was not lonely. This was not only because he was still a member of the National People's Congress who visited foreign countries or accompanied foreign representatives to travel around China as a member of the NPC's Foreign Committee, but also because he had a whole room of books to accompany him.

In an evening of fire-like sunset, I interviewed General Li Xuge as scheduled. He had not reached his sixties yet, and was still fit. Though he had already retired, he still kept the short military haircut which he had worn for decades, as if he was still waiting for the call to war. He had a generous and tolerant character, as he was in good health. He was still a quick thinker, just like when he was on duty. Any interviewer would be attracted by him. His remarks covered politics, the military, philosophy and religion, and were full of wisdom. Before we could realise anything, the mind and value gaps between the older generation and a younger generation were bridged; or it could be said that, through his exceptionally profound philosophical ideas, many kinds of illusion could be generated in an interviewer's mind—did this commander of China's most advanced troop actually grow up from this land of China? Was it true that he walked into the war without the education of any foreign senior military academy? Actually, when you lift your head from his study, looking at the thousands of books of his personal collection, and the specially made aluminum ladder for picking up books, all your questions would be answered. And you would feel much comforted by this senior officer, who was raised and educated in China.

Eight years ago, I worked for General Li Xuge for five years as a young secretary in the headquarters of the strategic missile troop. So I could observe this exceptional general's image and deeds from an intellectual's perspective.

Compared to those military officers who had come up the ranks without much education, he was different; also, he was different from those cadres who barely read but focused solely on studying the newspapers and red-headed documents. Apart from his work, reading seemed to be the biggest hobby of General Li. And the width of his dabbling and depth of his reading indeed impressed many younger officers. Not only did he study Mao and Deng's works, he also read all kinds of military books from around the world. *Historical Events Retold as a Mirror for Government*, a book which could be difficult for a student majoring in Chinese literature, was his favourite and he had read it many times. What impressed the youth more was that he would always spare some time to read the popular magazines of the young. The ocean of books extended the life of a senior Chinese military officer, and also his field of vision and mind.

When he was talking about his past career, in the eyes of this old general, there was still a strong sense of longing. "We have to realise this reality," he said philosophically. "There is indeed a gap between our strategic missile troop and that of the US and Soviet Union. We have to admit our weakness. And we could work harder once we realise the shame. Also we must see the advantages of our army, because most of our soldiers came from the poor rural areas. This means that the steps of our soldiers will always be heavy in moving forward—this is our weakness, but it can be our strength as well. If our sword is not long enough, then we must step forward earlier. If we want to be better than others, we must rely on the exceptional persistence and toughness of our soldiers to make up for our weakness. It could be said that the men in our missile troop have used their heavy wings in accomplishing all our historical success, which is peerless compared to any other army in the world… "

The Chinese soldiers who had cultivated the land of knowledge were granted with the strong wings that would enable them to fly high into the sky.

The new sense of crisis injected a strong motivation to strive into generations of missile soldiers. The wise eyes of the Chinese soldiers had gone over the gate of the old wall of the 1980s. Compared with other armies in the world, it could be said that our young strategic missile troop had been left behind in terms of their overall quality and strength. We were still weak in terms of equipment and modernisation. When we realised that our swords from the old horizon were not long enough, the only thing we could rely on to make up for it was persistence and a spirit of striving, having realised our shame.

Therefore, when history had placed General Li in the position of commander of the Chinese strategic missile troop, facing the "hibernation" problem pointed out by the Western military analysts and the weaknesses of our army, he would encourage the soldiers whenever he went: "The Second Artillery Corps is a new strategic nuclear power, and what we are undertaking is unprecedented, without reference in history or the experience of foreign armies. We are different from any other army of China. Thus our soldiers cannot just rely on their books or superiors. Instead, we must start from our own situation and develop a strong and efficient strategic missile troop with Chinese characteristics." At the start of the 1980s, he raised the problem of developing the strategic nuclear power with Chinese characteristics, which showed his profound vision and foresight. He collaborated with his colleagues closely, and reformed the launching training which had been cultivated over many generations. Some of the working mentality and training models with special characteristics were promulgated, which led to many vivid dramas and pushed the launching trainings to many climaxes. The snow in the forests had not melted, and the many bleak mountains were still sleeping in that distant dream of winter. However, the launching field in the mountains was already filled with a dynamic atmosphere. The new and old soldiers were trained separately for the first time. In the past, when the new recruits arrived, they would be mixed with the old soldiers in the training—this old model of low level cycles was disrupted. All the sections of the strategic missile troop promulgated a new training model of training first before joining the old soldiers, with the soldiers of two or three years experience being placed in a higher level of development. The new recruits should start from the most foundational level of missile knowledge, including the basic operating actions as a launcher and the evacuation operations in nuclear conditions. And a conference for command deliverers was set up in the army. The battalion commander was circled by the grassroots soldiers, and a shifting command system was adopted. Teams consisting of cadres and technicians who supervised the technology operations were scattered in every part of the strategic missile troop. The hibernation problem pointed out by the Western analysts was quickly improved over one or two years.

The dust of history had covered the ancient battlefield of Chu and Han 2,000 years ago. On the ruins of the war between Chu and Han was erected the highest academy of the Chinese strategic missile troop. From the middle of the 1980s, the middle and senior ranked military officers were gathered here to conduct battle training. The instructors included white-headed professors and young lecturers. From the chiefs of the Second Artillery Corps to the responsible offers of each division, they all listened to lectures here. What they learned here consisted of knowledge about high technological wars, strategies under modern nuclear conditions, modern commanding, even the most recent Gulf War was included. Especially with the modern multi-media system which was connected to the launching field thousands of miles away, the officers were able to direct the trials and training through the large screen without stepping outside. The annual training had gradually narrowed down the gaps between us and the foreign armies…

What was more important was a mentality of striving ahead based on a sense of crisis, which has been deeply entrenched into each soldier's blood. Only with a strong sense of crisis can one develop the self-motivation to strive ahead. A strong inertia had pushed the wise eyes of the soldiers of the Chinese strategic missile troop to look over the eastern horizon, to look toward tomorrow, moving forward along an indefinite path of seeking…

3. In the green square matrix of 3 million Chinese soldiers, the honour of controlling the red button for launching the missiles always belongs to the few intelligent officers who graduate from universities. A Chinese soldier from Daba Mountain realises astonishing progress and transformation.

On the dark green mountains, a screen of rain was cast down. The giant green missiles were pointing to the rolling sky. The command deliverers were waiting for the orders with their heads lifted, expecting the best chance of launching in twenty minutes, as predicted by the meteorology team.

"Get ready in ten minutes!"

In the central control room located in the central commanding organ, all the irrelevant parties had been evacuated. Zeng Jiao, a master sergeant, was sitting in front of the operating panel where red lights were flickering. On his dark and unattractive face there was a look of exceptional concentration. His dexterous hands were operating hundreds of switches without any mistakes. His solemn face had attracted all the attention in the room, and his hands, which were used to farming, were tied closely to every soldier's nerve as they stood on each of the launching positions...

In the last three minutes before the launching, a magical view was suddenly revealed as the red sun emerged from the dark thick layers of clouds and its light was cast over the tall birches and between the white water and black mountains.

It seemed that the air in the valley had been frozen.

The launching process proceeded to the last countdown.

"Ignition!" The battalion leader delivered the last order.

...

20 minutes later, happy news came from thousands of miles away: the launching trial conducted by a soldier had created the highest precision record in history.

Beijing, in the office of Liu Huaqing, the Standing Member of the Politburo and Deputy Chairman of the Central Military Committee

When the secretary handed over the report to Deputy Chairman Liu, an old general who came from the same hometown Hong'an County of 100 generals and studied in the former Soviet Union navy academy, as well as contributing to the missile cause all his life, a comforted smile appeared on his face. While he waved his pen, he commented on the confidential file: *This task was completed very well, you must summarise the experience of this success and strengthen the quality of the Second Artillery Corps.*

In the green square matrix of 3 million Chinese soldiers, those who were able to operate the strategic missile were called the favoured ones of the gods. Those who were able to personally control the switches were very few, and this honour usually belonged to the university students who had graduated from the strategic missile academy. It was an attractive occupation, but also one with temptations and risks. Most of the generals of the Chinese strategic missile troop had achieved glory through this position. However, Zeng Jiao, the son of a farmer who came from Daba Mountain and had never been to university, was able to join this honourable line of work with the persistence gifted by the mountains.

When the comments of Deputy Chairman Liu were passed to the army, Zeng was full of tears. His comrades congratulated him with flowers from the slope. The faded memories came flooding back, making his vision hazy…

In the ancient Daba Mountain area, there was the devolving line of the Yangtze River.

An old and bleak song of the boat trackers could reveal just how long they had persisted, and also the poverty and isolation of this area. Yet this isolated mountain path was precisely the one which led Zeng out of the mountains and on to his path of studying and future military career.

During the second spring of the 1980s, a military train carried Zeng to the mysterious tribe of the missile troop. In the mountains of northern China, he spent the whole year with his battlemates in the wilderness, the drillers building silos for the missiles among the lonely mountains and moon. The persistence and toughness of a man from eastern Sichuan province heated his blood, animating his skinny body. His youth and blood sacrifice had been rewarded. Among those who joined the army with him in the same year, he was admitted by the Party first, and he was the first one to be promoted as the squad leader, and was selected for training first, which made him an exceptional soldier.

But it is the accidental events in life that can change one's fate.

When Zeng had his dream of becoming a young military officer, the disarmament policy which cut off 1 million soldiers and shocked the whole world was promulgated, affecting the army he was in. A big group of engineering soldiers whose hands were covered with calluses were sent to the missile troop in excitement and confusion. Zeng's dream of promotion was ruined by this change after four years of hard effort. Facing the oriental swords standing in the launching field and the tens of thousands of circuits and mountains of parts inside of the missiles, he felt as if he were confronted with a giant mountain. His battlemates who came from his hometown told him, "Your promotion is not possible now, and as an old soldier who has served your term, you have to learn about the missiles from the basics. What can you achieve? Just let it go, and wait until we can retire from the army. Let's return home and form a construction team to make money!"

In the cold winter night, as he was hesitating at the crossroads of fate, Zeng sat alone on the slope near his camp, frustrated. He looked up at the sky, which was full of stars, searching for the one which mastered his own fate. After four years of military service, he understood one thing: along the tough journey of life, what could decide one's fate were only a few choices; if one made a mistake, life-long regret awaited. Should he return to his hometown and repeat the bitter life of his father's generation? Or grasp the last chance during his military service to learn from the basics, which might lead him to a new glorious stage of life as a missile launcher?

Zeng stood up, and walked confidently back to the camp.

Luoyang, the ancient capital of nine dynasties

When Zeng walked out of the book shop with a big pile of

books on scientific technology, his cheerful feelings were frozen. He was only thinking about buying books just now, but after that he couldn't repay the 8,000 *yuan* debt owed by his family, which was due this month. Even his money for food and other affairs was spent. After much consideration, he had to lower his life standard, buying kilos of cold buns and pickles to get by for a few days. Before he returned to the army, he bought the ticket by borrowing money from the wife of his old friend.

Beijing, Wangfujing Book Shop

The book, *A Complete Guide to Integrated Circuitry*, attracted Zeng's eyes like a magnet. Looking at this book, which he has been searching for for three years, he wanted to buy it instantly. But once he saw the price, he was shocked—it was 190 *yuan*. For ordinary people, this might not be expensive; but for a soldier who owed a lot of debt, it was unacceptably expensive. He hesitated for a while, and eventually he had to tell the shopkeeper in embarrassment, "Excuse me, can I read it here for a while longer? See, my hands are clean..."

On that day, he spent the whole day making excerpts from the book.

During the night, the old Company Commander Wu Jianmin was walking around in the company office. Then he patted Zeng's shoulder suddenly. "Don't you want to be the best launching controller? Ten years ago, there was a platoon leader of the Second Artillery Corps who managed to memorise three missile circuit maps, and this record has not been broken till now. If you were capable of memorizing all the five electric circuit maps, then you would be unbeatable!"

It was late autumn. The maple trees were on fire in the mountains of northern China, colouring the whole area red. And the wild chrysanthemum had invaded a shabby cottage stored with tools. Zeng covered the windows tightly with blankets, and the missile controlling diagrams were separated into a few hundred pages and stapled around the little cottage. As the papers flew around like leaves, the data on the papers shone and flickered like stars. In the evening, the company commander walked inside with a bowl of noodles, and asked him why he didn't go for dinner. He answered, massaging his blood-streaked eyes, "Didn't I just have breakfast?" The company commander forced him to take a walk outside.

Once he started to walk on the devolving path through the mountains, he took out the cards full of reference numbers from his pocket and began to memorise them. Unaware, he suddenly fell and rolled into the stream at the bottom of the slope.

On New Year's Eve, the snow was everywhere. The smoke of gunpowder from fireworks was carried away by the strong wind in the fields of northern China, while the soldiers who had just finished their dinner gathered in front of the TV set, singing and waiting for the bells of the New Year. Zeng has just taken his wife and son to the club of his company, but was still living in the cottage with the military overcoat covering himself. All his heart was tied to this kingdom of diagrams. He was a man of passion. The papers, pencils and bread crumbs on the floor were turned into a land he cultivated with his piousness, nurturing the sparks of inspiration and power of comprehension. The dawn of hope eventually smiled at him. At around midnight, his 2-year-old son was having a high fever. The sounds of sobbing from his wife were heard by the political instructor who was checking the guards. He rushed to the cottage and asked Zeng out.

All the more than 180 pages which were taken down from the calendar recorded the hard efforts and costs Zeng had spent in the field of scientific technology: the diagraphs he had drawn were a metre high; the pencils he had used up could form a pile. Finally he was capable of drawing the entire electrical schematic diagraph of the missiles' controlling system without any mistake; and he was very familiar with the working principles, technical and malfunctional phenomena of the nearly 100 machines on the missiles. He became the living circuit of the missile troop.

The hell-like torment eventually led him to success, a holy lecturing podium.

In the spring of 1991, Xi'an, the ancient capital city

A few dozen senior generals and officers ranked above colonel from the Chinese strategic missile troop gathered here for training. The military training champions and experts were invited here to perform and deliver lectures. Lieutenant General Li Xuge, the Commander of the Second Artillery Corps, who was familiar with the missiles, was gazing at Zeng while he drew circuit diagraphs on the podium for thousands of university graduates. General Li pointed at the most complicated part of the diagraph and nodded at Zeng.

The professors and trainees at the scene were all worried about this ordinary soldiers.

With some contemplation, Zeng started to draw on the blackboard confidently. Two hours later, a precise diagraph of the missile-controlling circuit was presented in front of all the people.

In the intense applause, an old professor said repeatedly in astonishment, "Wonderful, wonderful! It's hard to imagine an ordinary soldier without a university education could accomplish such things."

Those arrogant university graduates had to admit that they were impressed. "Even for the smartest among us, it would take at least one year to memorise all the diagraphs. But he took only 180 days, it cannot be explained simply by intelligence and knowledge..."

If we traced Zeng's bitter life journey, it was not hard to explain his success.

Zeng's hometown was not far away from Baidicheng by the Yangtze River. It is a place full of ancient historic stories and fascinating fairy tales. But God didn't grant Zeng this mercy; instead, his childhood was more about poverty and suffering.

Circled by mountains, in White Crane Plain, all that Zeng's family had were a shabby grass cottage and an old set of cotton blankets. Due to the hardships of raising her children, Zeng's mother, who was 40 years old, had had tuberculosis since over ten years ago. She had to rely on medicines to support her dying body. In order to pay for her treatments, Zeng's family had sold out all their valuable possessions; but they were still heavily burdened by the debt of nearly 10 thousand *yuan*. Not long after Zeng joined the army and left home, his father, Zeng Zhaolu, gathered his two younger daughters in front of him, and said guiltily, "I am sorry for you. Your elder brother has left for the army, and I could not manage to farm the land alone. You two are over ten now. As a girl, so long as you are literate, it's enough. You should come home and help me. Then your brother would be doing his job easier in the army." The two girls, who were still holding onto their dreams of education, had to put aside their schoolbags and take the heavy load of survival upon their fragile shoulders. Lanchun, the elder one of Zeng's sisters, who was 13 years old, had to follow other young girls in the village and went to Dongguan in Guangdong Province to be a migrant worker ...

In the late autumn of 1987, the cracking sounds of fireworks brought Zeng's family cheerfulness and happiness for the first time. Perhaps it was because of some directions from God, or just to finish the last wish of her life, but Zeng's mother, who had been sick in bed for more than 10 years, insisted that Zeng should have his wedding with his fiancée, Mao Guoxiu. When the couple walked into their wedding room, there was a comforting smile on her mother's skinny and sallow face. Before the red character for happiness pinned to the wall had faded, a telegraph from the army arrived: *Please return to the training field as soon as possible.* It was in Zeng's hands on the seventh day of his wedding. His mother, who was lying in bed, grasped her son's hand and said, "I am dying now, maybe this is the last time we can see each other. You must work hard in the army."

Zeng nodded, sobbing ...

Waves of strong wind from the north had crushed the leaves of autumn into dust and mud. A telegraph — *Your mother has passed away, please return soon* — was handed to Zeng as he was undertaking a competition. Holding this telegraph, feelings of sadness and conflict rolled and swirled in his heart. As the eldest son of his family, he was supposed to return home for his mother's funeral. But he was responsible for the competition. If he left, the marks of his troop would be worse; if he hardened his heart and chose not to return, he would be marked as not being filial in front of his father and other local people forever. However, loyalty and remaining filial couldn't all be preserved. After some struggle in his soul, he decided to stay in the training field.

When he stepped on the red soil land with his No.1 certificate of the competition, his mother had long since been placed beneath the yellow soil forever. Walking into his home, his father roared, "Why did you come back so late? What kind of son are you? How many times can your mother die … "

Crows were hovering around in the dark evening mist. Zeng placed his certificate solemnly in front of the tombstone of his mother. For the whole night he sat there, having a spiritual conversation with his mother as tears rolled down his face.

The shadow of misfortune always hovered over this unfortunate family.

One May afternoon in 1990, Mao Guoxiu, Zeng's wife, was boiling the herbal medicine in an aluminum bowl for her father-in-law and had given a bowl of rice to her five-year-old son, Songsong. She then went to feed the pigs in the yard. Suddenly, a heart-broken cry came out of the room. With her heart trembling, Mao rushed back to the room crazily. Her son had knocked over the chair and his entire right arm was inside of the boiling pot of medicine. She picked up her son instantly. As she gently uncovered his sleeve, skin and flesh fell down, revealing white bone. The villagers had sent them all kinds of local medicines to cure her son's injury. But instead of curing the injury, her son's condition worsened and the wound became infected. For a couple of days, he had a high fever and was in a coma, without even the strength to cry. She was worried that her husband who was in the launching field might become distracted if he knew, so she hid it from him for half a month. But one night, her son fell into a high fever. Mao had to carry her weak son more than 15 kilometres to the township hospital. Zeng's elder sister, who couldn't stand this situation any more, sent a telegraph to Zeng. However, at that time he was busy inspecting the missiles with other experts. The only thing he could do was to write his wife a letter to explain his situation, along with 100 *yuan*.

After a month, Zeng returned home, full of anxiety and worries. He was shocked to see that his wife, who was young and pretty, had aged very much. Seeing her husband suddenly, she couldn't believe her eyes, and threw herself into his arms.

"I am sorry," she cried. "I didn't take a good care of our son… "

Zeng patted his wife's back silently, not blaming her. He already owed too much to her.

He rushed to the bed to see his son. The boy was still sleeping, so he gently lifted the towel covering his arm. He saw the muscle on his son's arm was already rotten, blood oozing out. Though he was a tough man who barely cried, he couldn't keep the tears from streaming down. During his 20 days at home, he took his son to hospitals during the day and stayed with his son throughout the night, taking care of him. Perhaps he was hoping that he could make up for the lost days to his son. It was the first time he had spent 800 *yuan* on him, money which he borrowed from his battlemates. In order to find a kind of herb which could cure burn wounds, he walked more than 50 kilometres to pick it from the cliffs; in order to supply more nutrition to his son, he often went to the rivers for fish and shrimps. He couldn't tell for how many times he had sucked the blood out of his son's arm, or how many times he had chewed up the bitter herbs and applied it to his son's wound…

His piousness had touched God. His son was saved, but a permanent disability was left on his arm.

Disasters seemed to have formed a bond with this family. Four months after his son's injury, one afternoon, his wife Mao went to collect firewood in the mountains alone. She saw a tree on the red soil cliff, and went to chop it. But unexpectedly, she awakened the poisonous wasps hidden in the tree. They engulfed her within seconds, and she was stung so badly she lost consciousness and fell into the valley.

After half a month, Zeng received an unexpected letter from his mother-in-law while training to be a master sergeant in northeastern China. In the letter, she told him that after the fall his wife had needed eight stitches for the wound to her head, which left her with severe brain concussion and permanently disabled. His reins of rationality could no longer restrain his emotion. He ran up to the mountains as if crazy, and cried out towards his hometown which lied beyond the desert...

As the steps of history moved hurriedly into the 1990s, many people replaced the sacrificing idols in the shrine with material enjoyment. But the 3 million Chinese soldiers still regarded the national interest as the highest principle of their life, and strived to excel beyond themselves in all respects, in order to place the Chinese army on the path to victory in facing the challenges of the 21st century. For this, their families suffered and sacrificed much. But their spirit of sacrifice for a higher purpose was peerless compared to the soldiers from any other country. It was precisely these sacrifices that accounted for the greatness and loftiness of the Chinese soldiers.

Zeng Jiao, who came from the red soil land, had carried the rare heavy burden of his family, but with more than ten years of training in the military and the genes of persistence inherited from the older generation of soldiers, he refused to give in to continuous disaster and refused to lower his elegant head. He firmly believed that, so long as a soldier was not defeated by himself, and kept holding up the torch of faith, he would definitely be able to step out of the swamp and embrace the glory of his life.

From an ordinary soldier to an exceptional missile launching controller, Zeng Jiao had transformed his life as a soldier with his tough determination. He was promoted as a lieutenant as an exception. In the summer of 1994, he was awarded honours by an order issued by Chairman of the Central Military Committee.

4. In the minus 40 degrees snow, the new generation of Chinese rocket soldiers battled the cold iron with their young bodies, and let their determination and weapons be tested together.

In the middle of the 1980s, an old man stood atop the peak of the era and the history of the oriental state. As if wandering in the courtyard, he looked over at the earth, which had lain under the threat of the cold war for nearly half a century. Although at that time people were living in a generally peaceful world, the wars in some areas were still going on and people there were bleeding. However, this great oriental statesman had influenced nearly a quarter of the entire human population and the development of history, waving his arm bravely and declaring to the world: China would decrease the army by 1 million.

When many Chinese field corps, which had great battle achievements and honours, were making their last salute to the sky before they disappeared from the PLA, this senior man, who had influenced the last two decades of the 20th century, signed his name to an important military report.

As a result, under the background of the disarmament policy, a new trial regiment was born in the Chinese strategic missile troop in the forests of the snow field.

In the eyes of an outsider, as the special force within the special force, the soldiers of the trial regiment would have been thought to enjoy a fancy occupation with first class working conditions and the best living environment, perhaps with a modern scientific experimenting hall, facing big screens and controlling all the buttons on the panel...

But the hard reality would crush such a rosy picture. Lin Gang, who graduated from the highest engineering academy of the Chinese strategic missile troop, joined this trial regiment with his graduation certificate as an undergraduate. Originally, he thought the regiment, which had mastered the most advanced weapons of the republic, must have been stationed right beside the cities or at the gate of the research institutes. Yet when he departed the city at the end of his graduation, what greeted his eyes were mountains and huge forests. What shocked him was that the beloved new-born of the Chinese strategic missile troop were stationed in a primitive and remote valley. The waist-deep snow had covered the vigorous green of the mountains, and also the silver fantasy of many generations.

At that moment, this young man, who had never spent a day in the green missile matrix, reached an important conclusion: the Second Artillery Corps was actually the valleys. The most advanced army was synonymous with the most primitive. It was a huge regimental staff cramped in a 20 year old company office that was presented in front of him. The regimental commander, political commissar and the general staff shared one big bed. Every section was assigned one table, which meant every unit could only have one drawer. The canteen was in a shabby building with walls that did not stop the wind and a floor frozen with ice. When the soldiers were having their meals, they had to put on their leather overcoats and tremble as they ate.

In the afternoon when this regiment was set up, the political instructor of the 1st company arrived at the gathering location in the remote mountain area, stepping on the snow. When he walked into the camping area with shabby buildings, the whole area was so quiet that he could hear the roaring wind. He was shocked — where were the soldiers? He was relieved to eventually find more than 20 soldiers who were trembling in a corner. "Are you the soldiers of the 1st company? I'm sorry I'm late."

As they heard that he was the political instructor, the soldiers stood up from the big cold bed and circled him. Before they could talk, some of the soldiers started to cry. "If you were not here today, instructor, we would be dead from the cold." There were some freshmen who were transferred here from the recruitment. The political instructor said repeatedly, "Don't worry, we'll settle here immediately. Let's cover the windows first and then warm the sleeping platform." However, as he looked around, the political instructor was astonished as well. There were holes in all the walls — how could they start a fire? He asked the soldiers to look for spades and shovels, and made mud to repair the walls. But to make mud, they would need hot water. After they had searched through the camping area, apart from the few old stoves, they couldn't even find a pot. The political instructor was so anxious that he sweated. They were located in an isolated area miles away from the headquarters of the regiment. The area was not populated. What could they do? Gathering his thoughts, he came up with a solution. The soldiers were directed to dig into the snow for the old pots. It was not a dead end. They found an old pot at the bottom of the mountain near their camp, which was abandoned by those who boiled asphalt to build the road. But this was the life-saving pot for the 1st company. And so, in the quiet forest, cooking smoke rose again…

The cruel and unmerciful natural environment was freezing the soldiers' determined, youthful bodies. But not every soldier could reveal the greatness of their soul from the start. They were human after all, so they also had all kinds of strengths and weaknesses. Li Zhiguo, who was an old soldier, had submitted his application to his original army to join this new regiment after he heard that they would control the most advanced weapons. After the first day, the hard reality had crushed this dream and he often tried to ask for a transfer from the political instructor. Having been repeatedly rejected, one night, he walked out of the political instructor's room and kneeled down to the moon. "God, you must save me from this unbearable torment…" The noise attracted lots of attention from the other soldiers.

Also, there were many other soldiers pretending to be sick. One even faked insanity and tried to commit suicide in order to avoid spending one more day in the company. So the company staff had to keep an eye on him all the time. One afternoon, he escaped the supervision of the soldier who was looking after him, and walked into the mountains alone with his bag and ropes, causing a shock among the company cadres and the whole company to have to go looking for him…

The first regimental commander Ding Fengqi could no longer

resist the surging hot blood and anger in his heart. He was a strong northern man with a standard short military haircut. In the deep big eyes under his thick eyebrows there arose a fire of anger, replacing the usual gentleness. He gathered all the soldiers of the regiment on a snow field circled by the forest. As he cleaved the air with his arm, he said, "All these soldiers, men who requested a transfer, please open up your eyes and look at this snow field under your feet. Here lies the heroes of the Anti-Japanese War, and also the shame of we Chinese soldiers. These heroes are looking at us and mocking their descendants: are you a real man or a coward? I repeat, if you have some balls, stay and start a career here with us and wash off the shame and regret to build the spirit of the new generation of rocket soldiers. If you want to be a coward, please leave, you only need to leave us a small note. I, Ding Fengqi, will release you instantly…"

With his genuine words full of honesty, Ding had lit a fire in the cold wilderness. As for the education in loving the Second Artillery Corps, loving the battlefields and duties full of the army's own characteristics, it had sparked the souls of the soldiers.

A group of unsettled souls were settled down in this kingdom of snow. Before they had been completely settled down, the orders of their tasks had been issued to them.

The reality before the trial soldiers was extremely harsh. With the early warning aircrafts from the US and other Western countries hovering above them all the time, our soldiers were trying to catch up with their 3 to 15 minutes record of reacting to a launching order. The responsibility of setting up a new operation model for the new weapons through trials was laid on their shoulders.

For them to realise the goal of conducting the launching tasks in the same year of their establishment was no less than a modern fairytale. Some old generals who had spent many years in the missile troop worried about them a lot. A couple of days before, they couldn't even be called an army — were they able to realise this historical leap? For an army with the blood of toughness and persistence inherited from the Chinese nation, the Chinese army seemed to be capable of creating all kinds of miracles.

A group of experienced technicians were sent to the research institutes and factories of the Astronautical Ministry to study the functions and operations with the engineers and technicians there. The missile soldiers who remained started to learn from the basics with the new teaching materials.

Before the winter had passed, northern China was still immersed in its dream-like silver world. To test the maximum adaptability of the new missiles in complicated meteorological conditions, the newly established missile team put their young bodies to the test against the cold iron without hesitation.

In the arctic village, mid winter

The border of China seemed to have reached the end of the sky and earth. The horizon disappeared as the indefinite sky was ripped open into a giant crack. The bright day and dark night coexist on this planet, but it seemed that there would never be night here. To the far end of one's vision, it was all an indefinite silver world. The minus 47 degrees icy point had frozen the mountains in death-like silence. All of a sudden, everything disappeared between the heaven and earth, leaving only the mysterious sound of nature. Within a second, a wind storm arose and threw the falling leaves and snow into the frozen forest. With the snowy fog around, the soldiers of the trial regiment had to trudge on the field carrying the new weapons, in search of the coldest area in China, in order to obtain the adaptability data of the weapons.

During the day, the temperature of the arctic village dropped to minus 40 degrees, and it would go down further to minus 47 degrees during the night. Since it was so cold, people's breath could be frozen, and more than 95% of the soldiers faced the risk of incurring frostbite on their face and limbs. Even so, the soldiers were going to use their bodies to operate this newest missile and undertake the harshest tests of nature. Midnight was the coldest time in the arctic village. The soldiers were awoken by a sharp whistling from their warm dreams. They had to carry the modern equipment and start their operation in a hurry. As the wind of midnight shredded the soldiers' cotton coats, it lanced their bodies like needles. Initially they would feel some pain, but later they became numb and lost feeling. But the trial of the weapons was not allowed to pause. After seven consecutive hours of operation, the soldiers' eyebrows and mustache were frozen, which made it hard for them to talk. However, they kept up their meticulous work. Qi Dewen, the hoisting command deliverer, had still not had his 19th birthday. He was skinny and fair-skinned, with a child-like face. The moment people saw him, he struck them as a child. When he was performing his duty in the operation, he had to get into the narrow missile storage and take down a few rods and plugs of a few companies while checking whether there was anything left on them, despite the piercing cold wind. Once he got the order from his company commander, he took off his cotton coat, leather hat and gloves, and got into the storage with only an operation suit. Once his hands were on the iron, they were stuck. He said repeatedly, "My hands are stuck!" Before his battlemates outside could react, he tried to breathe out hot air and detach his hands from the cold iron. But this ruthless coldness meant his lips got stuck on the equipment as well.

"Don't worry, Qi." Soldiers outside rushed inside at once. After all of them tried to breath out hot air, Qi's hands and lips were finally detached. When his battle mates eventually took him out of the storage, this child-like soldier was frozen and bleeding from the wounds on his lips and hands.

When a female expert from the Astronautical Ministry saw it, she was touched and burst into tears. Embracing Qi with her arms, she tried to warm this frozen young soldier with her body. She said, "My son is as old as you, but he still could not leave our care. And you … what a good soldier … "

Once the silver fairy tale was ended, the soldiers of the trial regiment had to enter a new journey. They carried the new missiles and facilities to undertake adaptability tests under wind storms, pouring rain, long journeys and high temperature conditions. With their life and blood, they began to battle the silent iron again.

The western desert area

In the desert, where the wind speed was 15 miles a second, the soldiers of the trial regiment started the weapons test. In a second, dark clouds began to roll over the desert as the wind storm arose with the sand and stones, rendering the sky yellow and dark. As the sand storm roared, it seemed that it was going to engulf the soldiers. Even the camel thorns, which were called the soul of the desert, were pulled up from their roots. However, the soldiers stood still. They endured the power and abuse of nature along with the iron.

In southern Xinjiang, during the summer

Sunlight dropped from the cloudless sky and set the red soil land of July on fire. The earth was burned into unconsciousness, and the willows were moaning in pain. On the launching pad, the ground temperature had reached 58 degrees celsius. If one poured a bowl of water on the ground, it would turn into steam instantly. However, the soldiers of the trial regiment had to conduct the tests under the high temperature here for more than ten days. They had already taken off their inner clothes and were only in their operation suits, but sweat still immersed the suits until they were covered by salty sweat stains. When a squad of command deliverers collapsed, another squad came up and replaced them; every few minutes, there would be one person falling down …

After they had experienced the hell-like trial in high temperature, they felt like there was no difference between getting into or out of the hell apart from different feelings. As a result, this heroic team had integrated the strong motivation of determination into the process of the Chinese strategic missile troop's integration into the world, and created many new achievements. At the cost of their bodies, they successfully completed 11 important tests which provided 100 thousand pieces of precise data and more than 400 pieces of valuable information. And they had completed training materials of 2 million characters, building a strong army.

After a few months, in one of the control halls of the headquarters

On the huge screen, there was the scene on the launching field thousands of miles away in front of the generals from the Central Military Committee, the headquarters and the units in Beijing. This was the first trial launching of the new strategic missile, and also a demonstration of the qualities of the soldiers from the Second Artillery Corps. General Zhang Aiping, who was the former Defense Minister, was sitting in the chief position. As he looked around and had a sip of tea, he told his old subordinate, General Li Xuge, the commander of the Second Artillery Corps who was sitting in front of them, "Xuge, this is the first time the newly organised trial regiment has launched the new missiles."

Commander Li nodded, smiling, and didn't say anything. Actually, any words were not necessary at that moment. The soldiers led by him would prove through their loyalty and capabilities that they were the best.

On the launching field, they had entered the final countdown. The few hundred experts and technicians who were part of the design and construction had been evacuated to the grass field. There was no laughter, nor was there the sound of the wind, only a longing heart which was waiting for the long expected moment.

The soldiers calmly and steadily controlled the most advanced weapon of the Chinese Army, with perfect procedures and actions. Their completion of the preparation had been reported level by level to the master commanding department.

"Ready to launch!"

"Ignition!"

"Take off!"

The new missile flew up in yellow flames and flew up to the sky towards the infinite universe ...

"We succeeded!" someone said. The frozen atmosphere in the general controlling hall melted, and many high-ranking officers came forward to shake hands with General Li Xuge.

General Zhang walked slowly to the telephone connected to the launching field, and he congratulated all the soldiers of the trial regiment on behalf of the State Council and the Central Military Committee.

On the launching field thousands of miles away, people were cheering like boiling water. After countless days in their sweats, the soldiers of the trial regiment saw their tears fall down in the desert as they caressed the missiles …

5. The history of different eras always resemble each other. In an autumn of the 1990s, the new favoured one of the Chinese strategic missile troop was born by the bottom of Yanshan Mountains. General Li Xuge, the commander of the Second Artillery Corps, was going to retire soon. He told Gao Jin, holding his hands, "The history of the strategic missile troop will be turned to a new page in your hand."

History always develops slowly along the track of inheritance.

The first generation of the missile soldiers, who were called the morning sun of the young republic, were gathered at Yanshan Mountains. They had made the first step as the first strategic missile battalion of Asia with enormous difficulties and determination. After decades of sufferings, the life seeds of the "No.1 battalion of Asia" had morphed and reproduced into many clusters of strategic rocket armies in the mountains and deserts of China.

It was the cycle of history.

After 35 years, the autumn sky of Yanshan Mountains was as blue as if it has been cleaned by the sea. Inside the astronautical city circled by red walls by the Yongding River, a brand new missile battalion of the Chinese strategic missile troop had lifted its proud head, revealing its courage and determination as the most favoured one of the Chinese Army.

Under the directions of the battalion commander Gao Jin, the dark green missiles were going through every stage of the launching process with great precision and order. Their loud commands, close collaborations and skilled movements had gained waves of applause from the generals and colonels from the headquarters who came to visit.

At the end of the launching performance, the soldiers of the battalion saw the chiefs off. Suddenly, General Li Xuge returned from his car and came towards Gao Jin. He grabbed his hands as if he still had the blood which came from the trial base in the deserts of northwestern China. "The first Chinese strategic missile battalion was set up here, today your battalion is set up here as well. The history of our strategic missile troop will be turned to a new page in your hands. Young man, you are carrying a heavy responsibility now. Do not fail the favour of history..."

This scene was etched in the memories of this young battalion commander.

In the second summer of the 1990s, after the red flag of the Soviet Union which had dominated the world for more than 70 years fell down all of a sudden, the cold war structure that had existed since the end of the Second World War collapsed overnight. The hot spots in the world had cooled down. However, the next wave of competition for the strategic power of the 21st century started immediately. The US had increased its budget for developing high technology weapons by 15%. Russia, which was left behind after the collapse of the Soviet Union, also strived to develop "New Concept" weapons despite its power decline. The Western European countries didn't want to be left behind, and began to adjust their military budget and investments to ensure the development of important weapons. China, which was playing a more important role in the peace of the world, was facing both opportunities and challenges at the same time. The new generation of soldiers grasped this transformation of history and leaped towards the path of a stronger and more efficient army. Therefore, a new strong army with long swords was born in China. Gao Jin, as an outstanding staff officer of battle, was luckily appointed to be the first battalion commander of this new strategic missile troop.

But the first step was difficult.

On the southern slope, under heavy rain and strong wind, wild thistles and thorns covered the land. In an abandoned area of shabby factory buildings, Gao led a group of officers with university degrees and old soldiers here to start the first step. However, what was in front of them was frustration. In the dimming light of candles, the humid air on the shabby ceiling had formed a layer of "cold tears" which kept dripping down on the soldiers' beds. With the waves of cold wind carrying the sounds of dancing and music at the nearby clubs, more loneliness was added to this military camp.

The soldiers' emotion had dropped to zero degrees. Sun Jinming, an officer with a university degree who used to harbour romantic expectations and dreams before he joined the missile troop, came to Gao Jin. "Battalion commander, please be honest with me. How is the future of our battalion?"

What could Gao say? His heart was filled with rolling thoughts and feelings. Since the preliminary training, they had built the skeleton of the battalion. For more than a year, they didn't have any training materials or equipment — even the notebooks were paid for by the cadres themselves. The new missiles were still under development. It was not known when they could be distributed to them. However, with the toughness and persistence in his blood and his long term military experience, he knew deeply in his heart that once these new missiles were distributed to them, they would be the trump division of the entire army.

The next morning, Gao led a group of soldiers to the mountains behind their camp. They chopped down two trees and some bamboo, then built an arch gate for their camp. Gao wrote down "Gate of Entrepreneurship" on the top, clearing the doubtfulness in people's hearts.

As the midday sunlight cast a helmet over the soldiers' fate, Gao led them to make a vow in front of the "Gate of Entrepreneurship." His inspiring speech encouraged all the young men, "Everyone is eager to have his own achievements and write a glorious page in his life. Today, we have been chosen by history to learn and master the most advanced weapon of China. Let's continue the glory of the strategic missile troop as soldiers of the 1990s."

This solid faith had inspired the soldiers' determination to walk towards the world with steady steps. He directed the soldiers to build roads, clear thistles, maintain the launch pad, and build walls. After their hard work, the land under their feet was transformed from a ruin to the cradle for a new troop. Facing the challenges of not having any equipment or training facilities, they made their own models for training. All the soldiers looked for and found many abandoned paper boxes. With their dexterous hands, they made 37 new operation panels for the new missiles. They made a stunning copy of the panels of the operation systems. The troop which used this paper model eventually mastered the operation procedures and techniques of a new missile. With this achievement, they continued the legend of the "No.1 battalion of Asia".

When they spread the seeds of entrepreneurship over poor land, they could harvest a golden spring.

In October 1992, Gao and his subordinates started their operations on the real new missiles for the first time. They tried to suppress their excitement.

With the orders delivered, all the command deliverers quickly stood at their own positions. Every movement was perfect, which impressed the chiefs—they have never seen the missiles, how could they develop their skills? After they realised that the soldiers gained their skills with paper models, they had to give them a thumbs up. The general designer of the carriage rocket and the new missiles, Chen Futian, patted Gao's shoulder in excitement. "Young man, after giving the weapons to your troop, we can rest our hearts in peace."

A year later, deep in the desert of northwestern China

A new missile which was designed by China was launched and flew into the sky with thunder and lightning. Gao and his battalion cooperated with the General Astronautical Corporation to finish the launching task successfully, symbolising the fact this new troop already had the actual capacity to enter battle. When the remains of the missile were discovered in the distant desert and sent to the camp of the battalion, Gao and his battlemates welcomed it in a line. With pairs of hands touching the remains of their hard work, they burst into tears with pride and excitement...

The tornado was roaring, the rains were pouring. Tens of trainees with bachelor degrees were standing still on the field, waiting for the commander of the 1st battalion to deliver the dismissal order.

At this moment, Gao was having a fever of 39 degrees when the military surgeon gave him an injection. However, the thundering storm had refreshed Gao's mind. He felt an intangible power calling him.

He got out of bed, despite the objections of the doctors, and took down the needles before he returned to the field. Immediately, the thundering sounds of steps, calling and the storm on the field had formed an orchestra.

After the drill, Gao gave his comments; his whole body was wet. He saw in satisfaction that, although the storm was going on, none of the soldiers had moved or blinked or become absent minded, as if they were statues carved out of rocks in the storm. His comments were full of the courage of a soldier as well. "I don't want to give you a hard time. But the war doesn't care about the weather. You should be grateful to nature, since it gave you such a big present before your graduation."

After the drill he returned to his dorm. Once he stepped inside, Gao fell down onto the ground.

An officer with bachelor degree was confused about this approach and came to him. "We are an army of high technology, whose expertise is in mastering the missiles. Why are you training us as if we were the field army?"

Gao answered confidently, "Why does the West Point advance in the football games? Just in order to give their trainees some exercise? No! The real purpose is to develop the battling spirit of the soldiers, including their bravery and manner."

He took out the materials he had edited about the foreign armies.

It told them, although West Point was famous for its comfortable environment and advanced facilities, it valued the approach of harsh drilling to strengthen the bodies of the trainees and their persistence. Every year when the freshmen enrolled, they had to undertake 16 hours of physical training every day, which was called the "best training" by the foreign military experts; the prior Supreme Commander of the Soviet Union, Zhukov, who had led the 6th Tank Division, could undertake the survival training during the winters of the outer Caucasus in minus 50 degree celsius cold during the 1980s. The French army would go to the deserts every year to conduct large military exercises; the British parachutists often placed their soldiers in remote mountain areas.

The conclusion Gao reached was, "As the high technology troop, we are facing the crueler wars of the future, which have higher requirements for the qualities of their soldiers. Many unimaginable miracles were actually achieved with strong determination. We have to find more difficulties for ourselves, and strengthen our determination in harsh environments. The hard work we do will become the happiness of victory in the future…"

He told the officer seriously, "If you find it hard, go back and complain to your father, who has been working the whole year on the land."

As a punishment, Gao asked him and the company where he is subordinated to practice their military steps under the midday sunlight for a month.

As the sun burned southern China in July, the blue smoke of heat steamed the soldiers on the training field. In order to develop the courage and persistence spirit of the soldiers, Gao invited two fighting experts from the armed police to train them. During the practice, the stones and pieces of glass on the ground terrified them. Gao stepped forward without hesitation. "I will be the first!" Then he started to leap forward as his legs tightened and arms extended out…one time, two times, three times, his hands were cut, his elbows were hurt. He shed his blood and sweat on the ground full of sand and stones. "So long as I can do it, you cannot fall down." The battalion commander's powerful voice and body had set an example for all the soldiers. After a week, although all the soldiers got darker and thinner and their uniforms were covered with salty stains, they gained a soldier's courage and strength.

In the early spring of 1991, the Gulf War started, which further affected the nerve of Gao tremendously.

He borrowed the videos from the military intelligence department, and watched them five times, locking himself up in his room. The high technology weapons and command, telecommunications, operational and intelligence system C 31 had shocked him deeply. A new sense of crisis surged in his heart. Beside his ears, the tragic sound of the March of the Volunteers kept going on. Did this nation have to be beaten up and endure bloodbaths before it could realise what they should have done?

It was not Gao's paranoia. As an experienced staff officer of battle, he understood deeply that their officers were not interested in studying the wars, but were keen on socialising and dealing with their superiors. Those who joined the army for self-interest had only increased in number. Some had taken the training tests as games and cheated; and they did not take the military exercises seriously. He clearly realized that this army which was formed by farmers could not be transformed into a modern force in the 21st century if we could not sever the narrow-mindedness and ignorance entrenched in our blood.

As Gao maintained the tenet of "soldiers should only care about wars", he told his subordinates, "We long for peace, but how can we escape war? An army without education is weak and cannot withstand an attack. A commander who doesn't know about high technology will become a big problem for the army…

"If our sword is not long enough, then let's just take a step forward!" Ambitious Gao was always looking forward to tomorrow. On the launching field and the lonely military camp, or in the bed of the Astronautical Compound in Beijing, even during his reunion with his wife once a year, he fixed his eyes on the books, consuming all the knowledge of modern technology available. He dabbled in thousands of books, including history, politics, military and also the more difficult monographs of theory. He had collected and read much literature from all around the world, and even developed a rich interest in architecture. He said, "Our generation of soldiers should not be ignorant. The level and angle of our thinking should be comprehensive."

It was because of his eagerness and obsession for knowledge that Gao mastered the working principles of the new missile system and its operation and commanding procedures. Not only was he familiar with the 15 critical parts and testing reference data, but he could independently complete the operation at the primary positions. Additionally, he had completed technology notes and an academic thesis of 1.5 million characters.

Late autumn of 1993, the Astronautical Compound in the desert of western China

A new oriental sword stood pointing to the blue sky proudly.

The launching process had entered the final hour. The battalion commander Gao was sitting in the master control room and delivering every order. All of a sudden, the ground facilities and computer data started to show some abnormalities. The experts from the Astronautical Ministry had checked all the computer programs but could not find the problem. A chief designer of the missile fainted due to anxiety. Gao volunteered to lead Huang Chengfei and Li Zhenglian, the two technicians, to go through all the electrical maps in their mind several times, and took out thousands of programs. After four long hours of effort, they eventually found out that the problem lay with the computer program's original design, and they had avoided a big risk for the launching platoon.

Some white-headed experts called Gao their hero, and they all requested that Gao and his battalion should be awarded with the 2nd class award. Some cadres from the headquarters in Beijing were impressed by his thinking, speech, words and way of regulating the army once they met him. They said, "Gao was born to be a soldier. He has displayed the hope of a 21st century professional soldier."

A commander of the missile troop valued Gao very much. He joked to him many times, "You were not born in the right time. If you were born earlier, during the war, there would be enough wars for you to fight ... "

As a professional young military officer, who could know that Gao had been supported by a strong family. They lay behind his success. For all these years, he had been separated from his parents, wife and daughter by thousands of miles. He took the battle fields in the mountains as his home, and treated his warm home as a hotel. Every time he went back to Fuzhou to visit his family, his wife, who had been living with her parents, had to take him to his cousin's place just to spend a short month-long vacation. Having a tough life and sacrificing fun as a young man was nothing to Gao. Since he had chosen an occupation as a military officer, he had to be ready for sacrifice. However, what gave him the most pain was some people's indifference and discrimination against soldiers.

During the spring festival of an earlier year, Gao, who was having a vacation in Fuzhou, took his wife and daughter to visit his parents-in-law. His mother-in-law prepared a rich banquet for Gao, who came from the mountains, and her younger son-in-law, who had migrated to Japan. During the family dinner, the guy who had just migrated to Japan six months ago said to Gao in a sarcastic tone, "I dare say, my brother, that the salary of you Chinese soldiers is probably the worst in the world, but you seem to be more arrogant than the American soldiers based in Okinawa. It seems to me that the Chinese people are entitled to call you 'the big soldiers' … "

Gao pounded the table with his fist, which shook the entire table, "Shut your stinky mouth. Look at the fake foreigner look of you — how long have been in Japan? How could you forget where you have come from? Do you know anything about the Chinese soldiers? You do not deserve to comment before me … "

The reunion spring festival banquet had been ruined by these two sons-in-law who disagreed with each other, and the whole family were enormously upset.

After he returned to his room, his wife, Zhao Yanbin, could not restrain her anger. "They look down upon us because we don't have money. You'd better leave the army as soon as possible. I don't believe we can't go abroad and make money."

Actually many members of his wife's family were doing business in southeastern Asia. His parents-in-law had tried to persuade them to try their luck overseas many times. The two senior people deeply believed that with Gao's capabilities, if he could work abroad, he would definitely be no worse than anyone else. But Gao could not forget our nation, which had been through hundreds of years of suffering and shame. What he hoped for was that, with his generation, the Chinese soldiers would not provide any chance for any foreign armies to make achievements in this country. He said to his wife, "He could insult me, but he mustn't insult our army, our nation and our country…"

Gao told his wife a secret that he had kept for a long time. "The only gap in my career in the army is that I have never fought a war. If there is a high technology war in the future, I must be able to achieve something!"

Those were the words of a battalion commander whose troop had mastered China's most advanced strategic missiles.

Chapter 9

Our People, Our Land

1. Behind a strong army, there must be tens of millions of strong supporting families. It was our people who lived on the yellow soil and red soil who were supporting us — the new great wall.

Our army had come to the Forbidden City after they stepped out of the red soil and yellow soil mountains. After four decades, although the city life had washed away the colour of soil from the officers' faces and the fruits of modern civilisation had attached themselves to the sons of the farmers who had married city girls, we could not hide the cruel reality that, no matter how handsome they were or how civilised their manners were or how much they tried to hide their time with the yellow soil and transform themselves into a city man, the farmer's blood in their bodies could not be changed.

The 800 million Chinese farmer population decided that this army would be constituted largely by the famers, which destined the core of the greatest army to be composed of the kind and hard-working Chinese farmers. It was these qualities that supported this army's persistence and toughness. In the meantime, it was also the weakness in the farmers' blood that withheld the progress of the Chinese army's modernisation. These mixed qualities of the Chinese farmers had become both the biggest fortune and the weakness of the Chinese army.

Even so, people should not ignore an objective fact — it was the honest, kind and quiet people from the yellow land that supported China's most advanced nuclear power...

There were two events in the last winter of the 1980s which happened in the southern China missile troops and which have proved the above observations, though they had opposite outcomes.

A young soldier who was born in a cadre's family had joined the missile troop. Afterwards, deep in his heart, he could not help but harbour a sense of superiority toward most of the soldiers, who came from rural areas. His father was an middle-level cadre, and his mother was the wife of a official. Perhaps because he had had more experience, never did he take the leaders in his company seriously. He regarded the military rules as nothing and did what he wanted to.

One Sunday, in order to go to a little town many miles away to see the outside world, he took a ride on a farmer's tractor without getting approval. Unfortunately, he was involved in a crash, fell into a deep valley and lost his life.

His mother rushed to the army after a long journey. It was the biggest pain of life to lose one's son at an old age. The army gave her enormous sympathy, and took care of her as much as they could just to make her feel at home. The leaders blamed themselves for not being able to regulate the army more strictly, and apologised to her. However, their piousness didn't receive understanding from the soldier's parents. Their requests conflicted with the army's policy, which had already been mixed with sympathy. Within the possible area of the policy, the army could do their best to satisfy their requests. But the army was indeed not able to satisfy their requests of granting their son the title of martyr and compensating the family with a large sum. Therefore, after the disguise of colourful and polite discussions was shredded, the official who had spent all his life in lecturing people gave the local military leaders enormous difficulties, making them fearful. The dead soldier's body could not be cremated, and the dead had become the condition and bargaining chip of the living against the military. Of course, it was not uncommon in China then.

The deadlock had been going on for more than three months.

The families of the dead soldier had spent more than three months messing up in the military camp, until they started to find it boring and returned. However, this experience left a shattered image of the government officials in the mind of the soldiers.

Compared to these decent and eloquent city people, those farmers who were ugly and quiet could show an understanding and generosity that would make this country regretful and leave the army in tears ...

2. Facing their only son, who died on the missile battlefield, the old mother didn't cry. Her only request was to take away her son's bowl and chopsticks ...

The autumn rain was falling in the northern mountains.

Waves of cold wind coloured the dark green trees into a mass of blood red. The white fog of rain was spread over the valley, creating which spotless white curtains and rendering the atmosphere solemn.

As the retirement order arrived, Wang Hongshan, an old soldier from Gucheng County, was undertaking the last construction work with his battlemates in their wet and muddy cotton padded coats. In three hours, they would take off their uniforms and return home. The underground caves were as higher than a ten-storey building. As the squad leader of the construction team, Wang was directing the whole squad to drill for the last round. When he lowered his head while working, of course it didn't strike him that the God of Death would attack him from the cold autumn rain. An egg-sized stone fell down from nowhere through the safety net and hit him right on his head. As his safety hat shattered, he collapsed immediately and fell into unconsciousness. After he was hospitalised for seven days and seven nights, the doctors were not able to save this young man's life.

Heaven cried for this anonymous soldier.

The bad news carried the cold rain to Wang's hometown, Guxian County in Hebei Province. The leaders from the Civil Affairs Bureau and the army came to an ordinary yard of the countryside in Gucheng County. During the 1980s, this family had been wandering in poverty, which astonished them.

There were two shabby grass houses circled by their neighbours' brick houses. Wang's father, who was paralysed, was lying in bed, and his mother was also elderly and sick. The only thing which had some value in this family were their two shabby cupboards. The family had only Wang's 28-year-old sister to rely on. The comrades from the army and the cadres from the Civil Affairs Bureau could not tell them the bad news after they had seen this poor family.

When the old couple heard that the people from the army had come to take them to visit their son, they were so excited they could not get to sleep. His mother packed up the red dates and shoes sister had made for Wang throughout the night. They even got up early to make pastry for the journey. Before their departure, Wang's father asked his wife to come to him, and he told her, "When you arrive at the army, you should try to convince the chief that Hongshan should go home. Our family need his support. His sister is already 28, and she cannot afford more time to wait…"

His white-headed mother stepped on the train to the south with the comrades from the civil affair bureau and the army. Throughout the journey, the old lady didn't sleep at all and could not resist her pride. She praised her son as a countryside mother: "My Hongshan was born in a poor family. It was unfortunate for him. But even so, he has a good personality. He is an only son but we never spoiled him. Ever since he was young, he was an honest boy, and everyone in the village school praised him. He didn't want to remain in the yellow land for life like us, and said he wanted to join the army so that he could achieve something. Actually we didn't want to let him go, because this family of the old and sick needs him. But he was determined to go. I discussed it with his father and decided to let our son go as he wished. Since he joined the army, he would send us money each month. Initially he sent us from 5 to 7 *yuan* each month, and it was higher every year—now it is 10 *yuan* a month. We are poor, so no girls want to marry into our family. I have been worried about it. My boy wrote to me that he didn't want to get married for life, the silly child." As the old lady stopped here, she signed, and smiled bitterly. "In order to find my son a wife, I have asked around all my friends and relatives. When it comes to my son, he is perfect, he has already joined the Party in the army, and is valued by the chief and was promoted. What is his rank? My bad memory... Oh! I remember, he is a squad leader. But when it comes to our family, all the girls just turned away. It were us who held him behind. A family of the old and sick, who wants to jump into hell? This spring, originally I had found a girl for my son. She is illiterate but honest and healthy. A family like us do not have a choice. Before Hongshan could meet her, we had spent this much" — the old lady extended three of her skinny fingers — "300 *yuan*. It may not be enough for a meal, but I have to borrow around for half the month. As a poor woman, nobody dares to lend me money. I have hidden this from my son and he just needs to come back and get married. I am not worried about the money. This time I will ask Hongshan to come home with me and get married. So his sister can get married ... "

The old lady was talking to herself as if she were telling a distant fairytale.

The comrade who accompanied the old lady could not resist his sadness after hearing her story, and went to the washroom alone and cried. God was so unfair — why did he have to impose all this misfortune upon a kind old mother? He could not tell the bad news to the old lady.

After he dried his face in the washroom, he returned to the old lady and accompanied her. The old mother patted his hands. "You belong to the same army as my son, how is he?"

He tried hard to keep the tears in his eyes and nodded quietly.

He didn't dare to break the dream of an old mother cruelly, but he could not imagine that when she faced the cold reality she would be able to handle the pain of losing her son at an old age ...

However, nobody could have imagined, when the old lady was looking at her son who would never wake up again, that she would be so peaceful. She didn't cry or scream. It was as if she were a mother caressing her sleeping son. She touched her son's face again and again, murmuring, "Shanshan, you are sleeping so deeply. Son, why are you sleepy? Why don't you want to look at your mother...." She put her face of life-long suffering against her son's cold face for a while, and suddenly turned back to the leaders of the army. "Chiefs, you don't need to accompany me here. Please give us some private time so that we can have some conversation." The leaders of the army worried that she could not handle this shock, so they refused to leave and began to cry. The old lady fainted and collapsed...

After a whole night of nightmare, she woke up to hard reality. Her beloved son was no longer the Shanshan who was sleeping quietly in the cradle while she sang him a lullaby. And he was no longer the son who she has been waiting for all these years and who had returned to his mother's embrace. The white-headed mother's face was covered by tears, and the tears streamed down and fell on her son's cold cheek. The old lady tried to make her son sit up, but no matter how hard she tried, her son could not sit up. She cried, "Hongshan, your mother's come to see you, please sit up for me!" As she tried to open her son's eyes, she eventually realised that her son could no longer open his bright eyes. She put all the red dates into her son's pocket, and said in trembling voice, "Son, these are your favourite red dates, I have been saving these for you for a whole year."

Then the old mother put the new shoes which his sister had made on her son's feet and said, "Hongshan, my son, put on the new shoes made by your sister and go on your way. Your father cannot live any longer with his body. Don't worry, me and your father will come to see you…"

The soldiers who accompanied the old lady were all crying, and they kneeled down in front of her, telling her genuinely, "Madam, please don't be sad anymore. Hongshan is gone, all of us are your sons…" She wiped away the tears on her face and pulled up the soldiers, saying, "Stand up! Stand up!" She turned from sad to happy: "If I could have all of you as my sons, it would be my luck."

The old lady was leaving, and the army did its best to solve some problems for her. But she didn't want anything, and didn't ask the army to do anything for her. Finally when the leaders of the army came to see her off, the only request she made was pitiful. "I have brought you much trouble, and now I am leaving, I have no other requests. All I want is to take my son's bowls and chopsticks home. When I have my meals, I can't eat without seeing my child…"

What a kind mother; what a poor God of the soldiers!

She had sacrificed her only son to the Chinese strategic missile cause, and never did she think about any rewards. On the contrary, she had hidden the enormous tragedy of her family and her own sadness deep in her heart, sharing the pain only with her weak shoulders and poor body. Compared to those who had cars and food but could not forget about preaching to others and pressuring the living with the dead by asking for too much from the Party, an old lady from the countryside did not have much wisdom. And in some people's eyes, she was even ugly and pathetic. But it was people like her who had continued the spirit of this nation, and upheld the historic relics of understanding a larger justice.

You have to respect the greatness and tragedy in their silence.

You have to be impressed by the loftiness in their weakness.

Ten years later, when I shot a documentary and returned there, I traced this hero's mother's story in Gucheng. The end of this family was indeed tragic, as expected. Wang Hongshan's father could not take the shock of losing his son and passed away after him. Wang's sister put away the red clothes of her wedding and vowed not to get married forever. She lived with her mother and lived a poor life. However, the old lady, not long after she returned home from the army, suffered from delusions since she missed her son so much. Everyday when the sun set, she would sit by the road in front of the village and call her son's name gently, "Shan, where are you, come home. Your mother is waiting for you, where are you? … "

A poor family had swallowed the bitterness because they couldn't forget about their country. A group of people who could never leave the yellow land had upheld the sun of the east.

3. As his son lay beside the missile battlefield, the army exhausted what they had and sent 4,000 yuan to save the life of a father who had never left the mountain. But what the father received was just a note of debt …

A train from Sichuan Province stopped at an ordinary small station by the green forest in southern China. Nie Caigui, who was in a farmer's outfit and seemed to be fearful and quiet, came down from the platform, trembling with a deputy director from the Civil Affair Bureau of Yunyang, Yunnan Province. A team of colonels and lieutenants were already waiting for them. Before Nie could realise anything, a cry of "Salute!" struck him suddenly and the team of officers saluted to him with their eyes, as if they were receiving the inspection from the low-class farmer. Nie fell into confusion, since he has never been through this kind of serious situation. He didn't know what to do after the initial confusion and embarrassment. In a hurry, he took out the Hongtashan brand cigarettes from his pocket and gave them to the officers one by one. He heard that there was something that had happened to his son, who was in the army. Before Nie left home, as a man who has been fearful all his life, he decided to spend 12 *yuan* which he saved for months in buying this packet of high-end cigarettes. It was prepared for the chief of his son, in order to leave a good impression on him. His actions confused the officers who came to welcome him. According to their prior experience, when the officers took the soldier's parents here, usually it was because the soldier was involved in something in the army, or had made sacrifices on duty or died of disease. For these parents, they were treated like a god by the soldiers, who took solicitous care of them, in order to set the dead at peace and to avoid any trouble. Therefore, when the relatives of the soldiers came down from the train, they would be circled by a spring-like warmth. However, in seeing this man from Sichuan Province, these officers, who had handled lots of funeral affairs, were confused and uncomfortable. It was always the officers who would offer cigarettes to the soldiers' parents. It was a twist in this situation, and how could it be? Actually so long as they had known more about the background of Nie's family in the countryside, it would not be hard to explain what was happening...

Zhongyang Village, Yunyang County

Nie's family was not a native family. In the countryside where the power of native family clans remained strong, a few generations of

Nie's family could not lift their heads and be decent men without being bullied by other powerful families. Nie Caigui lost his parents when he was young and was raised by his uncle. In his memory, the men of Nie's family could never have their own status and reputation on this land. They couldn't carry their hoes on their shoulders on their way back from the farming land, and they had to pull the hoes to the land. To do otherwise would be regarded as disrespectful to the big family clan of Zhongyang Village. At least, they would be beaten; or worse, they would deprive them of their properties. At one time Nie Caigui, as a passionate young man, decided to let go of this dishonour and break this rule. So he carried his hoe on his shoulder and decided to walk out of the village decently. But before he could make it to the gate of the village, several young men from the powerful family rushed up to him and slapped his face in front of the crowd. "You damned bastard, how could you carry your hoe on your shoulder? Do you want to cheat the ancestors? Be careful or I'll break your legs…" Nie tried to argue with them, but after a beating which left him with lots of injuries, he had to give up and no longer dared to break the rule…

The bullies were not limited to carrying hoes. When it came time to allocate land to each family, Nie's family was allocated to the land which stood in the middle. When they had to water the land, no other family would allow them to go through their land, so the Nie family had to buy a plastic tube and carry water through the tube into the land. After all these sufferings, they managed to make it to the late autumn of 1990. As the eldest son, Nie Caigui went to join the army, and a plaque of "honourable family" was hung on the door of Nie's family. Chiefs from the county and the town governments would come by and visit Nie's family from time to time. All of a sudden, to the shock of the entire Zhongyang Village, the few powerful families started to show some respect to them, and only then did Nie start to develop some self-esteem. The villagers began to treat Nie's family in an entirely different way:

"Father Nie, congratulations, you are an honourable one for the army now. Do not pull the hoe on the ground, carry it on your shoulder!"

Coming from a life-long bully, he thought the sun must have come up from the west and answered repeatedly, "Yes, yes."

"Why do you need to use a tube to water your land? Just go across our land."

And he answered them with the same words.

The morning he sent his son to the road beside the village, Nie Caigui, who had never smiled, could no longer smile because the muscles on his face had cramped. But he couldn't resist his cheerfulness; and as he leaned on his son's shoulder, his eyes were full of tears.

"Son, you are the only honourable soldier in our family, and because of you we can raise our heads in front of the other villagers. You must work hard in the army, and bring honour to our family. Go…"

His son nodded, tears on his face, and left.

They didn't know that this would be the last time they would meet.

After half a year, his son passed away. It was not war time — was it because he had done something bad? If that was so, the Nie family would be dishonoured again. Once he heard that people from the Civil Affairs Bureau had sent him a letter, the old man pulled his hoe on ground on his way home, even his feet becoming weak.

The cadres from the Civil Affairs Bureau thought he was mad, and comforted him, "Uncle, you son is fine in the army. He is just sick, and he wants to meet you."

Actually he knew clearly that, if his son was fine, how could they have asked him to go to the army? His son must have made trouble. Before he left, he told his wife, "Don't sell the tube, we may need it again…"

Once he stepped into the camp, so long as he saw anyone in an officer's uniform, he tried to give him a cigarette with a trembling hand. He looked like a coward farmer who was trying to beg the powerful.

What worried the old man most was how his son had passed away. Originally, Nie Xingqian was assigned to the missile troop to build a silo for the missiles in Black Water Gully down by Black Stone Mountain. He was responsible for stirring the cement. On that day, for no reason, the pump was not working very well. Sometimes it worked, sometimes it didn't work. But if one pounded on it, it started to turn again.

On that day, when the pump stopped, and the electrician came and pounded on it with a wooden stick, it started to run again. Then he turned to the new soldier Nie Xiangqian and said, "Watch this thing and stay still, I will go get the wrench."

Not long after the electrician had left, the pump stopped again. While other people who needed water were calling, Nie tried to imitate the electrician and pounded the pump until it worked. After he hit it with a stick, he was drawn to the electrical machine— as one who had no knowledge of electricity he used an iron stick to hit the machine. The electrical machine leaked, and the strong electric current burned his whole body. When people rushed to him, he had stopped breathing. The cadres from his company said, "Uncle, we are sorry, it was our fault that your son was sacrificed on duty..."

Nie Caigui's heart suddenly became peaceful. He didn't cry — on the contrary, he comforted the cadres. "Don't say that, my son is not educated, and couldn't perform his duty loyally. He brought trouble to the army. 'Sacrificed on duty' is the best comment, do not say anything more..."

The battalion commander, political commissar, company commander and political instructor formed the first row in carrying the wreath for Nie Xiangqian. Regimental commander Zhou Yiping, who was called the modern General Barton, had smoothed his roughness and gazed at the people from the red soil land. Even he, who was used to the funerals, still burst into tears. All the soldiers of the battalion stood solemnly on the uncompleted battlefield and saluted by taking off their hats. The old man had never seen this before, and knelt down to give his gratitude to the regimental commander and the soldiers.

The cadres accompanying him rushed forward and helped him up. "Old father, do not do this. Stand up, stand up!" The old man still knelt down and said honestly, "This is courtesy. In my hometown Yunyang, when others come to help with the funeral, the host of the family must kneel down, otherwise it is impolite..."

Thanks to the persuasion of the deputy director of the county Civil Affairs Bureau, who had come with him, the old man didn't perform the full ritual. But the actions of the old man had grasped the soldiers' hearts. Not only did they feel sad for him, but also that they owed a debt which could never be repaid.

Therefore, they hoped to compensate him more economically.

However, the financial compensation was only slightly more than 1,000 *yuan*, as stipulated on the red-headed document. And it was already raised after multiple requests from the army. It was even lower a few years ago, when it was only just over 400 *yuan*. Compared to the airline compensation, which was 60,000 *yuan* per person, the life of a Chinese soldier was worth almost nothing.

However, these soldiers wanted to do something for this old man. Within their power, they could only do it in their own way. The soldiers from Nie Xiangqian's company initiated a donation, and soldiers of the entire battalion participated in it. The charity initiative was spread throughout the whole battalion…

The compensation and the donations were more than 4,000 *yuan* in total. But for a poor rural family, it was already a large sum of money. What kind of paper should they use to wrap the money? Red paper was for weddings—if they used that it would be condemning their son to death. But black or white paper would be another provocation to the old man. In the end, they used the official envelope to wrap it up.

When the 4,000 *yuan* was sent to the old man, he was confused and fearful, since he had never seen such a large sum of money. With his hands trembling, he said, "It was such a large sum of money, it was unsafe on the railway, how can I take it back?"

Out of helplessness, the regiment commander had to post the money to him.

The old man was leaving. Before his departure, his face turned red, as if he still had something to say. The regimental commander could understand what he was thinking, so he asked him gently, "Father Nie, do you have anything that needs our help?"

The old man hesitated. Eventually it was still the deputy director of the Civil Affairs Bureau who told the commander what the old man wanted to say: "He had a younger son and wanted him to replace his brother..."

Regimental commander Zhou's eyes were wet. He grasped the old man's hand and answered him silently: what a good man; what a good god of the soldiers. After they had sacrificed one son to the army, they wanted to send the other son to the army. This was the power source for our army, which enabled us to be ever-victorious on the oriental land. However, after some contemplation, he hesitated. According to the iron-clad military rules, only the blood brother of the martyr could replace him, but father Nie's son could not enjoy this entitlement. In order not to let the old man down, he comforted him. "I will give you a reference letter, stating that your elder son was sacrificed on duty and your younger son needs some special treatment when he applies to join the army next year. You can take this letter to the recruiters, what do you think?"

Nie Caigui nodded, and answered in satisfaction, "Yes, yes."

The old man left, having completely understood.

Three months later, the leaders of the regiment received the old man's letter unexpectedly. In the letter, he said that he hadn't received the money—the post office only gave him a green note of debt. Regimental commander Zhou was furious after he read this, and he pounded on the table with his fist. He told the director of the political department, "Damn it, it's money that cost our soldiers' blood and life, how dare they embezzle it? Go, send a cadre and find the leader in that county. If they don't return the money, I must bring this issue to the provincial government, even to Beijing..."

They were our god, our father.

4. A young soldier from a rich farmer's family, and a pair of senior people who had experienced much, were brought to Beijing at the last moment of their son's life by the plane sent by the Central Military Committee.

This story happened during one summer in the middle of the 1980s. The newly established missile troop in the deep forest of the southern mountains had entered the last stage of its testing process. On that afternoon, soldier Jiang Zhongxiang from Yunnan Province was conducting waterproofing works in the underground nuclear caves with another soldier, Jiang Hongjun, and the squad leader Wang *Yuan*zhi. After they had applied a thick layer of asphalt on the ground, the tunnel was filled with a repugnant smell due to the bad ventilation system. A kind of blue smoke arose in the cave, engulfing the three working soldiers. Perhaps because they had been overly exhausted, the squad leader Wang *Yuan*zhi lit a match and started to smoke. It was a severe violation of the operation procedure, but he ignored it due to carelessness. After he had lit the cigarette, he threw the match on the floor. Instantly, after a thundering blast, the combustible gas in the cave was lit and a fire was started. Waves of heat rolled towards the three soldiers. The squad leader Wang and Jiang Hongjun ran to the outside, but Jiang Zhongxiang, who was working inside, was shocked by this accident. The rolling smoke made him lose his sense of direction, and the heat burned away his consciousness. He moved to the deep smoke out of instinct, without realising that it was an underground cave in a tube shape which only had one exit. The tragedy happened inexorably...

When the dark smoke got to the exit of the tunnel, Wang and

Jiang crawled outside, their whole bodies burned with only one piece of pants left. They said in a low voice, "Accident happened … Jiang Zhongxiang was still inside." After they said so, they collapsed on the ground …

The company commander Song Guangzhu, who was directing the constructions outside of the tunnel, started to organise a rescue operation immediately. He led eight soldiers inside, before they could reach 40 metres inside of the tunnel, they were forced out due to the heat and smoke. After breathing some fresh air, they ran inside a second time. Although this time they had entered the cave, they didn't find Jiang. The third time, the anti-toxic equipment was delivered to them, and the soldiers rushed inside and searched through every corner. Eventually they found Jiang cramped in the last corner, disfigured with burns. When the platoon leader took him into his arms, the flesh on Jiang's arms fell off …

The ambulance rushed to the army's hospital with its blue spinning light on like a streak of lightening.

Jiang was in a dangerous circumstance, with 95% third degree burns all over his body. What was worse, it was the summer time of southern China, and the hot weather was another danger to the deeply burned soldier. But the life of an ordinary soldier had gained the full attention of the strategic missile troop. In order to save his life, the Party Committee of his regiment all attended him at the hospital, and asked the hospital to spare no efforts in saving Jiang's life. They also sent people to the capital city of the province, which was thousands of miles away, to buy an air conditioner. But, as an army's hospital located in remote mountains, it was restrained by its facilities. That night, Jiang reached the brink of death several times. The hospital applied to transfer him to the best burn wounds hospital, the 304 Hospital in Beijing. But there was thousands of miles of distance from the southern forest to Beijing. When the train arrived, it would be too late. The only solution was to apply for assistance from the air force and send the injured soldier to Beijing. The life of the soldier had concerned the highest commanders of the PLA ...

Commander of the Second Artillery Corps, General Li Xuge, and Political Commissar Liu Lifeng called the Central Military Committee and the headquarters personally to ask for a flight. After General Zhang Zhen, the then Deputy Chairman of General Staff, had received the phone request, he put away all his other important issues and instructed the helicopter to fly to the forest and carry Jiang to a military airport, from which he would then be carried to Beijing by a special flight. The Logistics Commander General Hong Xuezhi also instructed 304 Hospital to spare no efforts to save this soldier.

On the same day, at 3:13 pm, a helicopter landed in the green forest at an old airport abandoned by the KMT. Following a police car, the ambulance carried Jiang to the helicopter.

In the county which was abandoned by God, tens of thousands of people came out of their homes and stood at both sides of the road. More than ten jeeps followed the ambulance to the old airport, and scores of leaders came to see this ordinary soldier off. Under these circumstances, people who didn't know anything might have thought there was some high official being sent to the hospital. At this moment, Jiang's trachea had been split, so he could not talk anymore. But his mind was clear. The Regimental Political Commissar He Xianzhi grasped his hands: "The chiefs from the Central Military Committee have sent a special flight to take you to

Beijing. Jiang, you must hang on here and survive this. Cooperate with the doctors, we are all waiting for you here ... "

A string of tears fell down from Jiang's eyes. He nodded silently.

The helicopter flew into the rolling dark clouds, as the roaring sounds of thunder came from the distant sky.

Jiang left with the wind, but behind him, in the missile troop, this event was like the thunder of a peaceful era ...

If you knew the history of the Chinese strategic missile troop and Jiang's family background, this story would have been a fairy tale if it had happened a few years ago ...

Jiang joined the army as a first generation commune member. "Commune member" was an unfamiliar word to the young people of the 1990s. It was the ending point set by Deng for the end of Mao's people's movements, which cancelled the special names for those who suffered from the class struggles. Following the light of equality, the descendants of the prior landlords and rich people were granted the same right to enter universities, join the Party and be promoted. As a result, the strategic missile troop, which was famous for its prior political background check, opened its doors to the descendants of landlords and the rich. This was something one could hardly imagine happening in the past. Jiang Zhongxiang was born in a prior rich farmer's family in the middle area of Yunnan Province. His father had inherited tens of acres of land and livestock. Usually they would farm their land by themselves, but when it came to the busy seasons they would hire workers. Before they could enjoy more of their comfortable life, the country was liberalised and the whole family had to swallow the bitter fruits of time. Jiang Zhongxiang, who had lived through the 1960s, could remember, ever since his childhood, never having had any

of the happiness an innocent child should have had. His parents
were classified as the targets of class struggle and one of the four
types of people who were criticized and struggled against under
the dictatorship and forced to swept the street. He and his sister
developed low self-esteem. When the children of the poor farmers
were having fun, they could only stand aside and be envious,
sighing at the unfairness of life—why couldn't they be born in
an ordinary family, to avoid this black ring above their heads?
Or perhaps it was because he had been living under harsh social
conditions which left trauma on his heart. His personality became
lonely and weak. He wasn't talkative, let alone social. He spent all
day in his own world with his head lowered. From the 1980s, when
Chinese politics started to relax, these people whose background
belonged to the "commune members" began to have their own
spring. In October 1983, when Jiang Zhongxiang put on the green
military uniform, his father Jiang Zicong, who had been living in
fierce political suppression, was so excited the night before his son
left home for the army that he couldn't even fall asleep. He talked
to his son by the fire throughout the night. When dawn came, his
face, which was full of suffering, revealed a smile. He told his son
repeatedly, "Our family eventually will have a tomorrow. It is all
thanks to Deng's policy. Son, you must work hard and excel… "

His son had undoubtedly become the best soldier in the missile
troop. But now his son was riding on the flight sent by the chiefs of
the Central Military Committee from Beijing to the hospital. The
families of Jiang all felt the great honour, as well as the fear and
anxiety…

With the company of an officer from the missile troop, Jiang's
mother, sister and cousin traveled thousands of miles to Beijing.

The ancient capital extended its warm arms to welcome these passengers from the southwestern border. If not for their son, they would not even dream about stepping into Beijing. Indeed, Beijing didn't belong to them. Compared to the prosperousness of Beijing, the clothes of Jiang's mother could no longer hide the poverty of that red soil land. A black linen shirt in the old style covered this old woman's skinny body, which had been through the sufferings of time. The popular red headband also covered the old woman's complicated feelings. After decades of suffering, this old mother had become fearful and timid. They thought their son's life could be saved after he was sent to Beijing. But hard reality crushed this mother's last hope. The experts in Beijing didn't save Jiang's life. The last time the mother saw her son he was covered in white gauze. And his face, which was disfigured by the burn wounds, could no longer be restored, no matter how much make-up was applied. As soon as she saw him, she fainted…

From then on, this old mother washed her face with tears. She no long spoke a word, although she was quiet originally. Zhang Gushun, the director of the political department who was sent here to handle the funeral affairs, immediately spent 500 *yuan* to buy some clothes for them after he saw these poor families of Jiang, hoping to replace their native style clothes and defend against the hot summer in Beijing. However, they avoided these offerings carefully, no matter how hard the military tried to squeezed the money into their pockets…

In the hotel of the army, what people heard was the cries of an old mother.

The bone ashes of Jiang were returned to the southern forest where he used to fight under his mother's protection. The missile troop held a solemn funeral for him, and Jiang's leaders and battle-mates all attended his funeral. The people who came to see him off occupied the entire hall. And the eulogy delivered by the leaders was full of regret, and the tears of the soldiers were full of sincerity and thoughts for him. The old mother who had been living in the gaps of life and political discriminations had never imagined that after her son's death he would enjoy such honour and special treatment. She didn't know how to talk in this situation, but asked her daughter to say something on behalf of their family: "All the leaders and Zhongxiang's battle mates, I am here to kowtow and thank you. I am an old woman who doesn't know how to talk in this situation. Zhongxiang had a short life, but he enjoyed the good times. During the last days of his life, the chiefs in Beijing and the leaders of his army showed much concern for him, a child with a "commune member" family background. His life was so valuable he was taken by airplane to see doctors in the royal city. Even if he was a son from a good family, could he enjoy such treatment? Our families could never dream about this. But Zhongxiang is not lucky enough to deserve all this, and he left us still. He has failed the hope of all the chiefs. We are satisfied, and we have no other complaints. Zhongxiang was glorious when he was alive, and he died in honour, having received so much love from so many people. Only in this good army can we have this ... we will take half of his ashes home, and half will be left in the valley, to accompany you and guard his battlefield ... we are leaving now, thank you!"

The old mother left the army without asking for anything and returned to the ancient border of southwestern China. The army didn't forget this sick old mother; every year, Zhongxiang's battle-mates who had come from the same place would be granted with a few more days of vacation to help this family with farming work and chores. This has never stopped over the past few years…

However, on the red soil of southern China, an old couple had to pass the last stage of their life in loneliness…

5. A retired old cadre, father of an ordinary soldier, didn't shed any tears at his son's funeral. He faced the mountains where his son's body lay, and called his son's name for an hour, tears all over his face…

It was a gloomy day at the end of 1993.

The first snow of the winter had covered the southern mountains with a mass of white. The coldness was frozen on the land — ice covered the trees, and the fog fell down, dressing the forest in some ancient wild style.

My distant warm family in Beijing asked me to return home early, but I had to wander around in this mountain forest and interview the strategic missile troop there. The soldiers had raised the heavy wings of the Chinese army's modernisation, and the tragedy and greatness of their life had made me inseparable from them.

During the winter nights in the mountain area, the wind in the forest was roaring, making hoarse and imposing sounds as the cold current caused people to tremble. At an informal discussion of the strategic missile troop's brigade office, a group of men's faces sat, lit by the fire besides them. These officers, who had just stepped out of the era of construction and stone and into the era of the rocket army, still had silent hearts that could not be separated from that period, although their adventures of blood and stones had ended. When it came to the soul-stirring part of their story, these tough men's tears dropped down. They had witnessed too many deaths.

Wang Siwen ("Siwen" means "classic" and "polite"), a soldier whose face was like his name, was sitting in a corner and listening to the regimental commander, company commander and squad leader tell their stories. The beard on his lips and the unmoving muscles on his face suggested that he was calm and mature. When it came to the point when almost everyone was about to finish, I lifted my head and looked at him with a smile. "For the whole night, only you didn't saw a word. Could you please say something…"

Instantly, a blush appeared on his face. As he gradually recovered his cool, he said in a low voice, his head lowered, "I have a friend who came from this same town. His name is Wang Binwu. We were high school classmates…" He swallowed and looked at me.

"It's a pity that he is dead." He stood up suddenly, and placed a thick pile of diary books and letters on the table in front of me. He said, "These are his things, please have a look when you can…" Before he finished, a string of tears rolled down his face. "He was hit by the stones in the tunnel from a landslide. It was early morning, May 21, 1991. I will never forget that dark day. After the explosions, the tunnel was filled with smoke. We, the 3rd platoon, went into the tunnel to clear the stones. After we had conducted a risks check, Wang Binwu was moving stones. Suddenly, a bowl-sized stone fell down from above. I just heard the sound of his security hat…"

As he stopped, Wang Siwen buried his face in his hands and cried out loudly, his shoulders trembling. The solemn air in the room grew even more gloomy. After a while, he wiped away his tears and said in a hoarse voice, "I held him up, and shook him, and cried. 'Binwu, wake up, look at me. It's Siwen!' His body was soft and weak, and he didn't answer me. We moved him out of the tunnel and sent him to the hospital as soon as possible. The doctor felt his pulse, and checked his pupils. He said Binwu was already gone, and we should carry him back. All the soldiers of our platoon knelt down in front of the doctor, and begged him to save him. The doctor looked at us with sympathy, and left shaking his head ... "

Wang Binwu died before he could celebrate his 18th birthday. He had spent no more than half a year in the army. He was an only son, His father was a veteran cadre but couldn't walk, and his mother was not in good health. He didn't need to join the army, because his family needed him. But he insisted on it. Since his father used to be a soldier and knew more than him, his father didn't stop him by force, and let him follow the army. Before he left, he entrusted all his family affairs to his classmates.

His biggest dream of life was to become a command deliverer who had mastered the oriental giant dragon. However, fate sent him to become a soldier who built silos for the missiles. As an 18-year-old young man, of course he could not handle the heavy labour. There was a time when Zhou Wenkui, the regimental commander, came to the tunnel to inspect our work. The platoon leader asked Wang Binwu to clear any dangers. He raised a stick to poke the arch above, but couldn't do it because he was too short. It was the regimental commander who came to help him and got rid of the stones. Perhaps because the regimental commander felt sorry for him, he specifically requested the military affairs department to transfer Wang to be an orderly of the chief in the security platoon of the regiment office. It was supposed to be the best chance for Wang to leave the dangerous construction sites, but he refused to follow the transfer. The military affairs department tried several times to transfer him, but he didn't go to register. At one point the regimental commander forced him into a car, but he escaped.

His battlemates said that Wang Binwu seemed to be a pretty weak boy, but he was actually quite stubborn. If he had made up his mind to work in the missile troop, nothing could change his mind. He had a cousin working as a cadre in an armed police regiment in Shaanxi Province. He wrote to Binwu several times, trying to persuade him to work for the armed police, who were stationed near the city. The transfer orders kept coming, but he just refused to leave. He said, *after I finish building the missile battlefields, I would like to become a real missile soldier.* After he joined the army, every day he would review his math, physics and chemistry textbooks. His goal was to enter the highest college for the Chinese missile troop — the Military Engineering Academy in Xi'an — and become a great platoon leader of the launching battalion.

On the morning the accident happened, for no reason, he insisted on asking for leave to go to town. That day was the day for discipline inspections, which limited the number of soldiers going out, but he just had to go. He urged the platoon leader to grant him leave. Since he was favoured by the leaders of the company and battalion, his leave was granted. People thought he was going to the town for some urgent matter, but in fact it turned out that he spent more than 100 *yuan* to buy lots of medicine and medical appliances. When asked why he did so, he said the doctors of our company had taken leave to return home, and what if any accidents happened on the construction site? These things could be of some help.

Nobody had ever expected, that night, that he would be the first one to have to use the things he bought…

His parents rushed to the army from Hubei Province, which was thousands of miles away. The army sent a special car to bring the couple to see their son. On that day, the sky was grey and cloudy. The old couple requested to see their son's classmate, Wang Siwen, once they arrived. But Wang had gone to the forest in the mountain alone, to cry in the grass fields he used to visit with Wang Binwu. The company found Wang Siwen that evening. Once he met Binwu's parents, he burst into tears. Uncle Wang threw away his crutches and touched his head. Although his body was trembling, no tears fell from his eyes ...

On the day of the memorial service for Wang Binwu, the leaders of the regiment all came. The service was set up in the canteen, and sad music was mixed with cries ... However, uncle Wang was smiling and comforting his son's battle mates. He even asked them to take care and avoid dangers, and to finish the works left by his son.

The next day, accompanied by the company commander, uncle Wang visited each squad, and offered each soldier a cigarette. The old man placed his crutches against his back, and leaned on the wall to light the cigarettes for each soldier. Although sweat rolled down his face, he kept smiling. In the smoke, each soldier's eyes were full of tears ...

After he had lit the cigarettes for all the soldiers of the 1st company, the company commander asked whether he had any other requests. After some contemplation, he said in a hoarse voice, "Please show me the place where my son died."

Uncle Wang said he wanted to walk down the path his son had walked. It was an uncompleted modern nuclear storage cave. Usually, no one was allowed to step inside unless authorised. But they broke this rule for a veteran who had already taken off his uniform. Following his son's political instructor, the old man limped towards the dusty and dark tunnel with much difficulty. Many soldiers were battling with the stones and mud, bareback and wearing only a pair of pants. After seeing them, he could easily tell what his son was like when he was alive. The political instructor led Uncle Wang to the place where his son died. And he pointed to the uneven stones above, saying, "Binwu was hit by the stones falling down from there…" The old man slowly put down his crutches, and bent down to touch every stone. Without any facial expression, he lifted a stone which had his son's blood on it, cold sweat rolling down his face as the dark yellow lights cast their glow on his wrinkled face. He touched it again and again, and eventually told the political instructor, "Please ask someone to take this out for me, I want this and my son's ashes together…"

Under the blood sunset, a string of blue smoke rose from the distant mountains towards the sun. As the mountains and the land joined together in the distance, only the blood red colour of the sun remained.

Uncle Wang asked his son's friend, Wang Siwen, to come forward, and told him seriously, "Take me to the places where you and Binwu used to go."

The two came to the slope across the camp. Facing the missile storage caves, he turned to Wang Siwen. "You can return earlier, but I want to be here alone for a while…" Wang Siwen insisted on staying, but Uncle Wang forced him to leave. Out of helplessness, Wang Siwen had to hide in some wild camellias not far away from the old man. Uncle Wang thought Wang Siwen had left. Facing the valleys which his son had offered his body to, the old man burst into tears, having not shed a tear since his arrival. He screamed to the valley and battlefields, "Binwu, my son, where are you? Your father has come to see you… Binwu, can you hear me… Binwu… my good son…"

The old man cried to the valley for half an hour. His voice echoed around the valley until the sun fell beneath the mountains. The fog on the pines turned into strings of tears, and the valley replied with sobbing sounds like drums and tides.

After he returned, Uncle Wang held his son's ash box and the stone with his son's blood, and left.

6. When the Chinese strategic missile troop rose suddenly on the Eastern horizon, the soldiers knelt down to the people, their god …

The early spring of 1994, a mountainous area in southern China

After 12 years of construction, the nuclear missile construction project was completed as scheduled. An engineering team which had fought with the Americans in the Korean War had finished building silos for the strategic missiles in the mountains. They joined those who had mastered the giant oriental dragon.

The restructuring of the troop and the reorganisation of the veterans was undertaken simultaneously. After saluting to their flag for the last time, the celebration ceremony was held. Those retired soldiers who had sacrificed for this team and the martyrs' families were all invited, and were arranged in the middle section on the primary rostrum. During the 12 year period, ever since this team had arrived in the mountains, lives had been sacrificed, and many injured. Looking at these people who had lost their sons, husbands, fathers, and these people of the yellow land who were still in poverty, many soldiers felt sadness surge in their hearts and tears fall.

However, these humble parents of soldiers never had any despair. They had left their beloved ones on the missile battlefields and the mountains, as if it were the will of God. They didn't need the living to remember them, or award them with honours, because it would be a disturbance and blasphemy to the dead, as well as another pain for them. Although, due to their loss, many of them were widows and orphans, lonely old people who indeed lived a hard life, never did they ask for anything from the army. On the contrary, more of them showed remarkable courage: they wished to have their younger children serve the missile troop.

Zhou Wenkui, the Regimental Commander who was going to leave the army after 25 years of service and return to Shaanxi Province, had looked at these families of the soldiers, and told me with complicated feelings, "History is always the same. I remember during the 1970s, a soldier of my squad who was from Shandong Province sacrificed his life in the landslide in the underground tunnel. His father carried his 15-year-old younger son to the army for his older son's funeral. He was just like the families here with a broad heart and a grand sense of justice. He didn't shed a tear, nor did he ask for anything from the army. When the chief of the regiment asked what else he needed, the old man took his younger son in front of the chief, and said, 'My older son is gone, now I will give my younger son to the army, and let him replace his older brother and continue his work.' Now we are living a better life, but the people of the 1990s are exactly the same as the past. They have a deep attachment to our army, and would be as generous and calm as before in handing their sons to us. This is the luck of the Chinese soldiers and the Chinese nation!"

The late autumn sun rose from the red maple trees.

On the parade-ground besides the missile battlefields, the soldiers by, sunlight cast upon their faces. Seeing the new rise of the green troops from this mysterious forest, and with the soldiers seeing the people who shouldered the army, many could not help but kneel down suddenly. This was the first time the soldiers had knelt down to their God. Yes, the soldiers of our great army, and this republic, were supposed to kneel down for the people once …

Chapter 10

The Quivers of the East

1. The soldiers of the US strategic air force and the Soviet Union strategic rocket army were all university graduates. The controllers of the missiles were all postgraduates and doctors.

When their vision went beyond the mountains to the world, the Chinese strategic missile soldiers found their own location in this historic leap.

Humanity's step eventually trudged towards the gate of the new century. In the last 10 years of the 20th century, history suddenly revealed an unpredictable and conflict-riven world.

On February 5, 1991 the Gulf War started in the deserts of the Middle East, pointing the way toward the war of the future—from traditional wars to the future war of technology. Although this war only lasted for a week before it ended, the shock it left on this planet has not faded, and it has attracted the attention and concern of militaries all around the world.

On July 31, 1991 the US and Soviet Union officially signed a treaty to reduce nuclear weapons. In 20 days, the red flag of the

Soviet Union, which had been flying over the Volga River for two thirds of the century, suddenly dropped down. Following the collapse of the Warsaw Treaty Organisation, the cold war which dominated human life for half a century officially ended.

On May 29, 1992 China, the US, Russia, the UK and France, the five nuclear countries, reached an agreement on the principles of nonproliferation of weapons of mass destruction, and it became another hot topic of the world's progress toward peace.

As the world's hot spots cooled, the UN peace force successfully organised the vote in Cambodia, the last place of racial discrimination in Africa elected a black president, the long-term hatred between Israel and Palestine was finally reconciled, allowing the Palestine President Arafat to return to his homeland, and the treaty signed between the US and North Korea relaxed the tension between Seoul and Pyongyang.

Although these regions were still experiencing troubles that concerned the whole world, the sun of peace was roaming around the roof of mankind and a relatively stable world peace had come. In making use of this historic opportunity, the countries around the world started the biggest disarmament movement ever seen since the end of the Second World War: the US, the UK, France, Germany and the Commonwealth of Independent States all declared the number to be reduced by 2000, which amounted to more than 3 million. There would not be another big war within this century. But the competition for the control of initiatives on economic and military strategy had already started. A real quality contest was omnipresent in every corner of the world.

In the US: the budget for new weapons research and development had been raised by 15%. According to the Pentagon, there were 21 critical technologies in the next decade of national defense science which could ensure its leading position in the new century, so they were given the utmost importance. From the 1980s onward, the amount of nuclear weapons had increased 45% and the precision of the strategic nuclear weapons increased 1.5 times. As the development of the space shuttles, space base, ocean base and continent base missiles and stealth airplanes were all put into use, they became a symbol of the fact we had entered the age of overlapped sky and nuclear capabilities.

Russia, which shares a long border with us: even with much difficulty, and although the strong red army bloc had lost its prior glory due to political and economic upheavals, its military modernisation had not stopped for even a day. They were still developing the "new concept" high technology weapons, to strive to catch up with the West in terms of the quality of their weapons. The 20 thousand nuclear bombs scattered around the Russian territory were still pointing to every corner of the world.

The UK and France, and those middle-sized nuclear countries, had always considered that maintaining certain nuclear advantages was an effective means of nuclear threat. Accordingly, they adjusted their defense budgets to ensure the development of their high technology weapons and the purchase of critical equipment. The quantity and quality of their nuclear weapons were all on the path of development.

Japan: Japan emphasised their air and ocean force, and facilitated the research of all possible means of defense against the most advanced strategic missiles. It also actively participated in all the peace maintenance actions around the globe, and strived to join the line of military big powers.

The European nations further deepened their progress of integration. They established a rapid deployment force of 50 thousand soldiers, who aimed to handle crises from the arctic to the Mediterranean. The US also expanded its rapid deployment force. Even India, which didn't attract much attention, not only had their own aircraft carriers and nuclear weapons, they also strived to develop their own advantages, hoping to find their own opportunity in the struggles between the big powers…

Observing the whole world, everyone felt that it would be a difficult century.

China, which had been in its reform and open door stage, started to play an ever more important role in world peace. However, a group of incongruous figures had been engraved in the hearts of the Chinese strategic missile troop soldiers:

100% of the junior officers of the US strategic air force were university graduates, and had undertaken systematic trainings. And all the officers in charge of the operation systems held a master's or doctor's degree. Further, all the officers of the Russian strategic rocket army were university graduates or post-graduates. Most of the middle or senior level officers among them had been trained by military academies. Many of them had master's or doctor's degrees. General Schwarzkov, the Commander of the Allied Force of the Gulf War, had an IQ 25% above average. Of the seven members of the core leading group headed by him, five had a master's or doctor's degree, while the other two had undergraduate degrees but had been trained by West Point three times. In 1988, the graduation thesis of students from the junior and middle level commanding colleges in the UK was on the topic *Potential threats to the UK under the current developments of the world's hot spots*;

while our officers of the same level were writing on the topic *How to choose the breaking point in a 200 metre attack*.

When we put our eyes above the mountains of China to the world, we could see the differences. The soldiers of the Chinese strategic missile troop had to think about their past and the imminent future seriously — When the materials to build rocket and aviation equipment could render the oceans into rivers, as the Chinese soldiers who mastered high technology weapons discovered, what can we rely on to win the war of the new century?

Facing the ocean of shallow articles and immersed in more and more drinking and feasting, the Chinese aircraft carriers were eaten up, as were the Chinese high technology defense careers. A colonel of the missile troop commented on this situation with much worry: if we continued this trend, in the future wars, we would have to pay for what we had done. The steps of the Chinese army towards the world were heavy, but when every night the TV broadcast the tragic song *March of the Volunteers*, which recorded the history of this nation, the new generation of rocket soldiers had their own thoughts, which were different to those who were enjoying the prosperity: why did our nation only come to realise thing once we were forced into a corner and half-beaten?

The idea of striving for development was based on a sense of crisis. Only with a strong sense of crisis could one have the self-motivation to pursue development. The ambitious missile soldiers were always looking at tomorrow, and making rapid steps as they strove forward…

Almost every one of the soldiers was looking for their own place in search of the historic leap. A group of figures had revealed an irrefutable reality: in 10 years, although the glorious traditions would still be running in the rocket soldiers' veins, our weapons and equipment would have undertaken historic changes, and the quality of the Chinese strategic missile troop have undergone a fundamental development.

We built the swords for 10 years.

Before 1985, less than 40% of the officers in the Chinese strategic missile troop had associate college degree; but when it came to the 1990s, this percentage had risen to 70%. Presently, we are moving to 90%, and the majority of the officers of the launching battalion are university graduates. Many officers of the brigades' and regiments' political departments of the missile regiments are university graduates, and many postgraduates also has joined the missile teams.

In the middle of the 1980s, the pioneer of Chinese nuclear weapons, Professor Qian Xuesen, predicted that by the end of the 20th century 100 percent of the Chinese strategic missile troop officers would be university graduates, and the middle and high level officers would be composed of postgraduates and doctors.

Professor Qian's prediction would no longer be a dream!

2. From being a child cowherd to an expert of missiles was no longer the honour of the Chinese soldiers. History had pushed the new generation of commanders to the front stage.

If we went back to the 1970s, we would see many of the officers of the army had contempt toward modern knowledge. Even in the most advanced part of the army, the strategic missile troop treated the intellectuals from the military academies as waste. The leaders, who didn't have much education, lacked insight. And this had caused the education structure of the strategic missile troop to slip to a low point. The news *A Child Cowherd Became an Expert in Missiles* was regarded as explosive news and published by the PLA Daily and the reference publications of Xinhua News Agency.

In the early autumn of 1979, journalist Chen Jinsong, who was stationed with the Second Artillery Corps, went to interview a missile base in the northern forests. At that time, the reform has just started, and the Chinese people were longing for knowledge and modern human capital. Under these circumstances, this army, which had been hesitating around the political circle, started to strive for modern knowledge under the directions of Deng Xiaoping. The political publicity departments began to realise that the army needed an example of a studying culture to lead their way. Therefore Zhang Wen, the commander of a launching battalion, entered their mind. Whether from the perspective of weighing the value of an example or from a journalist's perspective, Zhang undoubtedly was the best choice. This commander, who had directed more than 10 launchings, had attracted the journalist's intense interest. He joined the PLA before the dawn of the new China burned away the shadow of the old one. Before this, he was a child cowherd without any education. During the war, he learned some Chinese characters with the cultural instructors. After the liberation, he was promoted to be the commander of an artillery company. Then he was sent to the military rapid-education centre to study, which turned him into a small intellectual overnight. Relying on this advantage, at the end of 1958, when the recruitment of the No.1 Battalion of Asia began across the PLA, he was elected. From then on, Zhang started his connection with nuclear weapons.

From a child cowherd to an expert in missiles, Zhang had realised a three-level leap of life. The article *From an Illiterate to the Leader of a Launching Battalion* was also a miniature of the history of the strategic missile troop. The path of Zhang towards success undoubtedly represented the older generation of rocket soldiers' trudge to modernisation. The scene of a child cowherd becoming an expert in missiles has become a picture of struggling for scientific achievements.

Under the lonely lamp during the dark night, Zhang worked hard to memorise the technological reference figures; in public, Zhang also asked questions to ordinary soldiers despite their differences in rank; at the critical point of launching, Zhang dared to overcome risks and dangers with calmness.

...

A report of no more than 3,000 characters had made Zhang famous across the army. The leap from a child cowherd to an expert in missiles also helped Zhang realise the leap of his life.

In a few years, the media not only brought him a reputation, but also blessedness. Zhang was later promoted to be the Deputy Chairman of General Staff, Chairman of General Staff, Deputy Commander and Commander of the strategic missile troop, and subsequently became one of the generals.

We certainly mean no offence to General Zhang—actually he deserved his luck, since he had grasped the rope of the god of fate and caught up quickly.

However, time was also cruel. The chance of a child cowherd becoming a pilot and expert in missile was quickly overcast by the nation and the army's higher pursuit for better talents. In the eyes of the later generations of officers who graduated from the missile academy and local universities, the older generations' news story-telling about their own experience seemed to be pathetic and absurd. Because, deep in their mind, it was the comprehensive talents who could match the most advanced troop of China. Although the old generations had suffered a lot, and had peerless perseverance and toughness, their lack of education could not be made up for by later rapid education; moreover, the education during one's teen period was usually critical in deciding his later way of life and thinking. The Chinese army had experienced lots of difficulties and turnings during their modernisation, none of which was irrelevant to the army's connections to this unfortunate yellow land and many of the high officers who used to be illiterate cowherds or workers. When they stood on the higher point to consider the modernisation of an entire army, it was always because either their lack of education or their farmers' blood rendered them incapable of making progress …

Therefore, when history pushed the new generation of generals to the front stage, these middle and high level officers who had been through many trainings from military academies no longer took the history of "child cowherd becoming a missile expert" as an honour. Instead, they bravely placed themselves against the background of international society, looking to improve their own qualities. From their calm and confident steps and wise eyes, you felt as if you had already seen the dawn of tomorrow.

3. The strategic missile troop was waiting for the Chinese "Millers" and "Symphil". The vacancy of the history was the shame of the Chinese soldiers.

More than 30 generals, experts and professors were concentrating on the big colour screen, waiting for the large comprehensive simulation system of strategic missile technological training to be born.

Following the launching orders, the large complex simulation system immediately reflected the sounds, lights, electricities, forces, figures and the pictures on the screen, the missiles entering the battlefields.

"Last minute!"

"Ignition!"

When the commander delivered the last order, a giant silver dragon shot up into the sky and lanced through the heavens. On the screen, there was soon a group of figures showing up, as the missile quickly entered the stage of mock flight. Soon after, the last period of the missile flight appeared. After the missile hit the target, a mushroom shaped cloud arose on the desert, turning blood red …

In the operation hall, a wave of applause replaced the prior silence. The Chairman of the Chinese Systematic Simulation Association Wen Chuanyuan and nuclear industry expert Professor Yu Daguang could not resist their excitement and stood up: "Brilliant, Wonderful! This simulation system is not only the most advanced one in China — some of it could be said to be among the most advanced in the world … "

"It's very real! I could never imagine something like this!" A general from the Headquarters in Beijing pounded on the table and said in excitement, "This is what we are waiting for, the Chinese 'Millers' and 'Symphil'!"

. . .

During the 1920s, in London

A British engineer, Lanchester, first invented the "battle situation digital model", which was quickly adopted in militaries worldwide.

Simulation systems had become the best method of training without casualties for armies during the peaceful era. For the past century, this model has been through several adaptations, and become more and more advanced, from digital simulation, mechanical simulation, computer simulation to laser simulation and the high technological simulation system, like the US "Millers", the British "Symphil" and German "Tasili" systems. Before the US strategic air force touched the Titan, Minuteman II, or Pershing missiles, they had to operate on Millers simulation system for 2 weeks, which amounted to 30 hours in total. It was required that the average time of operation be 20 times per person. Before that, they were not allowed to enter the launching silo and touch the real missile. When it came to the 1980s, the nuclear big powers, like the US, the Soviet Union, the UK and France, had already adapted their simulation systems from only replacing the real launching process to being used for trials of the nuclear weapons, which would provide more and better referral figures for battles. This way of training, which combined training and real launching, could reduce the number of experimenting missiles from 20 to lower than 10 before they were delivered to the army—the UK had made it to 6. Further, it significantly reduced the failure rate of the launching process.

"What the foreign armies have, we should have. History has left a blank page to the Chinese rocket soldiers, and it is our shame." General Fu Beichi was already the Director of the Chinese Strategic Missile Academy when the No.1 Battalion of Asia was established after their training in the Changxindian base. He had stood up from the last stage of his career and realised the Chinese "Millers" dream…

The research works for developing the simulation system for

the strategic missile training was started on Bailuyuan by Ba River. More than 100 experts, scholars and professors gathered on the flag ship of the high technology, commencing a historical advancement. Professor Deng Fanglin, who had a short figure and was raised by the side of Wei River, had been looking forward to realising this dream ever since the early 1960s.

It all started from the autumn of 1963. The No.1 battalion of Asia had already expanded to the size of a regiment and was sent to the deserts of the northwest for a launching task. As the first generation of graduates of the Missile Engineering Academy, he followed the missile regiment to the site in order to supervise the technological and scientific analysis.

The middle-range missile was designed by our own. Because we didn't have any modern testing facilities or any analytical system to decide whether the launching would be successful, nobody could tell the result. We could only rely on the instincts and experience of several senior experts and instructors. Even so, the launching time was delayed many times. After more than two months, the company commander of the launching company eventually delivered the order of ignition as the controller pressed down the button with a trembling finger.

They received an unexpected success. And the whole launching field was overwhelmed by boiling excitement. But the image of the controller's trembling finger had been engraved into Deng Fanglin's memory. With this gambling way of launching, a minor problem of any component could cause unbearable consequences. Let alone that the launching time had been delayed for two months due to their uncertainties about the hundreds of elements on the missile—it was not easy to make sure all the data was correct.

Therefore, Deng Fanglin dreamed about having a simulation system with which they could test the missile first and detect all the potential problems before the actual launching. It could be said that his imagination back then was exactly like the Millers system in the US. But the Cultural Revolution which engulfed China shattered his dream.

When he woke up from this nightmare, and the Chinese soldiers could observe the world with calm and objective eyes, the foreign simulation systems had already entered the computer and laser age. But we still remained at the same zero point, which was one century behind everyone else.

However, when the 1980s waves of reform surged in China, it provided the Chinese strategic missile troop with a historical opportunity. The Headquarters of the Second Artillery Corps approved the project, led by the Military Engineering Academy, to develop China's first simulation system, and all the material and human support necessary was guaranteed...

The Chinese "dream of Millers" eventually came. The experts from the Engineering Academy, Deng Fanglin, Huang Xianxiang and Guo Ximing, were invited to direct this massive systematic project, which involved the most advanced technologies. General Fu Beichi set up a goal for them: leaping over the first three stages of the world's simulation system development and striving for the most advanced level of the late 1980s. And they were required to produce a simulation system which could combine laser visions, speech synthesis and identification, and three dimensional real time images.

Effectively, they had to go down a path that had taken foreigners six or seven decades in two or three years. It was a sheer fantasy.

However, the stubborn Chinese soldiers who had been living in the remote mountains persisted in trying to realise this dream.

Deng Fanglin and four of his postgraduate students took on the core part of the research, which concerned simulating the movements of moving missiles. But the "dream of Millers" was not so easily realised. Simulation language, digital models, and laser images all formed giant mountains that blocked their way. As they closed their eyes and thought about the trembling finger, and the simulation system of the US which could test the missiles before launching, Deng Fanglin developed a strong sense of crisis.

In a few months, he and his students had completed the design. Nevertheless, this data needed to be processed by large computers. Given the cold war situation, these kind of computers were forbidden from being exported to red China. But luckily, China's first large computer, "Yinhe", was born in the National University of Defense Technology. In order to promote "Yinhe", the university declared that they would provide a free trial of three months for domestic users. Thus, Deng Fanglin decided to let his students Li Yuqiao, Wang Shicheng, and Mu Jianhua jointed a class in the graduate school of the National University of Defense Technology.

Hunan Province, Juzizhoutou

This was where the young Mao Tse-tung studied and composed poems. Li Yuqiao and his two other classmates worked upon the first problem of the simulation system project—a program that would digitally model the missile trajectory. Their objects were very utilitarian — not for a master's degree, but for the "Yinhe" Computer. Before them, seven other research teams had arrived, all experts in computer technology. They didn't take these three young guys from their Engineering Academy seriously. Even the director of the Speech Synthesis Room, Professor Huang Kedi, thought they were too young and might not be able to get any results.

As a result, they were arranged to be the last team to use "Yinhe". However, within twenty days they had overcome the speech synthesis. They had won the first round. And they impressed the other computer experts.

The other seven teams failed the last round, leaving them only 15 days before the end of the free trial period.

The three young students decided to spare no effort. They walked into the lab with a box of bread and soda water. The eldest, Li Yuqiao, allocated tasks to the three of them. He was responsible for the programming. Wang Shicheng was responsible for providing the time domain, and Mu Jianhua for picking up the frequency domain. Each of their tasks were chained together. After eight days of work in the lab without sleeping or stepping outside, eventually they realised their goal.

When they left the lab that morning, it was exactly one week before the end of the free trial period of "Yinhe". The three students cried together and celebrated with beer and sausages. But before they could raise their glasses, they fell asleep for three days…

After the success of his three students, Deng Fanglin allocated the most advanced research subject—three-dimensional real time image generation and reflection—to his student Lu Aihong, who was only 22 years old. The subject required that Lu reflect the three-dimensional movements of the missile in action on a high resolution screen. Based on the referral figures, the computer had to generate 25 pictures in one second. Lu used the most popular and advanced IMB-PC program from the US and worked for two months, but could only generate 25 pictures in four seconds, suggesting a possible failure in the works.

Deng Fanglin came to his student in time, patting his shoulder. "The problem is with the tool, not with you. I believe you are capable, now the critical point is to produce a new computer…"

At that time, the advanced computers were not allowed to be sold in China, and the "Yinhe" weighed a few tons. Even if it could be used, it was not suitable for the missile troop. So the only solution was to invent their own computer. Thus, Li Yuqiao completed his studies and returned to Xi'an to design a fast and light computer with the Northwest Industrial University. After a winter's work, a computer which could calculate 40 million times per second and was 1000 times faster than the IBM-PC but only slightly bigger was produced. It was the No.1 scientific achievement in Shaanxi Province that year.

Lu indeed didn't fail his mentor's expectations. Building on Li's achievements, he spent eight months designing tens of thousands of programs, eventually putting the real time images of the missiles in action on the screen.

Deng Fanglin and four of this students had achieved unprecedented success. Also, Professor Huang Xianxiang and his students, who were responsible for the simulation of the lift-off of the missiles, were not willing to be left behind. They set their target on a laser simulation, which represented the most advanced technological achievement. At that time, a joint venture company in Shenzhen had just imported the first laser VCD player of China. After doing their best to persuade the company, they were able to get the player. After three months of hard work, they were able to first solve the problems that resulted from the different speeds of the computer and the laser VCD. They then recorded the lift-off process of the missile on the biggest laser VCD through Beijing Film Studio. A year later, China's first computer-controlled laser simulator was produced in Shaanxi Province, the most advanced in the world at the end of the 1980s. The company which first tried to develop this project had to learn from the Missile Engineering Academy and request to buy the patent rights at a high price.

After the hard work of more than 1,400 days and nights, they finally arrived at the hall of success. All the parts of the comprehensive strategic missile training and launching simulation system were completed.

The steps of history entered the 1990s. China's comprehensive strategic missile training and launching simulation system had eventually emerged in the oriental land.

The Chinese "Millers" and "Symphil" could compete with the Western countries on the same level…

4. The later stories of the No.1 battalion of Asia. The young high-ranking officers who came from the cradle of China's missiles was no less outstanding than that of the foreign countries…

When I was just about to finish this long nonfiction work, some old people who had spent some tough times with the missile troop kept telling me that I must write about the people who joined the No.1 battalion of Asia later. Because it was also an important part of the history, and was both splendid and tragic. After all, history was not interrupted, and many young people asked me the whereabouts of the No.1 Battalion of Asia and how their descendants were.

Their whereabouts are always the secret of the republic, but their later stories can be told to comfort those who still have affection for this heroic troop.

It could be said, as the old and favoured one of the Chinese strategic missile troop, that the No.1 Battalion of Asia was forever lucky. During its 30 year existence, it had already achieved many famous "Number Ones" among the missile troops.

It was the first troop to master the P-2 missiles sold by the Soviet Union.

It was the first troop to launch a mid-range missile designed by China.

It was the first troop equipped with China's large-sized nuclear missiles.

It was the troop of the Second Artillery Corps that had produced the most high-ranking officers.

It was the troop that generated the most talents. Most of the 2nd level heads of the Second Artillery Corps came from Changxindian base and the No.1 Battlion of Asia. Captain Zhao Quanfang, who later became the Deputy Chief of the Organization of the Second Artillery Corps, told me that, "Since they became the No.1 Battalion of Asia, this troop has had nine commanders. If you were to write about their stories, you cannot avoid the 5th Commander, Ge Dongsheng… "

In the early autumn of 1994, when I was interviewing the retired former Commander of the Second Artillery Corps, Lieutenant General Li Xuge, the old man got excited as we came to the training reform of the strategic missile troop. "In exploring the reforms to training, Ge Dongsheng's contributions cannot be ignored… "

Actually, I am not unfamiliar with Ge Dongsheng. In China's

strategic missile troops, he has always been a rising star of the young high-ranking officers. He came from Shandong Province, and had a tall build. He was famous for his honesty and astute way of managing the army. As to his unusual military career, it started in 1963 when he joined the No.1 Battalion of Asia in Liangzhou in northwestern China from his hometown Wucheng County. First a launching controller, he was promoted to Chairman of General Staff of the regiment at the age of 33. The next year, he became the youngest regimental commander, and was promoted to be the Chief of Staff of the strategic missile troop at the age of 37 as an exception to existing standards, becoming the youngest deputy chief army level officer at that time. At the age of 44, he was a major general and the commander of the missile troop, and also the youngest high-ranking officers of the missile troop. By now, he had been working on the chief army-level position for five years, and had personally commanded 11 different missile launches.

Perhaps it was because of his unusual life experience, but for the past years, he has been a target of the media. However, without explanation, he always adopted a friendly but evasive attitude towards journalists. When CCTV's military channel entrusted a journalist to invite him to be part of a 15 minute long special show, he stubbornly rejected this rare opportunity, one which would have been much valued by others; some journalists from the military newspapers had requested an interview from him many times, but he always replied, "The comrades working for the media are very sensitive and acute, and I am happy to be friends with them and welcome suggestions about my work. As for the interview requests, please leave me alone…"

It was not difficult to understand him. In China, this ancient land, we have already become used to the phenomena that people who were not working on some causes think about those who did, and inevitably envy them. If one was too elite, how could other people live under his shadow?

There is an old saying: "If a thriving tree is taller than the other trees in the forest, the wind must destroy it." It has always been like that from ancient times. Undoubtedly, my interview request was rejected as well. But God didn't shut all the doors. It is human nature to try things which are challenging. Since I could not interview him directly, I sorted out a list of the people who knew him very well, in order to know him obliquely...

When the sunlight of winter was cast over the ancient capital of Beijing, I interviewed Colonel Pan Wu of the General Staff in his headquarters, who used to be his subordinate for a long time. There was only one topic in our interview, which was how Commander Ge Dongsheng carried out the training reform.

In Pan's words, there was a kind of pride which was close to reverence. "I have followed Major General Ge for many years. From him I learned passion for the cause. He was not the type who was conservative and always followed tradition. He always came up with new things to explore the missile troop's training. When he was the regimental chief staff officer, he was young and passionate about his work. The former Commander of the Second Artillery Corps, Lieutenant General Li Xuge, found him and asked him to solve the 'hibernation' problems of our army, which concerned the half year gap when the army could not battle due to the change of soldiers. He put all his heart into this research. First he separated the old and new soldiers, then transited the integrated training team to the new soldiers' training camp. After 10 years, the current

Commander of the Second Artillery Corps Lieutenant General, Yang Guoliang, decided on a new name for it: the 'training regiment'. This training model was widely adopted by the Second Artillery Corps. When he became the Corps' Chief staff officer, in order to realise what Chairman Deng wanted — 'using missiles to fight a guerrilla war', or a mobile combat order — he spent all his time in the army exploring a launch training regime which put the battalion commander in the centre. And this training regime had pushed the army to an advanced level in terms of launching times and relevant procedures. In 1987, he became famous during a military exercise which was attended by corps' staff from the headquarters and other bases. In 1990, when he was promoted to commander of a missile unit, he advanced the idea of making use of the intelligence and technology advantages of the factories under the Astronautical Ministry to serve our training program, and to promote improvements of the training facilities in the corps, which could reduce costs. He was the kind of reformer who would do something novel but also effectively…"

The Section Chief of Training from a missile unit stationed in the southern tropical forests, Zhang Junxiang had followed a transfer order to work for Commander Ge Dongsheng for two years. When I asked him about Commander Ge, he said after some contemplation, "Commander Ge is a professional soldier who would spend all his energy in the training and battles of the missile troop. He always reminded his subordinates that they should be strict and astute in training and managing the troop. He hated the undisciplined way of managing the troop. So he always adopted a typical soldier's manner and outfit wherever he went. He was just trying to set up a positive example for his subordinates, and he resented those who were fake and lied to their superiors. There was a time a news correspondent had written a false report, which published an event plan as if it had already been completed. He criticised the correspondent harshly in front of other cadres. He said we were the strategic nuclear threat power of China, and the very existence of the missile troop formed a formidable threat. What we relied on was our power, which could strike out at critical moments. Of course, people like us who controlled the nuclear buttons never wished for the upgrade of the nuclear gate; but in order to defend the peace we must rely on our power and ability to battle. Without real capability nuclear threats are only empty words. Certainly we were not bragging about the terror of nuclear war; actually we didn't want to fight a war. But to ensure we could fight once a war was initiated, we had to train the soldiers well. Just like the ancient school of military strategist, we should defeat enemies without waging a war, so that nobody dares start a war imprudently… "

Section Chief of Publicity Meng Haijun was the last person I interviewed. He talked about his top superior from a cultural perspective, saying "Our commander's biggest habit is reading. Under his direction, even those eccentric intellectuals would not feel lonely and suppressed. If you were a talent, you would definitely be valued. Maybe I am a bit paranoid, but maybe only the person himself could feel the value placed in himself by the leader. When you interact with him, the most prominent impression you get is from his wide thinking, which extends to many areas. Sometimes people felt that they could not follow him. Not only is he familiar with the special missile and launching knowledge, but he also dabbles in the areas of intelligence, telecommunications, and meteorology. As to the areas of war and nuclear strategy, he also has done some research and has produced lots of theses published in *Military Academia* and the *PLA Daily*. Even in the areas we are good at — literature, history, philosophy, arts and aesthetics — he sometimes makes us feel embarrassed at our ignorance..."

By the end of 1993, I had completed the peripheral interviews. When I was living in the guest house under Commander Ge Dongsheng's management, I took the chance during our visit to direct our conversation toward his works and life. However, to my surprise, he didn't take the bait. All the topics that night concentrated on war and peace, humanity, literature and philosophy. I was constantly impressed, excited and touched by his wise comments and rich knowledge. Originally I wanted to make another appointment, but he had business scheduled. Therefore when I actually started to write about him, I suddenly realised that all I knew were some general points provided by his subordinates. I could only give readers a general sketch of this young commander of the Chinese strategic missile troop, without highlighting his soul and eyes...

I can only apologise to my readers. But based on my instinct, this trump army, the No.1 Battalion of Asia, always maintains its power and elegance quietly.

Once you have lived, worked or studied here, you would be affected and transformed by this spirit. It would be entrenched in your blood forever and benefit you all your life.

After I left the missile troops in the southern forests and was on my way back to Beijing, I suddenly came up with a strange idea. If the God of fate had provided the Chinese soldiers with a historic stage to begin a contest, these young generals like Ge Dongshen and Wang Benzhi, who I wrote about in this book, would not be less outstanding than the foreign generals...

Do you believe it?

5. When the Chinese Defense Minister General Chi Haotian inspected a missile troop stationed in the south, he wrote, "The power of our nation depends on the Second Artillery Corps!"

Another day started as the sun rose from the peak of the east. The resonant sounds of military bugles echoed in the forests of the valley.

In the summer of 1992, General Chi Haotian, the Defense Minister, inspected a missile troop in the south accompanied by the former commander of the Second Artillery Corps Lieutenant General Li Xuge. In the underground storage caves circled by forests and mountains, Minister Chi gazed at the large strategic missiles, which were shooting the Greater Dog in the sky, bow outstretched. As the instructor delivered clear and loud commands, the rocket soldiers followed them closely. Every command deliverer performed their tasks perfectly. This high-ranking officer, who had battled with the trump general of the KMT, General Zhang Lingfu that year, stated in excitement, "You are a first class army, with first class equipment, training and soldiers. The launching performance you gave me has impressed me enormously..."

Later, General Chi waved his writing brush and wrote for the soldiers, "The power of our country depends on the Second Artillery Corps", which expressed his appreciation for and expectation toward this army of high technology nuclear capability.

Afterwards, a large group of senior staff officers, cadres and journalists from the headquarters and military media entered into the underground storage caves and watched the swords of China.

They said, in the critical moments of our nation when we are under attack, it is probably the strategic missile troop which will save us ...

In the northern mountains and southern forests, a Chinese phoenix was moving and rising into the sky from the Kunlun mountains ... This is the quiver of the east and the roar of China.

Chapter 11
The Weight of Balance in the World

1. History has played a big joke upon mankind — the five permanent member states of the UN who won the Second World War were all in possession of nuclear weapons. Was it an accidental event or the sadness of mankind?

The year of 1995 was an unusual year in human history. In this year under the ancient Chinese calendar, there would be two years occurring together. From the mysterious astrological compass, an ominous stellar was revealed in the sky. Some astrologists thought it would be a year of disasters, fortunes and confusions. Thus, just after the bells of the Year of the Pig stopped, in some cities and rural areas of southern China, red clothes became popular overnight, while red lanterns were hung under the roofs in the northern cities ...

Chinese people are used to use their own way of thinking in living their life. But, no matter how Chinese people thought about 1995, it was a lucky year for everyone on this planet. 50 years ago, the US, the Soviet Union, China, the UK and France collaborated on the European and Asian battlefields and won victory. From then on, the following half century was no longer haunted by a Third World War, though wars still went on in some parts of the world.

A peaceful era for half a century could be considered in all aspects a victory for the anti-Fascist war, and should be valued by all the peoples around the world.

Actually, in Europe, the ceremony of the end of the Second World War had already started in April 11, 1994, when the 50th anniversary of the Normandy Landing had come. The US President Clinton, French President Schmidt and British Prime Minister Meijer with the veterans of the War all returned to Normandy to hold a memorial service for the sacrificed soldiers on that day. The ceremony for the European battlefields would reach its climax in around May and June, while the Asian battlefields would continue celebrations till September. It was said that the Chinese leaders would attend the grand ceremony held in the Great Hall of People in early September to celebrate this great and victorious day.

Reviewing the history from the 1990s, although the war had gone and justice had won, there was no real winner overall. What the war left behind was an injured planet and 60 million deaths…

However, what saddest was that the victims of the wars became the creators and invaders later.

Everything started from Yalta.

February 4, 1945, the famous resort of the former Soviet Union by the Black Sea—the beautiful Crimea Peninsula

The three major leaders, who had already triumphed in the Second World War—the US President Roosevelt, the British Prime Minister Churchill and the host, Secretary General of the Soviet Union Communist Party Stalin, all gathered on the white beach by the blue Black Sea. As they looked to the beautiful sunny sky as the war faded away, they discussed the fate of mankind after war over coffee. During this one week meeting, not only did they decide upon Europe's division of power, they also decided that the US, the Soviet Union, China, the UK and France would constitute the five permanent states on the UN Security Council. Two months later, 282 delegates from 50 countries passed the UN Charter in San Francisco, confirming the historic status of the five powers.

After hundreds of years of weakness, humiliation and suffering, finally China had gained a decent position in the international community. However, shortly after that, people began to realise that God had played a big joke on them — the five permanent states on the UN Security Council were simply all those who had developed their own nuclear capabilities one by one after winning victory.

Was it only a fateful coincidence or an accident of history?

Actually, on February 11, when the 32nd president of the US, President Roosevelt, flew over the Black Sea on his wheelchair with the victorious fruits of the war, the Manhattan Project directed by Oppenheim was nearly completed. All that he lacked was an opportunity to test this new power before he died 60 days later, leaving the record of serving four consecutive terms of presidency and the nuclear bombs brighter than the sun to his deputy Truman, who was the son of a farmer in Missouri.

On August 6, 1945, without much consideration or hesitation, Truman replaced Roosevelt and signed the request to drop the atomic bomb "Little Boy" on Hiroshima, a request submitted by General Stimson. Three days later, "Fat Man" was dropped on Nagasaki, causing 200 thousand deaths. At the moment when the giant mushroom clouds arose, people thought Truman had gone insane. He was terrified but happy. He was guilty of this moral crime but felt cheerful for the power. He said he had never been so happy before. He seemed to believe that he was the most powerful man in the world, that he had won the fire of Prometheus but did not know how to extinguish it.

Undoubtedly, by dropping the two atomic bombs, Truman had facilitated the surrender of Japan. But he had also cast a nuclear cloud over the head of mankind. Thus, although the Second World War was ended, humanity walked into a more terrible nuclear winter…

The Kremlin

The Soviets were shocked by the power of the atomic bombs the US had dropped on Japan. It was no less than a mass of dark clouds blocking the sunny sky over the Red Square. Before this, Stalin had already known from the KGB that the Americans were conducting some trials of a new kind of weapon. In the same year, when the heads of the US, the Soviet Union and the UK gathered in Potsdam on July 17, Truman tried to reveal to Stalin that the US was going to have a new powerful weapon, but this didn't raise his attention. Nevertheless, when the US possessed the power of nuclear monopoly, he lost his former calm. He asked the five most famous nuclear scientists to his office in the Kremlin, and told them as he walked around, "My only request to you, comrades," taking the tobacco pipe from his lips, "was to provide us with atomic bombs as soon as possible. You have to know, the Hiroshima event has shocked the whole world. The balance has been destroyed, and providing this bomb will help us to avoid this threat."

After he sent away the scientists, Stalin sighed and told the Chairman of General Staff, Supreme Commander Zhukov, "I pray for the people of the Soviet Union wholeheartedly. Luckily it was our ally who first invented this atomic bomb and not Hitler, the swine. Otherwise, the Russian nation would face an enormous disaster. Comrade Georgy, we have to be fast before we lose all our advantages … "

The explosions of the US atomic bombs undoubtedly facilitated the progress of the Soviets.

But the success of the Soviets was closely related to the secret help offered by the American nuclear pioneer Oppenheim. After the collapse of the Soviet Union in the 1990s, according to the articles of high level officials of the KGB, at that time Oppenheim probably thought from the perspective of the power balance and concluded that the US should not dominate this threatening weapon alone; or he was sympathetic to the red world and intentionally revealed some confidential intelligence from the Manhattan Project to Hlefetz, the special agent in San Francisco, arranging for scientists who later escaped to the Soviet Union to work for him. Seven years later, the US President Eisenhower fielded severe allegations against Oppenheim's loyalty to the US. After he received the letter from the Director of the CIA, Edgar, that suggested Oppenheim might be a spy of the Soviet Union, the President moved to take away many of his titles and cancel his eligibility to access military intelligence, claiming that he had an unclear relationship with the Communist Party which had caused him to delay the research of the hydrogen bombs. So it was that the most outstanding nuclear physicist in human history suffered from 10 years of persecution due to McCarthysim. It only ended in 1963, when the Kennedy government granted him the Fermi Award, partly restoring his reputation.

No matter why Oppenheim chose to do so, he increased a

balancing weight for the peace of human world. On August 29, the Soviet Union exploded its first atomic bomb in the deserts of Kazakhstan, giving the US a big shock. Truman issued an announcement of only 125 words, stating that the US would continue to develop hydrogen bombs. Two years later, the US exploded an even more powerful and destructive hydrogen bomb.

The Soviet Union was unwilling to be left behind, and followed the path of the US. In a year, the Soviets exploded the same bomb. From then on, the nuclear competition between the two super powers had commenced, lasting half a century. During this period, evolving between the US and the Soviet Union, humanity's nuclear weapons experienced different stages of development, moving from their infant stage toward a full blossoming. Between the initial stage of fanatical pursuit and the relatively calm balancing stage, there could be said to exist four stages. The first stage was the US era of nuclear power domination, during which the US adopted a containment policy against the socialist bloc and stood atop the human world, seeing in nuclear weapons a tool which they could harness to end war. The next stage was the era when the Soviets had produced their own nuclear weapons and gradually caught up with the US, the two powers competing for nuclear advantage to dominate the world, and forming a balanced state in the end. The third stage was the era when the UK and France had joined the nuclear club, and especially when China exploded its first atomic bomb in 1964, breaking the monopoly of the US and the Soviet Union. As the only country in the third world which possessed nuclear weapons, China joined the balance of power. The fourth stage was another round of competition between the US and the Soviet Union.

Humanity was brutally placed under the nuclear threat, and even the inventor of nuclear weapons had to sigh out of helplessness.

January of 1953, the grass field of the White House

Truman, who was almost 70 years old, was retiring and going back to his hometown. In his last State of the Union Message he declared sadly to the Americans and all the world, "…We have made a bigger bet in the pursuit of peace than ever. Now, we have entered the atomic age. The existing technological reforms are radically different from those of any previous wars. If there was war between the Soviet Empire and the free states, this would not only dig the grave of our enemies, but also bury our own society…In future warfare, one party could annihilate millions of people, big cities, great civilisations and the fruits of hundreds of generations with one strike."

The US President, who was the first one to slaughter tens of thousands of civilians eventually discovered his conscience when he was about to leave the White House and return to his ordinary life.

Wasn't it too late?

2. When can we raise the spirit of a great country? The status of a great power is not dependent on the size of our territory or population, but solely determined by whether we possess nuclear weapons, with which we would have the ticket to any major political organisation. The rise of the middle-sized nuclear states, like China, the UK and France, have become important weights for the balancing of power.

Mankind was led to the "nuclear winter" by his own intelligence.

For any sensible ruler of a big country, choosing to build nuclear missiles was not a wise choice. But the post-war period was a black vicious circle from which humanity could never escape. On the one hand, they condemned nuclear weapons as the origin of all the evils, while on the other trying to enter the nuclear club at all costs.

This conflicting and confusing psychology was the result of the special status and effect of nuclear weapons in international politics and on the military stage. George Bondi, the US intellectual who was famous for writing *The Nuclear Strategies of the US*, used to say with great wisdom, "For a country, only if you possessed nuclear weapons could you have access to all the major political organisations in the world."

Another author, John Newhouse, who has written *The War and Peace of the Nuclear Age*, said, "All countries have realised that the nuclear age is indeed distinct from any prior era, at least in terms of the relationship between big powers. It is nuclear weapons, not traditional factors, which determine the status of a big power."

Perhaps it was exactly because of this that the statemen and generals of all the countries were realising more and more clearly that nuclear weapons were irreplaceable by any normal weapons. They could go beyond the defence line of the enemies and direct the war to the inner area of the enemy's territory, rendering the strongest enemy susceptible to its attack. Therefore, once a country had access to nuclear weapons, it had an equal position against a superpower. Consequently, all countries wanted nuclear weapons. In obtaining nuclear weapons, the UK and France had changed their usual style of obeying the US's instructions as its allies, insisting instead on following their own paths.

From the era of Churchill during the Second World War to the "iron lady" Thatcher and Major; from the "empire on which the sun never set" to the little brother of the US, Queen Elizabeth and her subordinates were determined to follow their own path when they faced the same Anglo-Saxons who had gone to the American continent for gold.

August 6, 1945, London, the Prime Minister's residence on Downing Street

When he heard the news that the Americans had dropped an atomic bomb upon the far East, fat Churchill jumped up from his chair. "Isn't it a good news?" he shouted to the Foreign Secretary, Sir Aiden. "The American cowboys have done a good job, taking revenge for our failure in India and Burma. No matter what, I have to celebrate…"

That evening, the London radio and the *Times* all published a poetic announcement in prose style from Churchill, who used to be a journalist and author: "Thanks to God's blessings, the scientific efforts of the UK and the US have exceeded all the efforts of the Germans… All the hard work constitutes that genius which will be recorded in US history, perhaps as the biggest victory of mankind… We must sincerely pray that these horrible powers will be used to maintain peace between countries…"

All the people around the world fell into confusion, Churchill, who had been wise throughout his life, could be as silly as this? How could he regard the American achievements as theirs? Actually it was certainly painful to share other's achievements, and Churchill was no exception to this. When his poetic prose announcement was broadcast across the country, the defense secretary and Supreme Commander Montgomery were called to the office of the prime minister. Changing from his usual intellectual manner, he said determinedly, "The UK must have this epoch-making weapon, to threaten those enemies who are equipped with nuclear weapons. The UK must master all the primary new weapons as a big power..."

However, it was sad that Churchill wasn't able to lead the research for this mysterious weapon. As the war ended, the indifferent British gentlemen abandoned their wartime Prime Minister...

Churchill left No.10 Downing Street on a cold rainy day. The first post-war Prime Minister Clement Attlee continued Churchill's secret proposal. When Churchill rose again in 1951 and returned to the Prime Minister's residence, he was surprised by the progress Attlee had made in terms of the atomic bombs...

After all, the Americans' ancestors used to be the subjects of Great Britain and lived a nomadic life under the same blue sky. With the same Anglo-Saxon blood and their days of battling in Europe together, the American cowboys helped the British on their way to the nuclear club. No matter whether it was core technology or intelligence, the US spared no efforts, and eventually the British were able to succeed. On October 3, 1952, they completed a nuclear trial in Australia and became the third nuclear power of the world.

General Charles de Gaulle felt a heavy sense of loss and crisis all of a sudden, as if the entire sky of Europe—from the Rhine to the English Strait—was covered by a mass of nuclear clouds.

The US generals who were in charge of NATO hadn't even notified France before they installed nuclear weapons. Their range covered France. At the same time, the eternal competitor of France, the UK, was able to master the nuclear weapons and recover their strength in the international political arena. And Germany, who treated France like a slaughterhouse, was returning to the path of rearmament under the encouragement of the US. What upset the French most was the war in the Suez Canal on July 31, 1956, in which France was manipulated by the three nuclear powers. In the last few days of the joint adventure of the UK and France, it was the Kremlin who showed off their nuclear weapons in Hungary, and the UK who later betrayed France by giving in to US pressure, causing France to lose its colonies and old sphere of influence in the Middle East.

General de Gaulle, a strong nationalist, could not bear this humiliation.

Palais de l'Elyseè, Paris

In September 1958, General de Gaulle asked the commander of NATO, General Lauris Norstad, to his office. He requested that he report to him about the state of nuclear weapons arrangements in France.

General Norstad congratulated de Gaulle on his return to power, and de Gaulle politely expressed his gratitude. After some greetings, finally they came down to business. The French President asked the American general to talk about the nuclear weapons installed in France and their targets. General Norstad looked around at the staff in the President's office. "OK, Mr President," he said. "But only if I can talk to you alone."

"All right," said de Gaulle, though not without some unpleasantness. He signaled to his two cabinet members to leave.

"It's a pity, Mr President, that I can't answer your question…" Though the commander of NATO was not embarrassed at all, and didn't seem to take the French political leader seriously.

"General, I think you don't understand, this is France..." de Gaulle's face turned red as blood surged to his brain.

"I am sorry, your excellency, but the US president didn't honour me with this power..." The Commander of NATO spread his hands helplessly.

De Gaulle felt that he has been nastily humiliated, and said in anger, "General, I want you to understand this: from now on, any responsible French leader would not tolerate this kind of answer."

General de Gaulle swore that they would produce their own nuclear weapons. In the opening paragraphs of his memoir, he stated: "If it were not him who stood on the front line... If France is not great it is not France. The US would not give a non-nuclear country the status of a great power. In order to take a share in the world's leadership, France could not live without nuclear power."

February 13, 1960, Reggane, Sahara

A mass of mushroom clouds rose above the desert in North Africa. When the French president de Gaulle, who was by the side of the Seine River, heard the news of the nuclear test, the battle-worn general sent a public telegraph to the French nuclear scientists and soldiers. The first line of the telegraph stated, Long live France! From this morning, it has become more powerful and proud.

General Albert Buchalet, who was responsible for the French nuclear project, said, "The success of the French nuclear test gave General de Gaulle the political resources to access meetings of the great powers. The passion in the telegraph showed the people the long-term lonely efforts he had made in order for this day to come..."

If it could be said that Churchill and de Gaulle were developing nuclear weapons under the pressure of being excluded from the circle of great powers, then the first generation of CPC leaders, represented by Mao, were developing China's strategic nuclear power under the pressure of the west's economic sanctions and nuclear threats.

As the No.1 country of the East, China has a large territory and biggest population in the world, but since the middle of the 19th century, it has been vulnerable to the bullying of powerful countries. Foreign politicians could determine the fate of an ancient nation with 5,000 years history as easily as their coffees. Even if we created eastern civilisation, in the eyes of the westerners, we were never a great power. It was not only because of the poverty of China, but because China didn't have the power to be part of the world leadership. Mao and Zhou, the old generation of Chinese leaders, came from the old world, which they shattered. They witnessed how Chinese were slaughtered by invaders and the indifference of a great nation who watched their people being massacred. Therefore, when Mao directed the young CPC to power, his ever-burning Chinese blood motivated him and his colleagues to restore the glory of the nation.

However, if not for the last US ambassador of the Truman government, Stuart Leighton, leaving China in a hurry, along with the 20 years long blockade against China, the Korean War, the nuclear threats of the US and the threats made by Dulles during several tense events across the Taiwan Strait, the secret nuclear project of the CPC wouldn't have progressed at such a fast pace. On October 16, 1964, China exploded its first atomic bomb and soon, on October 27, 1966, it successfully tested a middle-range nuclear missile. And it was unique for a country to conduct nuclear tests on its own territory. On June 17, 1967, China exploded its hydrogen bomb, which was only two years and eight months after its first nuclear test. Its speed was much faster than the US, the Soviet Union, the UK and France. And the world acknowledged China as a nuclear power.

The strategic nuclear power of China arose on the oriental land, greatly increasing the defense of the PLA. It could support the spirit of a great power, as had been expected by generations of Chinese. By lifting the status of China in the international arena, we were able to have more weight in international politics and diplomacy. Even the superpowers had to take the Chinese seriously. In the white paper report issued by the US Congress during the early 1990s, it was said that, "China's nuclear weapons stablised the hostile relationship between China and the Soviet Union, and also rendered the US incapable of threatening China for concessions like the 1950s."

During the long period after the Second World War, the US and former Soviet Union shared the balance of power. However, following the development of the UK, France and China, a triangular structure of power was formed. It represented a multi-polar balance of power in the world which was relatively stable and peaceful. Any leaders of a nuclear power did not dare to initiate war recklessly, thus delaying or avoiding a new world war, and gaining 50 years of peace for mankind…

However, humans are pathetic. The sounds of the doves of peace were the sounds of horrific peace, with the heavy nuclear clouds above the sunlight of peace…

3. Since the Second World War, there has been in total no more than 26 days of no war on earth. The Chinese people, who were undertaking reforms and pursuing the open up policy, craved peace more than ever. But peace was not something that could be begged for. The Chinese strategic missile troop has already grown larger and played a vital role in defending the national security.

Let's continue to focus on the last day of the Second World War during the 1940s.

On August 9, 1945, the US dropped the "Fat Man" in Nagasaki. The Japanese, who were already exhausted by the war, eventually collapsed after this strike. Emperor Hirohito finally announced unconditional surrender. On September 2, the Foreign Minister Mamoru Shigemitsu signed his name on the instrument of surrender on the American fleet U.S.S Missouri with his hands full of the blood of the Asian people...

The Second World War ended at this moment.

The Commander of the Pacific Allied Force, McArthur talked about his state of mind on the last day of the war in his memoir: "Ever since my early childhood, I had never cried. But that day I was so excited that I burst into tears..."

The five-star-general shed the tears of the victory.

But the Chinese shed the tears of losing 300 million people.

...

With the war long gone, the ruins of the cities left by the war were restored. The earth, bombed by humanity, grew the vigour of life again and produced bitter olives... The time was like smoke and dreams.

From 1945 to 1995, for half a century, there wasn't another world war. This period was three times longer than the period between the First and Second World Wars. This means that the industrial civilisation of half a century's development had washed away the barbarian and bellicose tendencies of humanity, leading them to maturity and development.

However, just as the sun could never shine on every corner of the world, the doves of peace could never cover the entire sky. Under the olive tree of a general peace, the wounds of partial war have never been salved.

When the China National University of Defense recruited for postgraduates of international strategies, the interviewer used to give out a question to the candidates: "Do you know how many days of peace existed since the Second World War?" None of the candidates could answer this question, and the white-headed interviewer would say with a bitter smile, "Only 26 days."

For 50 years, which was more than 18,000 days, there were only 26 days of total peace on this blue planet — what a mean number!

Actually, just after the end of the Second World War, all kinds of new wars across the globe immediately began. The former leader of the Allied Forces, the US had fought two large wars during the 50 years of the post-war era, one of which was in Korea and didn't make sense to American historians and strategists and was totally an error of the leaders. And it was the Commander of the Allied Forces, General McArthur, who became the Commander of the UN Allied Forces and fought a war with the Chinese and Koreans that they could never win. Compared to his splendid achievements on the Pacific Ocean, this time General McArthur lost badly. He was removed from the commanding department of the US Army stationed in Japan in a dishonourable way. The other war was in the jungles of Vietnam. The Johnson government pulled the US through the swamps of the southeast Asian tropical forests, which left a permanent trauma on the American's nerve and influenced the values and life of several generations. When it came to the 1970s, from Southeast Asia to black Africa, there was a war every three or five years. Some of them were the national liberation wars, but more were started because of the economic, territorial and national conflicts which deprived humans of their rationality. It left a nation and its people with heavy disasters to their country and development, disasters which are still visible...

The Fourth Middle East War in 1973 cost $10 billion.

The Ogaden War in 1977 cost $55 billion.

The Iran-Iraq War in 1980 cost $200 billion.

The Falklands War in 1982 cost $63.8 billion.

The Gulf War in 1991 cost $250 billion.

And the civil war in Afghanistan, which lasted for 8 years, ruined the country and turned millions into refuges.

The Bosnian War has been going on for there years without any hope of peace. Already 200 thousand people have lost their life.

The Rwanda genocide in 1994 cost 2 million innocent deaths.

During the 50 years after the Second World War all kinds of partial wars have caused the loss of life and assets no less grievous than during the Second World War.

All these traumas have reminded people that although humanity shares the same planet, the Goddess of peace does not grant her mercy equally. The prayer for peace coexists with the pursuit of wealth, regional hegemony and national conflicts on this planet.

The people are piously praying for peace.

Since the 1980s, the wave of pacifism that has overwhelmed the world shows the instinct of humanity after thousands of sufferings. Now, peace and development have become two of the major themes of the world. The collapse of the Cold War structure and the change from confrontation to conversation and the relaxation of tensions has seen international politics move from a bipolar system to a multipolar world. A new and relatively stable era of peace has come.

Since the middle of the 1970s, the Chinese people have commenced reform and pursued an open up policy with unprecedented bravery and determination. They joined in the changes occurring in the world with ambitions and strong steps. For this ancient nation, which has suffered so much, this may be the last chance.

Deng Xiaoping grasped a historic chance for the Chinese, waving his huge hand of history to open the gates of the Forbidden City, gates which had been shut for years. China has been developing by an average of 10% each year, the fastest developing country in the world. Even those arrogant Western political theorists and intellectuals, so proud of their superiority theories, had to admit that the 21st century was the century of China's rise. From this it can be said that the Chinese nation has been craving a stable and peaceful international environment more than ever, especially in China's surrounding areas. We long for peace, but peace can't be begged for. After a century of being invaded, enslaved and slaughtered, it was clear that a nation that solely relied on begging and the mercy of others could never have a future. Only the strengthening of its own power can ensure its position in this contemporary, competitive age.

Following the start of the 21st century and the end of the Cold War, the two superpowers, the US and Russia, adopted adjustments to and restraints upon their strategies, which produced a strategic vacuum in the world as the boundaries of their influence became unclear. In those areas where the relativity of power was unstable fierce competitions was waged between nations on all levels. The struggle for the next century had already commenced. The competition for resources and markets would become the hot spots of the next century.

For China, to secure the surrounding areas with its strong national defense power and ensure its reforms and developments became critically important. However, given the general trend of history, to battle a large country with normal defense powers is unrealistic, and would impose unbearable fiscal and economic pressure. Additionally, it can be concluded from the Gulf War that an army with normal weapons would collapse instantly when confronted with advanced ones in a modern high-technology war. Only with an army of effective nuclear weapons could one threaten enemies effectively in an emergency. After three decades of construction, Chinese nuclear power has entered a stronger phase for national security and world peace. As China enters the giant triangular structure of power, nuclear power plays an important role in determining China's status as a major power. It should be concluded that we should not forget Mao and the other old generation of leaders' foresight. Their wisdom and efforts, the strategic missile troop and the soldiers' struggles in remote mountains, have allowed us to gain our current advantageous position. It was they who raised the umbrella of peace and supported the spine of this great country…

It is hard to imagine: if it were not for those tough days of struggle, what would China be like today?

4. Despite the end of the Cold War, the nuclear winter continued. The West had imposed harsher nuclear checks against Iraq and North Korea, and wouldn't let third world countries enter the nuclear gate.

China is the only country of the third world which possesses nuclear weapons. The countries of the third world were not only impressed by China's achievements in the nuclear sphere, but envied the fact that China no longer needed to be threatened and manipulated by the big powers. Thus, for the past 10 years, they spared no efforts in developing their own nuclear weapons, in the hope of joining the nuclear club.

The first successful attempt was made by Israel. Standing in the tiny land of Tel Aviv and eastern Jerusalem, the Jews, who had suffered from Hitler's massacre, returned to their ancestors' land in 1948. But from that day on, they found that they were circled by the hatred of the Arabs. For 40 years, they have fought four large wars with the Muslims. They realised clearly that, if they lost any one of these wars, their nation would no longer exist. So they had to win every war. And every time they won, they found that they could only rely on themselves.

When the first war broke out in 1948, as they tested their own power for the first time, they discovered the irreconcilable hatred and hostility that came from the entire Arab world; the second war was the Suez War in 1956, which they fought with the French and British. Eventually they realised that allies like the US, UK and

France were not reliable; the third war was the Six Day War during June of 1967. In the first few days of the war, none of their allies were willing to stop the ruthless Nasser. But with their persistent army, they won the war and put the Sinai Peninsula and Golan Heights in their territory. The fourth war was the Middle East War during 1974, which rendered the Arab world incapable of initiating another war. Of course Israel paid a heavy cost for its victory. Gradually they came to realise that, in order to survive the hatred of the Arab world, apart from a strong army, they had to have nuclear weapons. They were totally competent in developing nuclear weapons, as most of the best nuclear physicists were Israeli, like Einstein, Oppenheim and Teller. Also, the French scientists and manufacturers seemed to be exceptionally lenient to the Israeli in terms of nuclear technologies. Although Israel has never declared that they possess nuclear weapons, everyone knows that they were ready long ago. In 1974, the President of Israel, Katzir, said, "Once we need this weapon, we will have them, even within just a few days." In 1984, the Science Minister of Israel, Professor Neyman, said, "15 or 20 years ago, Israel had nuclear potential even though it was in an isolated and defenseless situation. But we haven't leapt over the nuclear gate…"

The words of Professor Neyman seemed to contain some evasiveness. However, so long as we look at the recent argument between Israel and Egypt over the issue of non-proliferation of nuclear weapons, the reasons for Israel's nuclear power would be made clear…

And look at the rise of the nuclear power of Israel and the strivings of India and Pakistan. India is a large country of Asia, with a territory, population and history equivalent to China. However, in terms of its international status and influence, there is a striking distance between the two, especially since India has formed long term conflicts with its neighbor Pakistan over what was once eastern Pakistan and Kashmir. They almost went to war over these issues, and both have suffered loss. Therefore both parties wanted to develop nuclear power to threaten each other and compete. After more than 20 years of efforts, India was already capable in terms of aviation technology and strategic missiles that could enable them to launch satellites. And their atomic bomb project had showed some signs of existence. Pakistan was not willing to be left behind, and their nuclear technology was close to maturity. By the end of this century, both of these two countries had the potential to develop nuclear weapons.

Perhaps it was because of the closeness of their social institutions that both India and Pakistan adopted a policy leaning toward the US, and the West remained silent regarding the nuclear weapon projects of the two. But the West applied a different policy to Iraq and North Korea when they attempted to enter the nuclear gate, imposing harsher checks on them.

The Gulf War in 1991 was provoked because of Iraq's invasion of Kuwait. The Allied Force led by the US started Operation Desert Storm against Iraq. On the one hand, they intended to contain the arrogance of Saddam; on the other, they also intended to suffocate the nuclear project of Iraq. Because Saddam relocated his nuclear facilities prior to the Operation, the Allied Force didn't hurt him. Therefore, after the war, the UN could only force him to make concessions through economic sanctions and accepting the inspections of the International Atomic Energy Organisation. Although Saddam cooperated reluctantly with the experts from the International Atomic Energy Organisation, the sanctions imposed by other countries brought Iraq's economy to the brink of collapse. He had to take back his ambition to dominate the Islam world and open Iraq's nuclear development facilities to the inspection of the world.

The nuclear problem in North Korea has increased tensions in the entire far-eastern region for some time.

From the second half of 1993, South Korea, Japan and the US have been drawing attention to the nuclear problem of North Korea, with the goal of preventing it from entering the nuclear gate and disrupting the military balance of the region. On March 15, 1994, after the inspection of the International Atomic Energy Organisation, both parties kept arguing over the inspection process and results. Debate was so fierce that the tension in the Korean Peninsula increased. The US declared that if North Korea didn't stop their process of turning nuclear materials into military weapons, they would restore the US and South Korea joint military exercises and install "Patriot" missiles in South Korea. Later, following the former US President Carter's mediation, Kim Il-sung eventually agreed to accept the inspections of the International Atomic Energy Organisation just a few days before he passed away and the delegation groups of the US and North Korea in Geneva recommenced their negotiations. Eventually they reached an agreement: North Korea agreed to accept the assistance of international organisations and turn their heavy water to light water.

A shock on the Korean Peninsula finally faded away...

The West, led by the US, spared no efforts in preventing this third world country entering the nuclear gate. The first reason was the fear that nuclear power would be in the hands of immature politicians or warlords who would bring disasters to humanity. The other reason was that their own nuclear power status would be challenged by other countries. Thus, instead of letting them realise it, they'd rather kill it from the beginning.

However, whether these efforts would pay off was hard to say. According to the *New York Times*, Western intelligence departments had discovered that, since the collapse of the Soviet Union, uranium and plutonium which could be made into nuclear weapons was constantly being smuggled to the West and put on sale. There were 53 smuggles in 1992, 57 in 1993, 77 in 1994. In August last year, a Columbian who had been studying in Moscow for many years was arrested by Munich police on his flight from Moscow to Munich carrying 12.6 grams of plutonium-239, which could be made into nuclear weapons. And the loss of the Commonwealth of Independent States in terms of nuclear technologies and nuclear physicists were headaches to the US. According to the estimates of the US Defense Ministry, by the end of this century, there would be 15-20 third world countries capable of launching missiles, and half of them would possess nuclear weapons.

Despite the end of the Cold War, the nuclear winter continued...

5. The tragedies in Nagasaki and Hiroshima were all history, but the atomic bombs hanging in human city wall were not swords for observation. The amount of atomic bombs possessed by humanity were enough to bomb this planet three times over...

Early 1980s, Hiroshima, Japan
A 12 year old girl whose name was Michiko was affected by her

father's nuclear-stained blood. Originally she should have had her own childhood and beautiful dreams, but all these didn't matter to her anymore. Cruel death was gradually dragging her away. Some old people told this young girl that, so long as she piously made 3,000 paper birds, God would defeat her disease. The young girl believed them, and so she made the paper birds day and night, eventually making 3,000 paper birds, which were put all around her house and bed. She was immersed in her tale-like world, and with 3,000 paper birds she felt she was the richest and happiest person in the world. But the promise given by the adults wasn't realized — the 3,000 paper birds carried her to heaven.

Young Michiko was gone, the youngest victim of atomic bomb. But the 3,000 paper birds she piously made became flying doves of peace in the city of Hiroshima...

It has been 50 years since the events in Hiroshima and Nagasaki. When the memorial halls were erected on the ruins, the nuclear radiation and the walls remaining after the waves of fire were still there. Those bodies which had been forged into the cemetery pillars were still there, brutally presenting the demon parts of the human soul and quietly commemorating the disasters brought by the Japanese militarists to the Asian people, including the Japanese themselves.

However, in Hiroshima, it was hard to find the prior horrible scenes of the ruins after the atomic explosion. The Japanese, who never wanted to apologise to the Asian people, engraved their own sufferings after the atomic explosions on the most prominent monument in Hiroshima. After all the history has already passed, that period of pain has already been buried by the dust of history. Nevertheless, the atomic bombs hanging in human city wall were not swords for observation — the sword of Damocles could fall on people's heads at any moment.

Just when the young Japanese girl died, on the evening of March 23, 1983, the 40th president of the US, Reagan, announced the "Star Wars" project under the feet of the Statue of Liberty, and that he intended to create "a defensive measure against the horrible threats of the Soviet Union". He continued as an aged hero, "I hope all our efforts tonight can change the progress of human history." The Star Wars project of this old US President brought all of the major powers into a new round of military contestation. The Western European countries advanced jointly the Eureka Program, and the former Soviet Union promulgated *The Comprehensive Scheme for Scientific and Technological Progress*. Even Japan had put out a Strategy of Scientific Development. The US appropriated $26 billion for the Star Wars Project, but George Bush senior, the successor of Reagan, basically stopped the project. Yet the influence and shock it caused lasted until the end of the 1980s and early 1990s. According to *Jane's Defence Weekly*, the US and the former Soviet Union had increased their long-range nuclear missiles by six percent. At the end of the 1980s, the US installed the most advanced "Guards of Peace" missiles, and the former Soviet Union installed more developed missiles, the SS-24 and SS-25. In the 1990s, the Strategic Rocket Army of the former Soviet Union was expanded with another 11 newly equipped missile troops. The UK and France were not willing to be left behind. The UK spent 740 million pounds to purchase Trident missile systems from the US to replace the Polestar missiles. In 1990, the UK invested RMB 11.5 billion *yuan* in nuclear weapons, while France invested as RMB 26.8 billion *yuan*. By the end of 1994, the total number of nuclear missiles in France had increased by five times compared to the 1980s, its destruction area expanded by 120%. Now humanity uses thirty thousand dollars per second to make weapons. Nevertheless, in poor Africa, every five minutes, there is a child dying of starvation or disease. But over the heads of humanity, there are at least 50,000 nuclear missiles, 95% of which are in the hands of the US and the former Soviet Union. If there is a nuclear war, then the 50,000 nuclear missiles which cover the earth could bomb the planet three times over. If so, it would not be a problem of injuring the planet, but making it a dead one.

Luckily, it was always rationality that took hold. After 50 years of war, third atomic bomb was never exploded.

Actually, facing such a large nuclear arsenal, now it has reached the point when nobody dares to recklessly touch the red button. It is the only choice, placed in front of such a cruel reality. During the 1950s, the US forced their containment policy against the socialist movements with nuclear power as part of their massive retaliation strategy. The former Soviet Union was no better and raised their nuclear rocket strategy and aggressive attack strategy. All these strategies were the primary measures for crushing each other with nuclear weapons. Because of the balance of power, the US's massive retaliation strategy went bankrupt. After the 1960s, the Kennedy and Nixon governments changed the nuclear strategy of the US to a flexible reaction strategy and realistic nuclear threat strategy, while changing the targets of their nuclear weapons from the cities to primary military targets. This situation lasted until the 1980s. Eventually the US and the former Soviet Union realised that nuclear weapons were double-edged swords, and not only could they threaten enemies, but also oneself. No one can destroy all the nuclear weapons of their enemy at one time, and this would incur unbearable retaliation. In the end, they concluded that there would be no winner in a nuclear war. It was painful to admit one was not a hero. The two superpowers, which had been blindly pursuing nuclear weapons, finally walked out of this dark circle, a circle which had confused humans for half a century, and sat down together at the nuclear reduction negotiation table. After 10 long years of negotiation, the former president of the US, George Bush senior, and the President of the former Soviet Union, Mikhail Gorbachev, signed the first stage Strategic Arms Reduction Treaty on July 31, 1991. After a year and a half, President Bush and President Yeltsin signed the *Second Stage Strategic Arms Reduction Treaty* on January 3, 1993, in Moscow, which indicated that humans had made a step towards destroying nuclear weapons. But there was still a long distance before we could achieve full nuclear disarmament...

6. Deng Xiaoping said, without atomic bombs and missiles, we could not enter the big triangle, and we couldn't have achieved our current international status. To make the swords into ploughs has always been the dream of the Chinese soldiers!

1983, the Great Hall of the People, Beijing

Deng Xiaoping, who was the Chairman of the Central Military Committee, met the Canadian Premier Trudeau. Invited by the guests, Deng talked about international affairs and the past and future of China with his typical wisdom and profundity. When the guests asked him about the development of China's nuclear weapons, this great man, who had been through so many political difficulties, replied to him in a precise and striking manner that could attract and touch the other party. He said that the limited development of our nuclear weapons presented a balance that indicated to others that they would incur consequences if they attacked us. Then he smiled the solid and confident smile of a great stateman and said, "If it were not for the atomic bombs, missiles and satellites, we could never have entered the big triangle." Deng's words were precise but profound, deeply revealing that China treated the nuclear weapons as its last defense measures and would not strike first with them.

Yes, after the explosion of China's first atomic bomb, the Chinese Premier Zhou Enlai announced to the whole world that China had developed nuclear weapons solely for self-defense. He promised that we would never be the ones who first use nuclear weapons, that we would never use them on non-nuclear countries or entities, and that we would strive to abandon and destroy all nuclear weapons. This epoch-making statement was gradually accepted by some major nuclear powers.

No matter when, humanity always needs peace and friendship.

People cannot forget war, and not because they miss it. The Chinese soldiers have never thought about obtaining military medals by using nuclear weapons on another's territory, and would not allow a foreign military to seek honour on our land again.

To make the swords into ploughs has always been the dream of the Chinese soldiers.

Chapter 12

Saying Goodbye to Nuclear Winter

October 1983, Washington, the US

The "post-nuclear war world" academic conference was held by the International Atomic Energy Organisation in Washington as scheduled. The majority of the Congress, which was controlled by Democrats with a minority of Republicans, were arguing about the appropriations for the "Star Wars Project" advanced by Reagan. An academic thesis advanced by five American scholars to the conference solemnly envisaged a theory of human life in "nuclear winter". After careful calculation and reasoning, this theory warned the leaders that if the US and the former Soviet Union attacked a major city in a nuclear war, then the waves of heat and smoke generated by the nuclear explosions would cause a mass of clouds in the atmosphere of 1 or 10 km that could cover the sunlight but could not stop the nuclear radiation. In this way, the northern hemisphere would be covered by long nights for a couple of weeks with temperatures dropping to minus 15–25 degrees. In this situation most creatures, including humans and plants, would be extinct.

It was not a horrible delusional world created by the scientists.

An atomic bomb is strong enough to destroy mankind. But the total number of nuclear weapons hanging over the heads of mankind has reached a level which could create 200 nuclear winters.

As far as the period when the 33rd President of the US, Eisenhower, was in power, he had already done a nuclear test in the desert of Colorado. After the test, the radiating dust and smoke covered the sky, and all that was left was loneliness and sadness.

In fact, the loneliness and sadness were not limited to the initiators alone, but also the whole human race.

Nuclear winter is the last tomb that humans dig for themselves. It was never their original intention.

. . .

Our ancestors were a tribe of imagination. During the primitive stages of human civilisation, they used a leaf to cover their private parts. As they lived in the forest, placing their heads on the mountains while listening to the roaring of the animals, they became obsessed with the beautiful long night they saw after looking to the sky. All of a sudden, the plants around them grew colourful wings while their bodies sunk down. Their wings of imagination flew. So there were the stories of Chang'e, and the Palace of Heaven where all the gods lived, and also the flying goddesses in Mogao Caves and the eternal aviation dream of a nation...

The aviation dream has been worshiped by generations of people, and gradually was made a reality.

The alchemists of the Han and Tang Dynasties worked tirelessly; and though they didn't invent the drug for eternal life with their alchemy stoves, they produced the first fire of human civilisation—gunpowder and primitive rockets.

The notorious alchemists used their sorcery to facilitate the birth of a new era; a group of Taoist priests who roamed around ushered in the Qin Emperor's early dream of weapons and the Great Wall. It was the rocket dream that motivated human civilisation.

Since the time of the northern Song Dynasty, the Chinese army has had gunpowder weapons. During the wars between the Song and Jin, the Jin's bombs, "Zhentianlei" (thunder shaking the heaven), eventually shattered the Zhao family's Song Dynasty.

When Genghis Khan led his rolling cavalries to attack the castles in Baghdad, the flying explosives roared by. The entire European continent was still in the grip of the medieval era…

Chinese gunpowder and primitive vockets were sent to the Arab and the Europe Successively.

However, in just a few centuries, Europe rose while the Chinese empire fell. Why? It was an ancient vicious circle, in which all the students of this empire could achieve prominence in the bureaucracy so long as they could compose some standardised essays. Even the most outstanding scientist of the Ming Dynasty, Shen Kuo, set his ultimate value in the bureaucracy instead of science…

How could Chinese civilisation remain strong if it went on like this?

When the Westerners' sharp weapons broke the thick red walls of the Forbidden City — when the Sino-Japanese War of 1894–1895 struck down the oceanic great wall of the Chinese soldiers — when the Allied Eight Powers shattered the last bit of dignity of the Qing Empire — there seemed to be no other choices left for the Chinese.

After 400 years of journeying, rockets returned to their homeland in China. But it was no longer a simple cycle. The Chinese still had to start from zero…

The rocket dream burned with glory, but also tragedies.

Glory and dream, dream and tragedy — there wasn't a strict line between them.

When a primitive rocket propeller pushed him up, Wan Hu, the pioneer of the Ming Dynasty, hasn't expected that he would represent the first great tragedy of mankind.

On October 4, 1957, when the first Soviet satellite was sent into the universe, thus truly realising the dream of flying to the moon, it was a glorious moment for humanity.

Although there were defeats and failures, astronautic and missile technologies are still pushing human civilisation forward. Evolving around the space development represented by nuclear astronautic technology, the new revolution would take place in the areas of breeder reactor magnetohydrodynamics, conduction, laser and magnetic suspension technology, which moved us into the "era of plasma".

Following the USA's promulgation of high border strategies, humans have already stepped into an age where the universe and the nuclear overlap. The concepts of territory and borders have been fundamentally changed. Especially after the maturing of the space shuttle and space station technology, humanity's competition on earth and ocean have extended outward to incorporate the entire universe. The concepts of territory and security of the United States have adopted three changes:

If there is no security on the ocean, there is no security on land, which represents the change from land borders to land-ocean borders.

If there is no security in the sky, there is no security in either land or ocean, thus representing the change from a land-ocean border to a sky-land-ocean border.

If there is no security in space, then there is no security on land, ocean or sky, representing the change from a sky-land-ocean border to a high border.

However, the Chinese security concept is still located in our own territory. Whenever it comes to our territory, this would include the entire 9.6 million square kilometres territory and the coast line of 18,000 kilometres. But we have forgotten the infinite universe above, where there is an unsettled border line. Therefore, when foreign satellites and space shuttles approach our space, apart from hiding, there would appear to be no other solution…

Every nation and every country should have its own high border, just like everyone should have the sky of his own childhood.

Just as I was about to finish this book in Beijing, which I started last summer at my hometown in Yunnan Plateau, (and Beijing would never be the home of my heart), I suddenly remembered the autumn nights in my hometown. I remembered the starry sky used to belong to be me when I was in my grandmother's arms. My literary awareness began with fairy tales of counting stars as bonfires of hope. I have spent every cool night in autumn searching for the hope and expectations of my life by counting stars.

Therefore, on the quiet road in Banqiao town before dawn, in the straw piles on the red soil land, the stars which provoked a passionate young boy's dreams have led him to search and struggle as he travelled great distances. When I talked to the stars and flew in the universe, it seemed to be that there was no more threat of war, sin, ugliness, fake kindness, nor darkness…

After roaming around with the Chinese missile troops in the remote forests, I washed off my last bit of tan in the capital city. But eventually I found the starry sky and my attachment to a hometown which only belonged to childhood. If there is an "if" in history, if there is an "if" in life, we wouldn't need war, missiles, atomic bombs, killings nor nuclear winter. There would only be the beautiful fairy tales of my grandmother in the village courtyard during the autumn nights. There would only be the melodious songs of the shepherd boy in the fields during spring.